"Ms. Malek's marvelous storytelling gifts keep us deliciously entertained!"

—*Romantic Times*

THE HUNTER AND THE HUNTED

"What are you going to do with me?" Amy demanded, tugging on the ropes that held her bound to the pole.

Malik Bey said nothing, merely walked in a circle around her, surveying her as if she were the blue ribbon heifer at the county fair. The scrutiny made Amy intensely uncomfortable and she was finally able to look away from him. At that moment he stepped forward and lifted her chin with his finger.

He studied her face, and at such close range Amy was able to study his. He had the longest eyelashes she had ever seen, so thick and dense that they made his eyes seem huge in his olive-skinned face, and when his lips parted, she had a glimpse of strong white teeth. He stroked her chin absently with his thumb, looking her over, and she shivered at the touch, mesmerized by his stare. Then she realized that she was submitting to this humiliating examination without a struggle and she jerked back from him angrily. He smiled slightly, which infuriated her even more.

"You'll never get away with this," she hissed.

Enjoy *The Panther & The Pearl* by Doreen Owens Malek from Leisure Books.

Doreen Owens Malek

Panther's Prey

LEISURE BOOKS **NEW YORK CITY**

A LEISURE BOOK®

June 1996

Published by

Dorchester Publishing Co., Inc.
276 Fifth Avenue
New York, NY 10001

Printed in the United States of America.

Panther's Prey

Chapter One

Constantinople, Ottoman Empire
July, 1895

Malik Bey crouched behind an outcropping of rock and watched the plume of smoke from the train coming closer. Below him the open, sandy plain spread away to the horizon, narrowing on the right to the depot he could just see in the distance, its tin roof reflecting the sunlight. He had chosen the station well; it was isolated, and the train stopped long enough to take on new passengers and refuel. His men could surround and board it before the conductor or any of the travelers knew what was happening.

One of the horses neighed and Malik glanced behind him, shaking his head. Anyone might be in the hills above them; silence was essential. The offending handler controlled his mount, and Malik glanced back at the train, now coming around the bend and looming larger. He looked up at the sun, which would be in the conductor's eyes and aid the bandits in their task. The train should be loaded with business people, embassy aides, and tourists, all on their way to Constantinople and all in possession of jewelry and money.

Gain was the goal, after all.

Malik had no ethical qualms about robbing the train, no more than he would have about strangling the Sultan, if he could get his hands on him. Malik would do whatever was necessary to free the Turkish people from the oppressive grip of Abdul Hammid IV, the absolute dictator of the Ottoman Empire, which included Turkey and all of its dependent territories. If stealing was required, Malik would become the best thief in the Empire, and if killing was required, he would become the best assassin. Liberty was the goal, and nothing else mattered.

The train began to slow down, and its whistle blew loudly. Malik raised his hand, signaling his band to get ready. He grabbed his horse's bridle and mounted in one smooth motion, raising the scarf around his neck to cover the lower part of his face. Only his large, dark brown eyes showed above the printed cotton, eyes marked by glossy black brows and lashes the same shade as his anthracite hair. Malik was remarkably handsome, an attribute which he could have used to advantage if romantic pursuit was important to him, but he lived for his quest of a free Turkey.

Revolution was his constant occupation.

The train let off steam, hissing as it glided closer to the station. Malik cantered into position at the head of the group of mounted men, his hand still raised, watching the scene below. When the moment was right, he lowered his hand abruptly, and the bandits thundered down the slope, horses' hooves kicking up showers of dust as they rode.

The passengers on the train looked up in alarm as the horsemen materialized from the hills, seemingly by magic, swarming around the train as it inched toward its destination. The conductor pulled the emergency cord, but the Turks boarded before the train had even come to a standstill, leaping from their well-trained horses, which trotted away a few paces and waited for their masters to return.

Malik waited until he saw the two men who had been designated to handle the conductor land on the train, then burst into the caboose through its rear door. He ignored the screams of the women passengers and drew his pistol on the first man who stood to face him. The hero subsided, sitting back down slowly, his eyes wide as his plump wife clutched his arm fearfully.

Malik grabbed the empty sack tied to his waist and shoved it in the face of his would-be attacker. "Give me all your money and valuables and no one will be hurt," he said in English, for the couple looked Western. They scrambled to obey, dumping everything in the cloth bag, and Malik moved carefully down the aisle, stopping frequently as the travelers stripped themselves of their belongings and cash. His men did the same in the other cars, and Malik was not forced to repeat himself, not even for the Turkish passengers, who already had the idea and knew more about the local bandits than the tourists did. As he came to the end of the car, he saw an old man who looked far less prosperous than the rest extracting a few coins from his frayed pocket with trembling fingers. As he extended the money to Malik, the younger man pushed his hand away.

"Keep it, grandfather," Malik said gruffly in Turkish. "It is for you that I fight."

He turned to face the full car and scanned the faces quickly again, looking for women young and pretty enough to bring a good price on the slave market. There were none. He was strapping the sack, now heavy with booty, to his belt once more when his lieutenant, Anwar Talit, dragged a struggling teenaged girl through the door from the next car and said, "What do you think?"

Malik looked at the young woman, who was small and plain, with wispy brown hair tucked into a chip bonnet. She stared back at him in terror.

Malik shook his head, glancing through the train's grimy window for his horse.

"She's young enough," Anwar protested.

"Not worth the trouble," Malik said decisively, and Anwar released the girl, who almost fainted with relief. One of the other passengers caught her as she sagged to the floor.

"Are the others finished?" Malik asked Anwar.

Anwar nodded.

"Any women worth taking?"

"No, that one was the best of the bunch."

"Let's go."

Both bandits leaped from the train and dashed for their horses. The passengers reacted in various ways to having survived the incident with their hides intact. The men blustered and coughed, avoiding each other's eyes, and some of the women whimpered or sobbed, but it was clear that the outcome could have been much worse. Grandfather's pocket watch or a ruby ring was nothing to give up in exchange for a steadily beating heart.

Malik vaulted onto his horse and trotted in a circle around the stopped train, marshaling his men and making sure they were all mounted and ready to go. Then he shouted for them to head for the hills, and they streamed after him at a gallop, vanishing as quickly as they had appeared.

Amelia Ryder glanced out at the roiling water through eyes that were misted with tears. She was about to dock in Paris, there to board the Orient Express south to Constantinople. She had never been out of Boston, and this trip to Turkey should have been the biggest adventure of her life. But the reason for the journey was her parents' deaths, and their will specified that she be relocated half way around the world to live with an aunt she barely remembered.

It wasn't fair. She was almost eighteen. Her birthday was in just ten months, but the court-appointed guardian had insisted that custody of the "minor child"—just hearing herself referred to that way made Amy furious—should go to her father's sister. And her father's sister, Beatrice Ryder Woolcott, just happened to live in the capital of the Ottoman Empire with her rug dealer husband. It was all too foreign and bizarre; Amy didn't want any part of it, but here she was anyhow, on her way to meet Aunt Bea.

Amy had fought this fate with as much initiative as she could muster, but due to her age and inexperience that was very little. She had testified at her court hearing that she would much rather live with her best friend Abigail Cutter's family until she turned eighteen, but the judge had ruled, predictably, in favor of her father's will. So she was packed off on this trip in the company of her mother's friend Mrs. Spaulding, both of them still in a state of shock over the Ryders' sudden deaths in a carriage accident.

One moment Amy's young, healthy parents were alive, on their way to an evening concert. The next a runaway horse on a rain-slicked street where the gas lamps were out had ended their lives. And Amy had been forced to withdraw from Miss Pickard's Finishing School in Brookline and leave her old life behind for a new one in the mysterious East.

For years Amy had heard her parents discussing Bea's husband James and his cousin Sarah's involvement with the "pasha," whatever that was, in hushed whispers, as if it were some scandal to be shoved under the carpet. Apparently this pasha had "bought" Sarah from the Sultan while she was visiting James and tutoring the Sultan's daughter, and then the pasha had kept Sarah in his harem against her will. Amy remembered how the horrified sympathy of her family had turned to shock when they heard that Sarah had fallen in love with her purchaser and *married* him! And now the courts were sending Amy to live in the midst of these people! Did it make sense? Of course not, but it was happening. All because Bea Woolcott was

Amy's only surviving relative and an underaged young woman could not be trusted to live alone or without the supervision of family. It was twisted logic, but it had come to rule Amy's life.

"You'd better fasten your cape, my dear. The wind is picking up," Mrs. Spaulding said at her side.

Amy obediently tied the grosgrain bow at the neck of her blue wool traveling cloak, leaning on the railing and gazing out across the gray water. She wondered how long it would be before she could see land. She would only be in Paris for two days, but Mrs. Spaulding had promised that there would be enough time for Amy to see some of the sights before they had to board the train. The judge had given Amy an advance on her trust fund to pay for her passage to Turkey and for Mrs. Spaulding's round trip. Amy got the rest of the money on her next birthday, and until then she had to do what she was told like a good little girl.

"And button your gloves, Amy. This sea mist can chap your hands," Mrs. Spaulding added.

Amy sighed, closing her gray cotton gloves at the wrist and wishing that her companion would develop laryngitis. Mrs. Spaulding meant well, but she took her duties too seriously, barking orders at Amy as if she were training a dog. Amy couldn't wait until the older woman was on her way back to Boston, even if it meant that she herself was left alone in Turkey with the shadowy Aunt Bea.

A gong sounded behind them on the deck of the ship, and Mrs. Spaulding said brightly, "Tea time."

Amy turned from the railing and followed Mrs. Spaulding's sweeping skirt across the deck.

"Will you stop pacing around the room, Bea?" James Woolcott said irritably to his wife. "Amelia is not due to arrive at the station until tomorrow. Wearing a hole in the carpet now isn't going to change anything."

Beatrice dropped into a chair and sighed heavily. "What am I going to do with a teenaged girl?" she asked despairingly. "I haven't the first idea of how to entertain her."

"You won't have to entertain her, Bea, she is going to *live* here. It won't be a continuous garden party."

"But she's left all her friends behind. She'll have no one to talk to about her problems, her dreams. A girl that age needs conversation and companionship."

"She can talk to you."

"She hasn't seen me since she was five, James, since we came to Turkey when you started your business here."

"So it may take some time, but you'll get to know each other eventually. Fretting about it in advance isn't going to help."

"What could my brother have been thinking?" Beatrice murmured, almost to herself. "He knew I had no children of my own; how could he imagine I would be suited for this task?"

"He was thinking that you were his sister, and he wanted Amelia to be with family if anything happened to her parents. Now go upstairs and finish arranging the vases of flowers in Amy's room. I'll send Listak along to help you. We do want Amy to feel welcome, don't we?"

Beatrice nodded, her marcasite earbobs jangling. She tucked some stray ginger hairs into her chignon as she stood, saying, "Did you order the goose from the butcher in the Kapeti bazaar?"

James nodded. He had already answered that question twice, but reminding Beatrice of that fact wasn't going to help her state of mind. He waited until she had left the room, her striped bombazine skirt whispering along the bare floorboards between the rug in the salon and the tile in the hall. Then he sat down in the chair she had vacated and filled a pipe.

He was a little more concerned about Amelia's imminent arrival than he had allowed his wife to know. He really wasn't comfortable with shouldering the responsibility for his brother-in-law's child either, but James was a very practical man. He saw no help for the situation, so he had decided to accept it as graciously as possible.

No one had anticipated that the provisions of the Ryders' will would ever be enforced; Amy's parents had both been under forty and the idea that they would die together in their prime was so remote as to be almost unthinkable. But it had happened, and now a grief-stricken, unhappy girl was on her way to his home, saddled with a fate she had even tried litigation to avoid.

James lit his pipe and drew on it, reflecting on the years he had spent in the Ottoman Empire, years which had made him a rich man despite the difficulties of running a business in a foreign country. He had dealt successfully with the hostile climate, the language barrier, and the mercurial rule of a despotic Sultan, not to mention his cousin Sarah's complicated involvement with the pasha of Bursa, and had emerged a winner. He had augmented his original rug-exporting business to include woolens, pottery, and native handicrafts, and he was now one of the wealthiest foreign residents of the empire. He would not be inconvenienced by an underage chit who was going to be free to leave his care in less than a year.

James saw his duty and was willing to do it. He'd provide a home and supervision for this girl until she came into her trust fund and, he hoped, got married to some suitable young man. They were less plentiful in Turkey than they were in Boston, but he was already working on that, making sure Amy would receive invitations to the homes of the embassy attaches and military officers stationed in the area. From the daguerrotype he had seen, the girl was very pretty, and she had had the best of private educations in New England. Unless she had an insufferable personality, she should be married by the time she was twenty, and James's problem would be solved.

He puffed away contentedly, gazing around his luxuriously appointed living room with satisfaction. One of his finest silk rugs was the centerpiece of the salon, which was decorated in the cluttered Victorian manner with the objets d'art and bibelots Bea had selected over time, culling many of them from his own inventory. His wife was proud of her home, but she still missed her New England roots and she still suffered monstrously from the heat. It was at its worst now in July, and it was one of the few problems James's wealth could not solve. But all in all, James was content, and he did not expect that the new arrival would disturb his peace or prosperity very much.

He rested his pipe in its holder and got up to pour himself a snifter of brandy.

Malik dropped the last coin into the pile and said, "Three hundred and forty-three kurush."

Anwar grinned.

"And five rings, three gold bracelets, several watches, and an emerald brooch," Malik added, gesturing at the glittering tangle of jewelry next to the money. "Take it to old Gupta at the bazaar in the morning and see what you can get for the lot. Should be at least two hundred more."

Anwar nodded.

Malik rose and stretched, glancing around the cave where his men sprawled in various attitudes of relaxation, enjoying a respite after the successful raid. A fire burned in a corner, and several figures crouched around it; despite the searing heat of the day, the desert nights were cold. Malik wondered how long they would be able to remain in this mountain crag, for the Sultan's janissaries were always looking for their hideout, and they were forced to change locations frequently.

He looked back at the stolen hoard with satisfaction. That should be enough to buy arms and supplies for another couple of months, as well as outfit the new recruits. The rebel numbers were increasing daily. With each new outrage perpetrated by the Sultan, each new massacre or rout or execution, more volunteers came to join Malik's band. Some of them were barefoot and in rags, but all had one thought: to depose the Sultan and replace him with a democratically elected ruler. It was their only hope for a better life.

One of the camp women approached him and held out a jug of *raki*, the fiery clear liquor which turned white when water was added to it. Malik drank it straight, taking a slug from the bottle and then handing it back to the woman. Her gaze lingered on his face, but he didn't look at her, merely going back to his reverie.

The woman turned away in disappointment.

Malik raised his head and watched his server walk away, aware of what she was thinking. It seemed cruel to treat her so brusquely, but he knew that the slightest encouragement would have her trailing after him like a puppy, and he had no time for such entanglements. He was planning a raid on the next train likely to be loaded with Western gold, but in a different spot to thwart the escort the Sultan had ordered.

Malik had read about it in the Constantinople paper, which faithfully described each rebel raid as if documenting the exploits of a foreign army. Unlike many in his band, Malik could read, thanks to the education his brother Osman had provided. Before Osman Bey ran off to Cyprus with the Sultan's daughter, Princess Roxalena, he had been the Captain of the Sultan's halberdiers. This privileged position had allowed him to pay for a British tutor for his siblings and a maid for his mother. Malik took great satisfaction in knowing that the largesse the Sultan had provided through Osman was now enabling his younger brother to fight that tyrant more effectively. And now that Osman was established on Cyprus, thanks in part to the jewelry Roxalena had smuggled out of the Sultan's palace when she left, he often sent contributions to Malik's cause.

Osman's hatred for his former master was no less than his brother's.

Malik retrieved a folded, handmade map from his cloak and spread it on the ground before him.

He had to organize the next raid very carefully, because both the rail company and the Sultan's men were now on the alert.

He smiled. They didn't know he was planning to expand his operation to include the passenger coaches that ran from Bursa and Constantinople to the outlying districts, to Pera and Meerluz and beyond, carrying well-heeled travelers from the cities to their destinations elsewhere in the Empire.

He was smarter than all of them.

Amy shot forward on her seat as the coach hit a rut. She clutched at her straw hat and glanced across the way at Mrs. Spaulding, who seemed unperturbed by the bumpy ride. The glories of Paris had faded fast in the haze and heat of the dusty train trip, and now Aunt Bea's husband had failed to meet them at the Constantinople station. He had sent a message instead, saying that they should take this coach to the suburban district where the Woolcotts lived.

21

Amy and her companion were sharing the short jaunt with four other travelers. There were two businessmen in vested suits, named Ames and Harington, and two spinster sisters in their fifties, who sat staring straight ahead with delicate lace handkerchiefs pressed to their noses. Amy couldn't imagine what the Misses Ransome were doing in Turkey and didn't care; her whalebone corset was pinching her mercilessly, and her lightweight silk traveling costume seemed to weigh fifty pounds. The bolero jacket with its leg-of-mutton sleeves was suffocating. The sun beat down mercilessly on the canvas top of the coach, and the unpaved road they were traveling had more holes in it than a tinker's stockings. Amy felt as if she had been traveling forever and would never, ever reach her destination.

She glanced out the isinglass window at the sandy desert spreading before them, dotted occasionally with patches of dry grass. The Woolcotts' settlement was supposedly just beyond the next bend in the road, but it might as well have been on the moon as far as Amy was concerned. If the wheels beneath her jammed into one more gully, she was going to scream.

Suddenly she saw two riders approaching from the open plain at a gallop. She stared at them curiously, aware from her reading that there was nothing out there except scrub and rocks. Her idle interest changed to alarm when the driver above them suddenly reined in the coach horses, and both arriving riders vaulted off their animals while they were still moving.

"What's going on?" Mrs. Spaulding said as they jolted to a rough stop, looking around at the others in consternation.

"There are two masked men out there," Amy began in a frightened voice, her reply ending in a gasp as the taller of the two arrivals pulled a pistol from his waistband.

"Oh, my God," she said, her eyes widening.

"What?" one of the sisters said, going paler than she already was. "What is it?"

"I think we're being robbed," Amy whispered.

The second sister screamed, just as the coach door was yanked open on Amy's side and the travelers were confronted by the two armed men.

The taller one locked eyes with Amy and said curtly in English, "Out."

Amy glanced at Mrs. Spaulding, who looked as if she were going to faint.

"Get out," the man said again, and Amy had no choice but to obey, moving to the door and then glancing uncertainly at the ground, which seemed very far away. The portable steps used by the coachman were still stored up on top with the luggage.

The bandit stepped forward and reached up swiftly to lift her down to the ground. Amy had a quick impression of supple strength before she landed on the packed dirt and yanked herself away, dusting her skirt with her hands.

"Now the rest of you, out," the bandit said, gesturing with his pistol for the remaining passengers to disembark. They did so, slowly, too terrified to object, as the second bandit hovered silently nearby. Amy looked back at the first bandit, whose gaze was fixed on her face. She stared back, mesmerized by the huge dark eyes, the glossy black curls tumbling over the smooth brow, the arched bridge of the nose partially concealed by his mask. He's young, she thought irrelevantly, then gulped aloud as Mr. Ames lunged for him, grabbing for the robber's pistol hand.

What happened next took place so fast that Amy hardly had time to register the scene before it ended. The bandit danced out of reach easily and then whirled instantly to crack his pistol over the back of the traveler's head. Ames dropped to the ground bonelessly, and the bandit looked up at the rest of the passengers, asking soundlessly if anyone else cared to try. They all stared back at him in horror, and after waiting a few beats, he said, "Give me all of your valuables. Now."

Amy stripped off her rings and bracelet, tossing them into the scarf the highwaymen had provided. She looked up while removing her garnet earbobs and saw that the coachman was gagged and tied to his seat above the cab; she hadn't even seen the second bandit at work. She glanced away quickly.

The first bandit waited until the pile of money and jewelry at his feet was complete and then said, "Back inside. Now."

The passengers scrambled to obey, happy that it seemed as though they would survive. The second bandit assisted the women into their seats, then hoisted the unconscious businessman to his shoulder and dumped him on the floor on the coach. As Amy moved to take Mr. Harington's extended hand, the taller bandit said in his clipped English, "Not you."

Amy's heart sank, and she glanced desperately at Mrs. Spaulding, who rose to her feet once more.

"What do you mean?" that good lady demanded. "You have what you wanted. Let her go."

"She comes with me," the bandit said shortly, urging Amy toward his waiting horse.

"I must protest," Harrington said. "This is an outrage—"

The tall bandit raised his pistol over his head and fired it. The travelers shrank back, stunned into silence. Then Mrs. Spaulding started to cry.

"The next one is for her if there's any more trouble," the bandit said shortly, then stuffed his pistol into his belt as the second robber continued to cover him. The first one put his hands on either side of Amy's waist and lifted her onto his horse. He then vaulted into place behind her and kicked the horse's flanks.

Amy waited until she sensed that he was distracted with controlling the animal and then flailed her arms, striking him in the face and trying to jump off the moving horse. The bandit seized her about the waist with an arm that felt like an iron band and said into her ear, "Try that again and you will be very sorry."

Amy subsided in despair as the ground sped by beneath the horse's hooves, and the sound of Mrs. Spaulding's hysterical sobs rang in her ears.

"Hold the smelling salts steady, Listak. The fumes will wake her up," James said to the servant, who wafted the bottle under Beatrice's nostrils. The older woman coughed and stirred, wrinkling her nose.

"Thank you, Listak, you may go," James said.

The servant padded silently from the room as Beatrice struggled into a sitting position, memory flooding back as she eyed her husband, then the sobbing woman who sat slumped in an armchair. Mrs. Spaulding's face was crumpled with misery, and her red-rimmed eyes were wet and swollen.

"Tell me it was a bad dream," Bea whispered to James, who was hovering over her, his expression concerned. "Tell me the man from the embassy was not just here. Tell me that Amy

26

has not been kidnapped."

"It was not a dream. Amy has been kidnapped."

Beatrice moaned and closed her eyes. "Oh, why do we remain in this cursed country where a Western woman is not safe? First Sarah, now Amy. It's like a recurring nightmare."

Mrs. Spaulding broke into fresh cries and bowed her head dramatically.

"You can't compare what happened to Sarah with this incident. Sarah volunteered to stay in Sultan Hammid's harem to teach the Princess Roxalena English, then was sold to Kalid Shah under Ottoman law. Amy was kidnapped by highwaymen."

"What's the difference?" Beatrice cried. "They were both treated as chattel by these Turkish infidels. Why can't we return to Boston where it is safe to walk the streets?"

"We can't return to Boston because my business is here," James replied patiently. "And bad things happen in America too, Bea; the war between the states was evidence of that."

Bea looked across the room at Mrs. Spaulding. "Don't give me a history lecture now, James—I will not be able to bear it. And where the devil is Listak? She should show Mrs. Spaulding upstairs so that she can rest."

"I'm all right," Mrs. Spaulding said in a small voice. Then, pressing her hand to her mouth, she added, "I feel so responsible."

"Nonsense," James said briskly. "There was nothing you could have done under the circumstances. Getting yourself killed would not have prevented what happened." He strode to the door and summoned the servant, then helped Mrs. Spaulding to her feet and led her to the hall, as the distraught woman leaned heavily on his arm.

"Go upstairs with Listak and lie down in the guest room. I have summoned Dr. Hilway. Perhaps he will be able to prescribe some laudanum for you so that you can sleep. If we hear any news, I promise I will come up and tell you."

Mrs. Spaulding nodded unhappily, then walked toward the stairwell with the servant. James waited until she had climbed the stairs and disappeared along the gallery before he went in to his wife.

"An official protest will be lodged with the embassy today," James said to her.

Bea shot him a furious glance. "Official protest, my eye. What good will that do? It's obvious the Sultan can't subdue these rebels, or they wouldn't be terrorizing every traveler in the country! This is all your fault, James. If you had gone back to the States to get Amelia, none of this would have happened."

"I couldn't leave the business that long, Bea. It doesn't run itself."

"At the very least you should have met the

train instead of asking two women to take the coach alone."

James sat next to her on the divan and patted her hand consolingly. "Don't be silly, Bea. These bandits are everywhere. Amelia could have been seized at any time, and my presence would not necessarily have made a difference. There were two men in the coach with her, remember."

"That's just my point—it isn't safe for any of us to be here!" Beatrice replied, her thin face pinched with worry. "And why did we have to move out of the city? We used to live within walking distance of the station. Being so far away makes us easy prey for these hoodlums."

"You wanted to move, Bea, to escape the heat," James replied wearily. "Don't you remember?"

Beatrice made a dismissive gesture. "Never mind that. Can't you exert some pressure through your business connections to get Amy back?"

"Not until we know who did it."

Beatrice threw up her hands in exasperation. "Everyone knows who is responsible for these raids. It's that wild brother of Osman Bey's, the one who thinks he's going to depose the Sultan."

"We can't prove that."

"You don't need proof. Even the papers say that he's financing his anti-government activities by robbing Western travelers and selling kidnapped women into slavery. And that's the fate in store for my brother's girl unless you do something about it!"

"If he's Osman's brother, he must be a decent sort," James said mildly. "I don't think he will hurt Amy."

"I'm sure he won't—she's much too valuable a commodity to damage. She'll be worth more in good condition, don't you think?" She covered her face with her hands.

"Calm down, Bea."

"You're calm enough for both of us. It strikes me that you were a lot more upset when Sarah disappeared. Is that because she's *your* cousin and Amy is related to *me?*"

"Don't be absurd, Bea, I know very well that there is great cause for concern. But both of us getting into a state is not going to solve this problem. As soon as the embassy opens in the morning, I will be there, and I promise you I will do everything in my power to get Amy back."

"Have I been talking to myself, James? The embassy isn't going to help you! Didn't you learn that ten years ago when Sarah was taken? Diplomats can't affect the behavior of rebels who don't care about anything except raising money for their cause."

"Then what do you suggest, Bea?" James asked in a tired voice.

"Call in the only person who might have a chance of negotiating with them."

"And who is that?"

"Kalid Shah."

Chapter Two

"Mother, why is the sultan of the United States called the president?" Tariq asked, looking up from his book. His wide dark eyes, so like his father's, were lively with interest.

"There is no sultan in the United States, Tariq. The president is chosen by the people, who vote for him. The office of head of state is elected, not inherited," Sarah answered.

"So there is no crown prince, like me?"

"No."

"But then the people don't know who their president will be until the last minute," Tariq said, puzzled.

"That's true. But they have a chance to change things if they don't like their present leader; they are not stuck with him until he dies."

The boy shook his head. "It's very different from Turkey, isn't it?"

Sarah sighed. "Yes, it is. Now go back to the geography lesson, please. I'll have a quiz ready when you're done."

The boy groaned but bent his head obediently. Sarah smiled to herself and walked down the aisle of the Orchid Palace schoolroom, built for her by her husband. She was now teaching about twenty students, three of them her own children, the rest a continuously changing group of palace tots whose parents took advantage of the free education. She stopped next to the desk of her daughter, Princess Yasmin, who was laboriously copying out a list of English words, which were lined up next to each other like little soldiers. She had inherited Sarah's mania for neatness, as well as her fair coloring and independent nature. At the back of the room, Sarah's servant Memtaz played with Prince Nessim, who at four was too young for school but liked to play "letters," calling out the names of English and Arabic characters with equal enthusiasm.

Kalid's face appeared in the glass window of the door as he tapped on it. Sarah walked over to the door and opened it, admitting her husband.

"Lunch time," he said.

"In a few minutes."

"Can we take a nap?" he asked, grinning.

Sarah smiled, feeling her face grow hot. After ten years, he was still the most attractive man she had ever met. Nearly forty now, with some gray threads running through his coal-black hair, Kalid still exuded the same sexual energy which had captivated Sarah from their first meeting. It was difficult to remember now that she had hated him then and had spent the first months of their relationship fighting with him continually.

"How was the tax collector?" Sarah asked him, referring to his morning meeting with the Sultan's representative.

"Angry, and now I am too," Kalid replied. "No wonder the rebels are gaining adherents every day. If the Sultan tries to squeeze one more drop of blood from the people of my district, I think there will be open revolt."

"I had a letter from Roxalena today," Sarah said quickly to change the subject, which was not a pleasant one. She reached into the pocket of her capacious bengaline skirt and produced it. Sarah favored wearing Western dress in the classroom; it made her feel once more like the public school teacher she had once been.

"What does she say?" Kalid asked, picking up one of the English readers and examining it.

"That Osman has been away for two weeks and she misses him. That the baby is just beginning to talk, but he only says, 'wet' and 'eat.' "

"That's all he needs to say," Kalid replied, laughing. "Come on, Sarah, let the nippers go. I'm starving."

Sarah clapped her hands and the children erupted from their seats, the three Shah children dashing for their father. He entertained them for a few minutes and then shooed them off for lunch with Memtaz.

"Alone at last," he said, his British accent, the legacy of his time at Oxford, strong as always when he spoke English. "You spend too much time with this kindergarten and not enough with me."

"You're busy all day with Bursa's affairs."

"Never too busy for you. Now come along— Kosem is expecting us in her apartments, and then we should have time for a short 'rest'." He kissed the back of her neck.

"How is Kosem feeling today?" Kalid's aged grandmother was now confined to her couch most of the time, but her mind was as agile as ever.

"A little tired. But she was calling the cook on the carpet when I saw her, so there's no cause for concern."

Sarah chuckled. They left the classroom and stepped into the marble-floored hall just as Turhan Aga, the captain of Kalid's guard, appeared around a corner and bowed.

"What is it?" Kalid said to him impatiently,

eager to get away with his wife.

"A message from the pashana's kinsman, James Woolcott. It was hand delivered to me just now," Turhan said.

"James?" Sarah said. "What does it say?"

Kalid unsealed the envelope and opened the missive, scanning the lines rapidly. "He says that he will be traveling to Bursa shortly and requests an immediate audience with me when he arrives," Kalid replied, his expression puzzled.

"That's all? Nothing to tell you what it's about?"

"Nothing." Kalid nodded to Turhan, dismissing him.

"That's odd. Will you see him right away when he comes?" Sarah asked.

Kalid put his arm around her shoulders. "Darling, of course. Now don't worry. It's probably nothing serious. You know that your cousin's wife has a flair for the dramatic, and she is doubtless behind this. Come along—Kosem is waiting."

Sarah followed him, not as certain as her husband that there was no cause for concern.

The ride across the sandy flatlands seemed to last a long time. Amy was too scared to struggle any further, so she sat before the bandit on the horse and tried not to think about the fate in store for her as the scenery passed in a blur.

Would she be raped and then murdered? If the objective of her captor was robbery, then why had she been taken? In her present state, she couldn't think clearly and couldn't formulate a plan of action. When the horse made a sudden turn and began to ascend into the surrounding foothills, she stirred, looking around at the changing terrain. The bandit's arm tightened warningly.

Amy subsided, feeling dwarfed by his size and strength. He was much taller than most of the Turkish men she had seen, and the body pressed to hers was slim but very muscular. She had no chance against him, so her only option was to bide her time and see what happened.

They climbed steadily for a while, the horse picking its way along the rock-strewn path between crags, the clopping of the second horse's hooves signaling that her captor's companion was right behind them. Amy had just about decided that her back was broken from the jouncing ride, which made the passenger coach seem like a pleasure craft, when they arrived at a clearing where several tents stood around a central campfire. Veiled women tended smoking cookpots, and at the far end of the glen Amy saw a cave hollowed out of the rock where another, smaller fire was burning. She hardly had time to take it all in before her captor jumped down from the horse and lifted her to the ground after him. Before she could move, he whipped a rope from under his saddle and bound her hands with it, then led her stumbling to a nearby tent.

All the inhabitants of the camp stopped what they were doing to stare at the oddly dressed newcomer, her hat lost on the road, blond hair tumbling loose from its knot, the ripped and stained hem of her blue silk skirt trailing on the ground. Amy refused to look at any of them, keeping her head high and her eyes focused on the distance until she was inside the tent, where more women waited.

Her captor tied her to a tent pole and issued several curt orders in Turkish, which Amy did not understand. Then, with one last glance in her direction, he turned on his heel and left the tent.

Amy looked at the women, who were staring back at her with frank interest. Then she glanced quickly around the tent, spotting a crude, hand-printed flyer stamped with a half moon and a star lying on the dirt floor, its incomprehensible text partially obscured by a muddy footprint. She realized with a sudden shock that this was one of the broadsheets distributed by the rebels against the Sultan, a call to arms which appeared at uncertain intervals whenever the insurgents had the facilities to print it. She had read a description of such notices in a British newspaper article while waiting for the coach.

Was she in the hands of the anti-government rebels, who bartered hostages for anything they needed to continue their fight? Or had the flyer been brought in carelessly by a group of bandits, who stole only for their own profit and had taken her merely for sport, to be passed around from man to man until they tired of her? Or was there some other, worse fate in store for her, too horrible even to imagine? There was no way to tell, and all the prospects were terrifying.

The oldest of the women, who seemed to be in charge, unbound Amy's hands as she barked at her companions. They seized Amy's arms when she began to struggle, holding her until a young girl entered with a steaming cauldron full of hot water. She dumped it into a footed, cast-iron tub as the old lady, wearing an expression of exaggerated innocence, indicated it with her hand.

Amy eyed her and then the waiting tub. The old woman raised her brows, as if to say, "All we want to do is give you a bath."

Amy subsided and the women holding her released her arms. Amy knew that she needed a bath, probably more than she ever had in her life. The trip had been hot and dusty before she was kidnapped, and her struggles with her captor afterward had only added to the grime adhering to her skin, hair, and clothes.

"I'll take a bath if you get all of these people out of here," she said to the old woman.

The response was a blank stare.

Amy made a sweeping gesture to include all of her audience and then jerked her thumb to indicate distance.

The old woman shook her head; the black veil wrapped across her forehead and sweeping down to her shoulders wrinkled with the gesture.

Amy shrugged "All right, you stay," she said, pointing to the crone.

The old woman nodded and put her hand on the shoulder of the girl.

"The two of you?" Amy asked.

They stared back at her impassively.

Amy sighed. "Fine," she said resignedly. "Get rid of the rest of them."

The old woman clapped her hands and said something in Turkish. The remaining women filed out reluctantly, glancing over their shoulders as they went.

Amy was left with the old lady and the girl, who went to a chest in the tent and removed from it a stack of rough towels, a folded gown, and what looked like a lump of wax. As the girl came closer, Amy realized that the lump was homemade soap.

The camp dwellers regarded her expectantly, waiting for her to undress.

"Turn around," Amy said, making a spinning motion with her finger.

They didn't move.

41

Amy turned her back on them and ripped off her clothes, which were in tatters anyway. She heard the women exclaim behind her when they saw her boned corset, the girl bursting into giggles. Amy had trouble getting out of it and finally had to stand still, humiliated, while the women unlaced her. Then they watched as she loosened her stockings from her suspenders and pulled off the rest of her underthings, murmuring admiringly when her body was finally revealed. Amy jumped into the water immediately to escape their scrutiny, gasping when she realized that it hadn't cooled off as much as she'd anticipated. The girl left the tent at once and returned with a pail full of cool water, which she quickly added to the bath to make its temperature more tolerable.

Amy was acutely embarrassed to be bathing under the interested gaze of these two strangers, but her desire to get clean overrode her discomfiture. She lathered up with the strange soap, which had a resinous texture and smelled stongly of pine, a pleasant enough fragrance but a strong contrast to the scents from Worth and Cacharel that Amy customarily used. When the old lady lifted Amy's hair off her neck and removed the last remaining pins from it, Amy did not object. She bent her head as the girl dampened her hair and the crone lathered it, the two of them chattering to one another, doubtless commenting on its pale color, which the uniformly dark Turks found unusual. When Amy was ready to be rinsed, the women brought more warm water, dousing her until she held up her hand and stepped from the tub.

They dried her with the scratchy towels and slipped a light, almost transparent gown over her head. Its hem fell to her heels, and its thin sleeves belled at the wrist. They gave her slippers and a knitted cord to belt the waist, as Amy tried to look around unobtrusively, searching for a means of escape.

She had an inspiration when the older woman paused next to her, pinning a gauzy veil to her hair. Amy tapped her on the shoulder. The woman looked at her and Amy opened her mouth, miming spooning something out of a bowl.

The woman nodded, then said something to the young girl. The girl left immediately, and Amy saw her chance. The bath had refreshed her and given her time to devise a strategy. When the crone bent to replace something in the storage chest, Amy knocked her down and bolted past her, running through the flap of the tent. She turned immediately to head around the back of the tent and made for the woods.

She had gone only a few feet outside when she was seized so roughly from behind that she shot into the air with the halted momentum, her feet still moving. Two large men carried her, kicking and screaming, back into the tent and tied her securely, hand and foot, to its supporting pole as the crone supplied them with a gag to silence her screams.

Guards had apparently been posted all around the tent.

Amy sagged with frustration and stared daggers at her jailers, who finished binding her, their expressions impassive, and then left. The old lady sat down cross-legged on the ground and produced a bag from beneath her voluminous shawl. She took out a piece of embroidery and set to work, holding the cloth close to the small fire burning under the tent hole so that she could see.

Amy closed her eyes to block out the scene, concentrating on coming up with an alternative route for her escape.

Malik strode into the cave and sat by himself on an overturned boulder, shaking his head at the food offered to him by one of his companions. When the man tried to talk to him, Malik waved him off, grabbing a bottle of raki and rising again to pace around the confined space.

His men exchanged glances with one another, then looked away. They had seen Malik in this mood before, and it was best not to bother him, to leave him alone and let him brood. When he wheeled suddenly and stalked outside, they ignored him, continuing with their conversations, dice games, and makeshift meals.

When he had formulated his plans, he would tell them.

But Malik was not thinking about his campaign against the Sultan. He walked some distance from the camp to a clearing he knew, strewn with the stumps of lightning-struck trees and cooled by a nearby stream. He sat on its bank and watched the bubbling water rush by, sipping from his bottle slowly.

He could not get the woman captive out of his mind.

He had kidnapped and sold women before; it was a standard practice for his band. The captives were usually so panicked that they cowered and wept, on the verge of hysteria every waking minute until he finally disposed of them to some dealer, glad to have peace and the money at the same time.

But this one was different. She had looked at him with a very bold eye and had not cried once, not even when he had tied her up and dumped her in the tent to contemplate a very uncertain future. That was the moment many of them broke down and left dignity in the dust. But she had weathered it all and then attempted an escape, which bespoke a spirit and determination unusual in Western women. He had observed that most of them were pampered, coddled creatures who jumped on a chair if they saw an ant and went completely to pieces in reduced circumstances. Although this one looked and smelled as if she had been raised in luxurious surroundings, her attitude and actions belied her appearance.

Her appearance posed another problem. It was difficult to dismiss the image of a woman so gorgeous that she would turn any man's head. He had held her in his arms during the ride to the camp, pressed the slight, curvaceous body to his own, and inhaled the fragrance of her hair and skin. He had rarely seen eyes that color—gray without a trace of blue, like the ocean in the rain. And her hair! Pure beaten gold, like the minarets which topped the great mosque in the square of Hagia Sophia. Strands of it had blown back against his face as they were riding, soft as cornsilk and the same color, as fresh as grass.

Malik drained the bottle disgustedly and threw it into the stream, where it shattered against a rock. This rambling was unproductive and self-indulgent. He knew what he had to do and he would do it. He would forget her as he had the others and move on, never losing sight of his goal.

There was no other way to reach it.

James Woolcott sat in the office of Secretary Danforth at the American embassy and marveled how little the paneled chamber had changed over the years. The undersecretary he had first met when his cousin Sarah disappeared from the Sultan's harem was now the ambassador's secretary. The Kirman carpet had been replaced with one of Afghan design, but the red drapes, the gold tassels, and the bust of the late President Lincoln still remained. James was reading one of the framed diplomas on the wall when Danforth bustled in from the next room.

James rose and shook the diplomat's hand, noting that Danforth was even more portly and florid than when he had seen him last. The secretary was also still something of a fashion plate; he sported a full-skirted frock coat with braided trim, in a gray tweed unsuitable for the climate, and carried a gold topped cane.

"How are you, Woolcott?" Danforth said, indicating that James should sit again. "I think the last time I saw you was at the embassy tea about six months ago. You look prosperous. I hope that your business is still doing well?" Danforth sat behind his desk and picked up a single sheet of onionskin paper.

"Very well."

"Yes, I assumed so. Well, you are becoming a rich man and I, as you see, am still here." He sighed, perusing the letter he held. "I have your complaint in my hand; it was passed on to me by my attache. It seems that now your niece is missing." He dropped the page and folded his chubby hands on the desk before him. "If I re-call the circumstances correctly, I first met you when your cousin Sarah disappeared. I have to ask you, Woolcott, how is it that you have so much trouble keeping track of your female rel-atives?"

James stared at him for a moment, then said, "How is it that a country as powerful as the United States cannot guarantee the safe travel of its citizens through Turkey?"

Danforth, who should have been insulted by the jibe, merely waved aside the remark. "Come, come, Woolcott, don't fence with me. You and I have both lived here for years. We know what these people are like. If the Sultan isn't executing some harmless peasant for spit-ting in the street, the rebels are holding up trains and robbing passengers at gunpoint. We cannot change the culture; we can only try to hold our own and keep the diplomatic channels open, hoping that eventually the Sultanate will fall. In the meantime, we have issued an advi-sory to every U.S. citizen who applies for papers to travel to the Empire, describing the uncer-tain political climate of this area and the risks inherent in coming here. More than that we just cannot do."

James was silent.

Danforth looked down at the letter again. "Your niece was traveling with a chaperone?"

"Yes, a middle-aged woman, a friend of her

mother's. Mrs. Spaulding was not taken by the bandits."

"It seems that you would have done better to provide your niece with an armed marine from the barracks in Tripoli," Danforth said musingly, pursing his lips. "Is this Spaulding woman available for questioning?"

"Yes, I assume so. She was, of course, very upset when it happened, but I'm sure she would want to cooperate."

Danforth nodded. "And the passengers were robbed, but only your niece was kidnapped?"

"Yes."

Danforth nodded again. "It sounds like the work of the rebels to me."

"My wife thinks so, too."

"Your wife?"

"Amelia is actually my wife's niece, her brother's child. Beatrice thinks it was Malik Bey or his men."

"I agree. There are bandits abroad in the Empire who have no cause except lining their own pockets, but they don't take chances like this and they don't kidnap women for sale. They're not organized enough to house and transport them. Bey has quite an extensive and efficient organization and this type of thing is his trademark, I'm afraid."

"So what can we do?"

Danforth rose from his padded leather chair

and strolled around the room, his hands behind his back.

"The United States is in a very difficult position with respect to the rebels, Woolcott, and I'm sure you can appreciate why. They are seeking to remove a ruthless dictator from power and replace him with a democratic government, so we are of course in sympathy with their aims. But since they raise money for their operation by preying on well-heeled travelers, many of whom happen to be British and American, we have to condemn their methods."

"This incident wasn't just a robbery, Danforth. Amelia was kidnapped."

"Selling Western women into slavery is even more lucrative than banditry," Danforth said, shrugging. "From the description I have here, your unfortunate niece is just what these men are always looking for—young, blonde, and, I assume, untouched."

James nodded, not looking at Danforth.

"That explains why the other women on the coach weren't taken. They wouldn't be worth much."

"What can we do?" James said again.

"Well, the Sultan's government is the official one, as you know, and I will file a complaint with his representatives, but I wouldn't expect anything to come of that. If the Sultan could control the rebels, we would not be having this conversation."

"My wife thinks I should ask Kalid Shah to intervene in this matter."

"Kalid Shah? The Pasha of Bursa?"

"He is now a member of the family," James said, looking at the ceiling.

"Yes, I recall that your cousin eventually married her purchaser. Quite a turn of events there." Danforth considered the suggestion, biting his lower lip. "Shah has been trying to moderate between the rebels and the Sultan," Danforth said slowly. "He might be able to help."

"Then you think it's a good idea?"

Danforth widened his eyes. "It's worth a try. Like my government, Shah is caught between the two factions. He has a Western education, a Western wife and decidedly Western political leanings, but he is still the Sultan's man, and if the Sultan falls, he loses the pashadom of Bursa for his son."

"I assume that Shah hasn't been getting anywhere with the Sultan, or the rebels wouldn't be so active."

"Shah's been trying to win some concessions from Hammid to placate the rebels and work out a compromise." Danforth spread his hands to indicate futility. "But the Sultan is adamant about retaining his absolute power."

"That's how dictators always fall. They won't give a little to preserve what's left, and eventually they lose everything."

51

"Such is the lesson of history," Danforth said sadly. "And in this case, the Sultan's attitude toward the rebels is exacerbated by the fact that the oldest Bey brother ran off with his daughter."

"Yes, I know. Roxalena is Sarah's dear friend."

"Then you understand why the Sultan regards the Bey brothers as twin thorns in his side. Osman, his former captain of halberdiers, eloped with Princess Roxalena, and now Osman's brother is organizing a grass-roots army against Hammid. It's a very tense situation."

"And Amelia is caught in the middle of it."

"We all are, but she's in the most immediate danger. The rebels don't hang on to their captives long; quick turnover is imperative. We must act fast."

James rose. "I'll go to see Shah immediately."

"And I will meet with the Ambasador today to see what we can do from our end." Danforth reached out to shake James's hand. "Good luck, Woolcott."

"Thank you," James said.

He had a feeling he was going to need it.

Amy watched as the man entered and dropped the tent flap behind him. From his height and his eyes she recognized him as the first bandit who had kidnapped her.

"What are you going to do with me?" she demanded, tugging on the ropes which held her bound to the pole.

The man surveyed her without replying. He was now dressed in loose homespun trousers with a belted tunic slashed deeply at the neck. His coal black hair waved loosely over his forehead and his collar, and she saw that his mask had covered a thin, high-bridged nose and a wide, sensual mouth with a full lower lip. She had been right about his age; he was no more than twenty-five or thirty, but his intense, serious gaze bespoke a responsibility and a drive far beyond his years.

She could not tear her eyes from his.

"Answer me," she said. "I know you speak English."

He said nothing, merely walking in a circle around her and surveying her as if she were the blue-ribbon heifer at the county fair. The scrutiny made Amy intensely uncomfortable, and she was finally able to look away from him. At that moment he stepped forward and lifted her chin with his finger.

He studied her face, and at such close range Amy was able to study his. He had the longest eyelashes she had ever seen, so thick and dense that they made his eyes seem huge in his olive-skinned face, and when his lips parted, she had a glimpse of strong white teeth. He stroked her chin absently with his thumb, looking her over, and she shivered at the touch, mesmerized by his stare. Then she realized that she was submitting to this humiliating examination without a struggle, and she jerked back from him angrily. He smiled slightly, which infuriated her even more.

"You'll never get away with this," she hissed.

He removed the veil the old woman had pinned to her hair and ran his hand lightly over the flaxen mass, lifting it from her neck as if weighing gold.

"Stop touching me!" she yelled, close to tears at her inability to get away from him. She hated her helplessness, as well as the way he was making her feel.

In response he undid the single button at her neck and slipped his hand smoothly inside her collar, as if to sample the silken texture of her skin.

Amy reacted instinctively, not taking time to consider the rashness of her action. She spat in his face.

He looked surprised for a moment, then his expression hardened. He grabbed her collar and was pulling her toward him roughly when the tent flap lifted and the second bandit came in, calling, "Malik!"

Malik, Amy thought. Where had she seen that name? Then she remembered. Malik Bey was the sworn enemy of the Sultan, the rebel with an enormous price on his head whom she had read about in the newspaper.

Amy felt her throat close with fear. Her first guess had been correct then, and she was destined for the slave markets. That was why she had been bathed and handled so carefully, why this man was examining her as if she were some rare commodity. To him she was; selling her would bring him a fortune that he could then spend on weapons and supplies to outfit his men.

Amy refused to cry, but she began to tremble helplessly. Finding the flyer and the rebel leader in the same camp was not a coincidence.

She was lost.

The second bandit stopped short at the scene before him and then burst out laughing. He said something jokingly to Malik, but the rebel leader did not smile. He released Amy suddenly and then stalked out of the tent.

Anwar Talit dashed out after him and said again in Turkish, "Come on, let's strip her naked and have a look. That'll help to put a price on her."

"No."

"Why not?"

"I don't have to mistreat her to see that she's worth fifteen hundred kurush, maybe two thousand. She's very young, probably a virgin."

"Probably? I'll make sure!"

"I said no. If we start violating our captives, then all the men will want to do it and we'll be running an orgy here. The revolution will be forgotten. I must demand the same discipline of myself that I expect from my soldiers."

Anwar studied his friend and his face changed. "You want her, don't you?" Anwar said slowly.

"Don't be ridiculous. All she means to me is the price she'll bring."

"But you like this one. That hair, the gray eyes, the white skin. She's much more beautiful than any of the others we've sold. And she has spirit. You always respond to that."

Malik shrugged.

"Then why were you undressing her when I walked in?" Anwar persisted.

"I wasn't undressing her, I was merely seeing if the report I got from the women was accurate. She must be perfect to demand that much money for her."

"And?"

"As far as I was able to see, she is flawless," Malik answered quietly.

"Then take her. If it knocks a few hundred off the virgin price, what's the difference? She'll still bring more in one shot than we could raise with several train raids."

Malik swallowed hard, not meeting his gaze.

Anwar chuckled knowingly. "You should go to bed with one of the camp women every now and then, my friend. It does ease the tension."

Malik didn't answer, remembering the captive's yellow hair and creamy skin. "Let's sell her off as quickly as possible," he said abruptly. "Contact the Greek, Diomedes, the one who buys for the auctions in Medina, first thing in the morning."

"He's cheap, Malik. He won't offer what she's worth," Anwar said.

"Then call in Halmad from Beirut. I want the top price, but she has to be gone by the end of the week."

Anwar nodded, correctly reading the tight expression on his friend's face.

Obviously, Malik didn't trust himself around her.

Amy tried to get into a comfortable position on the ground, but she was bound so closely to the pole that she could only move a few inches. Darkness had descended and most of the camp was asleep, but she could see the shadow of her guards on the tent, moving slowly, a menacing puppet show backlit by the fire.

The women had left her alone at last, and of her captor there was no sign.

Amy had rejected the dinner the old woman produced, and since then she'd been ignored. The noise outside the tent had gradually diminished with nightfall, and the silence seemed to conceal a thousand threats. She had rubbed her wrists raw trying to loosen her bonds. Her legs were cramped and she was starving and she had a skull-cleaving headache.

And she was scared.

There was a sound outside and she quickly feigned sleep, cradling her head on her arm and watching the entrance through her lashes. Malik Bey came in and pulled his tunic over his head, exposing broad shoulders and sinewy arms to her view.

Amy quickly closed her eyes to slits, straining to see by the light of the banked fire and the smoky oil lamp sitting on a chest. Bey took a step closer to her and unrolled a woven floor mat from a bundle in the corner. He dropped his belt, his hand going to the knife stuck into the waistband of his pants.

Amy caught her breath, keeping still with an effort. He was clearly undressing. Was he going to *sleep* here? It made sense in terms of his desire to safeguard his investment, but the thought of having him so close by all night, breathing the same air, made her shudder inwardly.

He moved and she shut her eyes completely, listening tensely as he knelt next to her. She froze, trying to keep her breathing deep and even, as he touched her hair and then put the back of his hand to her cheek. Then he rose abruptly, sighing deeply, and she heard him go back to the mat and drop onto it, his remaining clothes rustling softly as he settled down.

Amy risked a look and saw that he was turned away from her, a cloak flung carelessly over his upper body. She watched as his respiration settled into a steady rhythm; then she stretched her legs to ease a cramp and tried to relax a little herself.

Why had he touched her so tenderly? It was hardly the action of a ruthless body broker who was preparing to sell her, but she knew that must be his plan. Why else would he have taken her? No one was bothering her sexually, and that had to be because he wanted to get the maximum price for an innocent girl. Was he staying with her tonight to make sure none of the other men interfered with her? Amy was hardly sophisticated in such matters, but she had been fascinated by the details of the newspaper article about the rebels and remembered it vividly.

The light from the oil lamp was blurring as her eyes grew heavy. She couldn't believe that she would sleep under such circumstances, but the events of the day had simply been too exhausting. Her mind drifted along the precipice of consciousness and then dropped over the edge.

Chapter Three

When Amy awoke, it was full day and the old lady was with her again.

Bey's pallet was back in the corner and he was gone.

"Where is your master?" Amy said to the old woman, who rose when she saw Amy looking at her and left the tent.

That accomplished a lot, Amy thought dismally, gazing down at her once spotless gown, which was now smeared with dirt from her night on the ground. Her head felt as if it were filled with cotton wool and her stomach was growling. She hardly had time to register these discomforts before the crone returned with a steaming bowl full of the same grayish meat Amy had rejected earlier.

"I'm not eating that," Amy said firmly, although she was already feeling lightheaded from hunger.

The woman placed it on the dirt floor in front of her. Amy shook her head.

The woman reached under her shawl, took out a leather pouch, and began to roll cigarettes impassively.

The girl who had helped with Amy's bath entered the tent and said, "Matka!"

The old woman glanced up and listened to the girl's message, then nodded. The girl left.

"Matka," Amy called.

Matka looked at her.

"You tell your master for me that I'm not eating this or anything else. I'll starve to death before I'll let him auction me off like a side of beef."

Matka didn't understand the words, but the defiant tone came through clearly. She looked down and continued to work, her expression neutral.

Amy passed the day in this fashion, refusing all meals while Matka continued to sit with her, going through her routine of homely tasks and ignoring Amy's outbursts completely. Amy was taken outside twice for walks with the guards and was subjected to the humiliation of being supervised by Matka while she relieved herself. It was dark again and Amy's leg muscles were screaming for more exercise when Malik swept through the tent opening and gestured abruptly for Matka to leave.

"Getting rid of my keeper?" Amy said, as the old lady vanished outside. "And she was such stimulating company, too."

Malik squatted before her, his eyes on a level with hers, and said, "You must eat."

"He speaks! What a miracle."

"You have eaten nothing since you came here."

"That's right, oh observant one. So if you plan to fatten me up for the slave market, you're going to be disappointed."

"I'll force you," he said smoothly.

"Then I'll bring it up again. If you think I can't, try me and see."

Malik sat back on his heels and said evenly, "You'll make yourself ill."

"That's right. And I'll be too skinny for you to sell me. What a shame."

"You won't be here long enough to lose much weight," he said, standing up in one smooth motion.

"What does that mean?" Amy demanded as he turned away from her.

He didn't answer.

"Turn me loose!" Amy yelled as he left, yanking on her bonds. "Don't leave me tied up like this, I can't stand it!"

Her voice echoed in the empty tent.

He was gone.

* * *

Sarah was correcting papers in her classroom when Memtaz entered and bowed, saying, "Pasha Kalid requests your presence in the audience room."

Sarah nodded. She dipped her pen into the inkwell one more time, made a note, and rose.

"Take my place here, Memtaz. All the children have their tasks, and I should be back before they finish." Sarah looked across the room at the bent heads as the Circassian slave bowed again.

"And if Nessim gets restless, just play that ball game with him until I return." Sarah went into the hall as quietly as possible, remembering the time when she couldn't travel anywhere in the palace without an escort of her husband's eunuchs. Now she flew through the corridors, her lightly shod feet almost soundless on the pink marble floors. The tapers of ten years earlier had been replaced by oil lamps, but they cast the same glow on the sandstone walls. Two halberdiers bowed as she approached, then banged on the carved double doors with their truncheons.

"Come," Kalid called from within, and the doors swung open to admit Sarah. She walked across the colorful bird-of-paradise carpet to the other end of the audience chamber, where Kalid sat with her cousin James in a small, plush anteroom hung with orchid silk. For friends and relatives Kalid ignored the large, formally appointed room where he received foreign dignitaries and used instead the cozy nook in which he felt more comfortable.

James rose to greet his cousin as Sarah offered her cheek for him to kiss.

"Dear Sarah," James said. "You're looking very well."

"I wish I could say the same of you, James. What on earth is wrong?" She looked at her husband and then sat next to him on the brocade divan he occupied, her eyes still searching his face.

"James has come to us with a problem," Kalid said.

Sarah looked at James, who had resumed his seat in a damask chair across from them.

James sighed. "Do you remember when I wrote you about Beatrice's niece, Amelia Ryder, who had been left in our care when her parents were killed?"

"Yes, of course. She was coming to stay with you, wasn't she?" Sarah said, glancing from James to her husband and then back again.

James nodded. "She never made it. She was traveling from the train station to our house by coach when the party was overtaken by bandits. She was kidnapped."

Sarah gasped.

"They think it was Malik Bey," Kalid added.

"Oh, no," Sarah whispered, clutching Kalid's

arm. "He deals with the . . ." she stopped.

"Slave traders. Yes, I know," James said wearily.

"Are you sure it was Malik?" Sarah asked.

"He fits the description Amelia's traveling companion gave. She said the bandit in charge was much taller than the other men, than the average Turk, and he spoke English with a British accent."

"Thanks to Osman," Sarah said softly. "And Malik is so brazen, he doesn't even try to disguise it."

"Why bother?" Kalid said. "Everyone knows who's behind these raids and they still can't stop him."

"The British papers write about him like he's Robin Hood," James said bitterly.

"James has asked me to intercede with the rebels and try to get Amelia back," Kalid said to Sarah.

"Will they listen to you?" Sarah asked.

Kalid shrugged. "Malik knows I've sought to avoid bloodshed by reasoning with Hammid, though I think he still sees me as the Sultan's man. But it can't hurt to try."

"Do you know where the rebels are?" James said.

"I have paid spies who can find them, go-betweens who have met with Malik before and know his haunts."

"You'll have to act fast, before Amelia is sold," Sarah said worriedly.

"If Malik wants to get the most for her, as I suspect he does, he'll have to wait for one of the bigger dealers to come to him," Kalid replied. "Traveling with this girl would be too conspicuous, not to mention dangerous, since her companion tells James she is spirited and probably would try to get away. I think I have some time, but I'll send a message right away."

"Thank you, Kalid," James said, relief evident in his voice. "You may be my only chance." He stood up and added, "I'll let you get to it."

"I'll be in touch as soon as I know anything," Kalid said, putting his hand on James's shoulder and walking Sarah's cousin across the audience room. Once James was entrusted to the escort who would see him out of the palace, Kalid returned to Sarah and wrapped his arms around her.

"So another proper young lady from Boston has fallen afoul of the nefarious Turks," Kalid said, his lips moving in her hair.

"She must be terrified," Sarah said. "I was."

"Of me?" Kalid said, holding her off to look at her. "You were not, *kourista*. You were spitting epithets every time I saw you."

"That doesn't mean I wasn't afraid," Sarah answered.

"Until I fell so hopelessly in love with you that

I did anything you asked," Kalid said, now kissing the shell of her ear.

"Strange, that's not exactly the way I remember it," Sarah said dryly.

"Do you remember the night we spent by the stream when I rescued you from the bedouins?" Kalid inquired softly, drawing her closer again.

"How could I forget that?" Sarah said. Then she looked up at him anxiously. "Kalid, tell me the truth. You're planning to go off alone to find Malik Bey, aren't you?"

"Not yet. I want to see how he responds to the inquiry first. Merely sending a message will be less threatening to him."

"He's not going to just hand the girl over to you."

"No. He'll want something for her, and I need to know what that is."

"Kalid, promise me you won't go looking for him. It's too dangerous."

Kalid shook his head dismissively. "I'm his only path to the Sultan if his campaign fails. He may not trust me completely, but he's not a fool. I'm worth far more to him alive than dead."

"Let's hope the same is true of Amelia Ryder," Sarah said quietly.

"Halmad is here to see you," Anwar said to Malik.

Malik put down the pistol he was cleaning and wiped his fingers on a rag.

It was dusk, and the moment he'd been dreading all day had arrived.

"Leave me alone with him," Malik said curtly.

Anwar left the cave and then reentered it seconds later with the slave dealer at his side. He waited until the two men had greeted one another before slipping outside.

"Anwar tells me you have a prize for me this time," Halmad said to Malik in his heavily accented Turkish.

Malik nodded. He didn't like the Lebanese, who dealt in human flesh from along the Nile into North Africa, across the Mediterranean into Europe and east into Asia, but Halmad had become a necessary part of the rebel enterprise. Since he had a massive shipping business following all the best trade routes, Halmad could pay the premium price, and if Malik was going to part with this woman who so stirred his blood, he was going to be well compensated for it.

"Where is she?" Halmad asked.

"She's nearby, don't worry. I want to know what you'll do with her first."

"I'd have to see her to be able to tell you that," Halmad said. "She's British?"

"American."

Halmad shrugged, negating the difference. "Blonde?" he inquired, smiling.

"Very," Malik replied shortly.

"And with the *gavur* eyes?"

"Yes. Gray, not blue."

"Young?"

"Still in her teens, is my guess."

"And you have not had her?" Halmad asked, brows raised skeptically.

"No. She is a virgin."

"How can you be sure?"

"Young American ladies of her class save it for their husbands, and she is unmarried. She has no wedding ring."

"How can you tell her class? Anwar said you kidnapped her from a traveling coach. It would seem then that you know nothing about her."

"I can tell her class from her clothes, her speech, the condition of her skin and hair and hands. She is well educated and well cared for; she has never done menial work."

Halmad frowned. "Then someone will be looking for her," he said worriedly.

"That's going to stop you?" Malik replied dryly.

"I don't want trouble with the American authorities."

"The Sultan can't find us. Do you think the Americans will do any better? Do you want to see her or not?"

Halmad threw up his hands. "Bring her in," he said.

Malik held up a warning finger. "I want to know what you plan to do with her. Will you bring her to the market in Beirut?"

"What difference will it make to you once you have your money?" Halmad replied. "You have never asked such a question before. You were counting the kurush before the woman had left the camp. What is special about this one?"

"I just want to know," Malik said unresponsively.

Halmad shrugged. "It would probably be Beirut—there is the most traffic through that market."

"Not at the Burnt Column," Malik said, naming the huge slave market in Constantinople.

"Of course not. I would never get enough for her there. Come now, Bey, you are wasting my time. Either bring the girl in here or I'm leaving, and I can tell you that I won't be so quick to answer your next summons."

Malik said nothing, but moved to the cave entrance and signaled to Anwar, who was waiting outside. Shortly afterward Anwar came in dragging a struggling Amy, who was wearing a fresh cotton gown, her hands tightly bound, her hair streaming loose over her shoulders.

Halmad stepped forward and looked her over with a professional eye, lifting her chin to examine her face in the lamplight and running his hands over her hair. Amy resisted as violently as she could, her defiant expression indicating that she knew what was happening.

"Very nice," Halmad said, nodding. "Two thousand at least. But she's a frisky filly—she

71

may be a problem to transport. Strip her and let me see if she's worth the effort."

Malik, who had known this was coming, stepped forward to unbutton the bodice of Amy's gown. Her head was down; she wouldn't look at him, but he could see the tears seeping slowly from under her lashes.

She was crying at last.

His hand fell away. "No," he said.

The slave dealer gazed at him in astonishment. "You expect me to buy her without seeing her?"

"I expect you to leave. I have changed my mind. She is not for sale."

Anwar stared at Malik, equally amazed, but said nothing, unwilling to disagree with his friend in front of an outsider.

"You brought me all the way out here for nothing?" Halmad sputtered. "You think I have nothing better to do than run around the Turkish countryside at the back and call of you rabble?"

"Anwar will compensate you for the trip," Malik said shortly. "Now go."

"Don't call me again," Halmad said angrily and swept from the cave.

Anwar glared at Malik, waiting for his instructions.

"Give Halmad five hundred and get rid of him," Malik ordered him.

Anwar shot Malik a disgusted glance, but he

turned to obey the order.

Malik looked back at Amy, who was gazing at him warily, her expression a combination of relief and fear; she was glad that Halmad was gone, but she didn't know what was coming next.

Malik met her searching gaze, then took the rope that tied her hands together and led her back to his tent. He didn't look up as he bound her to the pole; then he left immediately, not trusting himself to meet her eyes.

Anwar was waiting for him outside.

"Have you lost your mind?" Anwar demanded angrily. "Why didn't you let her go, you fool? To turn down that much money is madness!"

"Two thousand was not enough," Malik replied calmly. "She will bring more elsewhere."

"She will bring nothing because you won't sell her! Do you think I am an idiot? Halmad would have upped the price considerably if you had stripped her, as he requested. Now he's gone off in a huff, swearing never to deal with us again, and we're out five hundred kurush. All because you wanted to preserve the modesty of this *gavur* girl who obviously despises you."

"Halmad will cool down. And if he doesn't, there are other dealers. We'll get some in from Medina this week."

"And you'll refuse their offers too. That's your plan, isn't it, to turn everybody down and keep her here?"

Malik gazed back at him levelly. "You're jumping to conclusions. I know what I'm doing."

"You're lying to yourself, that's what you're doing."

"I don't tell you everything, Anwar. There are answers you'll learn only when the time is right."

Anwar was silent, but he looked skeptical.

"Don't worry," Malik said.

Anwar shook his head. "Malik, I don't care if you keep a harem as big as the Sultan's. But this woman could bring in a lot of money. What's worse, you made fools of us in front of a business connection we'll need in the future."

"Halmad needs us as much as we need him."

"That isn't the point. You're letting this girl interfere with the cause."

"I'm not doing that. I simply want to get more money for her, and I will."

"And if she knifes you while you sleep in the meantime?" Anwar said.

"No chance of that. I'm keeping her tied up."

"She's the one who has you tied, *agha*," Anwar said, and walked away.

Amy listened to the two men arguing outside, unable to make sense of the heated Turkish but glad that the discussion was keeping the pair of them occupied. When Matka was leaving the tent earlier, one of her crewel hooks had slipped out of her workbag, and the nearsighted old lady had not noticed it. Now the metal object lay just a few inches away from Amy, near her feet on the dirt floor.

If she could get to it, she could use it to unravel the hemp rope that bound her and get free.

Amy strained against her bonds, trying to get the toe of her right slipper near enough to touch the needle, but her awkward position didn't give her enough leverage to reach it. She tried again, huffing and puffing in the process. She looked up anxiously, afraid that she might attract the attention of the bandits. They went on talking, but she decided to wait until they were gone to continue.

It seemed a long time before they separated and left. She knew that the guards were still posted outside, but they were farther off and less likely to hear her. She began again, twisting and writhing until she was covered with a thin film of sweat and she had scored a rut in the ground with the heel of her shoe. She bit her lip in concentration; someone might come in at any time, and if she didn't succeed before Bey returned to sleep for the night, her chance would be gone. She stretched out her leg once more, her calf muscles straining with the effort, and finally knocked the hook toward her with the side of her shoe.

She felt a violent surge of triumph and bent

forward from the waist, wiggling the fingers of her bound right hand to touch it. She groaned aloud; it was still too far away. She blinked as salty sweat ran into her eyes and then licked beads of perspiration from her upper lip. She forced herself to pause, breathe deeply, and take stock of the situation.

She had to escape before more slave dealers came to look her over; she had no desire to repeat the day's humiliating experience of being paraded like an expensive whore before a prospective client, not to mention the horrible fate which would follow once she was bought.

She had to escape now.

Amy had known what was coming when Matka and the young girl arrived to give her another bath and a change of clothes. She had let them perfume her skin with oil of cloves and apply henna to her face and hands, but she had objected when they wanted to rub butter into her hair. The women gave up when she struggled, apparently because the dealer had already arrived and was waiting to see her. So she was presented with her oil-free Western hair unbraided and unbound.

Amy had no idea why Malik Bey had refused to sell her, but she was sure her reprieve wouldn't last very long. Even stranger than Malik's failure to consummate the deal was his objection when the trader wanted to disrobe her. Amy was sure it was standard for the buyer to inspect the goods before agreeing to a price, but she had no time to waste pondering the eccentricities of her kidnapper.

Her goal was to get away from him.

When her strength was restored, she tried to reach the hook again and was shocked when she almost grasped it. Maybe her rest had actually done some good. Heartened, she held her breath and made a desperate lunge forward, grabbing the hook with her thumb and forefinger.

She was so overjoyed that she had to restrain herself from shouting. She pressed the hook to her breast thankfully and then panicked when she heard a sound outside. She thrust the hook into the bodice of her gown, then felt the cold metal slip down to her waist, where the cord belt stopped it.

Footsteps halted by the tent entrance and she held her breath, listening. The camp rose and retired with the sun, and it was now dark. Malik was coming in to retire, and he left the oil lamp burning in the tent all night.

She would be able to begin work on her ropes as soon as he was asleep.

Amy closed her eyes, feigning sleep herself until she heard him discard his tunic and settle on the mat. She peeked through her lashes and saw that he was lying face down with his head pillowed on one arm. His position brought out the fine musculature of his upper arms and back, and Amy's gaze lingered on the slim torso and smooth skin, then moved up to the glossy black curls shining in the lamplight. She could just see his partial profile, the strong nose and sculpted mouth, and she looked away deliberately, not wanting to see him in this moment of vulnerability as a human being. This was her captor, her tormentor, her enemy. He could never be anything else.

Amy waited until he was breathing deeply and regularly, then took out the crewel hook and set to work. It took hours of picking at the woven hemp to get it to fray, and then unravel, but once she got one hand loose the process accelerated rapidly. Still, it was almost dawn before both hands were free. She rubbed her abraded wrists, which were chafed and bleeding, then bent to work the knots binding her ankles. When she finally stood unsteadily, she could see through the tent flap that first light was streaking the sky.

She didn't have much time.

She had spent long nights planning her escape, and she knew just what to do. She had noticed a spot where the tent's posting to the ground was uneven, creating a gap. She was slight enough to wriggle under the canvas, and best of all, the escape location was a distance from the guards. If she could make it to the woods, about thirty feet away from the tent, she'd be safe.

Amy crept soundlessly to the tent's edge and flattened herself on the ground, digging with her hands and pushing up the heavy canvas until she had created an opening big enough to admit her body. She began to crawl through it, glancing back once at Malik Bey to make sure he hadn't heard her scrabbling. Then she smelled the fresh night air and it urged her on until she had emerged on the other side of the tent, filthy and scratched, but free.

She glanced around anxiously, her ears pricked for sound, but she saw nothing and heard no one. She crawled on her hands and knees a little farther, then stood upright. She waited a beat, her heart pounding in her throat, then burst into the open and sprinted for the trees.

"*Kourista*, what are you doing out here?" Kalid asked, coming through the terrace doors and putting his arm around Sarah. "The sun is hardly up. It's too early for you to be wandering around half dressed. Come back to bed."

"I can't sleep," Sarah replied, glancing over the balustrade at the tiled courtyard below, where a palace guard paced his lonely route. "I keep thinking about Amelia Ryder."

Kalid took off his woolen robe and placed it over her slender shoulders. "I have already sent the message to the rebels. I'll make a decision about what to do when I hear their response."

Sarah looked up at him, his shadowy features barely illuminated by the lamps inside his bedchamber and the gray dawn. She had shared his suite in the *mabeyn*, or main court of the palace, with him for a decade now, and the harem stood almost empty, populated by his grandmother and a handful of aging female relatives. He had been monogamous since his marriage, and she still marveled that he had changed his whole way of life for her, for Sarah Woolcott of Massachusetts. But one thing was yet the same: he remained the pasha of Bursa, and the Sultan's lieutenant in the western empire. He might not agree with Hammid's philosophy or tactics, but he had managed to keep his position and his head while doing his best to give the people of his district some autonomy.

Sarah was afraid that might change, and soon. Amelia Ryder's kidnapping could upset the delicate balance Kalid had maintained for so long and force a confrontation. Kalid had hoped to keep the peace until Hammid died and left his more reasonable brother as his successor, but Hammid continued to breathe and Malik Bey grew stronger every day. Sarah could almost feel the pressure building, as if she were standing on a volcano from which steam was escaping as the ground rumbled beneath her feet. She knew that Kalid felt it too, but it was his nature to dismiss her misgivings in his protective way.

"I remember how strange everything seemed to me when I first came here," Sarah said suddenly. "And I at least entered Topkapi of my own accord. I wasn't snatched off a passenger coach by a pair of bandits."

"You accused *me* of kidnapping you," Kalid said, grinning. "I, on the other hand, looked upon the transaction as legal and binding, a legitimate sale."

"I still don't find that amusing," Sarah said crisply.

He laughed. "I don't think Hammid's palace has recovered from your visit yet," Kalid said. "I'm certain that Roxalena never did."

"It's hard to believe that she's married to Malik Bey's brother," Sarah said softly. "Osman always seemed so evenhanded and restrained, not the type to have a bandit for a brother."

"Osman ran off with Roxalena, didn't he? A lot must have been going on beneath the surface there. And Malik is not at all like Osman," Kalid replied.

"What do you mean?"

"I remember him as a lad when Osman used to bring him to Topkapi. Even then he was . . ."

"What?"

"Different. Intense, or . . ." he stopped. "Memorable."

Sarah stared at her husband. "You admire him, don't you?" she said.

Kalid shrugged. "Let's just say I think I understand him. If I hadn't been born to the position I hold, I might be where he is right now. Quite a few people in this country see Malik Bey as a courageous freedom fighter, not as a brigand or some sort of criminal. And you used to be the tireless champion of democracy, if I recall correctly. That's what Malik is fighting for, isn't it? I should think you'd be right with him."

"I might be more sympathetic to his cause if he hadn't abducted Bea's niece," Sarah said darkly.

"Or if his eventual success didn't mean the loss of Bursa for your son?" Kalid asked quietly.

Sarah didn't answer.

"Quite a dilemma for 'free the slaves, down with the despots' Sarah, isn't it, my darling?" Kalid asked. "You never imagined that your own child might have to sacrifice his birthright for your American ideals."

"Tariq would make such a fine pasha," Sarah said sadly. "He would be fair and wise and take this district right into the twentieth century."

Kalid tightened his grip on her shoulders. "The days of the Sultan and his system are numbered."

"Will you miss them?"

"I plan to survive them and forge a new government. With my family intact."

"Then you really are on Malik's side?"

"Let's simply say that I'm not on Hammid's," Kalid replied dryly. "I will work for some sort of compromise, but I can see that the chances for that are fading. I'll tell you this: when it comes time to fight, I will not take up the sword for the Sultan."

"So you'll go with Malik?" Sarah said. She couldn't quite believe they were actually talking about this; Kalid had always evaded the subject, as if the choice wouldn't have to be made, but Sarah knew he would never stand on the sidelines and let his fate be decided by other people.

When the armies faced each other, he would be on horseback leading one of them.

He kissed her forehead. "Don't worry about that now; the immediate problem is Amelia Ryder. If she's anything like you were when I met you, Malik has his hands full. I almost relish the thought of his dealing with an American woman from Boston—I've had the experience myself. Now come inside and let's have breakfast. The sun is up and Memtaz will be bringing the children soon."

Sarah took his extended hand and followed him through the terrace doors.

Malik saw that his captive was gone as soon as he opened his eyes. The ropes used to bind her were discarded in tatters on the dirt floor, and the burrow she'd created to get out was littered with freshly dug soil.

He leaped to his feet, pulling on his tunic and dashing out of the tent.

"Anwar!" he yelled, crashing into Matka, who was walking toward him carrying a bowl. Its contents flew out in an arc onto the ground.

His lieutenant emerged from a nearby tent, his face still groggy with sleep, his hand on his pistol.

"What?" Anwar called, looking around alertly.

"She's gone," Malik said, running for his horse.

"Who's gone?"

"The American woman. I'm going after her." Malik untethered his horse and then vaulted onto its back.

"How could she get away? You had her trussed up like a pig ready for slaughter!" Anwar replied.

"I don't know how, but she did it. I have to get her back." Malik kicked his horse's flanks, and the animal surged forward.

"You can't leave now—we've got to plan the next train raid!"

"I'll be back in time to do it," Malik called as he raced past his friend. "She can't have gone far. She's on foot."

Anwar stared after him in amazement, then looked at Matka, who was watching the scene with the empty pottery bowl still in her hand.

"Clean up that mess!" he barked at her, then stalked back into his tent.

Amy ran until the sun was sinking, her mouth

was dry, and her legs would no longer support her. She reached a clearing and fell to her knees on a patch of grass, then sprawled full length, staring up at the afternoon sky through a screen of intertwining leaves.

She was free, but she was also starving. She had no food or water, and she was lost in a foreign country where she didn't speak the language.

Suddenly freedom had its drawbacks.

She had known before she left that she wouldn't be able to bring anything with her. She was too closely guarded, and she didn't know where any supplies were kept in the camp. It had taken so much effort just to get away that she'd thought once that was accomplished she would be able to handle the rest of it.

Now she wasn't so sure.

The rebel camp was in a remote location; Malik had selected the spot for that reason. It was probably miles in every direction to another living soul, and she was still dressed in the gauzy gown and thin slippers she'd been wearing when she was shown to the slave dealer.

At the very least she would spend a chilly night.

Amy turned on her side and wondered what the coming night would be like in these woods, a night with no softly glowing oil lamps or welcoming fire, a night with whatever wild animals the hills contained coming out to prowl.

She shivered and decided not to think about it any more. She took off her shoes and dug her toes into the carpet of grass, closing her eyes.

She couldn't go any farther just now, and she might as well get some sleep.

When she woke up, she would see if there was enough light left to travel farther.

But after only a few moments of rest, she heard a muffled sound nearby and her eyes flew open immediately.

Malik Bey was sitting on the ground next to her.

Chapter Four

"Going somewhere?" he said.

Amy leaped up instantly and fled barefoot across the grass. She was fleet, and Malik was unprepared for her to bolt before his very eyes. She was halfway across the clearing before he caught her about the waist and brought her down. He pinned her arms as she kicked and writhed beneath him, flailing wildly even though it was obvious that she had no hope of getting away from him. For a second, as he subdued her, his face was pressed to her shoulder and his hair brushed her nose and mouth. It was surprisingly soft, smelling of the pine soap she had used herself, a rich contrast to the hard masculinity of his pinioning arms.

He raised himself up on his elbows and held

her easily, waiting for her to calm down, and when she finally did, their eyes locked. His face was inches above hers, the only sound their harsh breathing, accelerated from the struggle.

Amy stared up at him, her rage fading as she became aware of the muscular frame holding her fast, the sensual lips parted inches from hers. Everything about him became more vivid suddenly, as if her vision had improved: the black stubble covering his cheeks and chin, the wavy hair swept back from his forehead, the dark eyes boring into hers. His expression changed as he lay above her, his determination to control her melting into something else as she felt his body respond to hers.

"Are you going to rape me now?" she asked him, her expression contemptuous.

He released her suddenly, flinging her away from him and rising to his feet.

"If I had planned to rape you, I would have done so already," he replied quietly, facing away from her.

"And why have you restrained yourself? Is that privilege reserved for my purchaser?"

He turned and looked at her, saying nothing.

"I know exactly what's going on here. I know why I was taken and what you plan to do with me," she informed him, gazing up at him from her position on the ground.

"You know nothing," he answered. He walked away to the horse she now saw tethered a few feet away and took two blankets and a hand-stitched leather pouch from its back. When he returned, he sat on the ground and removed a tinder box and a tied bundle of sticks from the pouch.

"What are you doing?" Amy demanded, sitting up and pushing her hair back from her eyes.

"Starting a fire," he replied, striking a flint and holding it to the sticks. They smoked and then caught. He tossed the bundle on the ground and added bits of dried leaves and chips until it was blazing.

"Why?" Amy asked, taking a step closer to him.

"We can't go back in the dark. We'll have to stay here and return to the camp in the morning." He threw a few bigger sticks onto the fire, nudging them into the flames with his booted foot.

"I'm not spending the night here alone with you," Amy said and started to walk away.

He was at her side in two bounds and caught her wrist. "It is about time you realize that I am not the worst thing that could happen to you in this country," he said between his teeth. "Do you want to die of hunger or thirst in these woods? Or be devoured by hyenas? Do you? Or do you want to be set upon by bandits far worse than I, who will slit your throat and then desecrate your dead body until no one could tell that it had ever housed a human being?"

"I didn't realize there were degrees of brigandry," Amy replied, snatching her arm back and rubbing her wrist. "How interesting to know that there are men even you look down upon. They must be very low indeed."

"You should be thanking me for coming after you," he said, picking up more dry branches from the ground and tossing them onto the fire.

"Thanking you! If you hadn't abducted me in the first place, I wouldn't be standing in the middle of this wilderness having a pointless discussion with a common criminal. I didn't come halfway around the world to be treated like this!"

He put his hands on his hips and glared at her. "And how have you been treated? Have you been beaten or violated or starved? Tell me, for I would like to know!"

"Oh, that's right, I forgot. You're a great humanitarian because you gave your flunkies orders to feed me."

He strode away from her angrily, but she followed, sweeping in front of him to face him. "You must think I'm a simpleton. You're taking care of me to get the maximum price when you sell me to some scoundrel like that odious man Halmad. I felt I needed a bath after he just looked at me. You're maintaining me the way a farmer maintains the livestock in his pens. And you came after me to safeguard your investment and for no other reason, let's be clear about that, *agha*. So you answer me now, do I really have reason to be grateful?"

"Your president is not the only American who makes speeches," he said disgustedly, striding back to the fire and adding some larger limbs to it. "Come over here, sit down, and be quiet. Have something to eat."

She didn't obey but watched him remove a packet of food and a leather bottle of water from his pouch.

"Is that your kidnapping kit?" she said sarcastically.

"I keep it with my horse always, for emergencies," he replied, taking a long drink. Amy licked her lips and took a step forward hesitantly.

"How exciting to think that I qualify as an emergency," she said, but took another step.

He saw her movement and held out a woven sack tied with a string. When she didn't accept it, he set it on the ground.

"How did you find me?" she asked, finally walking over to the fire and sitting down next to him.

"I've been tracking people and animals through these hills since I was five," he replied, handing her the water bottle. "I had a horse and you left a wide trail. You were very easy to find."

She took a drink, guzzling the cool water, and he finally ripped the bottle away from her, alarmed.

"Drink slowly. Too much at once after a thirst is sick-making," he said.

It was strange to hear him using British expressions, stranger still to hear the Oxford accent emerging from his bandit's mouth. What an odd hybrid creature he was. If the newspaper she had read was correct, the daughter of his sworn enemy, the Sultan, was married to his brother.

And he certainly didn't speak or smell like her American idea of an outlaw.

"Did I drink it all?" she asked anxiously, the prospect of going thirsty again alarming her.

"There's a brook just through those trees," he said, nodding to the left. "I'll refill it in the morning."

She opened the sack he had produced and began to eat the contents—strips of dried goat meat mixed with raisins, berries, and split hazelnuts.

"This is like pemmican," she said, chewing.

"What's that?"

"The western people of my country prepare it for the trail. It's high in protein and keeps indefinitely without spoiling."

He grunted.

She chewed some more, thinking. "Look, can't we make a deal?" she finally said, striving for a reasonable tone. "You want money. I can get you money if you let me go."

He shot her a sidelong glance but said nothing.

"It's true. I have money, an inheritance from my parents. I'll be getting it in ten months."

"Ten months," he said, as if it were ten years.

"But if you just let me write home to my guardian, I can get an advance on it, and he will send a bank draft . . ."

"A bank draft from the United States of America?" he said, laughing. "Why not a cache of diamonds from the mountains of the moon?"

Amy stared at him; she had never seen him laugh, and she was charmed in spite of herself. His teeth were white and even and his chuckle infectious. She looked away.

"My aunt's husband has an export business in Constantinople. I was coming to stay at his house when you snatched me," Amy said, trying again. "He is wealthy, and I'm sure he would pay a lot of money to get me back."

Malik continued to eat as if she hadn't spoken.

"And my uncle's cousin is married to the—oh, what do you call it . . . I forget the title—the district commissioner or something . . ."

He held up his hand. "Enough! You Western women talk too much. Finish eating and go to sleep." He rose and stoked the fire, adding enough wood to keep it burning for hours. He shook out one of the blankets and tossed it to her.

"You don't believe me?" Amy asked, catching the woolen square. "It's the truth! Why do you think I was on that coach in the first place?"

"You could have been on that coach for a hundred different reasons, and I am not interested in any of them. What I am interested in is sleep. I've been tracking you all day and I'm very tired." He spread the second blanket on the ground and stretched out on it, closing his eyes.

"Why would you rather sell me into slavery than contact my family? I'm telling you they would pay to get me back!"

He opened his eyes. "If I were your family, I would pay to get someone to take you away. Now if you don't be quiet this minute, I will leave you here for the leopards." He rolled over deliberately, turning his back to her.

"Aren't you going to tie me up?" she said tauntingly.

"If you think of taking off during the night, you should know that what you will find out there is far worse than what you will experience here with me."

Amy threw the remainder of her pemmican to the ground disgustedly and stood.

"I'll just run away again, the first chance I get," she said to his back.

"No, you won't," he replied.

"Really?"

"Really. If I have to keep you chained to my

belt twenty-four hours a day, you won't get away again."

The certainty in his voice gave her a chill.

"I guess I forgot how valuable I am," she said spitefully. "Why don't you raise money for your sacred revolt by working for a living like any other decent person? But selling kidnapped women is so much easier, isn't it?"

"I worked for a living on my father's farm for ten years," he replied equably. "Then the Sultan executed my father and brothers, gave my mother and sister to his janissaries to be used before they were killed, and confiscated all of our property. Since then I've worked to execute him."

Amy sank to the ground slowly, silenced. "Why?" she finally said.

"My oldest brother Osman eloped with the Sultan's daughter, Princess Roxalena. Osman sent us a message and money to follow him, but he was betrayed and the message was intercepted. The Sultan took out his anger on the remaining members of the family. I was away at the time and so escaped the axe. I went on the run when I heard what had happened, and I've been on the run ever since."

"You had done nothing at all to make you a fugitive," she whispered.

"Exactly. But I'm doing something now. I won't rest until Abdul Hammid is dead and his government deposed."

Amy stared at the back of his head, wrapping her arms around her torso.

He turned to look at her, then sighed and sat up, pulling his heavy woolen tunic over his head.

"Put this on," he said.

She shook her head.

"Do as I say," he barked, rising and settling the tunic over her shoulders. It was warm from his body, and she couldn't resist snuggling into it.

"And come closer to the fire."

She shook her head again.

"You're in a desert climate—it's boiling during the day and freezing once the sun sets. You've been sleeping a few feet away from me every night in my tent—why does it bother you now?"

"It bothered me then," she whispered, and he stared at her, his eyes lambent in the firelight. The moment hung between them, the silence filled with things unspoken.

"I'll move away," he finally said in a low tone, and did so immediately.

Amy took her blanket and dropped it next to the fire, then lay full length on it, not looking at him.

In three minutes she was asleep.

Malik looked up at the night sky, picking out the constellations he had learned to identify from his tutor when he was a boy. He was exhausted but could not sleep, the proximity of the woman he had kidnapped keeping him awake.

He smiled to himself as he thought of the stories she had told him. She would have said that her father was President Cleveland and her mother Queen Victoria if she thought that would take her one step closer to freedom. He knew from her appearance that her family was well-to-do, and she would not have been able to travel so far from home if they weren't, but only a handful of American families could match what he would be able to get for her in the slave trade. Unless her name was Carnegie or Astor, his best bet was to sell her to a broker, and a Carnegie or Astor would not have been traveling in a shared passenger coach with a weepy companion. But he had to admire her for trying, just as he admired her escape attempts, even though they left him footsore and mind-weary.

She was brave, if not exactly a meticulous planner.

A hyena barked loudly from a safe distance and was answered by a low growl somewhere nearby.

His companion sat up, her eyes huge, and whispered, "What was that?"

Malik rose to his feet, drawing his pistol from his belt. He fired one shot into the air. They both listened to the scrambling sound as a large animal took off quickly through the brush.

Malik gathered more sticks for the fire, then sat again. Amy picked up her blanket and moved next to him.

He looked at her. "Feeling lonely?" he said, arching one dark brow.

She muttered something unintelligible under her breath.

"I beg your pardon?" he said.

"Do you think that . . . whatever it was . . . will come back?" she asked anxiously.

"If it does, I will be here," he said calmly.

Amy was surprised at how much his capable tone reassured her. No wonder so many people followed him and obeyed his orders without question. He inspired confidence.

"What time is it?" she asked, pulling his tunic closer about her.

He looked up at the sky. "About three. It will be light in a few hours."

"Do those animals prowl only at night?" she asked, looking around them.

He stared at her. "*Now* you are afraid? You run off from the camp armed with nothing but a pair of shoes and it doesn't occur to you to worry until a leopard is standing a few feet away from your campfire?"

"Was that a leopard?" she murmured, aghast.

"Maybe an Anatolian wolf, but most likely a panther, a leopard in the black phase before the coat turns color. It's the season for them."

She swallowed. He probably *had* saved her life by coming after her, it was true, but she couldn't forget his venal reason for doing it.

She shivered, as much from her bleak thoughts as the night chill.

He got up and gave her his blanket.

"I can't take this—you'll have none—" she began.

He held up his hand. "I am accustomed to the climate. You are not. Take it and go back to sleep."

Amy subsided, looking over at him as he sat with his back to a tree. The firelight played over his high cheekbones and arched nose, giving him a fierce aspect that daylight softened and transformed into a dark beauty.

"Your English is very good," she murmured, trying to get him to talk. She was still skittish about their four-legged visitor, and the sound of his deep voice had a soothing effect, reminding her that she was not alone. She studied him in the firelight, wondering how he would appear in Western clothing. With his exotic looks, he would definitely liven up a tea dance in Boston dressed in a herringbone sack coat and pipestem trousers.

"Thank you," he said.

"How did you learn to speak it?"

"Before my brother Osman eloped with Hammid's daughter, he was the Sultan's favorite soldier for many years, the captain of his guard and very well paid. When Hammid first came to power, he wanted to learn European warfare in order to train his own troops. He sent Osman to England to study with the British for two years and Osman learned to speak English there. He was very impressed with the language and the way of life, and when he returned here he hired a British tutor for us at home."

It was the longest speech she had heard him make, and his admiration for his brother came through. "He sounds like an extraordinary person," Amy said.

"He is," Malik said shortly.

"Does he know what you are doing now?"

"He does," Malik replied flatly.

Amy dropped the subject. "How do you keep up with your English?" she asked him.

"I have books, and I read the English-language newspapers from Damascus and Constantinople."

"It must be important to you," she said.

"It's important to my future plans that I speak and read English competently. I have to be able to talk to the Western powers if I expect their help for my new country."

"How do you practice conversation?"

"I talk to people like you whenever I get the chance," he replied.

"While you're abducting them? Short conversations, no doubt," she said, yawning.

"Yes. None of the others have run off and given me the opportunity for such a stimulating and extended exchange. Go back to sleep."

She sighed, her eyelids getting heavy. "Did you really come after me just for the money you can make when you sell me?" she muttered, her lips barely moving.

He didn't answer; then, to his relief, he realized that she had fallen asleep. He put his head back against the tree trunk and closed his eyes.

He did not want to sell her, and that was a fact. To anybody. But the opportunity to obtain so much money had him more confused than he had ever been in his life.

When he thought of what he could buy for his men with that fortune, his mouth watered. But when he thought of his captive being sold to some fabulously wealthy brute who would consume her as he did his dinner, Malik almost went wild with rage and pain.

Anwar was right. He knew his friend, and he had known from the first that the American woman would be trouble.

Malik opened his eyes again and looked at the slight figure of the girl sleeping on the ground. She was certainly beautiful, but it was more than that which drew him to her. He believed in *kismet*, fate, and as he accepted that it was his fate to lose his family and fight the Sultan, it was also apparently his fate to desire this woman. What mattered was how he managed

101

his fate. He had never had trouble doing that before, but this situation presented him with a new and different challenge.

She stirred and began to mutter in her sleep, becoming more agitated as he moved closer to her. He put his hand on her shoulder and she started, almost waking. He spoke soothingly and she settled down, turning toward him when he sat next to her. When he slipped his arm around her, she murmured, sighed, and let her head fall to his shoulder. He held her in his arms, inhaling the fragrance of her hair, her skin, absorbing the warmth of her body into his own. He drew both blankets over them, wondering how long he could keep her safe before the reason he had kidnapped her became more important than the feelings she now aroused in him.

Finally, just as the sky was beginning to lighten, he slept.

When Amy awoke the next morning, the sun was high and she was horrified to discover herself in Malik Bey's arms. She sat up abruptly and he started, then settled back down again, still asleep. She realized that he had tracked her all day yesterday and then had been awake most of the night; even a man with his obviously strong constitution would be tired.

This was her chance to get away.

It was clear he had planned to be awake before she was. That was why he had left her untied. If she went now, she could get a good head start.

She grabbed his food bag, looking around for his horse, but when her mind caught up with her actions she sank to the ground next to him, distraught. She couldn't ride his horse; she had seen it throw another man who had attempted to do so, to the vast amusement of the camp. The food bag was almost empty, and her slippers were ruined. She couldn't get far. He would just track her again, and find her again. She was no better prepared now to elude him than when she had first left the camp. And the thought of another night in the woods with the local wildlife was more than daunting.

The thing to do was go back with him and then get organized: hoard supplies, steal a pliant horse and a weapon, learn the escape route. It could be done, but it would take time and ingenuity. And if she was sold before she succeeded, then she would just plot again and run away from her purchaser.

She would get away eventually, but bolting without a plan was foolhardy. Her most recent adventure had taught her that.

Malik coughed in his sleep and she looked at him. The morning light made his black hair gleam like jet, and the lashes that lay against his dusky cheeks were as thick and curling as a child's. She could see a faint pulse beating in his bare throat, exposed by the deep V of his thin cotton shirt. Her hand went to the woolen tunic he had given her; she realized that he must have been cold without it.

What kind of person would abduct a woman to sell her into slavery and then strip the shirt off his back to keep her warm? Was he really just trying to maintain her health so he could make a profit? Or could there be some chivalry, some compassion, in the character of a man who would do such a thing in the first place? She had never in her life encountered a contradiction like him.

But then again, she had never met anyone who had been so wronged. If the story he had told her about the Sultan was true, she could understand why everything in his life was secondary to his pursuit of revenge. If her family had been tortured and killed at the whim of a mercurial dictator, maybe she too would be willing to do anything, even trade in slaves, to bring about that dictator's fall.

It was a notion that upset her conventional ideas of right and wrong.

A breeze whipped through the trees, and she clutched at the neck of her gown, glancing down at her hand. It was filthy, the knuckles gray, which was not surprising when she considered how she had spent the previous day. Where was the brook Malik had mentioned? She looked in the direction he had indicated, remembering the lump of soap she had seen in his bag.

She would have a bath while he slept. She retrieved the soap and set off through the trees.

It was only minutes after Amy had left the clearing that Malik sighed and opened his eyes. When he saw that the girl was gone again, he felt like an imbecile for the second time.

Would she never stop? Was he destined to spend the rest of his life stalking her? And why hadn't he tied her up when he knew that he was physically spent? Was she causing him to lose his mind? Irritated with himself and the situation, he charged to his feet and grabbed the water bottle lying on the ground, intending to refill it for the chase.

When he was a few feet from the spring, he stopped short. She was already there, stripped to the waist, washing.

He looked away, feeling like a voyeur, but then looked back, compelled by a force stronger than gallantry to watch her.

What he saw caused his mouth to go dry and his pulse to quicken. She had tied up her hair with the neckline ribbon from the gown, which was now pushed down to her waist, leaving her torso bare. She knelt on the bank and soaped her arms, and as she raised each one her breasts rose, the nipples puckering in the cool morning air.

Malik closed his eyes, his hands clenching

into fists. He wanted to taste that silken skin, take those pebble-hard nipples into his mouth, run his tongue into the valley between those creamy breasts. When she bent to rinse, he caught sight of the white, vulnerable curve of her back, the cleft at the base of her spine, and he imagined caressing it, then pulling the gown from her slender limbs and taking her on the dewy grass.

She turned to dry herself on his tunic and he stepped back, his heart pounding. He could not be found spying on her; he was too proud to endure even the thought of it, but he couldn't tear his gaze away from the alluring scene. To his disappointment, she loosened her hair and pulled up the gown, retying it at the neck. When he saw that she was finished he retraced his steps, crashing through the underbrush loudly as he approached to alert her to his presence.

She was waiting for him when he arrived, shaking out her damp hair.

"Surprise," she said. "I'm still here."

He said nothing, kneeling where she had lately been and filling the water bottle.

"Didn't you think I had run away?" she persisted, watching him immerse his head in the water and then come up, pushing back his wet hair.

"I thought your memory of last night would keep you with me," he lied, rubbing the stubble on his face.

"Why don't you grow a beard?" she suggested. "Wouldn't that be a good disguise in your chosen profession?"

He shot her a look and said darkly, "The Sultan's men wear beards."

"But growing a beard would change your appearance," she said logically.

"So would shaving it off," he replied, pulling his shirt over his head.

"I think you're arrogant," Amy said, looking away uncomfortably as he splashed his torso. "I think when you rob a train or sabotage one of the Sultan's outposts, you want people to know it's you. You see yourself as Robin Hood."

"It's the British papers who say that, not me," he answered, rubbing his hair with the tunic she had discarded.

"But I'll bet you love reading about it," she said dryly. "You've had a price on your head for years, and no one has turned you in for the reward."

He stood and she watched the play of muscles in his arms and back as he donned the shirt again. "The Sultan is not popular," he said. "Even those who are not actively working to throw off his yoke won't betray someone who is." He picked up his tunic and said, "Come on. It will take us most of the day to reach the camp. The horse will be slower with two on his back."

As she came closer to him, he took the rope

belt from his waist and said, "Hold out your hands."

"Oh, please don't tie me up again," she moaned.

"I don't want the sunlight to make you ambitious." He drew the knot tight and asked, as if he had just thought of it, "What is your name?"

"Amelia," she said defeatedly, as he led her forward by a dangling piece of the rope. "Amelia Ryder."

"What does it mean?"

She glanced at him. "Amelia?"

"Yes."

"Beloved."

He murmured something under his breath.

"What?" she said.

"There is a word for that idea in Turkish."

"How do you say it?"

"*Nakshedil*," he replied.

"Does it mean the same?"

"Almost. In Turkish it is more poetic."

"In what way?"

"The literal translation is 'ornament of the heart.' "

"How lovely," she whispered.

"There was a great sultana by that name, a Westerner like you. She was French, and her given name was Aimée de Rivery."

"*Aimée* means beloved in French," Amelia said. "That is my name, you're right."

He nodded. "Nakshedil was from Martinique; she was a cousin of Napoleon Bonaparte's wife. She was captured by pirates on her way to a convent school in France and sold into the harem at Topkapi. She spent the rest of her life there."

Amy shuddered. "That's awful."

He smiled. "She was very happy."

"How do you know?" Amy demanded.

"She fell in love with her captor." His dark eyes met hers and she felt her face growing warm.

"It happens, I am told," he added softly.

They reached the horse and he lifted her onto its back.

Chapter Five

Anwar Talit was worried. Malik had been gone since first light on the previous day, and still there was no sign of him.

Anwar knew there was reason for concern. He had seen the quiet ones before when they got the call, the cool ones who seemed almost indifferent to women until they met the single female who set them on fire. They became unreachable, transferring all the intensity they had previously devoted to a cause or a faith or a family to the object of their desire, drawn as if mesmerized to the woman who would destroy them.

He had never known his friend Malik to look at another woman the way he looked at the American captive.

Anwar moved out of the cave to walk across to his tent when another of the rebels, a former slave from Slovenia named Yuri, trotted up to him.

"There's a rider coming up the hill," Yuri said.

"Alone?" Anwar asked.

Yuri nodded his head.

"Can you tell if it's Malik?"

"I don't think so. It's not his horse."

"You and Selim go out and get him," Yuri said. "I don't care if he's by himself—it could be a trick. Take your pistols."

Yuri ran off to obey and Anwar began to pace. Whatever this was, he would have to deal with it, since Malik was not available. He wondered who would be foolhardy enough to come into the camp unescorted, who would even know where it was. His mind ranged over the possibilities until he turned and saw the visitor being dragged toward him by his rebel escort.

"Mehmed Trey," Anwar said. "What brings you to see us this fine day?"

Mehmed shrugged off the arms holding him and drew himself up to his full height, which was not very impressive. Mehmed was a part-time thief and full-time hustler, the illegitimate offspring of a British seaman's dalliance with a Turkish bazaar girl. Mehmed's mother had hauled him with her as she plied her trade throughout the Empire. Because of his peripatetic background, Mehmed could speak many of the Empire's dialects and had forged a shaky career as a go-between, trusted completely by no one but used by all sides because he could be counted upon to deliver a message for a price. He had no loyalties, and in a perverse way that made him reliable.

He was always very determined to reach his destination and thus collect his fee.

"I come to you from Kalid Shah," Mehmed said, rubbing his wrist where Yuri had held him.

Anwar folded his arms. "And what does the Pasha of Bursa want?" Anwar demanded.

"My message is for Malik Bey."

"Malik is not here," Anwar said.

"I won't get paid unless I can prove to Kalid Shah that I have seen Malik," Mehmed whined.

Anwar took a step forward and grabbed the man's tunic, hauling Mehmed upward until he was standing on tiptoes.

"I will give you something to prove that you have seen me," Anwar said quietly. "Now spit out your message before I set the dogs on you."

"I—I think I should wait for Malik," the little man said nervously, his eyes darting around at the ring of rebels who were closing in on him.

"I don't know how long he will be," Anwar said smoothly. "Speak now or I throw you out."

Mehmed swallowed, then said, "Kalid Shah wants a meeting with Malik Bey to negotiate the release of the American hostage you hold," Mehmed said.

"What American hostage? There is no such person here," Anwar replied, looking around at the faces of his friends. All of them were carefully impassive.

Mehmed shrugged. "I know nothing more about it. Kalid Shah said that Malik kidnapped an American woman from a passenger coach several days ago. The pasha wants to discuss the terms of her surrender to him."

Anwar said nothing, then pulled an amulet from around his neck and handed it to the messenger.

"Give this to Kalid Shah to prove that you have seen me. He will recognize it. Tell him he will have our response within three days."

Mehmed snatched the bronze charm and curled his fingers around it.

"Now go," Anwar said dismissively, turning his back on the little man.

As soon as Mehmed left, Anwar ordered the rest of the men to disperse. Then he gestured covertly for Selim and Yuri to come to his side.

"Selim, you follow Mehmed out and make sure he leaves without snooping around—and make sure no one is waiting for him at the bottom of the hill."

Selim took off and Yuri said in a low tone, "What are you going to do if Malik is not back in three days?"

"I'll come up with something. But let's hope I don't have to," Anwar replied. "How do you think Kalid Shah knew about the American girl?"

Yuri shrugged. "Maybe he read about it in the British papers. They report on all Malik's doings like he's a cricket star."

Anwar furrowed his brow. "Shah's in Bursa. The only British papers are in Constantinople."

"Maybe his wife gets the English language papers mailed to her."

"But why would he take such a personal interest in this one girl? The papers have been writing about the kidnappings for years and we've never heard from him before today." Anwar shook his head. "I don't like it. Something's up."

"I wish Malik were here," Yuri said, sighing.

Anwar made a disgusted sound. "No, he's off chasing that prize package he refuses to sell," he said darkly.

Yuri stared at him.

"Never mind," Anwar said, realizing that he had revealed too much. "Didn't Malik tell Nerisa to buy the British papers when she went into town to sell baskets at the covered bazaar?"

"Yes. She's probably waiting for him to come back to give them to him."

"Go and get them now," Anwar said.

Yuri walked off and Anwar went back into the cave, sitting down at a crude table and lighting a candle. The oil lamp was empty; he needed to make a supply run but was reluctant to leave before Malik returned.

It was so unlike Malik to run off the way he had that Anwar didn't know what to anticipate next. Where was Malik? How far would he go to find the girl? There was no way to know.

Yuri returned with a newspaper and dropped it onto the table in front of his friend.

"There she is," Yuri said.

The paper had been folded to expose a grainily reproduced photograph of Amelia Ryder, a studio pose showing her dressed in the Western fashion of several years earlier, with billowing sleeves, a wasp waist, and an upswept hairdo.

"Isn't that the girl?" Yuri prompted.

Anwar nodded. "I wonder what the story says," he added thoughtfully.

Yuri was silent. Neither one of them could read it.

"Malik will tell us when he gets back," Yuri finally said firmly.

Anwar didn't answer.

Sarah prepared the *chibuk* for Kosem, packing the old lady's pipe with sweet tobacco, tamping it down until it was ready, and then lighting it. She handed it to Kalid's grandmother, who smiled and accepted it, drawing on it deeply.

"You look worried, my dear," Kosem said.

Sarah poured a cup of thick Turkish coffee for Kosem, then one for herself. When a servant stepped forward to assist her, Sarah sent her from the room.

"I guess I am," she said, when the door had closed behind the slave. "I know that Kalid is going to get involved with Malik Bey and this kidnapped girl, and it's bound to be dangerous."

"What is my grandson doing now?" Kosem asked, exhaling a stream of gray smoke.

"He sent a message to the rebels, and they promised an answer in three days."

"And he's just waiting? That's not like Kalid at all."

"He says it's best to let the rebels take the lead. He's trying to get her back without incident, but I don't know if that's possible," Sarah said.

"And what about your cousin James?" Kosem inquired.

Sarah sighed and put down her cup. "Oh, he's dealing with the diplomats, but you know what they're like. They'll be talking about it until we're welcoming in the twentieth century."

Kosem snorted. "Kalid's father would have stormed the rebel camp and killed them all to get her back," she said.

Sarah said nothing.

Kosem laughed. "You don't have to hold your tongue for me, daughter. I can tell that Kalid is in sympathy with the rebels. I've been watching his actions since he assumed his father's throne, and I know what he thinks. He has grown more

Western with each passing day under your influence."

"If it comes to war, he will join forces with Malik and his men," Sarah said to her.

Kosem nodded slowly. "It would have been the last wish of my long life to see Kalid's son ruling from Orchid Palace. I have guessed for some time that my wish will not be granted." She smiled suddenly. "Do you remember when I tried to bribe you to have Kalid's son?"

Sarah chuckled. "I remember."

"You two were so in love, but always at cross purposes! It drove me mad. I thought I would die before I saw Kalid happily married and a father." Her smile faded. "And now you have three beautiful children—two sons—but Kalid wants a democracy." She sighed. "The world is changing and I suppose he must change with it." She reached over and patted Sarah's hand. "But not me. I am glad that I will die soon. I am too old to give up the harem."

Sarah's answering smile was roguish. Kosem had been announcing her imminent death for as long as Sarah had known her. The old lady was now past ninety.

Kosem suddenly took a ring off her finger and placed it in Sarah's palm. "I want you to have this," she said.

Sarah began to protest, but Kosem waved her hand dismissively. "Jewels disappear upon a death. The servants are unreliable. That belonged to Kalid's mother. You have always reminded me of her very much. She began as a captive too, like you, and like this Amelia Ryder who is causing so much concern."

Sarah nodded.

"I missed her terribly when she died," Kosem said, with a catch in her voice. "I almost lost my English before you came. It has been the comfort of my old age to have you here to talk to, *seker* Sarah."

Sarah could see that the old lady was getting tired and melancholy. She got up and spread a cashmere lap robe over Kosem's thin legs, encased in the silken *shalwar,* or trousers, that she always wore.

"You must rest now. Close your eyes. I will wait until you fall asleep."

"Keep the ring," Kosem whispered. "Promise me."

"I promise. Go to sleep."

Kosem sighed and let her head fall back upon the satin pillows on the divan. Sarah looked down at the ring she still clutched in her hand.

Kosem must really feel that death was near to part with it, Sarah thought sadly. It was a huge square cabochon emerald surrounded by magnificent pearls set in heavy gold, and the old lady had worn it daily.

· It was too much for Kosem to face, Sarah knew—the end of her life, the end of an era, the end of the sultanate in the Ottoman Empire.

Sarah looked around at the opulent apartment. It had remained almost unchanged since the day she had arrived at Orchid Palace as Kalid Shah's purchase, the latest addition to his harem. Then the quarters of the *valide pashana* had seemed as exotic and foreign as an opium den—the caged birds, the gilt mirrors, the inlaid furniture and hand-painted jewel chests, the ornate rugs and plush hangings. To her they had seemed the pathetic evidence of mere indulgence. Now Sarah saw that they were the accessories of a life, the life of a woman who had been raised with one goal, to please a man. In the tenth decade of her existence, Kosem still dressed every day in the full costume of a harem woman—the cashmere and silk shalwar, the embroidered waistcoats and jeweled *curdees*, the high-heeled pattens and satin *yeleks* with immense hanging sleeves slashed with crimson and gold. Her jewel collection was rumored to rival that of the Sultana and she inspected the pieces regularly, sending anything dirty or damaged to the palace artisans for cleaning or repair. She still wore the *yashmak*, the face veil which exposed only eyes and forehead, when she went outside the palace.

And she still asked permission of her grandson to enter a room, for he was her pasha, and a man.

It was true, Sarah thought, as she rose and

rang for the servant to return and watch over the sleeping Kosem.

The world was changing, and the *valide pashana* was too old to change.

There was tears in Sarah's eyes as she left the room.

When Malik arrived back at the rebel base with Amy on the horse before him, his men came from everywhere to watch his progress through the camp. There was silence as they dismounted and Malik led her, hands bound and head down, back to his tent. When he emerged soon afterward, Anwar was waiting for him.

"What is it?" Malik said.

"We have to talk," Anwar said.

"What's happened?" Malik demanded.

Anwar led him away from the camp, and they walked through the trees as Malik learned of Mehmed's visit and the article in the British newspaper. Malik took the paper from Anwar's hand and scanned the article quickly.

"Well?" Anwar said.

"She's a relative of Kalid Shah's wife," Malik said thoughtfully, remembering Amy's words at the campfire. So there was some truth in what she'd said.

"His wife?" Anwar said.

"Yes, he's married to an American, and this girl is a ward of the wife's cousin. She was coming to stay with the cousin in Constantinople when we took her."

"That's good news!" Anwar said eagerly. "Forget the slave traders—we can make a ransom demand of the pasha. He'll be able to afford much more than Halmid. Five thousand at least!"

Malik said nothing.

"Don't you see?" Anwar persisted. "Kalid Shah is immensely wealthy. He has a fortune in European investments made by his father before his death. Shah doesn't need to be pasha of Bursa or to do anything else connected with the Sultan. He could take his family and leave at any time. He only stays here because he's been trying to avoid civil war and a bloodbath for the people of his district."

"That's exactly why I'm reluctant to extort money from him. The Sultan's spies are everywhere, and when Kalid Shah pays us, the Sultan will know about it. The story is all over the British newspapers. When the girl is restored to her family, they'll report that too. Hammid knows that Kalid has been sympathetic to our cause. He'll think that the kidnapping was a sham we constructed to enable Kalid Shah to contribute to the revolution."

"So much the better for us!" Anwar said. "If Hammid sees Kalid Shah as allied with us, he'll know we're making big inroads in the western Empire." Anwar stopped. "Of course, you'll have to give up the girl."

Malik didn't answer.

"What are you thinking?" Anwar said.

"Kalid Shah has been a friend to us. I don't want to put Bursa at risk."

"What Kalid wants is not going to happen. Hammid will never compromise; he'll level the whole country first."

"I'm more worried about what might happen when Hammid learns that we have made the deal." Malik put down the newspaper. "It has to look like a hostile transaction."

"Shah wants to meet with you. Tell him that." Anwar hesitated, then moved back to what was, for him, the real issue. "Can you give up the girl?" he asked.

"For five thousand kurush, I'll have to," Malik said, and walked away.

Secretary Danforth accepted a cup of tea from Beatrice Woolcott and added a lump of sugar to it. He looked up as the servant, Listak, silently offered him a tray of comfits.

"Have one," James said. "My wife makes them from an old family recipe, using the local hazelnuts in place of Georgia pecans. They're very good."

Danforth selected a delicacy and dropped it onto the gilt-rimmed porcelain plate at his elbow. The china was the finest Limoges, in keeping with the rest of the appointments in the stately home.

James Woolcott was indeed prospering in Turkey.

"So the official word from the Sultan is that there is nothing he can do?" James said, continuing the conversation that the arrival of refreshments had interrupted.

Danforth nodded, his mouth full of nuts. He patted his lips with a napkin and swallowed before replying.

"He says that the people who kidnapped your niece are outlaws living under a death sentence. If apprehended, they will of course suffer the ultimate penalty, but until then no monarch can halt completely the commission of crimes in his country."

"In other words, go scratch," Beatrice said dryly, sniffing and flicking an invisible bit of lint from the tight cuff of her organdy sleeve.

"I'm afraid so," Danforth agreed. "The Sultan knows that our country is in sympathy with the rebels, so he's not going to lift a finger to help locate a missing American woman. Your niece is a victim of international gamesmanship."

"Then Kalid Shah is our only hope," James observed.

"I told you he would be," Beatrice said.

"Do you think this bandit will listen to him?" James asked Danforth.

Danforth set down his cup and dusted

crumbs from his fingertips.

"If he doesn't, you'll never see your niece again," he said gravely.

The side street just off the main thoroughfare was more like an alley, too narrow for much more than foot traffic and deeply rutted from the carts used to transport goods to the shops. The adobe structure at its end was low and dark, full of the smells of closely packed humanity and the dense smoke from Turkish tobacco. The babble of many languages formed a background noise as Kalid Shah loomed in the doorway of the *cayhanesi,* or coffeehouse.

Kalid was dressed like a British businessman in a three-piece suit, his *Kaffe* skin, vaguely European features, and Victorian beard enhancing the Western tourist effect. He spotted Malik Bey immediately at the back of the room. The younger man was disguised as a bedouin, with flowing robes and a headscarf obscuring his hair and the lower part of his face.

The disguise was a precaution. Malik had never been turned in for the substantial reward offered for his capture, but a desperate peasant in a moment of weakness might just recognize him and alter his fate forever.

The two men moved toward one another without haste, meeting next to a scarred table in the middle of the room. Kalid gestured for Malik to sit and then ordered two cups of *boza,* the fermented barley drink popular with the country's working class majority. He spoke in Turkish to the barmaid and then switched to English when he addressed Malik, to reduce the chance of their conversation being overheard.

"I am here to redeem the American girl," Kalid said. "What do you want for her?"

"Five thousand kurush," Malik replied.

"That's quite a bit."

"Not for a relative of your beloved pashana's," Malik replied dryly.

"The relation is not close—Sarah doesn't even know her. The girl is the niece of Sarah's cousin's wife. Were you aware of this when you took her?"

Malik shook his head. "I saw that she was young and beautiful and knew she would bring a fine price on the slave market."

"Then why haven't you sold her?" Kalid demanded, watching the younger man's face.

Malik looked away. "I tried. I couldn't do it."

The barmaid brought their drinks and Kalid handed her a coin. When she left, he leaned forward and said, "I'll give you ten thousand if you'll keep Amelia safe for three weeks and then turn her over to me at the end of that time."

Malik stared at him, unable to speak.

"I mean it," Kalid said. "I have the money with me."

"Why?" Malik finally said.

"If you hold her that long, the Sultan will be

convinced that I was reluctant to pay the ransom and had to think about it, finally relenting in response to pressure from my wife." He smiled. "It is well known that I indulge her, and sexual persuasion is a concept the Sultan will understand."

Malik nodded, his mind racing.

"I want to avoid any appearance of collusion in the kidnapping," Kalid said, "and there is another reason." He took a sip of the *boza*. "The Sultan has convened a meeting of all the district pashas for the twentieth. I hope to win some concessions for Bursa at that time, and if Hammid thinks I'm still holding out on your extortion demands, he'll be in a more favorable mood."

"Everyone says that you play him like an instrument," Malik said admiringly.

"I have to, *agha*," Kalid said, addressing Malik by the title that his men used. "He still has the janissaries, and they could lay waste to Bursa in a few days. The people rely on me to protect them. When I decide to fight, it will be when I've eliminated Hammid's personal army and am poised to win."

"Anyone else in your position would be long gone, living in luxury in a townhouse in London," Malik said.

"I'm not anybody else," Kalid replied shortly.

"Where is the money?"

"Here." He lifted a leather bag onto the

scarred wooden table. "I'm giving it to you now as a contribution to your cause because I think you may have need of it soon."

"Why? What do you know?"

"I received a tip yesterday from one of my paid informants. The Sultan is planning a raid on the Armenian section in Constantinople. He suspects them of working with you."

"When?"

"At dawn on Thursday. If you want to keep your allies there alive to fight another day, send reinforcements the night before and have them ready and waiting for the attack."

Malik took the bag of money and stood. "When we move against the Sultan, I'll make sure you're warned in enough time to get your family out," he said.

"When you move against the Sultan, I'll be with you," Kalid replied.

Malik extended his hand and Kalid clasped it. Their eyes met and held.

"I'll wager Amelia's a handful, isn't she?" Kalid said, his expression mischievous.

Malik nodded, smiling slightly.

"So was my wife, but well worth the trouble, I assure you. Take care of her."

Malik nodded. He understood.

"Good luck on Thursday. I'll send word to the camp with Mehmed when and where you can meet me to release the girl." Kalid rose and walked out of the shop.

Malik watched Shah's wide shoulders disappear through the narrow doorway, his pulse pounding, his fingers knotted around the purse in his hands.

He had heard many amazing stories about the pasha of Bursa.

Now he knew they were true.

When Malik returned to the camp that evening, he sent Matka out of his tent and ordered the guards away from the area. Amy watched, puzzled, as he knelt on the ground before her and pulled his knife from the sheath at his waist.

She drew in her breath, her eyes widening.

He slashed through her bonds with two strokes and said, "Stand up."

Amy rose unsteadily, her cramped legs almost giving way beneath her. Malik extended his arm and she took it, leaning on it heavily.

"We're going for a walk," he said.

Amy felt the eyes of the camp women on her as she and her companion walked past the cooking fires and the stand where the horses were tied, past the main guard post and into the trees. They walked a short distance to a clearing where fallen tree trunks and the remains of rotted stumps provided a natural seating gallery. Malik indicated for her to sit on a flat stump and then stood facing her, his arms folded.

"Why the dispensation?" Amy asked, holding up her naked wrists.

"What's that?" he asked. Apparently his English vocabulary was not equal to this challenge.

"Why no ropes?" she amended.

He looked down at the ground, then up at her again. "I have met with your kinsman, Kalid Shah, the pasha of Bursa."

Amy stared back at him triumphantly. "Oh, really? How interesting. I told you I wasn't lying about that."

"You never mentioned his name."

"I couldn't recall it immediately."

"I thought you were just trying another ploy to get—"

"You wouldn't even listen to me!" Amy interrupted him indignantly.

He held up his hand for silence. "It doesn't matter now. The pasha will be taking you back to your family in three weeks."

Amy stared at him, unable to comprehend it.

"You aren't tied up anymore because there's no further reason for you to attempt an escape. I have no plans to sell you to a dealer or harm you in any way. Kalid Shah has already given me what I want. You will be safe and well cared for here until he comes for you."

"He paid you?"

"Yes."

"How much?"

"Why do you want to know?"

Amy picked up a wood chip and turned it over

in her fingers. "Just curious. It would be a shame for you to go to so much trouble over me and not get what you were hoping for."

"I am well satisfied with the price," he said.

Amy said nothing.

"Well?" he prodded. "I would have thought you'd be happier at this news."

"I'm not sure I believe you," she said.

He eyed her warily. "Why not?"

"Why not? You're surprised? A trustworthy fellow like yourself?" she said dryly.

"What makes you doubt me?"

"Oh, let me see. What could there possibly be? Your past history, your present occupation, your sterling reputation, your honest face?"

"Answer me seriously."

"You could take Kalid's money and then sell me anyway. By the time he showed up here to collect me I would be long gone and you'd have been paid double for one hostage."

"Obviously, he trusts me."

"I can't imagine why."

"I am a man of my word."

She snorted. "What's that? Honor among thieves? Or is it kidnappers? Oh excuse me, what *do* you call yourselves, agha—heroes of the people?"

"We call ourselves men who want to be free."

"Please!" Amy said, standing up and clenching her fists. "Just tell me the truth for once! Why did Kalid give you the money now instead of when he gets me back? Isn't that the standard procedure? And why is he waiting three weeks to come for me? Something else is going on here, Malik, and I want to know what it is."

Malik said nothing. It was the first time she had called him by name, and hearing her say it with the native pronunciation his friends used clutched suddenly at his gut.

"Or are you lying to me about everything?" she went on, almost raving. "Have you just made all this up to confuse me?" She balled her fists at her temples, her knuckles white. "I don't know what to believe!"

"Believe what I'm telling you."

"Why should I? You might be lying to me about anything. Maybe the next slave trader you have lined up to inspect me can't get here for three weeks. You could be telling me this story so I'll be a good little girl and not give you any trouble until Kalid arrives to make the deal."

"You think too much," Malik said, picking up a stick and snapping it in half disgustedly.

"I've had plenty of time to think, tied up all day," she shot back.

"I've said that you won't be tied up anymore," he replied heatedly.

"Oh, thank you, my lord and master," Amy said sarcastically. "I'm so grateful for your kindness. And did I remember to thank you for dragging me off on horseback at gunpoint and installing me in this queen's-appointment hotel? Not to mention parading me like livestock before that insect with the nose ring and the turban. Why didn't you sell me to Halmad anyway? Wasn't the price high enough?"

Malik charged forward and grabbed her arms. "The price was fine. I just couldn't let him strip you as bare as a strumpet to inspect the goods!" he said furiously.

"Why not? Did you want to do it yourself?" Amy countered, staring up at him.

A throbbing silence fell as they heard what they had said. Neither knew what to do; too much of what they had been feeling had been exposed by the exchange.

Amy was the first to recover.

"You're hurting me," she whispered, twisting uselessly in his grasp.

He didn't move.

"I said, you're hurting me. Let me go!"

His fingers relaxed slowly, and Amy snatched herself away from him, rubbing her wrists.

"Go back to the camp and stay in my tent," he said abruptly, looking away from her.

"Aren't you going to put a rope around my neck and lead me there?" she said in the old taunting tone, but her heart wasn't in it. She was visibly shaken, her face pale.

"The sun is going down. If you want to take off and spend another night with the wolves, be my guest. I won't come after you this time."

"Why? Because you already have your

money?" she said nastily.

"Because you are a nuisance and a burden and I wish I had never set eyes on you."

There was a long pause. Then she squared her shoulders and lifted her chin, which was trembling.

"I hate you," she hissed, her eyes filling with tears.

"That's your problem," he replied.

One tear crept down her cheek, and she dashed it away in annoyance. Then she stalked past him, and he turned to watch her go. When she had disappeared through the trees, he took her place on the polished stump and put his head in his hands.

He should not be involved in this; he did not have the time. To say that he had more important things to do was a ludicrous understatement: the fate of his country was hanging in the balance and he was having spats with a spoiled American teenager who had already caused him more trouble than all the previous women in his life combined.

In short, he was risking his mission, not to mention making an ass of himself.

It didn't seem to matter. He was ensnared and he knew it. In three weeks she would leave and he would never see her again, but while she was with him he could not stay away from her.

He stood and began to pace, thrusting his fingers through his hair distractedly. He must stay away from her. He *must*. His agreement with Kalid Shah had left several things unspoken, and one of them was that Amelia leave the rebel camp as she had entered it.

The tension between them was causing them to fight, but he couldn't take her, even if she was willing to be taken, and even if he was dying of the need to sink into her so deep that he would be lost forever. It was no longer a matter of keeping her virginal for the slave trade; it was now a matter of honor. His honor.

He would not break faith with the pasha of Bursa, who was risking his life and that of his family to help the revolutionaries' cause.

Malik closed his eyes. Why was it so difficult to resist her? It wasn't just that she was ready and wanted him, even if her inexperience was confusing her and she didn't yet realize it herself. Her anger and her indignation, very real at first, were now becoming a defense; he could see through them to her true emotions. But he would have to let the moment pass, even though he knew it could never come again.

She would soon go back to her old life and forget him.

The thought was unbearable. He realized that he was clenching his fists in frustration and opened them immediately.

Malik stopped walking suddenly and looked up at the setting sun. Anwar would be searching for him, wanting to review the plan for their infiltration of the Armenian quarters.

When the Sultan's men arrived at dawn, the rebels would be waiting.

Chapter Six

The silence woke her. Amy sat up and looked around the empty tent. Malik's pallet was still rolled up, unused, and she realized with a start that he had not come back after their quarrel.

She wrapped a shawl around her shoulders and walked through the tent flap. It was the hour before dawn, when the birds began to stir and the women started the cooking fires. Amy looked around curiously and quickly realized what had disturbed her.

All the men and the horses were gone. The noise they made was absent, and the resulting quiet was unnerving.

The women moved about her like shadows, performing their routine tasks. They ignored

137

her as if she were part of the morning mist drifting through the trees.

Amy watched them, wondering why they were alone. There was no one she could ask. To her knowledge, Malik was the only member of the rebel group who spoke English, and her Turkish was restricted to a few necessary words and phrases.

Whatever was happening, all the others seemed aware of it. There was no alarm in their expression or demeanor, and their placid acceptance of the changed situation made her almost envy them their serenity.

She knew she could never be so detached. She always wanted to know everything about every situation, and sometimes that trait got her into trouble.

It was the longest day of Amy's life. She had no idea what was going on and there was no one to tell her. At dusk, when she could stand it no longer, she found Matka doing needlework and said to her in English, "Where are the men?"

Matka looked at her and shrugged.

"Malik Bey," Amy said, enunciating carefully, certain that Matka would understand that much. Then Amy gestured expansively, sweeping her arm to indicate empty space, and pantomimed looking around corners and into the distance. "Where is he?" she asked.

Matka's expression indicated that she understood, but she still said nothing. She went back to her sewing. Frustrated, Amy moved away, looking around for someone else. Risa, the young girl who had helped Matka to bathe Amy when she first arrived at the camp, walked past with a pail of water. Amy grabbed her arm and went through the same routine.

"Mahalle Armenia," Risa replied.

Even Amy knew what that meant; she had heard Malik use the term often enough. The Armenian quarter of Constantinople.

"Why?" Amy asked, lifting her shoulders and arching her brows inquiringly.

"Tanzimat," Risa replied. The revolution.

The revolution? Amy thought, watching Risa walk away. What did that mean? They were always occupied with the revolution; they lived for nothing else.

Then realization dawned, and Amy felt a cold finger on the back of her neck. Risa meant that the men were fighting; she meant that they were fighting right now. Malik and his band were risking their lives at that very moment, and the sudden knowledge made her feel naive and foolish.

War was Malik's occupation, his interlude with her just a means to that end. Why was she surprised that he had disappeared from camp to go off and fight the Sultan? He had done it countless times, and he didn't need her permission to continue on his chosen path.

Amy shivered, wondering if she would ever see him again. She wished that their last encounter had not been so ugly, so filled with bitterness and anger.

As soon as she realized where Malik was, she knew she didn't want anything to happen to him.

When darkness fell, she went back to Malik's tent to sleep. No one was paying any attention to her, and she could have walked right out of the camp; Malik must have known she would not go. After all, he was risking nothing by leaving her unguarded. He already had his money, and Amy's best way out of this nightmare was to wait for Kalid Shah. But there was more to it for her now. She wanted to stay and see that Malik returned safely. She knew the desire was childish. In just a few weeks he would be nothing but a memory, but the need to see him again remained.

She fell into a fitful doze, waking frequently throughout the night, but it was light before she heard the sound of horses' hooves and knew that the men were back.

Amy jumped up and ran out into the clearing as the other women did the same. She looked around frantically for Malik, but saw only the limp bodies of injured men slung across horses, tended by those who were still capable of riding. The returning rebels swarmed around her, greeted by their wives and families, but she couldn't find the face she sought. Then she suddenly glimpsed a glossy dark head, a slim torso covered with blood, and her vision went dark for a moment. When it cleared again, she saw with a sickening lurch of relief that the man with the wound was Anwar, and Malik was standing by his side.

Her heart still pounding in reaction to the spurt of fear she'd just experienced, she watched as two men lifted Anwar from Malik's horse and carried his still form into his tent. Malik followed them, walking past her without a glance.

The camp was busy for the rest of the day, but there was no sense of accomplishment in it. Rather it was the ceaseless activity of a hospital which prevailed, as everyone's attention focused on tending the wounded. Amy watched Anwar's tent until late afternoon, observing the comings and goings and Malik's tense expression whenever he appeared. Finally, as the women were gathering to cook the evening meal, he emerged and stalked across the clearing.

Amy ran up to him and said, "I can help you with Anwar."

This got his attention, as she had known it would. "What do you mean?" he demanded, looking down at her.

"I volunteered at a hospital in Boston for two

years while I was in school. I know a lot about nursing."

He snorted. "Oh, yes, I know about American volunteers. Did you ever actually see a sick person between the luncheons and teas and bandage rolling?"

"I assisted at bedside treatments and changed dressings and administered doses of medicine."

"And you had a civil war going on in Boston at this time?" he said dryly.

"We had criminals and police who were shooting each other," Amy replied. "I cared for them. What else do you need?"

"I need a doctor," he burst out in frustration, "but they're all too afraid of the Sultan to come here."

"Then I'm the next best thing. Will you let me take a look at him?"

Malik looked at her doubtfully.

"I want to help," Amy said quietly. "I may not be fond of your methods of raising capital, but I would not deliberately worsen the condition of an injured man."

He still regarded her measuringly, unconvinced.

"Is there anyone else here with experience in Western medicine?" Amy asked. "Is there anyone else here with any medical experience at all?"

"We've tended the wounded many times," he said stiffly.

"Has your best friend been shot before?" Amy countered. "What can it hurt to let me see him?"

He sighed resignedly. "All right. Come along," he said, and she trailed at his side as he entered the tent containing the injured man and several of his relatives. When Amy knelt by Anwar's side and touched his forehead, one of the younger women protested in a vehement burst of Turkish.

"What is it?" Amy asked, looking up at Malik.

"She doesn't want you tending him," Malik said shortly.

"Why not?"

"She says you're a foreigner and an infidel and have brought bad luck to the camp."

"She has you to thank for my arrival here, agha," Amy said. "Why don't you tell her that?" She bent over Anwar again, and the woman clutched her arm warningly.

"Look here, I'm not going to hurt him," Amy said. "Malik, tell her I'm trying to help. She has to trust me." She looked up at Malik. "You do, don't you?"

"If I didn't, you wouldn't be in here," he replied quietly.

"Then tell them all to go now," Amy said. "I have to be able to concentrate."

Malik said something curtly in Turkish, and the family left the tent one by one. When he was alone with Amy, he asked, "What do you think?"

Amy peeled the makeshift dressing back from

the wound and gazed down at the suppurating hole in Anwar's shoulder. It was jagged from the exit of the flattened metal pistol ball and charcoaled with the powder burn.

"Well?" Malik said anxiously.

"The ball exited on its own, so I don't have to probe the wound for it, and that's good. But the wound is infected. That's why it's oozing and his skin is so hot. He has a fever."

"What can you do?"

"He needs a poultice to draw the wound. I must have the herbs to make it and something to reduce his fever."

"We have nothing here—you know that," he said impatiently.

"Isn't there an apothecary in the covered bazaar in the city?" Amy asked. "You could purchase what I need there."

"Tell me what to get and I'll go. I'll be back in one day."

Amy stood and faced him. "I don't know the Turkish names. I have to see them."

It was a moment before the implication of what she had said reached him.

"I'm not taking you back and forth to Constantinople with me," Malik said flatly.

"Do you have any choice? I can ride well enough, so you won't have to carry me. Do you want Anwar to die?"

"We will attract attention!" Malik said. "You may not have noticed this, Amelia, but Turkish women don't have yellow hair and gray eyes!"

"Then we'll wear the bedouin robes you use for a disguise. If I keep my face covered and my eyes down no one will notice me. I only have to be in the shop for a short while. I can identify everything by sight. I was very well taught by an herbalist famous in Boston for his cures."

"This is a dangerous idea," Malik said quietly. "Anwar has not been fond of you. He was against keeping you here from the start. Why would you take the chance of being caught in the city with me, a man with a price on his head? The accomplices of state criminals are not treated very well by the Sultan."

"The same reason you'll take a chance on going. It would be wrong to let Anwar die when I think I can save him. I have seen others in the same condition, and if I get the medicine I need he has a chance. You don't want to lose your friend, do you?"

Malik thought about it. "If we're stopped, you must say that you're my prisoner and I forced you to come with me. Your kidnapping is well known. They'll believe you."

Amy smiled at him. "It's more or less the truth," she said. "Isn't it?"

He didn't reply.

"Do you still have the clothes I was wearing when I came here?" Amy asked.

"What's left of them," he replied. "Why?"

"What about the little knit bag I was carrying, my reticule?" Amy said.

"I think Matka put it away with the rest of your things," Malik said.

"There's a green bottle of medicine in it that was prescribed for me when my parents died. It's laudanum. If Anwar takes some of that, it will kill the pain and help him sleep, so that he'll be comfortable until we get back."

"Is it safe? Why were you taking it?"

"I had nightmares after my parents were killed. I took it to help me sleep. The spoon attached to the cap measures the right dose for me. If Anwar, who is bigger and heavier than I am, takes just that much at a time, every eight hours, he will be perfectly safe."

"Anything else?" Malik asked, listening intently.

"Yes. There's also a small wooden box in the reticule containing aspirin tablets. They'll reduce his wound inflammation and fever until we can get back."

"What's aspirin?"

"It's an acid the native people of my country used for many years. They boiled the bark of the aspen tree, which grows in the American west, and drank the liquid when they were ill. The Germans discovered its medicinal properties on their own about twenty years ago, but American physicians still don't use it."

"Why not?"

"Malik, we're wasting time. Can't we talk about this on the way to the city?"

"I want to know why American doctors don't approve of what you plan to give Anwar. Now."

"Most of my countrymen don't respect herbal cures; they think herbalists are quacks."

"What is a quack?"

"A charlatan."

He smiled. "What is a charlatan?"

Amy smiled too. "A reckless experimenter who pretends to knowledge he doesn't have. Don't worry, I've taken aspirin and it works. It will help Anwar, I promise you. He should have a tablet every four hours."

"All right. I'll send Anwar's sister for your bag and give her your instructions. She'll be nursing him while we're gone." He watched as she covered Anwar's wound gently, then held the back of her hand to his burning cheek.

"When were your parents killed?" he asked.

"Two months ago, in a carriage accident in Boston. The court awarded me to my aunt. I was coming to stay with her when you . . . interrupted my journey."

He offered her his hand and pulled her lightly to her feet. "So everything you told me that night in the woods was true?" he said.

"Everything I told you that night was true. I'm not a liar, *agha khan*."

He shook his head, lifting the tent flap for her as they went outside.

147

"What?" she asked.

"My language sounds odd on your lips."

"My language sounds odd on yours. You cannot imagine the effect of hearing Koroglu talking like an Oxford don."

He looked at her in amazement. "What do you know about Koroglu?" he asked.

"He's a Turkish folk hero, isn't he? I read about him in the newspaper. The author was comparing you to him."

He made a dismissive gesture. "Writers have fanciful imaginations. What I'm doing is not heroic but necessary. Go back to my tent, and I'll send Matka to you with the bedouin clothing."

Amy did as he said and was soon dressed like a nomad, with long robes and a heavy veil and the *yashmak* covering the lower part of her face. Malik led two horses over to the tent, one loaded with blankets, a water bottle, and his leather pouch.

"You told me you could ride," he said to Amy, when he saw her eyeing his horse uneasily.

"I can't ride your horse," Amy replied.

"True. I alone ride Mehmet."

"But that mare looks gentle enough," Amy observed.

"She is. Her name is Dosha. Let's go."

He held out his arms, and she stepped closer so he could lift her onto the horse. Dosha danced a little, and Amy reined her in gently.

The horse settled down and began cropping grass.

"Good," Malik said, and it was strange how that one small word of approval warmed her.

Malik gave a few instructions in Turkish to Yuri, who was standing by, his disapproval of their excursion evident on his swarthy face. Then they rode out of the camp as its inhabitants watched them in stoic silence.

They traveled through the morning, coming down out of the hills and then riding across the sandy plain until the direct heat of the sun forced them to stop. Amy followed Malik into a small copse where the shade offered relief. Malik dismounted first, then held up his arms to help Amy dismount. She bent as his hands encircled her waist, and for a second she felt his breath fan her face as he swept her to the ground.

"Are you tired?" he asked, as she sat with her back to a tree and closed her eyes.

"I'm all right. I just haven't been doing much riding lately. You're the one who should be tired. You spent all night coming back to the camp and you were fighting in the Mahalle yesterday."

He took a long drink from the water bottle and handed it to her. "How do you know I was fighting in the Mahalle?" he asked.

"Risa told me."

"Risa talks too much," he said darkly.

149

"I asked her where you had gone. I was worried when I got up and saw that all the men had left."

"I had advance word that the Sultan was planning a raid on the Armenian quarter, so we were there waiting when the janissaries arrived."

"Did you win?"

"We won the skirmish, not the war."

"Why is the Sultan against the Armenians?"

"They are separatists who want their own country, and my men don't want the country they now have. So for the moment we are allies, since we share the same oppressor." He grinned. "The Armenians dislike paying the Sultan's taxes as much as we do."

"And who are the janissaries?" Amy asked. "Everyone seems afraid of them."

Yeni ceri," Malik said, giving her the original Turkish phrase for the Sultan's guard as he removed a wedge of cheese from his pack. He offered it to Amy, who shook her head. "Conscripted men. They compose the Sultan's private army, soldiers taken from their homes as young boys and trained in his service. Their duty is to keep Hammid alive, and the penalty is death for any one of them who fails in it. So they generally succeed."

"They have no choice about joining his service?"

Malik gave a short bark of a laugh, cutting a

slice of cheese for himself. "No, the Sultan doesn't offer many alternatives. But the janissaries are selected from the Christian peasants, who usually have too many children to feed anyway, so it's really the army or starve. In the Empire, choice is a luxury most people cannot afford."

"But you want to change all that," Amy said.

He looked up at her tone. "Do you think it's just a dream?" he asked, removing a wheel of barley bread from the pouch and breaking off a piece of it.

"It seems as if the odds are against you," Amy answered him quietly.

"It will happen," he said. "I may not live to see it, but my actions today will pave the way for those who do."

"And that's enough for you?"

"It has to be. I won't live a slave's life. If I die young, at least I'll die like a man." He passed her a handful of olives and she set them on the ground.

"Will you please eat something?" he said. "We have another four hours to ride."

"It's too hot to eat," Amy said, removing the yashmak and fanning her face. "Are you sure we'll get there before the bazaar shuts down for the night?"

He nodded. "I've made this trip many times. You'll have half an hour before sunset to buy what you need and then we'll return to Anwar as quietly as possible."

"You're very fond of Anwar, aren't you?" Amy said.

"We grew up together in a *koy* not too far from here," Malik said.

"Koy?"

"A farming village too small to have a name. Anwar has been like a brother to me since we were both five, my right hand since we took up arms against the state. His life is as important to me as my own."

"Then we should go," Amy said, standing. "Time is crucial in fighting a fever. Anwar could dehydrate or develop a secondary infection—"

"Have you had enough rest?" Malik asked, rising in one motion as he interrupted her, not wanting to hear what else might happen to Anwar.

"I'll rest when we get back," Amy replied.

He put the uneaten food in the bag and hung it and the bottle back on his saddle. He then helped her onto Dosha, waiting until she was seated comfortably before he vaulted onto his own horse.

"Replace the veil," he said, "in case we run into anyone on the road."

Amy obeyed.

"How is your back?" he said. "If you haven't been riding for a while, you're sure to feel it."

"It hurts a little," she admitted.

"It will hurt a lot more tonight," he said, and kicked his horse's flanks.

Amy followed him out of the trees and back into the desert heat.

"Father, you promised me you would let me ride Khan this afternoon," Tariq said, tugging on Kalid's sleeve.

Kalid put down the book he was reading and said, "Khan is getting old now, Tariq. I'm not sure he can handle you."

"But you promised!" Tariq complained, sticking out his lower lip.

Kalid looked at Sarah, who was correcting a mathematics paper from her class. She held up her hand as if to say, Leave me out of it.

"I believe I said that I would think about it, which is not exactly a promise," Kalid said sternly.

Tariq waited tensely, his dark eyes watchful, unsure which way the wind would blow.

Kalid shook his head and rose. "All right, run down to the stables and tell Aleph to saddle him. I'll be along in a few minutes, and we'll take a few turns around the paddock. I want to make sure you don't kill my old friend."

The boy charged out of the room as Sarah said, "You spoil him, Kalid."

"I can't understand why he's so fascinated with that horse," Kalid observed.

"You can't?" Sarah replied, staring at him.

"You've told him so many stories of your exploits on that animal I'm surprised he isn't sleeping in the stable with it."

Kalid grinned. "Are you suggesting that I have exaggerated my glorious past to my son?" he said.

Sarah threw a gum eraser at him.

He caught it in midair, then crossed the room to sit at the table with her. He took her free hand in his.

"Can you stop for a moment?" he said. "I want to tell you something."

Alerted by his serious tone, Sarah pushed her stack of papers aside and sat forward, looking into his eyes.

"I have been waiting all morning to talk to you, but one of the children was always around," he said.

Sarah nodded.

"I have transferred a large sum of money to a bank account in London," Kalid said, "and this evening I will give you the papers and the name of the man in Lincoln's Inn who will be handling my affairs there in future. I want you to be able to take the children and leave here at a moment's notice if it becomes necessary. All you have to do is get to England, and you'll have enough to take care of all of you for the rest of your lives."

"I won't leave without you," Sarah said.

"Yes, you will," Kalid said firmly. "If the time

comes, you will do exactly as I say with no argument."

Sarah released his hand. "There's no life for me without you—you know that."

"Then think of the children," he said gently.

Sarah swallowed. "Are things that bad, Kalid?" she asked quietly.

"Not yet. But they could be. I just want to be ready."

"I thought the problem was solved. I thought Malik Bey said he would turn Amelia over to you when you asked for her."

"Bey did say that, but the Sultan is another story. He's volatile and unpredictable. His men are dealing with new outbreaks of rebellion every day, and Hammid blames Bey for all of them. The janissaries were roundly trounced in that raid in the Armenian mahalle and Hammid knows the Armenians are Bey's allies. If he manages to kill Malik before I redeem the girl, I don't know what will happen to her."

Sarah put her hand over his on the table. "How awful for you to be caught in the middle of all this," she said softly.

He stood abruptly. "I've been in worse spots. If Bey keeps his word, all should be well."

"Do you trust him?" Sarah asked.

"I did trust him when I looked into his eyes and saw Osman looking back at me. Let's hope I was not wrong and they are not that different after all. Now let me go after Tariq and make sure my horse survives his encounter with my son."

He walked out as Sarah stared after him unhappily.

She sighed and tried to go back to her work, but the numbers on the pages were meaningless.

Kalid was not an alarmist; if he was taking action to enable his family to leave the Empire, he was worried.

Sarah folded her hands on her work table and stared into the distance, lost in thought.

Constantinople straddled the continents of Europe and Asia along the narrow river of the Bosporus, the "throat" which opened into the Sea of Marmara, its gleaming waters then flowing on to mix with the blue Aegean. Amy was fascinated with the sight of the city as they neared it. Its minarets climbed toward a scarlet sky next to the domes of Christian churches, and its stone and wooden structures clung to the hills overlooking the edge of the land. A blend of east and west unparallelled elsewhere in the world, its name in Turkish, *Istanbul*, meant "into the city," as if there were and could be no other.

Amy had seen very little of Constantinople when she arrived in Turkey, spending most of her time in the train station waiting for the coach, so now she stared at the inner harbor, the "Golden Horn," filled with boats of all kinds.

Some were under sail, European schooners as well as Asian junks, but there were many more *caiques*, slim rowboats which slipped smoothly under the Galata Bridge with rhythmic oars hardly splashing. The traffic on the bridge was dense and noisy, a blend of Arabs leading camels, horse-drawn coaches, farmers herding bleating goats, nomads in trailing robes with donkeys, even Daimler carriages. Amy craned her neck backward as they turned down a dusty side street toward the market, and her horse objected to the change in pace; Amy leaned over to stroke Dosha's neck.

"Come on," Malik called to her, glancing up at the darkening sky. "This way."

Vendors shouted at them at they rode past, hawking *simits*, or crescent-shaped doughnuts, as well as grilled fish and lamb kebobs and *borek*, a flaky, cheese-filled pastry. By the time Malik and Amy reached the walls of the *Buyuk Charsi*, or enclosed market, the sun was low and some of the merchants were starting to pack up their wares. Amy followed Malik through the gate, gawking at the crowded aisles where each stall or open stand seemed to display some new and exotic item.

But their mission was to get back to Anwar as soon as possible, so she concentrated on guiding the horse until the lanes became too narrow and they got down to walk. She tried to ignore the manic scene around her—the squawking of live chickens and geese flapping in cages, the smell of drifting incense and meat grilling over charcoal braziers, the Europeans in homburgs arguing with turbaned rug and skin traders, the rainbow of varicolored costumes representing every ethnic group. It was all too much to take in. That would have to wait for another, better time.

They reached a turn, and the path beyond was just wide enough for two people to walk abreast. Malik stopped and said something to one of the barefoot boys scampering underfoot everywhere, shouting at one another or begging from the passersby. The child stopped and took the coin Malik offered, then accepted the reins of their horses, tying them to a pole.

"Will he stay with them?" Amy whispered, worried about their transportation.

"If he wants the rest of the money I promised him, he will," Malik replied, taking her arm and steering her into a doorway draped with ropes of garlic. A wooden sign depicting a mortar and pestle swung in the light breeze drifting in from the water, proclaiming the wares of the shop to the mostly illiterate population.

"Why garlic?" Amy asked, pointing to the garlands.

"An offering to the grey wolf," Malik replied.

Amy didn't know what that meant, but she was soon distracted by the interior of the stall. It was dim and crammed with shelves containing glass bottles and jars, some of them so dusty it seemed they hadn't been moved for years. They were filled with every form of plant and mineral life, indistinguishable from one another. She had to get a better look to determine what she needed. The slanting sunlight drifting in through the shutters did not provide much illumination, but even if Amy had been able to read the jar labels, the lettering was all unfamiliar.

The attendant pushed open the curtain that screened off the back of the shop and came forward, the dark eyes above her veil watchful.

Malik sighed, his face changing.

"What is it?" Amy asked anxiously.

"She's a Kurd. They're a mountain tribe, very independent. Even the Sultan deals with them at a distance, through their tribal overlords. I hope I can make her understand me," Malik replied unhappily.

"Don't they speak Turkish?"

"Some do, but most speak a language like Pharsi. They rarely come out of the eastern hills. Their women are bold, though it's still unusual to see one of them running a shop."

"What's the lettering on the jars?" Amy whispered.

"Arabic," he replied.

The Kurdish woman looked inquiringly at Malik. He said something to her in Turkish and she nodded, replying in a long stream of liquid syllables which made Malik look hopeful again.

"What did she say?" Amy asked.

"She's a Yezidi, a sect known for the supernatural and healing powers of its priests. This is her father's store. He sells his cures here and has taught her his art. She says you can look around and pick out what you want. She has samples from Europe and Asia and all over the world."

"First I'll need marjoram to reduce the tissue swelling," Amy replied, her eyes roaming the shelves. "My herbal instructor was English and the plants I want are mostly from England, derived from John Gardner's *Herball*. Maybe if you tell her why I require the plant, she can pick out the most likely candidates from what she knows, and I'll be able to identify it when I see it."

With Malik at Amy's side translating, the process went as quickly as they could have hoped. By the time they left, as darkness was falling, Malik's pouch was filled with not only marjoram but foxglove, lady's mantle, St. John's wort and marigold, mustard seeds and oil of wintergreen to extract the healing sap from leaves. Amy was so thrilled with her unexpected success that she didn't see the two men standing next to their horses.

But Malik did.

"Get behind me," he said suddenly, and she looked up, alarmed, as the two figures moved forward menacingly. When she froze, Malik thrust her out of their path and tossed the pouch at her feet.

The first man jumped Malik so fast that his motion was a blur; there was a swirl of clothing and then both men were struggling on the ground. Amy gasped and shrank back against the adobe wall of the shop, the flaring torch in a niche above her head illuminating a scene from hell. She saw a flash of metal and realized that Malik's attacker had a knife. She ran forward, but a long arm swept her up and a large hand covered her mouth, holding her tightly. She struggled fiercely, but was helpless in the grip of the second attacker.

Amy was forced to watch as Malik and his opponent rolled in the dust. She screamed behind the grimy fingers pressed into her teeth when she saw the knife sink into Malik's arm. He grunted, but somehow was able to gain leverage against the other man and flip him onto his back. Malik grabbed the hand that held the knife and slammed it into the ground repeatedly until the fingers loosened and dropped the weapon. Malik knocked it out of range and punched the man under him in the throat. The man's eyes bulged, then closed as his head lolled to the side.

The second man released Amy when he saw that his friend had lost the fight and lunged for the knife. Amy stuck out her foot and tripped him, and Malik got up quickly, kicking her attacker as he went down. He tried to rise and Malik kicked him again, then laced his fingers together and brought both hands down forcefully on the back of his neck. The man slumped and lay flat.

Malik held his good arm out to Amy and she flew to him. He embraced her and she buried her face against his chest.

"Are you all right?" he panted.

"Am *I* all right? You just got stabbed!" she cried.

He looked down at the cut in his tunic sleeve, which was seeping blood. "It's not bad," he said.

She could hear his heart pounding under her ear. When she put her arms around his waist, his grip on her tightened and he put his cheek against her hair.

"We have to go," he said to her. "Even in this alley somebody's bound to stumble across these two soon. The janissaries patrol the market at closing time to protect the merchants bringing home the day's take."

"Why did they attack us?" Amy asked, drawing back to look at him.

"The kid probably told them we were bedouins come into town to trade. After a deal they always have money."

"Why would the boy do that?"

Malik shrugged. "They gave him more money than I did, or he's a decoy they use to set up

162

their marks. The Sultan has turned us all into thieves. He has us preying on each other." He took her hand and led her away, increasing the speed of his steps until she was running to keep up with him.

"If they wanted to rob us," Amy said, looking back at the prone bodies as they flew down the alley, "why didn't they just take the horses?"

"I think they planned to have both our money and our animals," Malik said, untying the horses and handing her Dosha's reins. The horse, spooked by their haste, the close quarters, and the unfamiliar atmosphere of the market, reared and then took off down the alley, her hooves kicking up clods of dirt.

"Oh, no!" Amy wailed, lunging forward even though the horse was already long gone. Malik put a restraining hand on her arm.

"Let her go," Malik said. "She's trained to return to the camp, and we can ride double on Mehmet."

"She'll never go back all that way alone, Malik, and you can't afford to lose a good horse," Amy replied, still staring in dismay after the vanished mare.

"She *will* go back alone, and we have no time to waste," he said. "Get up on Mehmet like a good girl before we wind up in the Sultan's parrot cage." He lifted her bodily and she flew through the air, landing on Mehmet seconds before he did. She hardly had time to grab the pommel before the horse was trotting down the alley they had walked before, passing the Kurdish woman as she closed the shutters of her shop. Mehmet picked his way through the narrow passage and then gathered speed when they reached the wider street, finally cantering as they passed through the double gates of the market just as they were swinging closed.

"We made it," he said in her ear, a clear note of triumph in his voice.

Amy rested back against his shoulder as the scenery which had fascinated her before passed now in a blur. She was so relieved to be out of the market in one piece that she hardly felt the horse moving beneath her. Once they left the congested area behind them, the animal picked up speed, and Amy closed her eyes, content to feel Malik's arms around her and know that she was safe.

When she looked again, they were riding across the open plain and the moonlight streamed down upon them, making their path as bright as day. Mehmet, who seemed remarkably fresh for all his recent efforts, pounded along at a brisk pace, and Malik's solid presence behind her made her feel as if she were suspended in time and space, as if the ride would go on forever.

But she knew that it wouldn't. In just a short time Kalid Shah would arrive to take her to

Aunt Beatrice, and this chapter of her life would end.

Amy tightened her grip on the trim Asian pommel and looked up again at the glowing disk of the full moon.

She was not going to think about that now.

Malik drew in the reins and the horse began to slow down. Amy looked around, puzzled; there was a verdant area to their left, but it was not where they had rested on the way into the city.

"Why are we stopping here?" Amy inquired, as Malik jumped off the horse and lifted her down to the ground. "Isn't it too soon?"

"The horse needs a rest and so do you," he replied.

"I can keep going," Amy said.

"Then think of Mehmet. He's done this journey twice in a row, and now he's carrying both of us. If he collapses with our double weight, neither of one of us will get back." He took off the robes and the headscarf he was wearing and made a bundle of the clothes, tying it to his saddle. When he turned back to her, she saw that the left arm of his tunic was soaked with blood.

"Malik, I have to bandage that cut," she said firmly, discarding her own robes and walking toward him. "Give me the water bottle so I can wash it."

"We need the water to drink," he said.

"Then let me at least tie it off, for heaven's

sake—the blood is running down your arm!"

He sighed and looked annoyed but sat obediently on a patch of grass and held out his arm. Amy knelt next to him, ripping his sleeve back to the elbow to expose the cut on his forearm.

"Let me have your knife, please," she said.

He withdrew the blade from the sheath at his belt and handed it to her.

"Why didn't you use this when that thief jumped you?" she asked, cutting away the blood drenched linen.

"The more weapons exposed in close combat, the more dangerous the situation," he explained. "I knew I could overpower him. It was just a matter of choosing the right moment."

"What about your pistol?"

"Noise. I couldn't afford to attract attention."

"Doesn't this hurt?" she asked, wincing as she dabbed at it with the clean cloth of her discarded veil.

"Not anymore. Now it's . . ." he searched in vain for the English word.

"Numb?"

He nodded, watching as she cut strips from the veil and bound them tightly across the wound.

"Tell me, Amelia. What was it like to grow up in the United States with enough to eat and nice clothes and a big, warm house full of servants?" he asked challengingly, studying her face.

"It was absolutely lovely," Amy replied, looking him directly in the eye. "I would heartily recommend it to anyone."

He had the good grace to laugh.

Amy wrapped his arm with the makeshift bandage and then split the last piece of the veil, tying the ends securely to keep the binding in place. She handed him his knife when she was finished and said, "That should hold until we get back."

He flexed his arm, staring down at her work admiringly. "It should hold for a lot longer than that. You're a good woman to have around in a crisis."

Amy turned away from him, flushing with pleasure. Malik so rarely made such a personal remark that she was thrilled at the slight praise.

"You don't look as if you would know much about combat dressings," he added.

"How do I look?" Amy asked, facing him again.

"Ornamental," he said, and smiled.

She didn't smile back at him.

He rose and put his hand on her shoulder. "That's not an insult," he said softly. He tilted her face up to him with his forefinger under her chin. "The moonlight turns your hair and eyes to silver," he murmured.

Amy stood still, gazing up at him—at the black hair disordered by their ride, the rough stubble on his cheeks, the strong nose and full, sensual mouth, the wide dark eyes that seemed to see into her very soul.

At that moment she was his to command.

His hand fell away and he turned his back on her.

"You should see if you can take a nap," he said neutrally. "A little sleep will help you get through the rest of the trip."

Amy didn't move, her eyes filling with scalding tears of disappointment. She clenched her fists, trying to regain control, as he waited and then said, "Did you hear me?"

"I heard you," she whispered, stifling a sob.

"Are you all right?" he said to her back.

"Fine," she said in a louder tone, surreptitiously wiping her eyes with the back of her hand.

"Then come over here and sit down. You can't rest standing up," he said.

Amy obeyed, keeping her face in shadow so he couldn't see her expression.

"In just a few hours we'll be there," Malik said.

And in just a few days, I'll be gone, Amy thought.

She pillowed her head on her arms, so he couldn't see that she was crying.

Chapter Seven

The Woolcott home outside Constantinople had been planned to take advantage of every breeze, no matter how slight, since Beatrice suffered greivously from the heat. Both floors were surrounded by wide "sleeping porches," and the main rooms had floor-to-ceiling glass doors which could be opened to create a cross draft in high summer. Beatrice was sitting on the verandah outside the dining room, fanning herself with a letter she was reading, when James arrived home from work.

"I'm out here, James," Beatrice called when she heard his step in the front hall. James handed his hat to a servant and followed the sound of his wife's voice, bending to kiss her flushed cheek and note the dew on her upper lip as well as the wisps of ginger hair escaping from her bun. Bea had pale, freckled skin that turned scarlet in the heat and the kind of hair that wilted like lettuce when the temperature went above seventy. No matter how many times she changed clothes or wiped her brow with her crumpled handkerchief, the summer weather kept Bea, as her favorite author, Jane Austen, once wrote, "in a continual state of inelegance."

"What are you reading?" James asked, nodding to the letter Beatrice held.

"A note from Mrs. Spaulding, sent from Paris on her return journey," Bea replied.

James sat in a rush rocking chair next to his wife and asked, "What does she say?"

"She apologizes again for 'losing' Amelia and begs me to let her know the girl's fate," Bea said wearily. She tucked the note inside her sleeve and added, "As if we knew it ourselves."

Listak came through the doorway and handed James a brandy. The servant looked at Beatrice and said, "Would you care for anything, madam?"

Beatrice shook her head, hunting in her reticule for her bottle of cologne. She shook a few drops of the liquid onto a handkerchief and dabbed at her temples with the square of lace.

"You look tired, Bea," James said, sipping his drink.

"I haven't been sleeping well."

"The heat?"

"I've been having nightmares."

"About Amelia, I suppose."

"In the dreams, my brother comes to me and scolds me," Bea said dully. "He asks me why I couldn't do the only thing he ever asked of me, why I couldn't take care of his child."

"Amelia will soon be with us and you'll sleep well again," James said soothingly.

Listak appeared in the doorway once more and said, "Dinner will be ready shortly, madam."

"Bring Mrs. Woolcott a sherry, Listak," James said.

"I don't want a drink," Bea protested.

"Bring one anyway," James said to the servant.

Listak bowed and left.

"My descent into alcoholism will hardly change the situation, James," Bea said.

"A before-dinner sherry is not a descent into alcoholism, Beatrice, and the liquor will relax you."

"If only it weren't so hot all the time," Bea whispered, putting her head back against her chair.

"The rains will come soon."

"And then everything is a sea of mud. Oh, how I do miss Boston," Beatrice sighed.

Listak returned with the drink, and Bea downed it in two gulps. James signaled for Listak to bring another one.

It looked like it would be a long night.

When Malik and Amy arrived back at the rebel camp, they went directly to Anwar's tent. His sister Maya was tending the injured man, and when she saw Amy, she ran forward and fell to her knees, lifting the hem of Amy's gown and pressing it to her lips.

"Malik, what on earth is she doing?" Amy asked, pulling back, appalled.

Maya stood and took Amy's hand, kissed it, and then held it to her forehead.

"She's thanking you for helping Anwar," Malik replied.

"Is he that much better?" Amy asked, kneeling next to Anwar. She touched his forehead and found it cooler; his face, which had been contorted by pain, was smooth and relaxed.

"He is!" she exclaimed delightedly, and Malik smiled.

Maya said something in Turkish to Malik and he translated. "Maya says that the medicine you left made all the difference. His delirium has passed, and he spent a comfortable night."

"But the wound still looks nasty," Amy said, peeling back the bandage. "I'd better make the poultice right away."

"What do you need?" Malik asked.

"Boiling water, or water just as hot as possible, and a bottle of raki."

Malik gave the order to Maya, who vanished. He squatted next to Amy on the dirt-packed floor and said, "Anwar does look much better."

"The wound is still infected, but the poultice should take care of that. The aspirin will keep his fever down in the meantime."

Malik turned his head to look at her. "Thank you," he said quietly.

"You can thank me when he's up and around. I still have work to do."

"Are you sure you aren't too tired?"

"Just leave me to it. Send Maya in with the water when it's ready," Amy replied.

Malik slipped out of the tent as Amy removed the rest of Anwar's sodden linen, planning how to redress the wound. When Maya brought the water, she washed the torn flesh carefully, then disinfected it with the liquor. Then she soaked the herbs in the water, crushed them to release their sap, and made the poultice, applying it liberally and finally wrapping the wound with gauze soaked in oil of wintergreen.

By the time she was done, Anwar was stirring and Amy was almost asleep on her feet. Maya returned to administer another dose of laudanum. Amy nodded and smiled, taking the medicine back from Anwar's sister and then curling up on the pallet Maya had used.

Anwar would sleep for a while and so would she, and if he woke she was certain to hear him.

Amy was so tired that she thought she would

drop off immediately, but the previous night repeated itself in her mind endlessly, robbing her of rest.

Why had she cried when Malik turned away from her? Just a little while ago it had been her dearest wish to escape him, but she could not lie to herself.

Last night she had been disappointed to the point of pain when he didn't kiss her.

What on earth was wrong with her? When had Malik gone from criminal to potential lover in her mind? When he wouldn't sell her to the slave dealer, when he came after her in the woods, when he trusted her to tend Anwar? Had it happened so subtly that she hadn't noticed it until she was in love with him?

Amy turned restlessly and pillowed her head on her arm. *Could* she be in love with him—this thief, this kidnapper, this fugitive with a price on his head? True, she understood his cause now and why he had chosen the life he led, but was her feeling for him just proximity, the reaction of an untried woman to her first sustained, close contact with a young and virile man?

It would almost be a relief to think so, but Amy couldn't quite believe it. She wasn't that naive; she was pretty and an heiress and she had been pursued by men in Boston since she was thirteen. None of them had made her feel the way Malik did.

But maybe that urge was just base desire, the attraction of opposites, the yearning of a young body for its counterpart. She had thought of little else lately but getting Malik to make love to her, and her sense memories of him were so vivid that they disturbed her even now. She felt again Malik's arms about her as they rode, as he embraced her after his fight with the thug, as he lifted her down from her horse. She saw his face as he looked at her in the moonlight, saw the longing in his eyes.

And that recollection presented another puzzle. She *knew* that Malik wanted her—his every glance and touch indicated his need. Then why wouldn't he act on it? Was he sparing her for the shadowy American husband of her future? And if so, when had he acquired such a delicate conscience? For a man who'd been willing to sell her to slave traders a short time earlier, his reluctance to pursue her was strange behavior indeed.

Amy sat up, too confused to think any more. She couldn't sleep, and she needed something to do, a task to keep her mind from wandering back to the subject she wished to avoid.

She didn't want to think about Malik, or about the fact that she would be leaving him soon. She pushed her way through the tent opening just as a horse galloped into the camp and all eyes turned toward the new arrival.

Malik appeared from the cave at the other

end of the camp and greeted the newcomer; as he jumped down from his horse, Amy saw that it was Selim. He had a brief conference with Malik, who then turned to the camp and said something in a loud voice, which brought immediate cheers. Amy watched the rebels slapping each other on the back and embracing, wondering what was happening.

Malik walked over to her and asked, "How is Anwar?"

"About the same. It will be eight hours or so before we can tell if the poultice is working. Why is everyone so happy?"

"The Sultan has withdrawn his troops from the Armenian Mahalle."

"Is that a victory for you?"

"It's more than a victory. It's a sign that his grip is weakening, that he's losing his annexed territory. It's proof that our campaign is working."

"Congratulations."

He grinned. "Tonight there will be a *bay-rami*—a celebration."

"I'm sure your people could use one."

He studied her face, taking in her sincere but wan smile. "You look worn out," he said.

"I tried to sleep. I can't."

"Take some of that potion you gave to Anwar."

"We may need it all for him."

"You can spare half a dose, enough to make

176

you drowsy. There was almost a full bottle in your bag, and you didn't use much of it."

"I was afraid to become dependent on it."

"Was it very bad when your parents died?" he asked quietly.

Amy looked away from him. "Maybe I was spoiled and just couldn't handle adversity, but one minute I was part of a family, and the next I was . . . alone."

"I know exactly what you mean," Malik replied quietly, and when she looked into his eyes she saw perfect understanding.

Risa ran up to Malik and said something excitedly in Turkish. He held up his hand for Risa to wait and looked at Amy.

"Go back to my tent and rest," he said.

"But Anwar—"

"I'll make sure Maya tends him. You've done enough. Maya will bring you the medicine and then she'll sit with her brother."

Amy nodded.

He put his hand on her shoulder. "You can handle adversity," he said, and smiled.

Amy watched him walk away with Risa and then went back to his tent.

Amy awoke in darkness, to the sound of music. She lay in a semi-slumber, the oil lamp in the tent a blur before her half-closed eyes, listening to the tambors, violins, and flutes, watching the play of light and shadow on the canvas of the tent. She felt refreshed and relaxed, as if she had slept for a week instead of most of the day. When she stretched and finally sat up, she saw that she was not alone; Maya was sitting about ten feet away, holding a bulky package in her lap.

"Maya?" Amy said.

The young woman rose and came forward, kneeling and touching her forehead to the dirt-packed floor. When Amy moved to raise her up, she pressed the bundle she held into Amy's hands, and Amy unfolded it to look at it.

It was a dress—a gauzy handmade gown of finest Bursa silk in the traditional Turkish style, with bell sleeves and a high-cinched waist, exquisitely embroidered with red and gold thread in a Seljuk pattern of vines, leaves and rosettes. Amy stared down at the painstaking needle-work, ran the whisper-weight cloth through her fingers, and held it up to the light to see it better. It was the loveliest garment she had ever seen.

"Maya, this is gorgeous. Thank you for showing it to me." Amy said, handing the gown back to Maya.

Maya shook her head and gave it to Amy again.

"This is for me?" Amy said, shocked, pointing to herself.

Maya nodded vigorously.

"Oh, no—you must have worked on this for months. I can't possibly take it," Amy said.

Maya's face crumpled at her tone, and the Turkish girl looked as if she was going to cry.

Amy was nonplussed; she had no wish to offend Maya, but the gift was far too extravagant. It had probably been intended as Maya's wedding dress.

Maya suddenly grabbed her hand and began to tug Amy out of the tent. Amy followed, puzzled until she realized that Maya was bringing her to see Anwar. They passed a large bonfire in the center of the camp, around which the musicians were playing and many of the women danced. Amy did not see Malik, but she didn't have much time to look because Maya hustled her past the celebrants and into Anwar's tent.

Once inside Amy realized why Maya had been so insistent about the gift. Anwar was sitting up, propped on a pile of embroidered pillows and sipping a cup of broth.

He put down the cup and held out his arms when he saw Amy. She gave him her hands and he held them to his dry, cracked lips.

"Tessekur ederim," he said.

"You're welcome," Amy replied to the familiar phrase, snatching her hands back shyly. All this excessive gratitude was making her feel quite embarrassed.

"Elinize saglik," Maya added.

Amy looked at them smiling at her, two people who would have cheerfully throttled her a week earlier, and marveled at the complexities of life. She bent to check Anwar's dressing and then left, going back to Malik's tent, where she found Maya's dress crumpled on the floor.

Maya clearly thought Amy had saved her brother's life, and Amy realized that in a culture she was just beginning to understand, it would be an insult for her to refuse Maya's finest possession.

The music changed and Amy listened to a solitary voice, accompanied by a dulcimer, singing one of the plaintive Anatolian folk songs she often heard about the camp. The tunes were so sad that they could bring tears to Amy's eyes even though she didn't understand the words. Amy smiled wistfully as she removed the cover from the clawfoot tub and gathered soap and towels.

Even when the Turks were having a party, their melancholy nature came through in their music.

She picked up the large black iron pot Matka used to bring water and went in search of a boiling kettle. But when Matka saw Amy approaching the small fire she always kept going, she took the pot from Amy and filled it herself, then recruited Risa to get more. Amy stood aside as they filled the tub, then Matka dismissed Risa and went to stand guard at the entrance of the tent while Amy bathed.

It was clear to Amy that Anwar's recovery had

changed her status from camp pariah to camp heroine in the blink of an eye. Even taciturn Matka was suddenly solicitous.

Amy shuddered to think what might have happened if Anwar had died; could even Malik have saved her?

She had a long, luxurious bath, even washing her hair with the pine soap and rinsing in the clear water Risa brought. She dressed in the gown Maya had given her, which was a little too big, except in the bust where the fitted gold clasps pulled the panels of silk together tightly, molding the bodice as if she were wearing a corselet. The neckline was cut low, exposing the tops of her breast to an almost immodest degree. Amy threw the *feradge*, or cape, she had been wearing when disguised as a bedouin over her shoulders before she left the tent.

It was a warm, clear night, fragrant with the wild heliotrope that grew in profusion around the camp. Matka glanced at Amy's dress, her shining face, and damp and shining hair, and said, "Malik," pointing through the trees.

I must be about as subtle as a halberdier's truncheon, Amy thought as she watched Matka trudge back to the party. I didn't even have to ask.

Amy followed the path to the clearing, her feet as light as the fiddle music which now filled the air. She felt wonderful after her long nap and sure of what she had to do.

181

For once in her pampered, careful, well-tended life, she was about to take a chance.

Malik was sitting alone on a tree stump, smoking one of the cigarettes he could rarely afford and looking up at the star-filled night sky. He was wearing the tunic Amy liked best, dark blue and slashed almost to his waist, its color and style setting off his dark good looks and slim physique to perfection. His trousers were the same tan he always wore, tight and tucked into black boots. His hair had been recently brushed, taming its wild waves, and as she got closer she could see that he had shaved closely, revealing the slight cleft in his chin and the hairline scar on his upper lip.

He stood when he heard Amy approach and tossed away the butt, watching her as she stopped a few feet away.

"Why aren't you celebrating with the others?" she asked him, drawing the shawl closer about her.

"I'm celebrating alone," he replied evenly. "How are you feeling?"

"Much better."

"So is Anwar."

"Yes, I know. I saw him. Maya took me to visit him. She said, *Elinize saglik* and gave me this dress." She held out the skirt for him to see. "What does that phrase mean?"

"It means that your hands should have a long life. It's said to anyone who has done something wonderful—a cook who has prepared a delicious meal, an artist who has created a marvelous painting, or, as in your case, a doctor who has healed a patient."

"I see. Do you like the dress?" she asked.

"Very pretty."

"I think so too."

"It's a shame you won't have much use for it when you leave here," he said evenly, looking away from her.

It was the first reference he had made to her departure since the day he had cut her bonds.

"Don't you think my Aunt Beatrice will appreciate native dress?" Amy asked lightly.

"I think you will soon be back in hoopskirts and those ridiculous sailing sleeves you were wearing when I met you," he replied.

"Sailing sleeves?" Amy said.

"Yes, they look like billowing sails—you know what I mean," he said, gesturing.

"Leg of mutton," Amy said.

"Is that what they are called?" he asked, amazed, sitting again on the stump.

Amy nodded, smiling as she looked down at him.

"You must admit that Western women wear strange clothing," he muttered.

"I think I prefer this style of clothing now," Amy said to him, letting the shawl slip down her arms, exposing the low neckline of the dress.

His gaze lingered on her bare throat and

swelling decolletage before returning to her face.

"So do I," he said huskily.

Amy took a step forward, saying, "I'm so glad that Anwar has improved."

Malik smiled. "It's odd to think you're responsible. Before he was wounded, Anwar couldn't wait to get rid of you. And after his injury, he was unconscious and didn't know until today that you had effected his cure."

She reached out and touched his cheek. "I didn't do it for him," she said softly.

Malik stared at her for a long moment and then slowly closed his eyes, turning his head to kiss her hand. When she lowered it to trace the curve of his lips with her finger, he snaked out one long arm and drew her to him fiercely.

Amy gasped as he pressed his face to her exposed bosom, rubbing his skin on hers like a cat. She shuddered when she felt his tongue trail along her collarbone and then probe the valley between her breasts, his mouth so hot and wet that it turned her bones to water. When he lifted his head and opened the bodice of her dress, her knees gave way and he pulled her into his lap.

He had one nipple in his mouth before he had even seen it, his free hand greedily cupping the other. Amy sank her fingers into his hair and held him against her, her breath coming in short bursts as he sucked and nipped and teased, drinking his fill of what he had denied himself for too long.

He pulled the sleeves off her arms and shoved the dress down to her waist, kissing the white smoothness of her shoulders, the tender, blue-veined flesh of her throat and wrists and inner elbows. The sight of his dusky skin against her paleness, the feel of his strong hands roaming her bare back as his mouth caressed her, made Amy faint with longing. She clung to him, so enervated that she would have fallen without his support, when he stood suddenly with her in his arms and strode briskly to a patch of grass.

He flung Amy's shawl upon the ground, then set her down on it, sprawling full-length next to her, catching himself with one arm as he dropped. In the next instant, he had rolled Amy under him and lay poised above her, his liquid eyes filling the world.

"I have wanted you so much," he said thickly, his voice sounding strange, as if the admission had been wrung from him against his will. "So much, from the beginning."

"Don't talk," she whispered, blinking back tears as she pulled him down to her once more. "Don't talk."

The last was said against his mouth as his lips met hers for the first time, and it was a sensation she would never forget. She had been kissed before, by the boys who had courted her

185

back in Boston, but not like this. Malik was a man, and this was a man's embrace, powerful and demanding. His mouth was soft, a contrast with the hardness of his teeth and the hard body pressed against hers, and she could taste the faint tang of tobacco and the bitterness of raki on his lips. He kissed her again and again, his mouth fused to hers, his weight pinning her as he stroked her hair, running the silken strands through his fingers.

Amy slipped her hands inside the waistband of his pants and loosened his shirt, tracing the muscles of his back, which bunched as she touched them. His skin was hot, and she could feel his tension in the tips of her fingers. As his mouth moved to her cheek, her neck, she tore restlessly at his tunic.

"I want to feel you against me," she moaned, pushing the material away from his neck, where she could see a pulse beating strongly. He sat up abruptly and tore off the shirt, tossing it on the ground. When he lay back down, he held himself up on his hands, looking at her as she ran her finger down his chest, then gripped his shoulders to lift herself up and trace the same path with her tongue.

Malik groaned, holding her tightly as she put her arms around his neck and arched against him, sighing with the blissful sensation of his naked torso crushing her breasts. She wrapped her legs around him as her dress rode up unheeded, exposing the slim line of her thighs to his view.

Her innocent abandon inflamed him, and he felt his control going; he ground his lower body into hers, letting her feel his arousal fully. Amy responded in kind, digging her heels into the back of his thighs and kissing him wildly everywhere she could reach—his shoulder, his bicep, the prominent cord on the side of his neck. The virginal fears she had once harbored were forgotten in the intensity of her passion. The overwhelming need to join with him, to feel him inside her, was new to her experience but not to her imagination. This was the lover she had dreamed of in Boston when the pawings of some adolescent lothario left her feeling disappointed and unmoved. Here at last was the man she had waited for, the handsome and virile man whose need of her was so all consuming that it would carry them both away.

His hands, rough from farming and warfare and a life lived out of doors, stroked her skin as if handling the finest silk. He pushed her skirt up further and slipped one hand along her thigh, rolling back slightly, watching her expression as he touched her. She whimpered and closed her eyes, burying her face against his damp shoulder, listening to the runaway pounding of his heart as she strained against him.

"Will it hurt?" she whispered, her words muffled by his flesh, the muscles of his back as rigid as oak under her fingers.

She felt the impact of the question as soon as she asked it. His arms loosened, and to her astonishment he released her, rolling away and then sitting up with his back to her.

"Malik?" she said, sitting up too, suddenly embarrassed by her partial nakedness. She crossed her arms over her naked breasts and hugged herself. "What is it?"

He didn't answer, and she saw his palpable struggle to regain control. He sat for a few moments with his head bent and his arms propped on his knees, his respiration slowing visibly. Then he stood and retrieved her shawl from the ground, not meeting her eyes as he handed it to her.

"Put this on," he said, striving for a calm tone, but his voice betrayed him. It was low and gravelly, and she noticed when she took the cape that his hands were shaking.

He was not as steady as he wanted her to think.

"Malik," she said, trembling once more on the verge of tears, "what happened? What did I do?" She wrapped the *feradge* around her torso and flung the ends of it over her shoulders, heedless of the open bodice of her dress.

"You didn't do anything. Go back to the camp."

"Go back to the camp! Don't you want me?"

she wailed, unable to believe the change in him.

He closed his eyes; a blue vein in his temple pulsed visibly. "Of course I want you," he said between his teeth, "but I won't take you."

"But I want you to!" she protested, childlike, as if her desire obviated all other concerns.

He looked at her then, his expression contorted, as if he wanted to believe her but could not.

"You don't know what you want—you're a baby," he said, trying to convince himself as well as Amy.

"I'm a woman," she said, crying openly now, contradicting her words. "Was that a baby you just made love to? You're lying to both of us, Malik."

"Go back to the camp," he said again.

"Stop ordering me about as if I were one of your lackeys!" she cried, then covered her face with her hands. Her hair streamed over her bare shoulders, which shook with emotion as she strove for calm. It was an eternal minute before she looked at him again; by then, though her face was still streaked with tears, her expression was regal and composed.

"Is this your revenge on me for giving you so much trouble?" she asked. "Does it bring you satisfaction to humiliate me, to take me to the point of utter submission and then turn away?"

He almost went to her then, unable to let her think that of him, unable to endure the pain he saw on her face. But he knew it was dangerous to touch her, so he held his ground and merely said, "You're wrong."

"Then explain it to me."

"You wouldn't understand."

"Why not? Am I so stupid?"

"Amelia, I am not going to have this discussion with you. It's over. Accept that and go back to the camp."

She stared at him, her lower lip trembling, bunching the shawl at her waist with one small white hand.

"You're a vicious person, Malik," she finally said, her voice wobbly, "and I never will forgive you for this." She picked up her skirt with her free hand and ran out of the clearing.

Malik waited until she was out of sight, then sat back on the stump and dropped his head onto his folded arms.

He didn't move for a long time.

After that night, Malik steered clear of Amy, never returning to his tent, sleeping in the cave with the rest of his men. Time passed, he received a message from Kalid Shah naming the day and the hour for Amy's return, and each morning Anwar was better.

Amy stayed out of Malik's way, helping Matka and Risa with the chores, waiting for the ordeal to end. She counted on her fingers, aware that every sunrise meant she was closer to escaping

Malik's indifference. Soon she would be away from him where she could forget.

On the night before she was to meet Kalid Shah, Amy retired early. She had undertaken so many tasks that day to make sure she would sleep that the strategy actually worked. When Malik looked through the tent flap to check on her he saw that she was sleeping soundly.

He knew he would not be so lucky. He wandered the camp for hours, his mind filled with images of the woman he was about to give up— her face when he first saw her as she emerged from the coach, her pale hair glowing in the moonlight, her eyes closing with catlike pleasure as he caressed her.

The memories did not make for easy slumber.

He finally went to his customary spot to think. When he heard the sound of footsteps approaching, his mouth went dry. Was it Amy? But when he stood and looked through the trees, he saw Anwar, his left arm in a makeshift sling.

"Shouldn't you be sleeping?" Malik asked, as his friend sat on the ground with his back to a tree.

"I've been sleeping so much since I was shot that I've stored up enough for the next five years," Anwar replied.

"How's the arm?"

"Stiff, but I'm still here. Thanks to the girl."

Malik said nothing.

"Is she the reason you're out here in the middle of the night staring into space?" Anwar asked.

Malik met Anwar's eyes, then looked away.

"I know you're giving her over to Shah tomorrow morning," Anwar added.

"I guess I can't keep any secrets around here, can I?" Malik said dryly.

"Do you want me to come with you?"

Malik shook his head. "I think I'd better go alone."

"Are you sure there's no chance that it's an ambush?"

"No, Shah's been straight with me. He just wants Amelia back. He waited until now to convince the Sultan he wasn't in collusion with the kidnapping."

Anwar endured several minutes of silence before asking, "What went wrong between you and the girl?"

"Nothing is wrong."

"Nothing is *happening*, but something is wrong. You won't even look at her. You haven't spoken to her since the night of the *bayrami*, except to tell her when Shah was coming for her. What caused the silence?"

Malik sighed. "You know I was trying to avoid getting involved with her."

Anwar nodded.

"The night of the party she came after me and found me out here. I was feeling good—maybe

I'd had a little too much raki at the celebration—so when she touched me I just . . ." He opened his hands expressively.

Anwar sucked in his breath. "You slept with her?"

"No, but it was close. Very close. A minute more . . ." He broke off again, staring at the ground.

"What stopped you?"

"She said something that brought me out of it."

"What?"

"She asked me if it would hurt."

"And that reminded you she was a virgin?"

"It reminded me of what I was doing, not only taking her maidenhead but violating a trust."

"Hers?" Anwar asked.

"Hers and Shah's. It was understood between him and me that she would return to her family the way she left them."

Anwar studied his friend's face, only partially visible in the light of the waning moon.

"You want to keep her, don't you?" Anwar said quietly.

"I want to, but I can't."

"I'm glad you realize that."

"What bothers me the most is that she thinks I tricked her, led her on to humiliate her."

"And you didn't?"

"No! I just wanted her so much that I lost control."

"She *is* beautiful."

"It's not just that, it's so many things." He smiled faintly. "Who can say why one woman drives you wild and another leaves you cold."

"I don't have the answer, I only know I've never seen you like this."

Malik rose and began to pace. "I don't want her to leave here thinking that I'm such a yellow dog, but there is no other way. If I had told her that I promised Shah to leave her untouched, that would ease her feelings of rejection, but it might also give her hope that we could have something in the future, and that's impossible. I can't drag her into the danger and uncertainty of my life. I have nothing to offer a woman, especially a woman who once had so much."

"I can see that you have given this a lot of thought," Anwar said.

"I've had plenty of time since the Sultan withdrew his troops from the Mahalle. It would have been easier to be busy."

"What's our next move?" Anwar asked, rubbing his sore shoulder.

"The granary in Antakya, on the Syrian border. Our people there are starving."

"When?"

"Two weeks or so. We'll strike when the Sultan is preoccupied with entertaining the emissaries from Greece. Our palace spies say the Greeks are arriving for treaty talks at the end of the month."

Anwar snorted. "He's playing around with foreign policy while his own empire is crumbling. The man is an idiot."

"The more notoriety our activities attract, the more he will work to convince outsiders that he's still in charge. He'll play right into our hands."

Anwar walked over to stand next to his friend and put his hand on Malik's shoulder. "It may not seem like it at the moment, but it really is a kindness to let her go. She'll be sad for a while, but she'll get over it and go back to her old life."

Malik nodded.

"But tomorrow will be hard," Anwar added.

Malik didn't respond.

"Do you want to come back with me?" Anwar asked.

"No, I think I'll sit here a while," Malik responded.

"*Gecmis olsun,*" Anwar said as he left.

Malik thought about his friend's parting words as Anwar disappeared through the trees.

If only he *could* put his feelings for Amelia in the past, as Anwar had said, he might be able to get on with his mission—and the rest of his life.

Amy was awake before first light and dressed in the gown Maya had given her. Matka stood by silently as Amy wrapped her *feradge* around her shoulders and picked up her reticule, the only remnant of her Western clothing worth taking back with her. She put her hand on the old woman's arm and said, "Good-bye, Matka."

Matka surprised her by responding "Good-bye" in a touching piece of mimicry that brought a delighted smile to Amy's face. She nodded, thanking Matka for the effort, and stepped outside.

Malik was already waiting for her, holding the reins of Mehmet. Risa and Maya stood with him. As Amy approached, Risa held out a bag of *dolma*, stuffed vine leaves, a snack for the journey.

"*Afiyet olsun,*" Risa said. To your health.

"Thank you," Amy replied, taking the bag.

"*Gule Gule,*" Maya said, bowing with both hands pressed to her forehead. "*Tesekkur ederim serefinize Anwar.*"

"You're welcome," Amy said. "I'm so glad Anwar is himself again."

Amy then looked at Malik, who said, "Dosha picked up a stone and has gone lame. We'll have to ride double on Mehmet."

The two women stood back as Malik held the reins of the horse while Amy mounted, then handed the reins to her. He leaped onto Mehmet's back behind her and then turned the horse to the south.

"How far are we going?" Amy asked him.

"Not far."

When the horse trotted through the camp,

Amy saw that almost all its inhabitants had
come out to see her leave. They stood by in silence as she and Malik rode slowly past them.
Amy caught Anwar's eye as he stood by the entrance to his tent. He raised his hand in a curious little salute and Amy nodded.

Malik's horse gathered speed as they left the
camp, and Amy leaned back into Malik's shoulder as they headed downward toward the plain.
She wished she did not have to spend this final
hour in his arms, but at the same time she sa-
vored the contact she was about to lose forever.
The trek through the foothills that Amy remembered as long and tortuous seemed to pass like
a flash of lightning this time. When they
reached the valley and emerged onto the sandy
mesa, she could see a lone horse approaching
them from the distance. As they came closer,
she could see the rider, a tall, dark man attired
in an ivory tunic trimmed with gold. When they
finally met, he dismounted immediately and so
did Malik.

"Is this the little lady from America?" Kalid
Shah said, smiling as Malik lifted Amy down
from Mehmet.

Malik stood by as Amy turned and faced Sarah's husband. He was handsome in the European way, older than Malik, whose features
were bolder and whose skin was browner. But
Amy could see immediately what had caused

James Woolcott's cousin to turn her back on Boston for this man.

"I am Kalid Shah," he said, extending his hand as if meeting her at an embassy party. "I didn't bring a horse for you because I have a coach waiting about a mile away."

"Did you want to make sure I came alone, Kalid?" Malik said to him in Turkish.

"She is lovely, Malik," Kalid responded in the same language, ignoring the question. "Quite a test of your self-control."

"Can we go, please?" Amy said, afraid that she might break down if they prolonged the farewell.

"By all means," Kalid replied in a British accent more pronounced than Malik's.

Amy moved to Kalid's horse, but Malik put a restraining hand on her arm. When she turned to look at him, his dark eyes were full of feeling, as if now that he knew it was over he could reveal what he had been holding back before; a muscle twitched along his jaw.

"It is written on my forehead that I will not forget you," he said softly, quoting a Turkish proverb.

Amy swallowed hard but couldn't speak.

Kalid vaulted into his saddle and then held his hand down to Amy, who mounted behind him. When Amy looked back at Malik he was mounted also, watching them.

Kalid kicked his horse and they rode away.

Amy turned back once to look at Malik, seeing him through a screen of tears.

He was still in the same position, but when he saw her turn her head, he pulled on Mehmet's reins to bring the horse around, then took off at a gallop, sending up a cloud of dust.

Kalid rode briskly across the open plain as Amy hung on to him, the wind whipping her hair as tears streamed down her cheeks. When Kalid slowed the horse, she didn't even look up until he jumped to the ground and extended his hand upward.

Amy took Kalid's hand and descended from the horse, noticing that they were in a green oasis. An elaborate coach drawn by two geldings stood a few feet away, the liveried driver perched atop the high seat looking straight ahead.

"There's your transportation," Kalid said gently. "My wife is waiting for you."

Amy walked over to the coach, and Kalid opened the door and handed her inside. A beautiful blond woman with hair a few shades darker than Amy's was ensconced on one of the facing seats. She was wearing a navy traveling suit of tissue wool and a pert navy straw boater with an orchid ribbon tied around its brim.

"Hello, my dear," she said warmly. "I am your cousin Sarah. I understand you've been through a very difficult experience and I would like to help you."

Amy tried to answer, then shook her head, wiping her eyes with her fingers.

Sarah took a linen handkerchief from her sleeve and handed it to Amy.

"Are you all right?" Sarah asked.

Amy nodded unconvincingly, dabbing at her nose with the lace-trimmed square.

"Should I go ahead?" Kalid asked Sarah.

Sarah waved him away; he shut the door. Once he had mounted his horse, the coach lurched into motion and he followed behind it at a trot.

Sarah leaned forward and patted Amy's knee. "I've arranged with Beatrice and James for you to stay with me for a few days at the Orchid Palace. The respite will give you a chance to recover a little from this ordeal and enable us to get to know one another. Is that agreeable to you?"

"Yes," Amy said in a small voice.

"I think you'll find that we have a few things in common," Sarah added quietly.

Amy put her head back against the plush upholstery of the pasha's coach and closed her eyes.

"Would you like a lap robe?" Sarah asked. "You could take a nap on the way to Bursa."

"I know I shouldn't be tired, but somehow I am," Amy replied wearily.

"Emotional turmoil takes its own toll," Sarah replied, opening a compartment beneath her neatly booted feet and taking out a cashmere rug. She leaned forward to spread it over Amy's legs and added, "There. Just go to sleep. When we arrive you can have a bath and a change of clothes, a nice meal and a comfortable bed."

"Thank you," Amy whispered, her eyes flooding once more. She squeezed them shut more tightly to contain the tears.

Why couldn't she do anything but cry?

Sarah looked across the leather seats at the pretty, miserable, exhausted girl, and realized that she could have been gazing at herself ten years earlier, during her battles with Kalid.

Could this story possibly end as happily?

Chapter Eight

When Amy woke the next morning beneath a satin coverlet on a brocade sleeping couch at Orchid Palace, she could hardly remember the previous evening. It was all a blur: her arrival at the pink sandstone palace, her walk through corridors floored with marble and lit by flaring lamps, the forbidding halberdiers and scurrying servants, the dinner she could not eat served on a silver tray in a room draped with tapestries and carpeted with tasseled rugs. As she sat up and looked around, she realized that she was now occupying the inner chamber of a suite; the salon where she had dined was directly in front of her. The bedroom was just as ornate, with a wool rug worked with a green and silver trellis pattern underfoot and Afghan tapestries on the walls. A small bedside table held a golden bell ornamented with blue enamel. Amy picked it up and rang it experimentally.

The outer door of the suite opened immediately, and a tiny woman with waist-length black hair, wearing shalwar and an embroidered surcoat, came in from the hall. She walked gracefully through the anteroom and stopped at Amy's bedside, bowing deeply from the waist.

"Good morning, miss," she said in slightly accented English. "I am called Memtaz, and I have been assigned by the pashana to wait upon you during your stay at Orchid Palace. May I bring you some breakfast?"

"Just coffee, I think. Where is the pashana, please?"

"She is in the schoolroom, miss. She has instructed me to tell you that she can take lunch with you here in your suite if you would like that. But if you are too tired and would prefer to rest, she will see you at dinner."

"No, no, please tell her to come and see me at lunch. I'm afraid I wasn't very sociable yesterday, and I would like to thank her for her hospitality."

Memtaz bowed again. "As you wish, miss. I will return with your coffee."

The servant slipped from the room and Amy rose from the bed, examining the elaborate furnishings and the stack of books in English which had been left on a shelf near the door.

Everything had obviously been prepared with her comfort in mind, and she felt a surge of gratitude to her uncle's cousin, who had taken so much trouble to welcome a kinswoman she had never met.

Amy spent the morning bathing and dressing in the clothing Sarah sent in with Memtaz, then reading while stretched out across the bed, trying to occupy her mind so she would not think about Malik. At twelve-fifteen Sarah arrived, carrying a tea tray and wearing a peach-and-white silk bengaline dress.

"How are you feeling?" Sarah asked, placing the tray on a low table. "From what Memtaz told me, I gathered you were feeling somewhat better this morning."

"Yes, thank you," Amy said, studying the woman and her clothing carefully. Sarah's ensemble with its fitted bodice and striped, paneled skirt flattered her tall, slim figure. Her hair, the color of ripe wheat, was twisted into a chignon and she wore an exquisite cameo in the lace fichu at her throat. Her stylish Western dress struck an odd note in the atmosphere of Oriental excess which surrounded them, but Sarah seemed to carry off the effect with serene good humor. Amy wondered if clinging to the habits and dress of her past helped Sarah to maintain her sense of identity in the palace, where her husband's power and personality must dominate the inhabitants.

205

Sarah bent to kiss Amy's cheek. "I wasn't sure you would be up to seeing me so soon."

"I'm glad of the company. It was kind of you to send . . . Memtaz, is that her name?"

"Yes."

"Did you teach her to speak English?"

"No, she learned English from my husband's mother, who was British. Memtaz was given to me when I came here because she was one of the few servants in the palace who would be able to converse with me." Sarah sat in a silk-covered chair across from Amy and arranged her skirt across her knees, then poured the tea into two china cups. "I've ordered lunch for about one o'clock, but we can have this tea first and talk."

"Thank you for the clothes," Amy said, gesturing to the dress she wore.

"You're welcome. I had ordered that one for myself, but it was a little too small in the waist." She smiled. "I see it fits you very well."

"How do you keep up with the Western fashions?" Amy asked. "It must be a chore to have them sent here."

"I'm afraid that I take advantage of my husband's position," Sarah said wryly. "I get *Harper's Weekly* and *Godey's Lady's Book* in the mail from the boat train and then order what I want through a shop in Constantinople which caters to Western tourists. They're very happy to accommodate the pashana of Bursa."

"Do you ever wear Turkish dress?"

"Sometimes, usually on holidays. I did all the time when I was in the harem."

Amy stared at her, amazed. "So it's true that the pasha bought you?"

"Oh, yes. He bought me from the Sultan. I tried to tell them I wasn't for sale, but they weren't listening."

"No, Ottoman men don't listen very well, do they?" Amy said sadly. "I've discovered that for myself."

There was a long silence, then Sarah said gently, "Do you want to talk about it?"

"Yes, I suppose so. Yesterday, I didn't think I ever could but now I see . . ." She stopped.

"What?" Sarah said, handing her a cup and indicating the tray, which held cream and sugar and a small fluted dish containing moist slices of lemon.

"That it might help me to talk with someone who knows this country and its people," Amy replied simply, adding cream to her cup and stirring her drink.

"People like Malik Bey?" Sarah asked.

"Yes." Amy took a sip of the tea, which was strong and hot and scented with cinnamon.

"Are you in love with him?" Sarah asked bluntly, watching the girl's face.

Amy looked away in consternation. "Is it that obvious?" she asked unhappily.

"Well, let's just say that I noticed you weren't

207

overcome with joy to be escaping from the man who kidnapped you," Sarah observed with an understanding smile.

"I'm sorry I was in such a state," Amy said.

"You haven't answered the question."

"I must be in love with him," Amy said. "I only know that the thought of never seeing him again is breaking my heart."

"Is he in love with you?" Sarah asked.

"How could he be?" Amy lamented. "He let me go without a word!" Her mouth turned down, and she looked as if she were about to cry again.

"That doesn't mean anything," Sarah said. She sighed. Getting up and moving next to Amy, she put her arm around the girl's shoulders. "He could be dying of love for you and still stay silent. They are all proud and willful and independent, these Turks. Panthers, every one of them."

"Panthers?" Amy said.

"Yes. The panther is the symbol of my husband's family, but its traits apply to all of his countrymen. They are all fierce, silent stalkers. To show emotion is considered a sign of weakness." She sighed again. "They are difficult men to love. It's a pity they're so damned attractive." She picked up her cup and sipped.

"Your husband is difficult?" Amy said in surprise. "He seems so nice!"

Sarah choked on her tea and put down her

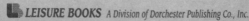

GET YOUR 4 FREE BOOKS NOW — A $21.96 Value!

Mail the Free Book Certificate Today!

Get Four Books Totally FREE — A $21.96 Value

PLEASE RUSH
MY FOUR FREE
BOOKS TO ME
RIGHT AWAY!

Leisure Romance Book Club
65 Commerce Road
Stamford CT 06902-4563

AFFIX
STAMP
HERE

cup. "Oh, my dear, you are seeing him after a decade of marriage and fatherhood have mellowed him. When I first met him, he was just as arrogant and overbearing as your Malik."

"Really? I never knew how much to believe of the stories I heard in the family. Gossip distorts everything so much."

"What you heard was probably a heavily filtered version of the truth. I never told James a lot of it—I was afraid he'd get some wild notion to challenge Kalid to a duel or something." Sarah rolled her eyes and Amy giggled.

"Kalid kept you here against your will?" Amy asked.

"Indeed he did. He gave an heirloom sword and quite a bit of money to the Sultan in exchange for me and then drugged me and carried me here from Topkapi. I woke to discover that I was his prisoner."

"Did you try to escape?"

"Of course. But the harem was heavily guarded and I was the *ikbal*, the favorite, so I was watched constantly. I ran away through the bazaar when we were on an outing once, and I was back here the same day, betrayed by someone loyal to Kalid."

"Did he punish you?"

"Oh, no, not directly. He was very clever about getting me to do what he wanted. He once threatened to whip little Memtaz if I didn't obey him in some trifling matter. He knew that it would pain me much more to see an innocent person suffer for my obstinacy than to endure the whipping myself."

"Did he ever . . . force you?" Amy asked hesitantly, coloring slightly.

"Never. He was very experienced with women and could see that despite my resistance, I wanted him. When I first saw him at Topkapi, I was dazzled and fascinated, powerfully attracted to him, and he knew it. That always gave him hope, but it took him quite a while to overcome my outrage at the way I had been taken from the Sultan's palace. By the time we got together, I was more than ready for him and, God help me, despite everything he had done, deeply in love."

Amy was silent.

"You are thinking about the similarities in our histories?" Sarah asked.

Amy nodded.

"That's why I wanted to discuss this with you. I, more than most people, can understand how you feel, how the conflict of falling in love with a man you should actually hate can tear you apart."

"I'll always remember how Malik made love to me," Amy said softly. "I know I'll never feel like that again."

"Never say never," Sarah observed mysteriously.

"What do you mean?"

The door to the hall opened and Memtaz entered.

"Ah, here is our lunch," Sarah said. "I think you will enjoy it. I ordered those dishes most acceptable to a Western palate. Afterward, you can meet the children and Kalid's mother. I'm sure she would be delighted to see you. Would you like that?"

"Very much," Amy replied, wondering about Sarah's previous remark.

Was there really any hope that she would see Malik once more?

Amy stayed three days at Orchid Palace, visiting with Kalid's grandmother, who fascinated her with stories of the heyday of harem life, and playing with Sarah's children. It was a brief and pleasant interlude before she had to deal with the next phase of her Ottoman odyssey—the arrival of Beatrice and James Woolcott.

Beatrice cried for the first ten minutes of the reunion, despite the fact that she probably would not have recognized Amy if she met her on the street. Once she was assured, repeatedly, that Amy was fine, and yes, she felt well enough to go back to Constantinople, and no, she didn't want to talk about any of it just yet, Beatrice began to calm down. She and her husband stayed the night at Orchid Palace, and Bea did her best not to gape over dinner at a vastly entertained Kalid, who cast amused looks at his wife behind Bea's back while Sarah kicked him under the table. When the Woolcotts and Amy departed the following morning, Amy did not know that Sarah stood on the balcony outside her bedroom, watching the coach leave the courtyard and silently wishing her the best.

Amy passed the time during the trip back to the city looking out the isinglass window of the coach and thinking about Malik. Trying to put him out of her mind didn't seem to be working; when she had kept busy during waking hours at Orchid Palace, she dreamed about him at night. She knew she could never locate him on her own, even if she tried; the rebels moved their camp at odd intervals, and Malik had made it clear that he didn't want to hear from her again. What was she going to do, traipse all over the hostile hill country by herself in search of a man the Sultan's troops couldn't even find, on the slim hope that he might have changed his mind about her?

It was hopeless.

By the time they reached the Woolcott house, a stately colonial on a wide, tree-lined street in Pera, the wealthy European suburb of Constantinople, Amy had resigned herself to going along with whatever arrangements Beatrice and James had made for her. She had nothing else planned, and they'd disrupted their settled lives to make room for her, worrying all through the weeks of her absence that she might be injured or dead.

The least she could do was cooperate.

After James had retired to his study, Beatrice and Listak showed Amy to an airy second-floor bedroom with French doors leading to the wide porch which faced the wooded grounds. As the servant unpacked her bag, Amy examined the capacious cherry armoire, the washstand with its porcelain bowl and pitcher, the brass bed with its frilly canopy and hangings, the Victorian wallpaper printed with cabbage roses and glossy leaves. There were gas jets set into the wall on either side of the bed; Pera was one of the few areas in the empire where gas was available to homes, as most Turks still made do with oil lamps, tapers, or even candles. Fresh flowers stood in tall vases on the highboy and on a side table covered with an intricate lace doily.

"This is lovely, Aunt Bea. Thank you so much."

"I'm glad you like it, dear," Beatrice said from the doorway. "It's been ready and waiting since the morning you arrived in Turkey, and Listak has changed the flowers every few days."

"I'm sure I'll be very comfortable here," Amy said.

Bea patted her sagging chignon and said, "I'm a little tired from the trip, I think I'd like to lie down for a while. Will you be all right until dinner?"

"I'll be fine."

"James and I will see you at six, then," Bea said, and disappeared, her footsteps hushed by the carpet as she walked down the hall to her room.

"Do you require anything else, miss?" Listak asked in her slightly sibilant English. She was standing next to the armoire, her hands folded.

"Oh, no, thank you, Listak. You may go."

"Will you need me to help you unpack your trunks later? They're in the closet. Mrs. Spaulding brought them with her from the coach."

"Don't worry, I can do that. It will help me settle in to put some of my own things around, don't you think?"

The servant bowed her head and left the room.

Amy looked out window, thinking of the contrast between this well-appointed home and the rebel camp where she had recently spent so much time. She should be grateful to be back in the lap of luxury, but of course she wasn't.

Amy frowned at her own perversity and decided to unpack her trunks. It would give her something to do.

In the month that followed, Beatrice made sure that Amy had plenty to do. The British and American embassies, oases of familiar culture to the European population, each had several functions a week, and Amy attended all of them. She sat through luncheons with embassy wives,

attended charity planning meetings, dressed up
for tea dances, and dressed formally for evening
affairs. Once the locals got over her exotic adventure in the hills, which Amy downplayed by
acting sprightly and discussing it dismissively,
they began to treat her as the eligible young
heiress she actually was. And it quickly became
clear to Amy that the routine Beatrice had os-
tensibly designed to keep her busy was in reality
designed to get her married.

Amy had never thought there were so many
Western men in Turkey; she had never thought
there were so many men anywhere. James was
known to be wealthy and successful, so his
pretty niece brought them all out of the wood-
work. She met junior officers from both garrisons, the sons of James's colleagues, the scions
of industrial families taking the grand tour, and
even the nephew of an Italian count. Anyone
watching her interact with these young men
would not have suspected anything was wrong
with her, unless they noticed the blue shadows
under her eyes which she had covered up with
alum, or the continual narrowing of her waist.
She took her clothes in herself to avoid comment from Beatrice, but nothing could disguise
the new prominence of Amy's cheekbones or
her total lack of interest in meals. Beatrice var-
ied the menus and ordered new desserts, but,
deceived by Amy's apparent gaiety at social
functions, she ascribed her niece's lack of ap-

petite to the heat, from which she also suffered.

If she had known her niece better, she would have been able to tell that Amy was unhappy. And Amy, trapped in her role of carefree young miss, vented her true feelings in letters to Sarah, who understood the younger woman's emotions only too well. Her responses calmed Amy somewhat, but in her darkest moments she actually considered marrying one of her eager suitors, since Malik appeared lost to her anyway. She would forget, she told herself; she would adjust and she would do what other people did when they abandoned hope of gaining their heart's desire but kept on living.

But somehow she wasn't ready to make that final break. As summer turned into fall and the days became less infernal, the nights even colder, and the rains came, she kept the flame alive, waiting, watching, for what she wasn't sure.

But she waited, just the same.

Malik tossed a heavy burlap bag of corn meal into the waiting wagon and looked around him, judging how much longer it would take to fill all eight wagons with the grain. He had picked a night with no moon to disguise their operation, but that meant his men were working by the light of oil lamps and had to move quickly. The soldiers who had been guarding the granary were dead, victims of a sneak attack, and the two night watchmen inside the building were bound and gagged.

As he watched the wagons fill up with the food that the Sultan hoarded for export while his own subjects were starving, Malik calculated how long it would take to finish the job and get away. The corn meal was destined for drop-off points around the country, where it would then be distributed to the people. Malik smiled slightly when he thought about the Sultan's reaction to this latest piece of larceny; he would just have to do without the revenue from the foreign sales. What a shame.

Dawn was breaking over the Syrian hills across the border when the last bag was loaded. As the caravan headed out through the alley behind the granary, an old woman answering a call of nature in a nearby field was startled to see the wagons rolling past her. She quickly rearranged her clothes and then stood in silence, watching what was obviously a covert mission. Her somber expression changed when she saw the young man standing at the back of the last wagon holding his finger to his lips. She grinned, then made a reciprocal gesture, waving with her other hand.

The Sultan was no friend of hers. What did she care if some bandits were robbing his storehouse? Good for them!

The young man bent, and two bags of corn meal went sailing through the air to land at her feet. She seized them and then blew him a kiss as the wagon reached a turn and hove out of sight.

There would be fresh *pida* bread for dinner that night, she thought, hurrying back to her house with her prize.

"You're a soft touch," Anwar said to Malik as the wagon carrying them rumbled along the dirt road, lurching heavily each time it hit a rut cut into the dust by the recent rain.

"Why shouldn't she have some?" Malik answered. "She's one of the people the Sultan has been raping for years."

"Nothing like leaving your calling card."

"She'll keep her mouth shut," Malik said, as they turned off the road and into a narrow lane leading to a series of caves, where they planned to store the haul until it could be moved.

"You trust them all too much," Anwar said. "She's poor, but that doesn't mean she's an angel, or your supporter."

"And being rich doesn't make a woman my enemy, eh?" Malik countered.

Anwar grabbed a bag as it lurched forward when the wagon's rear wheel hit a rock. "You're still thinking about her, aren't you?" he asked.

"I haven't stopped."

"What are you going to do?"

"Nothing."

"You're planning to go on like this?"

"Like what?"

"Driving yourself every minute to forget her. It isn't working, my friend."

"How do you know?"

"I know," Anwar answered in a tone which brooked no argument.

"So what do you suggest?" Malik asked.

"I have no ideas. It's your decision. I'm just telling you that brooding by night and pretending that everything is fine by day isn't fooling anybody, least of all yourself."

Malik was silent as the wagon creaked to a stop. He and Anwar jumped down and got in line to hand the bags inside the cave. There were men already assembled in there to stack them.

"Just do something," Anwar added, closing the subject. "You'll feel better."

"You're the one who told me to let her go, Anwar. Several times you told me that, with lots of reasons why it was the right thing to do."

"So I know everything?" Anwar said, grinning. "When did that happen?"

Malik shot him a disgusted glance and handed him a bag.

But once his friend looked away, Malik's expression became thoughtful.

It was a gloomy afternoon, threatening more rain, when Kalid knocked on the door of Sarah's schoolroom and then stood back to let her come into the hall.

219

"What is it?" Sarah asked.

"We have a visitor, and he wants to see you."

Sarah looked at him inquiringly.

"Malik Bey. I've been with him for the last hour in the *selamlik*."

The selamlik was a restricted area of the palace reserved just for men. Sarah put her hand on her husband's arm, alarmed.

"Kalid, he's a wanted man. What if someone saw him come here?" Sarah said.

"No one saw him. He came to the kitchens disguised as a beggar. He knows one of the skivvies—she's an old flame of Osman's—who smuggled him inside and then went to Achmed to say that Malik was here."

"And Achmed brought him to see you?" Sarah asked incredulously, wondering if her husband's aging *khislar* was getting sloppy.

"Achmed asked me first if I wanted to admit Malik for an interview," Kalid replied, smiling.

"And you, of course, couldn't resist the idea of having the Sultan's most notorious criminal under your roof," Sarah observed dryly.

"I was curious to find out what he wanted," Kalid said, his smile widening.

"All right, my darling husband, I'll bite. What exactly does he want?"

"Well, he *said* he wanted to ask me if I had accomplished anything at my district meeting with the Sultan, but I suspect he really came to talk to you."

"Why?"

"He knows I got nowhere with the Sultan. Bey reads the newspapers avidly, and all the English-language dailies reported that the Sultan refused any concessions to the rebels, that he won't consider a parliament or a shared government with elected representatives. So it's my guess that Bey came here on that pretext to get news of Amelia Ryder from you."

"Did he mention her?"

"Of course not. But I don't think he wants to see you to get the latest fashion news, do you?"

Sarah considered that in silence for a few moments and then said, "Did you tell him I would see him?"

"I told him I'd ask you if you would grant him an audience," Kalid replied.

Sarah nodded. "Give me ten minutes to get the children settled with Memtaz, and then have Achmed bring him to the audience room," Sarah said.

"Are you sure? It's your decision."

"I'm sure."

Kalid turned to go. "I'll have Achmed post guards outside the door," he said.

"I'm certain I'll be quite safe. Bey would be an idiot to try anything here, and I think we both know he's not an idiot."

Kalid looked over his shoulder at her. "I'll post the guards anyway."

Sarah went back inside and got the children

221

organized with their tasks, then hurried along the corridor and through an outside courtyard, glad of the freedom to move about alone. Kosem still thought it unseemly that Sarah ran around the palace without an escort, though Sarah was happy that she was now able to find her way through its labyrinthine passages on her own. It was a feat of navigation which had seemed beyond the talents of Dr. Livingstone when she first came to Bursa.

Achmed was waiting for her when she arrived at the audience room, wearing the sour look he always assumed when he disapproved of something. Sarah ignored it and gestured for him to bring in the visitor. He went to a side door and admitted Bey, who came into the chamber flanked by two halberdiers, each of whom had one of Bey's arms clamped in a huge fist.

"You may release him," Sarah said.

The guards let Malik go and stepped back.

"You may go," Sarah said to the guards.

They looked at Achmed.

"My husband said you would remain outside the door," Sarah said to him firmly.

Achmed bowed. "But certainly my master has no wish to endanger his wife . . ." Achmed began.

"Out," Sarah said. "I'll call if I need you."

The three men marched from the room, and Sarah turned to her guest.

"It seems my husband's khislar thinks you are a dangerous character, Mr. Bey," Sarah said.

Malik said nothing.

"Is this your latest disguise?" she asked, gesturing to his rags, as well as the enveloping cloak he wore, its hood hanging part way down his back.

"I find that these days I must employ a variety of disguises," he replied.

His voice was low and resonant, his English almost as good as Kalid's. Sarah thought that he was about as tall as her husband, but slimmer of build, with duskier skin and eyes as black as Jerusalem olives. Even with the wild hair and three-day stubble of the mendicant he was pretending to be, he was a romantic enough figure for Sarah to imagine his intoxicating effect on an inexperienced, seventeen-year-old girl.

"Why did you want to see me, Mr. Bey?" Sarah asked, sitting in Kalid's chair.

"I want to know if Amelia is all right," he said stiffly.

"Why should you ask about her? She was your victim and glad to escape you."

Malik's mouth tightened but he made no reply.

"Was she not?" Sarah asked innocently.

"You know she was crying when she left me," he said darkly, gazing at the floor.

"And why was that?"

223

"You'd have to ask Amelia."

"She isn't here, so I'm asking you."

He looked up then and turned on her a gaze so blazingly defiant, yet so full of pain, that Sarah could no longer maintain her schoolmarm pose.

"Look here," she said briskly, rising, "I don't know you, although I knew your brother Osman and can only hope that you have some of his fine qualities. I do know that you have habitually engaged in criminal behavior—"

"That's easy for you to say, living surrounded by luxury in a palace full of servants," he snapped, his eyes narrowing. "You'd resort to criminal behavior too if you had to exist the way most of your husband's subjects do."

"Mr. Bey, my husband has done more for his subjects than any pasha in the last three hundred years, and if you want me to help you, I would advise you not to take that tone with me," Sarah snapped back at him.

"All right," he said quickly, holding up his hand, obviously afraid that she was about to have him removed. Or arrested. "It's true that I have broken the law for my cause, but so have many others like me throughout history, including the founding fathers of your own country."

"You don't have to make a speech, Mr. Bey. As a Bostonian, I am well aware of the anti-government activities of the colonists who established the United States," Sarah said crisply. "That doesn't mean I want to discuss my cousin's ward, or her state of mind, with a wanted man."

"I was just trying to find out if she is happy," he said dully.

"Are you? Are you happy with your doings?"

He glared at her. "What does that mean?"

"If you had a shred of Osman's decency in you, I don't know how you could seduce that child and then send her back to us as if nothing had happened!" Sarah burst out, losing her temper.

Malik stared at her stonily as the back of his neck flushed a dull red. Then he said carefully, as if trying to maintain his own control, "I did not seduce her. She made the first move, if you must know, and I stopped it before—" He broke off abruptly.

"Before the result could be pregnancy?" Sarah said dryly, realizing that she had misunderstood Amelia.

He nodded curtly.

Sarah waited, sensing that he wished to say more.

"And now I've lost the chance to be with her forever," he blurted.

Whatever doubts Sarah may have harbored about his character were dispelled by the look of anguished frustration on his face. She could only guess what it had cost him to come to her and ask about Amelia, to admit that he felt the girl's loss as deeply as he obviously did. What a great leveler love was, Sarah thought. The hero of the Ottoman revolution had been reduced to this abject state by his passion for a slip of a girl.

"You want to see her again, don't you? That's why you really came here," Sarah said quietly.

He hesitated, then nodded. "I told myself she would be better off if I just let her go, but . . ."

"But you're miserable. I can tell you for a fact that she is as well," Sarah said.

He looked at her sharply, hope dawning in his eyes.

"I've had four letters from her in the month since she left us here in Bursa, and her heart has not changed. She's observing the routine her aunt has scheduled for her, but all she thinks about is you," Sarah said.

"Truly?" he said softly.

"Yes."

"But you know my situation, my life. Do I have the right?" he asked.

"You have any rights she gives you. Don't make the decision for her. If you go to her and she doesn't want to see you, she has a tongue to say so."

He smiled slightly. "Yes, she does." He thought a long moment and then said, "Where is she?"

"It will be dangerous for you to go there."

"It's dangerous for me to go anywhere," he said simply.

Sarah told him where the Woolcott home was in Pera, giving him the address. She described the street and the house and then said, "The rest is up to you."

He came forward and knelt at her feet, taking her hand and kissing it. Sarah, always a little startled by the dramatic gestures of the Turks, withdrew her fingers from his and watched him as he stood up again.

"Mashallah, haseki pashana," he said, and backed away from her until he was at the door.

Sarah called for the guards and the door opened.

She hoped that God would protect her, as Bey had said. She hoped that God would protect all of them.

Seconds after Bey had disappeared between the two halberdiers, Kalid came into the room.

"Well?" he said.

"He's handsome, he has the requisite mixture of arrogance and charm, and he's dedicated to a noble cause. I can easily see why Amy fell for him."

"I wasn't asking for a commentary on his allure, Sarah. What did he want?"

"He wanted to know where Amy was, just as you said."

"And?"

"I told him."

"Was that wise?"

"He would have found out anyway. James is a prominent businessman who's easy to locate and Malik is persistent. I just saved him the trouble of tracking Amy down and assured him that he would be welcome."

"How do you know that?"

"Kalid, I showed you Amy's last letter. What do you think her feelings are about Malik?"

"But considering his situation, shouldn't you have tried to dissuade him?"

"Would you have been dissuaded ten years ago?" Sarah asked rhetorically.

"Malik is not the type for half measures," Kalid said warningly. "He'll carry her off, you know."

"If she wants to be carried off, so be it," Sarah replied.

"Spoken like a true American, to whom all things are resolved by love," Kalid said.

"Don't give me your 'American' speech again, Kalid. If we're such a bunch of fools, why did you marry me?"

He put his arms around her from behind and kissed the side of her neck. "I just love to tease you about your nationality. You always rise to the bait. But you are well aware of the perilous situation Amelia will be facing. The consort of Malik Bey will have a dangerous career."

"And Beatrice will have the vapors again," Sarah sighed. "Guaranteed."

He grinned. "Beatrice has the vapors if the temperature rises five degrees. Did you see the way she was looking at me when she was with us? As if I were some headhunter out of the jungle, about to strip off and attack her."

"Maybe she was just hoping you would," Sarah said, and he chuckled.

"Speaking of stripping off.." he said, undoing the buttons at the back of her shirtwaist.

"Here?" Sarah said, looking around the room.

"Why not? I'll tell the guards we're not to be disturbed." He went to the door, and Sarah's mind wandered back to what she had just done.

She wasn't as confident about telling Malik where Amy was as she tried to appear.

Had she done the right thing?

Malik wasn't the type to delay using the information.

She would know very soon.

Malik crouched on the branch of the tree and watched the gaslight dim and then disappear in the Woolcott master bedroom. Amy's aunt was going to sleep. But there was still a light in the first-floor den, which meant that her uncle was working in there, and in Amy's room, where he could see her reading in bed.

He would have to wait.

The desire to just rush into her room and take his chances was overwhelming; it seemed a millenium since he had touched her, but he knew it was much wiser to bide his time until the uncle retired. Malik had been watching the house for several nights and knew the routine. The servants, who rose early, also retired early. The aunt went to bed next, and the uncle usually worked until about eleven-thirty in his office. By midnight Amy's light was the only one left burning, and that's exactly the way Malik wanted it.

He settled back into the crotch of the tree and wished he could have a cigarette. Waiting was so difficult; he had planned every aspect of this visit as if he were designing an assault on Topkapi and wanted to go forward with it. He had selected a tree whose limbs were stout enough to hold his weight and which grew close enough to the house to enable him to reach it with a rope. He planned to swing onto the porch from the tree and then enter Amy's bedroom through the twin French doors.

It sounded simple, but he knew that anything could go wrong at any time. If Amy's aunt couldn't sleep and decided to get a breath of air, if her uncle forgot something downstairs and got up to retrieve it, if Amy, despite the pasha-na's reassurances, had decided she hated him. . . . He sighed and resolved not to think about it. Any risky course of action always needed an element of luck, and he had to believe that luck would be with him this night.

The light in the den finally went out, and Ma-

lik waited half an hour after that before he
climbed to a higher limb, uncoiled the rope
from his waist, and screwed the hook on its end
into the trunk of the maple. He dropped a few
feet, testing the rope, and then began to swing
in slowly increasing arcs, getting closer to the
balcony of the Woolcott home each time. The
house was screened from the street by a heavy
growth of shrubbery and a grove of trees, but
at such a height there was still the risk of being
seen by a passing janissary on patrol. For that
reason he had worn dark clothing and chosen
not the tree just next to the house, but the one
most likely to land him in the correct position
quickly.

He kicked his legs repeatedly and finally
achieved a high enough arc to soar over the railing of the balcony. He let go of the rope suddenly and landed heavily on the porch,
stumbling and crashing into the wall. He recovered his balance and flattened himself against
the side of the house, his heart pounding, waiting for the lights and the voices and discovery.

Nothing happened. He waited for his pulse
rate to return to normal, then threw the rope
back toward the tree so it wouldn't be seen dangling from the second floor. He crept along the
balcony to Amy's room, looking quickly inside
and then stepping back.

She was lying on her side in bed with her
back to him, reading by the light of a lowered

gas jet. His respiration quickened again as he stepped forward once more and tapped on the glass.

Amy turned toward him convulsively, frightened by the unlikely sound of someone knocking on her balcony doors, but when she saw who it was, she threw back her coverlet and leaped from the bed. She ran barefoot in her nightgown across the carpet and yanked open the doors, throwing herself into his arms.

"Thank God," she said, standing on tiptoe to kiss him all over his face and clinging to him tightly, as if to make sure he was really there.

Malik closed his eyes in exquisite relief and pressed his cheek against her hair.

Chapter Nine

"Come inside," Amy said suddenly, stepping back and tugging on his hands. "Someone might see us from the street." She led him through the doors and closed them, drawing heavy drapes across the glass. Then she whirled and embraced him once more.

"I can't believe you're here," Amy whispered, burying her face against his shoulder. "Am I sleeping? Is this a dream?"

"It's not a dream. I had to see you," he said huskily, bending to pull her closer. "I missed you so much." He could feel her warmth and softness through the thin batiste nightgown she wore as if she were naked.

Amy raised her head to look at him in the soft light. His expression was unguarded, open, more vulnerable than she had ever seen it.

"Amelia, I have to explain . . ." he began, but she stopped him by putting a finger to his lips.

"It doesn't matter," she said. "You're here now; we have tonight. Let's not waste any of it going over the past. I had plenty of time to think when I thought I'd lost you, and I know what I want. Do you?"

He swallowed and nodded, his eyes locked with hers.

She took his hand and led him toward the bed.

"Make love to me," she murmured, reclining on the pillows and holding up her arms. "I don't care what happens after tonight—at least we'll have this to remember."

Malik needed no further invitation. He dropped next to her and enfolded her, stroking the silken skin of her bare arms, reminding himself that he had to go slowly, that no matter how ardent she might seem, she was a virgin who could be hurt or frightened easily. This was new territory for him, too; his experience with camp followers had hardly prepared him to deal with Amelia's eager innocence or reckless devotion. But fate had allowed him this reunion with her, and he could no longer deny them both what they most wanted.

Malik turned his head and kissed her gently, his lips hardly touching hers, pressing, then withdrawing, until she clutched him, locking

her fingers behind his neck and kissing him
back avidly. She felt the intrusion of his tongue,
the hardness of his teeth, as he enjoyed the luxury of kissing her deeply, searchingly, pinning
her to the bed with his weight. When this was
no longer enough, he lowered his mouth to her
bare throat, tasting the fragrant flesh there,
then traced the line of her collarbone with his
tongue. She sighed and arched her neck invit-
ingly, causing the neckline of her gown to open
further, exposing the creamy tops of her
breasts. He kissed each one lingeringly, closing
his eyes to savor the sensation, teasing the nipples through the thin cloth until Amy was
moaning and twisting restlessly under his seeking mouth.

"It seems a hundred years since I last touched
you," he murmured, his lips against her skin.

She sank her fingers into his hair and held
him to her, gasping as he pushed aside the bodice of her gown and took one rigid peak into his
mouth. Amy watched him as he loved her; his
breathing was ragged, his face flushed dark, his
lashes fanning his cheeks. She had never felt
such an overwhelming desire to yield and sub-
mit, to give a man whatever he wanted. Malik
drew back abruptly as his hands came up impatiently to pull her gown to her waist, then he
bent again and Amy sighed blissfully at the renewed contact. His mouth was hot, his hair soft
against her as he buried his face between her

breasts, his hands roaming the smooth skin of her naked back. He turned his head and placed his burning cheek on her belly, his absorbed, dreamy expression reflecting the intensity of his emotion. His lips, moist and swollen from her kisses, were parted, allowing a glimpse of his teeth, stark white in his swarthy face.

"I need you," he murmured thickly. "I never thought I could feel this way. I've thought of this moment every day since you left me."

"So have I," Amy said, stroking his shoulders, his upper arms, feeling the tension knotting his muscles through his shirt.

"Take this off," she whispered, tugging on his collar. He sat up, stripping off the tunic in one motion, the upward movement flexing his arms and exposing the sculptured ribcage under his skin. Amy looked at his broad shoulders, the strong column of his neck, the simple beauty of his young manhood, and her throat tightened with unshed tears. Removing the shirt had disordered his hair, and Amy reached up to smooth it back tenderly as he descended to her again.

"You have such beautiful hair," she said softly. "It was the first thing I noticed about you."

He kissed her again, murmuring against her mouth, "Your hair wasn't the first thing I noticed about you."

"What was?" she asked, closing her eyes as he

dropped a trail of kisses along the line of her jaw and then came back to her mouth, lingering there.

"Your skin, your eyes, your body, your scent," he answered, cupping one ripe breast and stroking the nipple until it hardened in his palm.

"My scent?" she sighed, losing track of the conversation as he caressed her.

"It's been with me since I first held you," he said huskily, "and now I am drunk with it." He lowered his head to her shoulder and embraced her fully; Amy gasped as she felt him, heavy and ready against her thighs. She moved sinuously beneath him in an instinctive response, and Malik came close to losing control, pressing her down almost roughly. He ran his hand along her bare thigh under her gown and her legs fell apart in unconscious invitation.

Malik ground his teeth and rolled off her, lying at her side with one arm flung over his eyes.

"What is it?" Amy asked anxiously. "Did I do something wrong?"

He held up his free hand, and she waited. When he looked at her again, he lifted her fingers from their resting place on his shoulder and kissed them one by one.

"You did everything right," he said, but his voice was congested. "It's just that I'm trying not to . . . rush you . . ."

"And?"

He closed his eyes. "It's hard to go slowly after

waiting so long," he finished lamely.

"It is for me too," she whispered, pressing herself against him again. He held her loosely for a moment, but when she embraced him more tightly, he was soon stroking her breasts, her abdomen, kissing her wildly as he pulled her gown from her limbs. She hid her face against his shoulder as he looked at her, then stiffened when he lifted her to him and she felt his full arousal against her naked body for the first time.

"Are you all right?" he murmured.

"Yes," she said, relaxing as he stroked the slender curve of her back, his hand slipping lower with each caress until she was clinging to him like a limpet, avid for more. He kissed her again and again, with an intensity that belied his earlier caution, and as her excitement increased her response grew more abandoned, carrying them forward on a tide of desire. When he turned her slightly and slipped his hand between her legs, he forced himself to pause and gauge her reaction. But she was too far gone to protest, her skin flushed and dewed with perspiration, her eyes closed.

"Do you like that?" he whispered, watching her face.

She moaned and her lashes fluttered. When he moved, she lifted herself toward him, begging silently, her body speaking for her. He gave her what she wanted, and when she reached for the waistband of his pants, he left her only long enough to remove them, then rejoined her on the bed.

This time when he pulled her to him and she felt flesh against flesh, she did not hesitate, but melted into him, twining her legs with his. He groaned with satisfaction as she caressed him eagerly, running her hands over his muscular back, his skin now fiery and slick with sweat. She grew bolder, inflamed by curiosity and her burgeoning need, and pushed him a little away from her, exploring his chest and belly with searching hands. He closed his eyes as she rubbed his flat nipples with a soft palm; he sucked in his breath when she traced a trail with her forefinger from his heart to his navel, then caressed the line of hair below it. When she reached for him, he held his breath, and when she touched him, his head fell back, a pulse beating strongly at the base of his throat.

Amy became lost in her own investigation of his body, the rough hair and silky skin, the contrast of hard and soft, so when his hand caught hers abruptly, she looked up in shock.

"Don't," he said curtly. His hand was trembling.

All of Amy's new confidence drained out of her in a sudden flood. When she drew back in consternation, he sat up suddenly and seized her, pulling her back down with him and covering her face with kisses.

"Don't look like that. I love you," he said huskily, pulling her arms around his neck. "I love you, I love you. You just don't know what you're doing to me. I want to be gentle, I don't want to hurt you, but you're driving me crazy."

There was no doubting him as he held her close, the runaway pounding of his heart and the drawn-bow tautness of his body mute evidence of his sincerity.

"I want to drive you crazy," she whispered fiercely, reaching up to touch his cheek. "I want you to want me as badly, as much, as I want you."

He groaned helplessly. "Can you question it?"

"Kiss me again," she said, and he complied, soon bringing her back to a pitch of desire that had her whimpering with each caress. His mouth consumed her body and, her shyness completely gone, Amy matched his ardor. She held him to her as he tongued her navel, trailed his lips along her thighs and belly, then moved lower, wrapping his arms around her hips and lifting her to his mouth.

Amy gasped, writhing away from him, but he held her steady, keeping her still with firm pressure until she felt the mounting pleasure and her resistance faded. She moaned softly, then moaned again, biting her lip as exquisite sensation flooded her body. She sank her fingers into his thick hair, digging her nails into his scalp, her head dropping back to the pillow in submission.

Malik's skin was aflame against her thighs, shining with sweat in the low light, the cords in his arms and back tight. When Amy could stand it no longer, she tugged him upward, flinging her arms around his neck when he rose to join her.

"Please," she gasped. "Please."

"What?" he said softly, his tongue in her ear. "What do you want?"

She sobbed as he touched her and found her ready—more than ready. She pressed upward into his hand convulsively.

"Tell me," he said huskily, enjoying the depth of her need, which matched his. "Tell me."

"You. Inside me. Now."

Unable to wait any longer either, Malik positioned her, putting her flat on her back and looming above her. He lifted her hips, and she locked her legs behind him.

"This . . . it may hurt," he said, barely able to speak.

She kissed him in silent reassurance, and he entered her as she did. The arms supporting him above her trembled with tension as he waited for her reaction.

"Yes?" he said, biting his lip, fighting the urge to plunge into her again.

"Yes," she answered.

He moved again, experimentally, and her

sigh of satisfaction reassured him. He relaxed and drew her into his rhythm, groaning deeply when her response increased his pleasure.

"I love you," she whispered, tears seeping from the corners of her eyes.

"I love you, Amelia," he answered, and proved it.

The sound of rain drumming on the roof woke Amy, and she stirred to find Malik sprawled across her, his head on her shoulder, his arm flung across her waist. She felt supremely happy and completely fulfilled, the slight ache in her loins reminding her of the experience she had just shared with the man in her bed.

Sleep wiped the care from Malik's face and made him appear to be her exact contemporary, his slenderness and glossy, unkempt hair contributing to the effect. The sheet was twisted under him, the coverlet drawn over his legs, his boneless sprawl indicative of total relaxation. Amy hated to disturb him, but she wanted to make use of the basin and ewer in a corner of the room. She shifted Malik's weight gradually, finally freeing herself as he slumped back to the bed, still asleep. She tiptoed over to the washstand and picked up the soap and towel, working away busily until she looked up to find Malik's eyes on her.

"I saw you washing once before," he said lazily.

"When was that?"

"The morning you woke up with me after you ran away. I came upon you when you were at the stream."

"And did you watch?" she said teasingly, walking back across the room and slipping into the bed.

He seized her and rolled on top of her. "Of course. I had to tear myself away and then make a lot of noise so you would hear me coming the second time."

"You are a sneak," she said, kissing the side of his throat.

"I think I knew then that I had to have you," he said quietly, turning to lie back against the pillows and pulling her into his arms.

"You put up quite a fight, anyway," Amy said.

"It was clear to me from that morning that I would lose," he said, tightening his grip around her. He waited a moment and then said, "Are you all right?"

"I'm perfectly fine. Never been better," she said, putting her head on his shoulder.

"I mean, are you bleeding?"

"I was, a little, but it's nothing."

"Are you sure?"

"I'm sure." She turned to look up at him and said, "Malik, what are we going to do?"

"I thought you didn't want to talk about it," he replied.

"Not then," she replied. "Not when I first saw you."

"Yes, you just wanted to drag me into bed like a huzzy," he said.

She sat up to look at him directly. "A what?"

"A shameless woman," he said. "A huzzy."

"That's 'hussy,' my friend. Do you speak English?"

"My English is far superior to your Turkish," he said, insulted.

"Anyone's English is far superior to my Turkish, and don't change the subject. We can't spend the rest of our lives in this bed. How are we going to see each other?"

"We'll see each other. I'll find a way."

"You took such a risk in coming here. Why did you wait so long?"

"I wasn't sure you would want to see me until I talked to Kalid Shah's wife."

"You went to Orchid Palace?"

He nodded. "I didn't know where you were."

"Of course not. When I left the camp you didn't exactly ask for a forwarding address."

"I tried to cut if off between us then, Amelia. I thought it would be best."

"For me?"

"Yes, for you. Certainly not for me. I felt as if I had amputated my arm when you left."

"But why? Why did you let me go in that cruel, impersonal way? I thought I would die of unhappiness."

"Amelia, I'm a criminal in this country, a fugitive. I have nothing and I'm likely to have nothing for some time in the future. My cause is just, but I don't even know if I'll survive to see it triumph. In the meantime I have to live from hand to mouth, from day to day. You saw that for yourself; you experienced it. I have no resources to provide for a wife."

"A wife?" she said breathlessly.

"Don't you want to marry me?" he said, watching her face.

She threw her arms around his neck. "Yes, yes!"

"You understand what marrying me would mean. You'd become a criminal too, just for sheltering me. Your life would be in danger, just like mine. You'd be on the move all the time, with no settled home."

"I don't care. I'd live in a tent with you." She started to laugh. "I *have* lived in a tent with you."

He smiled. "And you survived it pretty well." He pulled her back down on the bed and as she wrestled with him playfully she heard a slight growling sound.

"What's that?" she said, drawing back from him.

"What?"

"That noise. Was that your stomach?"

He shrugged. "Probably."

"When was the last time you had something to eat?"

He thought about it. "Yesterday?"

"Malik, for heaven's sake. You must be starving!"

"Not for food," he said, leaning forward to nibble the side of her neck.

"I'm going down to the kitchen to get you something," Amy said, eluding his grasp.

"You can't run around the house in the middle of the night," he said.

Amy got up and took a dressing gown from the armoire, pulling it on and tying it at the neck as she stepped into her slippers. "Why not? I couldn't sleep—I wanted a snack. In the unlikely event that anyone else is awake at this hour, that's a reasonable excuse for a trip downstairs. Just stay in here and after I leave relock the door—the key is in the lock."

He stood and grabbed her as she walked past him, wrapping his arms around her waist from behind and hugging her to him.

"Hurry back," he said.

She turned and kissed him quickly. "Malik, let me go. Listak will be stirring in a couple of hours and you have to get away before then."

He must have been really hungry, because he released her. She ran to the door, turning to hold her finger to her lips as he pulled on his pants. She pointed to the lock. After she went through the door, she waited until she heard the key turn from inside the room before running along the gallery and then down the carpeted steps in her slippered feet.

James had turned the gas jets to their lowest setting, but there was still enough light to see as Amy made her way through the first floor to the kitchen at the back of the house. The servants' rooms were just behind it, so she was careful to be very quiet as she went to the cold larder and quickly selected a leftover breast of chicken, a wedge of cheese and two apples, pushing aside a block of ice to reach a bottle of James's lager as an afterthought. On her way out, she grabbed three hardening biscuits that Listak had set aside for bread pudding, wrapping the hoard in the skirt of her gown. She moved swiftly back through the silent house, tiptoeing as she passed the Woolcotts' room and then gathering speed as she approached her own. She tapped lightly on the six-paneled door and it opened instantly.

"Yes?" Malik said inquiringly, as if she were one of the Turkish bundle women who went from door to door selling their wares.

"Stop clowning!" she hissed, shoving him aside and barreling into the room, sure that James was going to walk into the hall at any moment.

"What's clowning?" he said, watching with interest as she dumped her purloined treats on the bed. He selected an apple and crunched into it vigorously.

"You know—acting silly, like a clown in a Barnum circus," she replied, going back to the door and locking it.

His blank look conveyed the cultural gap which separated them; he didn't know what a circus was. His English was so good and their mutual desire so intense that Amy sometimes forgot they were the products of two different worlds.

"Never mind," she said, going to the French doors and pulling aside the drapes as he picked up the piece of chicken and attacked it, stripping it in seconds.

"It's still raining," she observed glumly. "You're going to get wet."

"I've been wet before," he said, chewing industriously as he came to stand behind her. "Thanks for the food."

"Consider it payment for services rendered," Amy said, looking back at him mischievously.

He laughed, putting down the chicken bone to pop the cork from the lager. He took a swallow of it and then said, "Gah," looking at the bottle as if it had bitten him.

"I'm sorry—that's all James had in the larder. I thought it was English beer."

"I've had English beer, and this is not it," he replied, setting the bottle on her nightstand.

"Do you want me to get you some water?"

He picked up a biscuit and disposed of it in three bites. "No. I want you to come over here and talk to me." He extended his hand and as she took it he led her to the bed.

"Talk?" Amy said. "We're not going to talk here."

"Yes, we are," he said, settling back against the pillows and pulling her down with him. "I want to know what you have been doing with yourself this last month."

"I have been following Beatrice's plan for me, which is to attend boring parties in order to meet boring suitors."

"Suitors?" he said, his eyes narrowing as he bit into the piece of cheese. "Men?"

"Of course, men. My aunt is determined to marry me off at her earliest convenience."

He was silent, watching her, the food in his hand forgotten.

Amy sat up and stared at him, astonished. "Malik, you can't seriously be jealous."

"Do you think I enjoy the idea of your being pursued by a horde of very proper and very suitable men?" he said.

"As opposed to unsuitable you?" Amy suggested.

He said nothing.

Amy took the cheese from his hand and put it on the table. "Malik, don't be ridiculous," she said, amazed that he could even be worried about it. "I have been crying myself to sleep every night over you!"

"You never considered forgetting me and doing what your relatives want?"

"I tried. I really tried to put you out of my mind and move on, but it didn't work. Some part of me was waiting, always waiting for you."

"You knew I'd come?" he said softly, reaching up to touch her hair.

"I hoped and prayed you would."

He pulled her back into his arms, looking around him at the well-appointed bedroom. "This beautiful house, this comfortable life—how can I ask you to leave all of it for me?" he said. His worried tone indicated that her earlier dismissal of this concern had not entirely convinced him.

"Don't start that again. Ask me. Just ask me." She kissed him, then kissed him again, hoping that her ardor would convince him that his fears were groundless.

He responded avidly, rolling her under him and untying the bow at her neck.

"Malik, we can't," Amy protested weakly, wishing they could. "There's no time."

"We'll make the time," he said.

When Amy awoke again, the sound of the rain was gone and a thin strip of sunlight slanted through the opening between the drapes. As she rolled over drowsily, she heard the distant sound of carriages clopping past in the street and smelled the faint but distinct odor of bacon frying.

She sat bolt upright, looking at the ship's clock ticking away on her fireplace mantel.

It was seven-forty in the morning. She would be expected downstairs at breakfast in twenty minutes. James and Beatrice were sure to be up and about, and Malik was still in the house.

She sprang into action, shaking his shoulder violently as she scrambled in the bed for her dressing gown.

"Wake up, wake up—we overslept!" she whispered, thrusting her arms into her robe and climbing out of the bed. She picked up his clothes and shoved them into his arms as he struggled to sit upright, blinking.

"Look at the clock!" she hissed.

He did so and then glanced back at her, fully awake. He jumped up and began to dress immediately. He had pulled on his pants and was yanking his shirt over his head when there was a knock at the door.

They both froze.

Amy recovered first. She looked at Malik, holding her finger to her lips, then called out, "Yes, what is it?"

"Miss Beatrice sent me to see if you were awake, miss," Listak said.

"I'm awake," Amy replied cheerfully.

"I have your coffee, miss," Listak said.

Amy groaned deeply and closed her eyes. When she opened them again, she pointed to the floor and mouthed, "Get under the bed," to Malik.

He dropped to the rug immediately and rolled under the four-poster. Amy ran over to the bed and dragged the coverlet to the floor to block the space where he lay from view.

"Coming," she said loudly, glancing in the cheval mirror as she passed it, then stopping short at her startling image. Her hair was wild, her mouth swollen and red, and there were dark smudges under her eyes as well as two passion marks on the side of her neck.

She looked like what she was, a woman who had spent an active night in bed.

Amy pulled her hair over her shoulder to cover her neck, twisted the key in the lock, then yanked open the door.

"Good morning, Listak," she said, her smile feeling stuck on her face.

"Good morning, miss," Listak replied, taking a step past Amy to go into the room.

"Let me take that," Amy said hastily, removing the tray from the servant's hands as she blocked Listak's path.

"Do you need anything else, miss?" Listak asked.

"No—no, I'm fine. I just slept quite late and I don't feel much like breakfast. Would you tell my aunt that I won't be in the dining room this morning?"

Listak bowed.

"Thank you." Amy barely restrained herself from shoving the door closed in Listak's face with her foot. Instead she stood smiling, with the tray in her hands, until the servant had walked away. Then she carried the tray to the bed, running back to relock the door before lifting the coverlet.

"She's gone," Amy said breathlessly.

Malik crawled out from under the bed, dusting his sleeves and brushing lint from his hair.

"The Sultan should see me now," he said dryly. "He'd be sure he had nothing to fear."

Amy giggled.

"May I have some of that?" he asked, indicating the tray on the bed.

Amy poured him a cup of coffee, which he downed black.

"Too weak," he pronounced. "European coffee is always too weak."

"That's American coffee, but we'll all try to do better in the future," Amy replied. "Now will you please apply yourself to the problem at hand—namely how to get you out of this house? It's almost eight o'clock; everyone is running around downstairs."

He was silent, thinking. "I could make a rope from some of your clothes—silk would be best, stockings maybe—and let myself down over the side of the house."

Amy shook her head. "Beatrice always does her gardening after breakfast when it's still cool. She'll be out there by the time we've fashioned anything strong enough to hold your weight. She'll see you."

"She'll see the rope I left hanging from the maple tree, too," he said, his expression grim.

Amy struck her forehead with the heel of her hand. "I forgot all about that! I have to go out there and get it!"

"You'd better hurry, before she finishes her coddled eggs and gets out her shears," Malik said. He went to the double doors and drew one of the drapes back slightly, looking out at the grounds.

Amy dressed quickly, throwing on a shirt-waist and skirt, not bothering to comb her hair. She went to her dressing table and took out her jar of alum paste, rubbing the covering mixture on the purpling bruises on her neck.

"Did I do that?" he asked, glancing back at her.

"Nobody else," Amy replied, applying petroleum jelly to her abraded lips with a pinky.

"I guess I got carried away," he said, looking abashed.

"We both did, or you wouldn't still be here," Amy replied softly, smiling at him.

"Go," he said, nodding at the door.

"Listak won't come up to make the beds until she's finished in the kitchen, so we have some time," Amy said. "Lock the door after I've left."

He nodded.

She blew him a kiss and slipped through the door.

Amy stood still and listened. She heard the clinking of china in the dining room and the murmur of voices, feeling a surge of relief that James and Bea were exactly where they should be. She crept down the stairs and peeked into the dining room. She waited for a moment, until her aunt and uncle were both looking down at their plates, before skulking past the glass doors and exiting through the front hall.

The grass outside was wet from the night's rain, soaking the hem of her skirt as she ran around the side of the house and into the maple grove. She glanced up at her room and saw Malik just behind the drapes as she dashed past. She couldn't remove the peg from the crotch of the big tree—it was too high—but she looped the rope on a lower limb, then shoved it into the dense growth of damp leaves. It wasn't perfectly hidden, but it was disguised. Satisfied that she had done her best, Amy scurried back into the house breathlessly, only to encounter Beatrice in the front hall.

"My dear, what were you doing outside in the wet?" Bea greeted her. "Your shoes are covered with mud."

"Oh, I just felt like taking a walk," Amy said, laughing gaily, hoping that Bea didn't notice the tinge of hysteria in her voice. "Everything is so fresh after the rain."

"It's been raining on and off for three weeks," Bea said, looking at her strangely.

"Yes, I like wet weather," Amy babbled, edging toward the stairs.

"Are you sure you're all right?" Bea asked. "Listak said you didn't want any breakfast."

"Yes, I'm fine—just not very hungry. I'll take some fruit up to my room." She changed direction and went into the dining room, grabbing two oranges and a pear from the silver bowl in the center of the table. Then she waited until Bea had gone into the morning room to write her letters before she bolted up the stairs.

Malik was waiting for her tap and let her into the bedroom. She handed him the fruit and said, "Put this with the leftover food. You can take it with you."

"Did you get the rope?"

"I couldn't retrieve it, but I hid it pretty well. Unless you were looking for it, I don't think you would see it."

"Have you got a plan?"

"I think so," Amy said, unlacing her wet shoes. "The carriage will come to take James to his office in a few minutes, and Bea should be occupied with her correspondence for a while."

"I thought you said she'd be in the garden."

"She must have decided it was too wet for pruning, but the morning room where she's working looks out on the garden, so you still can't leave the way you came. But once the coast is clear, I can take you out through the flower room. We shouldn't encounter any of the servants there."

"What's the flower room?"

"It's a sort of gardening shed attached to the house. You enter it from the back hall and it lets you out in the alley where trash is stored for collection." She stepped into her slippers, shoving her muddied shoes aside.

"That sounds good."

Amy looked up at him. "I don't know how you're getting back. I don't even know how you got here."

"I left Mehmet with Yuri's brother, who lives in the lower market district. He's keeping the horse for me. I'll pick Mehmet up and ride back."

"And how will you get to Yuri's brother's house?"

He pointed to his feet.

Amy ran across the room and flung herself on him. "I don't want you to go."

"I have to go," he said, his arms tight around her, his cheek against her hair. "But I'll return."

She tilted her head to look into his face. "When? When will you return?"

"I can't say. I don't know. But soon. As soon

as I can, I'll come to you."

"I won't be able to stand not knowing," she whispered, her voice cracking.

"You'll stand it," he said reassuringly. "We both will."

"I'll look for you every day."

"And one day I'll be here," he said.

Amy put her head back on his shoulder.

She felt him take a deep breath and then he added, "But just in case I'm not . . ." he began.

Amy clutched him. "Don't say it," she whispered.

"I have to say it. If something happens to me, I want you to know that after last night I could go through the rest of my life and never ask for more. The memory of what you gave me will sustain me through anything."

"Don't talk that way," Amy said, putting her hand over his mouth. "We'll make other memories—we'll have more time together." She started to cry.

"Shh, I don't want to upset you."

"You *are* upsetting me," she replied, sniffling childishly.

"Amelia, we can't be blind to our circumstances. I don't want to leave here regretting that I didn't tell you how I felt when I had the chance."

Amy was silent.

"I love you and I want you to carry that

knowledge in your heart always, no matter what happens," he said.

"I will," she said, standing on tiptoe to kiss him. He kissed her back, but refused to be drawn into a further embrace when she clung to him. He held her off gently and said, "Let's go. Your aunt can't have that many correspondents; she won't be writing forever." He picked up the leftover food he had wrapped in a pillowcase and walked to the door.

Amy followed him reluctantly, wiping her eyes. She opened the door and went into the hall, looking over the stairwell and down into the entry foyer. Through the glass panels on either side of the front door she could see carriage wheels and the forelegs of horses.

She turned and waved Malik back. "James's carriage is outside," she whispered.

Malik went back behind the door.

Amy waited until she saw James walk out of the house, his fedora on his head and his cane in hand. Then she signaled for Malik to follow her.

They went down the stairs and through the house as quickly as possible, Amy crooking her finger to indicate the narrow passage which led to the shed. She opened the flower room door, and the odor of humus and fertilizer overwhelmed them. Amy picked her way through the piles of clay pots, rubber boots, and racks of tools littering the cement floor to lead Malik to the outer door.

"Here it is," she said, her face mirroring her feelings at the prospect of his departure.

He sank his hand into the mass of hair at the back of her neck and wrapped the golden strands around his fist.

"*Allaha ismarladik,*" he said. "God protect you."

Amy touched his cheek. "And you."

He lifted her hand to his lips. "I'll be back," he said, and went through the door.

Chapter Ten

In the days that followed Malik's departure, Amy became a model citizen, eager to do everything Bea requested and loath to call attention to herself. Aside from a few minor escapades, like a midnight excursion with a ladder to dispose of Malik's rope and another nocturnal jaunt to wash her bloodstained sheet in the bathtub, Amy's behavior was impeccable. She replaced the sheet and missing pillowcase with duplicate items from Bea's favorite shop in Pera, but if Listak found Amy's linen suddenly fresher than it had been, she made no mention of it.

Beatrice, obviously relieved by Amy's increased appetite and newly relaxed appearance, threw herself into the social whirl with renewed vigor. She attributed Amy's resurgence to a finally complete, if delayed, recovery from her unfortunate experience with the rebels. She included Amy in her activities even more than before, seemingly proud of her niece's youth and beauty and finishing-school polish. And Amy tried hard to please, sincerely grateful for Beatrice's innocent efforts on her behalf and feeling slightly guilty that she was deluding her aunt.

But Amy knew that misleading her relatives was not a choice, but a necessity. They could never understand the way she felt about Malik; they regarded him as a criminal who preyed on Western travelers, on their friends and acquaintances. While they had no respect for the Sultan, they felt that the tactics of his enemies placed them also beyond the pale of civilized behavior. Amy accepted this and worked around it. They didn't know Malik or his background and experiences. They couldn't possibly grasp the strength of his motivation or the extent of his desperation. But Amy's love for him was the most important thing in her life, and if she had to deceive her family in order to be with him, she would.

One afternoon, about three weeks after she had last seen Malik, Amy was dressing for one of Bea's charity teas and wondering how long it would be before she saw her lover again. She trusted Malik and believed that he planned to return. But when? She missed him almost beyond bearing. She got through the days, since she was busy, but the nights were endless. She kept waiting for his tap on her balcony doors, but it never came.

Was he all right? Had he been hurt or killed in one of his frequent skirmishes, betrayed by a comrade or captured by the Sultan's men? It was hell to be in love with a man who faced such an uncertain existence, but he had chosen it and she had chosen him, so she endured the situation.

Amy dragged her thoughts away from Malik and examined herself in the pier glass in her room, studying the ensemble she had purchased in Paris before boarding the train to Constantinople. It was an afternoon dress of navy watered silk, with a high-collared bodice featuring a short, flared peplum and empire puff sleeves. Its fitted waist flowed into a plain, bias cut *fin-de-siècle* skirt. She had forgotten the dress until she unpacked one of the trunks Mrs. Spaulding had brought to the house in her absence. There she found it, still wrapped in Worth's pink tissue paper and resting in the signature box. It was a little too big when she tried it on again; she had put darts in the waist and made a few other alterations before donning it today. She was happy to see that the sewing skills she had learned at Miss Pickard's still served her well; she was the very picture of a fashion plate, sure to make Beatrice proud. She piled her hair on top of her head in the current upswept style and added her mother's favorite earrings, triple pearl clusters with pink jade drops.

She was ready.

As Amy picked up her reticule and prepared to go downstairs and greet Bea's guests, she couldn't help comparing the image in the mirror with the young woman who had left the rebel camp wearing Risa's wedding dress. Were they the same woman? Amy knew in her heart that they were, but she also knew that the rest of the world would have a difficult time reconciling the two contrasting aspects of her life.

Beatrice's guests were arriving as Amy descended the staircase, coming through the front door in their cone skirts and bishop sleeves, their carriages lined up in the circular drive leading to the house. Amy joined Bea and stood at her side, shaking the hands of the well-to-do matrons who filled the foyer, all of them nodding and smiling graciously as they were greeted. Amy had been trained to do this sort of thing in her sleep, and as she steered the women into the dining room for finger sandwiches and lemon cake and Earl Grey tea, she wondered what these stalwart wives and mothers would think of her wild night with Malik Bey. Would they be shocked, alarmed, disappointed? Envious? Or did they all have hidden memories of a secret adventure tucked away somewhere in their graying, well-coiffed heads?

Amy had an idea that some of them must; they had all once been young.

"I'm so tired of all this rain," Mrs. Ballinger said to Amy as she selected a watercress sandwich with the crusts removed. "It rained in England, of course, but it was a different sort of rain, soft and misty, not like the awful downpours you get here. Thank God the sun is out today."

Amy nodded and handed her a napkin, looking after her as she moved down the refreshment table. Mrs. Ballinger was the wife of the brigadier in charge of the British garrison in Constantinople, and she was the chairwoman of the charity fundraiser the women were meeting to discuss. The Victoria Mission Ball was held each autumn at the British embassy to benefit the foundling home attached to Her Majesty's Lying-In Hospital, the maternity facility which served the soldiers' wives. The foundling home had been established to care for the half-British by-blows the soldiers often left behind, and it had been expanded to accept orphaned or unwanted local children as well. It ran exclusively on contributions and its worthy cause appealed to the bored and underutilized wives of the British and American officers and businessmen stranded on foreign soil. The ball was the social event of the fall season and required a good deal of time to plan.

Beatrice had chaired the event the previous year.

Amy made small talk with the guests as they sampled the light fare before settling down to finalize their plans for the event. She was accepting a tray of iced ginger cookies from Listak when she heard Mrs. Ballinger say, "Did you see the news of the latest rebel raid in the paper this morning? That man Bey robbed a train full of tourists on their way to Hagia Sofia and absconded with all their valuables. One of the female passengers fainted and had to be taken to hospital."

Amy set the tray on the table and edged closer to the conversation as Mrs. Ballinger's listeners shook their heads and clicked their tongues. Amy saved all the newspapers James brought into the house to scan them for reports of Malik's exploits, but this morning James had folded the *Monitor* and stuck it into his briefcase to take to his office. She had intended to get another copy.

"I mean to say, it's not safe to travel anywhere with that man at large," Mrs. Ballinger went on. "I have wanted for some time to leave the city and view some of the outlying sights, Byzantine churches and such, but my husband will not allow it. He says that Bey sends these hooligans everywhere, and trains and coaches are their main targets. You'd think that with all the Sultan's soldiers, as well as the foreign forces here, someone could put Bey behind bars."

"It's a scandal," Mrs. Lambert agreed. "My neighbor wanted to send for her daughter, who had finished school in Sussex and planned to rejoin her parents here, but it would mean a coach trip, and with all the kidnappings . . ." She stopped short and looked at Amy, her face flushing scarlet. She fell silent.

"Oh, my dear, I am so terribly sorry," Mrs. Ballinger said quickly to Amy, looking equally chagrined. "I never meant to bring up an unpleasant subject. It was quite thoughtless of me to forget your recent experience. I'm very sure you don't want to be reminded about it."

"That's all right, Mrs. Ballinger, I know you didn't mean to upset me. But have you ever wondered why the rebels resort to such methods to obtain money? They have no other means of raising cash to oppose the Sultan, and I'm sure you would agree that almost any other form of government established here would be superior to his."

Both women stared at her, speechless with shock.

"Amelia, could you come here a moment?" Beatrice said from the doorway.

"Excuse me, ladies," Amy said smoothly, and joined her aunt in the hall.

"Amelia, what on earth are you doing?" Bea demanded, *sotto voce*, her expression bewildered and more than a little annoyed. "It sounded to me like you were defending those awful people who abducted you!"

"I wasn't defending the rebels, merely explaining their situation. Those women know how poor the locals are; they must look out their carriage windows as they drive through the streets and see them. If they were as hopeless and as miserable as the average Turkish citizen, maybe they too would resort to stealing in an attempt to change their lives."

"Mrs. Ballinger and Mrs. Lambert have both been here far longer than you have. They hardly need you to expound on Ottoman politics for their edification," Bea said tartly. "Now perhaps you should go upstairs and lie down. You are obviously not feeling well. I'll make your excuses."

Amy walked through the hall and ascended the staircase obediently, her campaign to please Beatrice in ruins. She stopped on the landing to look down at the first floor; Beatrice had gone back into the dining room and conversation had resumed. Satisfied that she hadn't disrupted the proceedings, Amy moved on, cursing her loose tongue.

What was wrong with her? She knew that nothing she said was going to change the fixed opinions of people like her aunt's guests, and if she kept making speeches justifying the rebels' conduct, her cherished secret would not be a secret long.

She went into her room and flung herself across the bed, wondering why she had come so close to revealing too much. She had been so careful, steeling herself to ignore thoughtless remarks and dinner table chatter, and yet when those well-bred ladies had torn into Malik, she simply couldn't keep quiet.

Why did she have such a lapse? Was it because sustaining the role of carefree debutante became more difficult every day that she didn't see Malik? At first his visit had buoyed her spirits and made it easier to play the part expected of her, but as time dragged on and he didn't come again, the strain of missing him was obviously telling on her nerves.

Amy sat up and unbuttoned her kid boots, dropping them on the floor. It would be several hours before the women left and she could sneak downstairs to see if James had brought the newspaper back. She wanted to see where the train robbery had taken place; in some strange way it helped her to know where Malik was, or at least where he had been.

But it only helped a little.

If he didn't contact her soon, she wasn't sure what she would do.

Kalid accepted the silver tray from the servant and removed the stack of envelopes, nodding in dismissal as he returned the salver. The girl retreated, bowing, and as she closed the door behind her, Kalid called to his wife, "The mail has arrived."

Sarah hurried in from the next room. A new shipment of mail was always an event for her; it meant a great deal to hear from friends and family when she was now so far away from them.

"Roxalena," Kalid said, handing her an envelope with a Cypriot postmark.

Sarah snatched it eagerly.

"Your friend Sophie from Boston," he said as he examined another missive, naming one of Sarah's former colleagues who still taught in the school where Sarah had once worked.

"You can see through paper?" Sarah asked archly.

"Brookline," Kalid said, tapping the canceled stamp as he gave her the letter.

Sarah took it and put it into her pile.

"Oh, and our invitation to the Victoria Mission Ball," he added, grinning wickedly as he held holding aloft a cream vellum envelope addressed in flowing script with an Italianate hand.

Sarah groaned and closed her eyes. "Is it time for that again already?"

"I'm afraid so, my darling. Time for the superior Westerners to display to the natives that they have not abandoned civilization and culture out here in the wilds of the Ottoman Empire." He widened his eyes dramatically.

"And time for the Sultan to show up with an outrageous entourage and terrify all the tea-sipping ladies."

"It is for a good cause," Kalid said, taking a drink of his coffee.

"I tell myself that every year," Sarah said, sitting next to him on the divan and putting her head on his shoulder.

"And every year you go and are the most beautiful woman there," Kalid said, bending to kiss the tip of her nose.

Sarah picked up the invitation, reading it. "Mrs. Ballinger is chairwoman this time," she commented.

"That old bat with the wart on her chin who talks like her mouth is full of marbles?" Kalid said.

"Yes. You remember—her husband is commander of the British garrison," Sarah replied, smiling at his description of the brigadier's venerable wife.

"I remember both of them. He always asks me how I enjoyed Oxford, as if I were there yesterday. I imagine he thinks it's the only thing we have in common."

"It probably is," Sarah said.

"My mother was as British as London Bridge, which I'm tempted to remind all of them every time they start waving the flag and looking at me as if I had just climbed down out of the trees."

"The women look at you like that because you are the most exotic, compelling, and sexual creature they have ever seen, and the men look at you like that because they know it." Sarah sat up and kissed him on the lips.

He laughed, kissing her back. "I thought nice American ladies weren't supposed to tell lies."

"I'm not lying; I'm speaking from experience." She lay back in his arms comfortably.

"So shall I say we'll go?" Kalid asked, nodding at the invitation still in her hand. "It seems a little ridiculous to attend a social function with Abdul Hammid when I might be shooting at him soon, but until that happens I suppose all the appearances must be preserved."

"Yes, let's go," Sarah replied. "I see no reason to break our perfect attendance record, and it will give me a chance to talk to Amelia."

"And check on the progress of the forbidden liaison?" Kalid said teasingly.

"Of course."

"You're a hopeless romantic."

"I know."

"And I'm so glad you are. Only a hopeless romantic would have left her old life behind entirely to begin a new one halfway around the world with the man she loved."

"I hope things work out as well for Amelia."

"You really like her, don't you?"

"She reminds me of me."

"Then she will be fine." He stood up, taking

her hand and pulling her with him. "If she has one quarter of your grit and determination, she will stick with Bey through any trouble and come out all right in the end."

"Where are we going?" Sarah asked, her mind still on the young lovers.

"Yasmin went to try on her new clothes for the Feast of the Flowers. I told her we would come and see her."

"I hope Memtaz can restrain herself; she tends to get carried away. When I think of some of the outfits she made me wear when I was in the harem . . ."

"I promise no transparent yeleks on the child," Kalid said dryly.

"And no jewel in the navel," Sarah added.

"Why don't we just put a corset and crinoline on her and one of those blouses that button up to the nose?" he said, as they left the salon and entered the hall.

"It isn't funny, Kalid. A shirtwaist might not be a bad idea. Between Memtaz and your grandmother, Yasmin will look like an odalisque before she's twelve."

"And you want her to look like a schoolmarm."

"You married a schoolmarm."

"I undressed her first."

Sarah burst out laughing. "I can never win an argument with you," she said.

"That's part of my charm."

They turned a corner and headed for the classroom, where Memtaz was keeping the children.

Malik handed Anwar the canvas bag and said, "Three pocket watches, two cameos, several gold rings set with stones, and a large sapphire brooch."

Anwar nodded. "How much cash?" he asked.

Malik looked down at the piles of paper on the table before him. "Forty British pounds, twenty-eight American dollars, and about a hundred kurush."

Anwar shook his head. "That's not much, considering that the risk of getting caught goes up with each raid. The janissaries are watching the trains."

Malik nodded. "And the travelers know about us by now and carry as little as possible with them."

Silence reigned as they thought about the problem; Malik looked out of the tent at the unfamiliar trees, wondering how else he could raise money. The rebels had moved their base soon after Amelia left, and he felt uneasy in the new surroundings.

His memories of her were associated with the old camp.

"Why didn't you rob the girl's house when you were in Pera?" Anwar asked.

Malik threw him a dirty look.

"Just a few pieces of silver? A couple of rings? They'd never miss them."

"Amelia's family is off the target list permanently, Anwar. Forget it."

"We have no reason to spare her relatives. *They're* not in love with you, and *they* didn't save my life."

"No."

"Well, we have to do better than this," Anwar said angrily, sweeping the paper money from the table.

"We will. I'll think of something."

Anwar sat on an upturned crate and looked at Malik. "Are you going back there again?" he asked.

"Where?"

"To her house."

"When I can."

Anwar sighed. "It's like putting your neck under the blade."

"I have to see her."

"I know that. I understand. But does it have to be at the risk of your life?"

"I risk my life every day, and so do you."

Anwar leaned forward, his elbows on his knees. "Look, I know you love Amelia, but there's something you should hear. Yuri just told me there's a rumor that the Sultan is tripling the number of janissaries in the Pera section. The Europeans have been complaining about the rising crime rate. Hammid is anxious to keep them happy and those Western trade dollars rolling into his treasury."

"He's turning us all into thieves," Malik said disgustedly.

"If the rumor is true, it will be even more difficult for you to get to her house," Anwar pointed out to him.

Malik shrugged.

"Let me go with you next time."

"No. If something goes wrong, the cause can't afford to lose both of us."

"So you think I can replace you if you die?" Anwar asked incredulously.

"Of course."

"Malik, you are blind. These people here listen to you because you're *you*, because they have faith in *you*. If you are killed, the band will fall apart and the cause will die."

"That's not true. No one man is that important."

Anwar stood and threw up his hands. "Fine. Maybe you're right. But if she means that much to you, go and get her. For good. She wanted to stay with you before—she'll come with you now. She understands what life is like with us. She's already lived it. You can't go on this way, running back and forth between her life and yours, tempting the Sultan's men to catch you at it every time. It's sheer madness."

There was a long pause before Malik said quietly, "I know that. I know."

Anwar exchanged a telling look with him and then bent to retrieve the bills from the ground.

"James has rung for the carriage, Amelia—are you ready yet?" Beatrice called down the hall.

"I'm coming," Amy replied, picking up her fan and moire reticule. She hadn't dressed for a formal event since she left Boston, and she had almost forgotten how heavy a gown of double-faced satin felt on the body. The pale rose ensemble she wore featured a scooped neckline and ornamental draped and gathered sleeves which stopped at the elbow. The short train on the trumpet skirt ended in the same draped and beribboned effect as the sleeves. Opera-length kid gloves and matching glazed-kid slippers completed the effect.

Amy picked up her cape, which was light-weight rose wool lined with satin to match her dress, and draped it over her arm. The marcasite hairpins which held her pompadour in place glittered as she turned her head, complementing the marcasite earrings and necklace she wore. She didn't even glance in the mirror as she left; if Malik wasn't going to see her, she was only concerned with making a nice impression.

"Oh, don't you look lovely," Beatrice said, beaming, as Amy met her in the front hall. "What a picture! Your dance card is sure to be full."

Amy smiled, glad that she had gone along with the dress her aunt had selected. Amy had been on her best behavior since her encounter with Mrs. Ballinger two weeks earlier, and it seemed that Beatrice had forgotten Amy's faux pas. Her aunt, incandescent with diamonds, was attired in a gunmetal-gray faille gown with dove-gray feathers in her upswept hair. Her eyes shone, and she was flushed with excitement. These social events were the high point of her life, a diversion which made her exile in Constantinople bearable, and Amy sincerely hoped the evening was a success.

James emerged from his den, attired in a swallowtail coat with silk-faced lapels, slim trousers, and a boiled shirt. He was carrying a top hat.

"Ladies?" he said, and offered Bea his arm.

The evening was cool, as the day had been for early October, and Amy tied the satin bow of her cape at the neck as she settled in for the ride on the seat across from James and Bea. It was a short trip to the British embassy, through the best sections of Pera to the heart of the ancient city, and Amy looked out at the well-appointed, gaslit homes they passed on the way, wondering where Malik was and what he was doing. The clopping of the horses' hooves and the swaying of the carriage almost made her feel that she was back in Boston, going out for the evening with her parents. But visible through her window were not the red brick colonials of Beacon Hill, but narrow cobbled streets dating back to the Byzantine era.

The embassy was ablaze, gas jets turned up to the highest setting, a yellow glow visible through every corniced window. The union jack was draped from the second floor balcony, fluttering slightly in the evening breeze above fluted Doric columns. Elegant carriages lined the crushed stone drive leading up to the porticoed entrance, its double doors standing open to admit the new arrivals. Amy and her companions walked up the wide stone steps past guards in red coats and white pith helmets and handed their wraps to a footman in the foyer. Then they passed beneath the largest chandelier she had ever seen and through an anteroom lined with gilt-framed portraits and into the reception hall.

Mrs. Ballinger stood on the red carpet in front of a marble bust of the Duke of Wellington, her smartly uniformed husband beside her as she greeted the guests and took their donation cards. As she handed Amy her dance schedule, Amy noticed that the older woman was wearing an ivory gown which set off to perfection the magnificent Burmese ruby around her neck. It was a cabochon stone the size of a pigeon's egg, set in a gold filigree base. Amy wondered how many of Malik's men could be outfitted and fed with the fortune used to purchase it, and then resolved to not to think along those lines for the rest of the evening. Such ruminations might lead to another outburst in defense of the rebels, and she couldn't afford to embarrass Beatrice twice.

James and Bea lingered with Mrs. Ballinger, and Amy moved on down the receiving line. The British Ambassador was at the other end of it, medals gleaming on a scarlet sash, and next to him stood his American colleague, Secretary Danforth.

"How do you do, young lady?" the secretary said. "I'm so glad to see you back among us again. Your disappearance had your uncle very worried, and I must say it was a great relief to all of us at the American consulate to learn that you were returned to him safe and sound."

"Thank you, Mr. Secretary," Amy said. "I wanted to come to your office personally to express my gratitude for your help, but my uncle told me you were out of the country for a while."

"Yes, I just returned. And thanks are not necessary, Miss Ryder. I'm afraid I did very little to effect your release. The credit for that goes to the Pasha of Bursa."

"Is he here?" Amy asked.

"Yes, he and his wife just arrived." His smile widened. "The women of your family are very lovely."

"How kind of you to say so," Amy replied. "With your permission, I think I'll go into the ballroom and look for Kalid and Sarah."

"By all means," the secretary said, nodding. "So nice to have met you."

Amy left him and went into the ballroom, where another Waterford crystal fixture poured gaslight onto the celebrants. The-floor-to-ceiling windows which looked out onto the courtyard were draped with crimson satin sashed with gold, and gilt chairs lined the dance floor for those participants who wished to take a rest. The orchestra launched into a waltz as Martin Fitzwater, one of the young officers of the British garrison whom she had met previously, materialized at her side to claim the dance listed on her card. Amy checked off his name with the little marker attached to the tasseled card by a golden cord and stepped into his arms.

She had danced several times when she spotted Sarah standing with a group of women near the ballroom entrance. Amy made her way through the crowd, and when Sarah saw her coming she detached herself from her companions and headed for Amy, holding out both her hands.

Sarah was wearing a pale green taffeta gown with a funnel neckline and triple-tier sleeves trimmed in Chantilly lace, its bell skirt split by a center panel of dark green silk.

"My dear, how lovely you look!" Sarah said. "I'm so glad to see you. I've been searching for you for over an hour." She kissed Amy on the cheek.

"It's not easy to find anyone in this crowd," Amy replied. "Where is Kalid?"

Sarah nodded to her left and Amy saw the pasha, dressed in a deep blue ceremonial robe bordered with silver, talking with a man in a sack suit wearing a monocle. When Kalid looked up and saw Amy, he gave her a very Western wink over the other man's head.

"He's such a flirt," Sarah muttered with mock indignation, and Amy giggled.

"And how are you?" Sarah asked, raising one delicate eyebrow. "Had any visitors?"

Amy smiled and looked down, the heat coming up in her face. "Yes," she said shyly.

Sarah pressed her hand. "Did he come to the house?" she murmured.

Amy nodded. "He climbed the balcony to my room and came in through the French doors."

Sarah closed her eyes. "An Ottoman Romeo," she said, sighing. She opened her eyes again. "He got away safely?"

Amy nodded. "I took him out through the flower room, but I haven't heard from him since. I'm worried."

"Don't worry," Sarah said reassuringly. "From everything I've heard, he's amazingly resourceful and I'm sure he's fine." She smiled. "Just busy."

Amy smiled back at her, then they both

turned as a man in his sixties came into the room wearing a white silk caftan, the sleeves slashed to reveal amber silk armlets matching the amber turban on his head. A white aigrette in the turban was studded with emeralds, as was the sheath containing his sword, and rings dazzled from his every finger. He was flanked by two massive men in loose shirts with baggy trousers fitted to their ankles, red sashes showing under their embroidered black waistcoats.

"The Sultan?" Amy asked.

Sarah nodded. "He never goes anywhere without his eunuchs, as if to remind everyone that he's living in the past. At least he's on his own two feet. He used to appear at all Western functions carried in a sedan chair."

"What is he doing here?"

"He's the country's ruler. If the embassy wants to remain open, the ambassador can't exclude him from an event like this," Sarah said simply.

"He doesn't look evil," Amy said, with a slight shudder.

"Men like him never do," Sarah replied grimly.

Someone tapped Amy on the shoulder, and she turned to find Martin back again. He bowed slightly.

"I know I signed up for just one dance," he said in his King's College accent, "but as you are free, Miss Ryder, may I have the pleasure once more?"

Amy looked at Sarah, who said, "Go ahead. But before you do, have you seen James?"

"No, not since I left him in the receiving line," Amy replied, and stepped into Martin's arms.

Martin made pleasant chatter about his posting to Turkey and his family back home in the West Riding of Yorkshire as he whirled her around the floor. When the musicians took a break, he invited Amy to join him for refreshments in the next room, but Amy declined, saying that she wanted to find her aunt. As Martin walked off, disappointed, Amy looked around vainly for Beatrice, then decided instead to get a breath of air on the terrace. The ballroom was stuffy from the crush of people despite the cool weather, and she walked to the end of the long hall so she could slip through the last set of doors unnoticed.

As soon as she set foot on the flagstones, she was grabbed from behind and a large male hand was clamped over her mouth. She struggled vainly as she was dragged into a clump of bushes by the side of the garden path.

"Amelia, stop wriggling!" Malik's voice said in her ear. "It's me."

Amy relaxed. He let her go, and she turned to throw her arms around his neck.

"Malik—oh, I'm so glad you're here!" she gasped, clasping him close. "I've been going crazy, imagining all sorts of horrible things. I haven't seen you, I've had no word from you—where on earth have you been?"

"Shh! Do want someone to hear us?" he whispered, holding her off to look at her. He took in her clothes and jewelry, her elaborate hair. "You look so beautiful," he added softly.

Amy's eyes widened and she put her hand to her throat. "Malik, you have to go!"

"I just got here," he said, smiling.

"But you don't understand—the Sultan is inside!"

"I know that," he said calmly. "I saw him arrive."

"But this is too dangerous. You could be picked up at any moment."

"Amelia, listen to me. I haven't been able to get near your house for the past several weeks. I had no alternative but to take this chance."

She stared at him.

"Several extra patrols of janissaries have been added to the Pera sector since the last time I saw you," Malik said. "Your street is the most heavily guarded, probably because it's the wealthiest. I've tried three times to come to your house and haven't been able to get through. I couldn't risk sending a note or a message to the house, so when I read in the newspaper about this party, I came because I knew you would be here."

A shadow passed across the windows behind

them, and they both drew back.

"You have been watching me from outside all night?" Amy whispered, relaxing as the shadow moved away.

He nodded.

"Just waiting for the chance to get me alone?"

He nodded again.

"Oh, Malik, I love you so," she said, standing on tiptoe to kiss him. He kissed her back, longingly, until she remembered their circumstances and pulled away from him.

"You have to go," she said. "It's too risky for you to be here and I'll be missed before long."

"Then I have to say good-bye for a while," he replied.

"No, no! If you can't come to the house, just tell me where to meet you tonight and I'll get there."

"Don't be ridiculous, Amelia. You can't run around the city by yourself after dark. You don't know the area beyond a few streets in Pera. You wouldn't last five minutes before being picked up by a patrol—or much worse."

"Then think of something!" she said, almost in tears. "I have to be with you tonight."

He considered a moment, then looked at the line of carriages waiting in the embassy drive, horses lazily chomping turf, coachmen seated on their boxes or conversing in groups.

"Did you arrive in one of those?" he asked, nodding toward the waiting conveyances.

"Yes, with James and Aunt Bea."

"Can you tell your aunt that you're not feeling well and want to go home early?" he asked.

"Yes, I suppose so. Why?"

"If you can ask them to go home with some of their friends and take the coach, I'll find a way to get into it before you leave here. Then you can slip me into the house."

Amy looked up at him, hope growing inside her. "Good," she said. "Good idea."

"Which one is it?" he asked.

Amy pointed. "Second to last before the drive curves left, with the blue doors."

He nodded. "I see it. Now go."

Amy kissed him again, quickly, and said, "I'll see you soon." She picked up her skirts and hurried back across the terrace, stepping inside just as the orchestra began to play a brisk czardas. She made her way around the edge of the dance floor, sighing with relief when she saw Beatrice talking with Mrs. Lambert. She went up to the two women and waited for her aunt to notice her.

"Amelia! I haven't seen you all night, and I've been wanting to talk with you. I've received nothing but compliments about you, and James and I are so proud."

"Thank you, Aunt Bea. I've been looking for you too. I'd like to ask a favor."

"What is it?"

"I wonder if I might leave early. I have a bit

of a headache. I've checked off all my dances, and I'll say good-bye to Mrs. Ballinger before I go."

"Of course, dear. I'm sorry to hear that you're not feeling well," Bea replied. "I'll send James to get your wrap."

"May I take the carriage?" Amy asked, holding her breath.

"Certainly. James and I will get a ride with someone else, or you can send the driver back for us."

Amy exhaled as quietly as possible.

"No need," Mrs. Lambert interjected. "William and I will drop you off at home, Bea."

Amy leaned forward to kiss her aunt and said, "I had a lovely time. I'll see you in the morning."

"Good night, dear," her aunt replied.

Amy found Mrs. Ballinger and had a mercifully brief conversation, and by the time she left the ballroom James was waiting in the embassy foyer with her cape.

"Maybe I should see you home," he said, as he dropped the wrap over her shoulders.

Amy froze. "No need, Uncle James. I don't want you to leave the party. I'll be quite safe."

"Are you sure? If anything else happens to you, Beatrice will be quite beside herself."

"I'm sure. It's a short trip and your driver has a pistol."

"Very well. But let me at least hand you into the carriage," James said.

Amy gritted her teeth but took his proferred arm, aware that if she protested too much, James was sure to think something was amiss. She waited as James instructed the driver and then ascended the portable steps, turning to smile at Bea's husband as he closed the door after her.

"Good night," she said, and waved.

"Good night, Amelia."

The driver removed the steps and climbed onto his box. He clucked to the horse as James went back up the steps. Amelia looked around frantically, trying to spot Malik by the light of the gas lamps lining the embassy drive as the horses ambled forward.

Suddenly both mares reared, and the driver yanked on the reins. The coach lurched to a sudden stop, and the driver jumped down to the ground.

"What is it?" Amy called to him.

"Maybe something in the path, miss, not to worry," the driver called back in his singsong English. "I'll have a look." He walked forward, holding his oil lamp aloft.

At the same instant the coach door opened, and Malik bolted through it, flinging himself flat on the floor.

"What did you do?" Amy hissed, lifting her legs onto the seat to accommodate him.

"I threw a rock onto the drive to spook the horses," he said. "Now be quiet and let's hope he doesn't suspect anything."

Amy removed her cape and dropped it over the man at her feet. She watched the driver look around and then return to say to her, "Can't see a thing, miss. Must have been an animal in the bushes that frightened the horses."

"All right," Amy replied. "Thanks for checking. You may proceed."

The coachman touched his cap, and the vehicle rocked as he climbed back up to his seat. When the horses started forward again, she murmured to Malik, "I think we're all right. Just stay where you are, and I'll get you out somehow when we arrive."

There was no reply, but a slim brown hand reached up and squeezed her ankle.

The trip back to the Woolcott home seemed to increase by several kilometers, and as they traveled through the streets near the house, Amy saw the patrolling janissaries Malik had mentioned. She hadn't been out this late since Malik's last visit and had not known of their presence. But they knew about her, or rather her family, as well as its mode of transportation. She saw two of the Sultan's men salute her driver as they passed.

When the coach finally pulled into the porte cochere next to the house, Amy sagged with relief. As the driver came to the door to hand her down, she said quickly, "May I ask a favor of you?"

"Yes, miss?"

"Could you go into the house and get my heavy gray cape from the entry hall closet? I know it's only a short walk inside, but I'm really quite chilled, possibly feverish, and the one I have here is too light."

The driver, an elderly Armenian who had spent his life humoring the baffling whims of rich Westerners in Pera, nodded resignedly. As soon as he was of sight, Amy pulled her wrap off Malik and said, "Go. Wait outside the flower room entrance. I'll let you into the house as soon as I can."

He scrambled out the door, and she saw him run for the shrubbery. When the driver returned with her cape, she thanked him effusively, slipping it on as if it were made of ermine.

"Oh, that's wonderful. Thank you," she said.

"You're welcome, miss."

"I appreciate your thoughtfulness," Amy added as she descended from the coach. "You can put up the horses now, as you won't have to go out again. Good night."

"Good night, miss," he said, leading the mares forward as she went into the house.

The house was quiet when she entered it; the servants were asleep, and Amy hoped that James and Bea would not return for another couple of hours. Amy stood at the kitchen window and saw a light appear in the stable. She waited, watching for the progress of the coachman's lamp from the stalls and up the outside steps to the room over the barn. When she saw the fuzzy glow stop in one place and felt sure that the driver was in for the night, she ran to the flower room door and yanked it open joyfully.

Malik stepped over the threshold and scooped her into his arms. She closed her eyes and pressed her face into his shoulder.

"I'm sorry it took so long. I had to wait for the coachman to go up to his room," she said, her words muffled by his shirt. "I was afraid he might see me open the door to you—this side of the house is visible from the stables but not from the window in his room."

"It's all right," Malik replied, setting her on her feet. "I saw him go. I knew why you were waiting."

They looked at each other in the dark kitchen.

"Let's go upstairs," he said huskily.

Amy took his hand and led him through the house and up to the landing, both of them treading lightly, alert to a creak in the floors or any other sound that might signal they were about to have company. They fled along the gallery and into Amy's room; she felt safe only when she had turned the key in the lock and sought the haven of Malik's arms once more.

He kissed her immediately, picking her up and carrying her to the bed. They embraced as fully as possible with Amy trapped in her voluminous gown. Finally Malik, frustrated by the dress, panted, "How do I get this off?"

She got up from the bed and turned away from him. "There are hooks and eyes down the back," he said.

He stood behind her and said, "Hooks and eyes?"

She pointed over her shoulder.

He wrestled with the metal closures and finally said, "I can't do it."

"Rip it," Amy said.

She heard the sound of cloth tearing, then felt his mouth on her bare shoulder as he pulled the bodice down to her waist. He yanked again and the capacious skirt fell to the floor.

"And what is all this?" he said, pulling at her strapless, heavily boned corset. He began to laugh. "It must take you an hour to get dressed."

"It laces down the back," Amy told him, ignoring his amusement. "Listak helps me."

He made a few swift gestures behind her, and the corset fell off into her hands.

"What did you do?" she asked.

"I cut the laces with my knife," he replied. He turned her to face him and picked her up again, setting her on the bed. He pulled off her stockings, discarding the rest of her clothes methodically until she was naked. Then he dropped next to her and said, "I think I'll take a nap now. I need a rest after all that work."

Amy flung herself on top of him and kissed the warm hollow of his throat, slipping her hands under his loosened shirt and caressing him.

"Still feeling tired?" she purred, straddling him.

"I'm reviving," he murmured, sucking in his breath as she moved one hand under the waistband of his pants.

"How about now?" she whispered.

"I'm revived," he answered, sighing and closing his eyes as she touched him.

"So I can tell," she said. "In fact, this part of your anatomy never seemed tired at all."

He seized her shoulders and rolled her under him, switching positions with her in an instant.

"You're a quick study," he said, nibbling the fleshy lobe of her ear.

"Americans learn fast. But I still feel I need more practice," she answered, holding his head against her as he turned his attention to her throat, her breasts. A silence fell as he made love to her; when he raised his head again, his face was serious. All traces of his teasing mood had vanished.

"I don't want anyone else to touch you like this," he said thickly.

"No one else has, and no one else will," she answered him softly.

"Promise me," he said, bending to wrap his arms around her waist, his mouth traveling down her supine body, leaving a hot, moist trail. "Promise me."

"I promise," Amy whispered, and then gave herself up to pleasure.

Amy was lying in Malik's arms, not sleeping, content to feel his body next to hers, when the sound of a carriage on the drive made her sit up and listen. She climbed out of bed, going to her dressing area where the window faced the front of the house.

"What is it?" Malik asked her, propping himself up on one elbow.

Amy saw James emerge from the Lamberts' carriage, then hold up his arms to help Beatrice down to the ground.

"My aunt and uncle are back home," Amy said, rejoining Malik. "We'll have to be very quiet until they're asleep."

"Were we making a lot of noise?" Malik asked, smiling. He held out his arm to enfold her. "I thought I was very quiet when I dismembered your dress."

"I'll have to have that repaired before Beatrice sees it," Amy replied. "She picked it out for me."

"I liked you much better in my camp, with nothing under your gown but you," he said.

Amy touched the scar left by the knife wound he got in the bazaar. "This healed nicely," she said.

"I had a wonderful nurse," he said.

"You have quite a few scars," Amy observed.

"And you're thin," he answered, tracing her collarbone with his forefinger. "I noticed the last time I was here that you had lost weight."

"I'm pining for you," she said, kissing his cheek. "Are you pining for me?"

He looked at her, his dark eyes intent.

"Yes," he admitted, and her heart turned over at his guileless tone as he said the word.

"I watched you for a long time through the window tonight," he added. "I saw you dancing with that Brit."

It took Amy a long moment to recall whom he meant. "Martin Fitzwater?"

Malik shrugged. "Sandy hair, long nose, weak chin."

Amy giggled at his account of the soldier's appearance. "That's Martin."

"You seemed to be enjoying yourself."

She stared up at him, trying to determine if he were serious. It seemed he was.

"Malik, you have to be joking. Martin Fitzwater is the biggest bore in the British army. He means well, but all he talks about is his family lineage. It's a fascinating subject to him, maybe, but a little less so to the rest of the world."

"You looked good with him. You looked right, you in that gorgeous dress and Fitzwilly in his scarlet uniform, sweeping around the floor together. I could tell he was interested in you."

"Malik, don't start this again. Are you going

to ruin the time we have together with this nonsense? I was putting on a performance, for my aunt and all the people there, trying to fit the image they have of what Beatrice's niece should be."

He sat up, clenching his fists, his face dark. "Can you imagine what it's like for me to be away from you, knowing that in my absence all the young bucks in both garrisons are chasing you down like hounds after a fox? Knowing that your aunt is doing everything possible to encourage them? Knowing that with each passing day your memory of me fades and the pressure on you to conform to her expectations increases? Sometimes I think I'll go mad just thinking about it."

"Don't you trust me?"

"I trust you. I don't trust your relatives, or your suitors, or anyone else who wants to separate you from me."

"Give me some credit. If they haven't influenced me so far, why should they in the future?"

"Absence doesn't make the heart grow fonder, as the deluded English like to say. It makes the heart forget. Each day that I'm gone makes you wonder if I will ever return. I know this, Amelia. You can't help but feel that way—it's human nature."

"Then take me with you," Amy said, pressing her body to his, winding her arms around his neck. "I can endure any hardship, whatever happens."

"Are you certain, Amelia? Don't make an impulsive decision that you will regret."

"How can you say that to me?" Amy demanded. "Do you think I'm some two-year-old who doesn't know her own mind?"

"I don't think that," he replied soothingly. "But you will be leaving your family and friends for a long time if you come with me, perhaps leaving them permanently. Can you stand that?"

"I can stand it, Malik. I can stand anything. I just want to be with you all the time."

His arms came around her convulsively, and he said into her ear, "Then you will. You have my word that you will."

"But when?"

"I can't say just yet. Soon. Pack a bag and hide it so you'll be ready to go in an instant."

"Do you really mean it? You're not just saying this to appease me?"

"I mean it. The next time I come here, it will be to take you away with me."

Amy drew back to kiss him and he began to make love to her again.

Malik left before anyone else in the house was awake, and after Amy saw him out she returned to bed, slipping into the dreamless sleep of a happy and satisfied woman. She rose again after James and Bea had eaten breakfast; her aunt had given orders to Listak to let Amy sleep as long as she wanted.

The weather was bright and much warmer, inspiring Amy to undertake some fall cleaning. She spent the day in meaningless chores, reliving the past night in her mind as she organized drawers, put away summer clothes, and stuffed tissue paper into shoes. She ate lunch from a tray and went back to work, finishing her tasks just as Beatrice returned from an afternoon of shopping.

Amy was humming under her breath when she joined James and Bea for dinner.

"You seem fully recovered from last night's malaise," Beatrice commented as Amy slipped into her chair.

"Oh, I feel so much better," Amy said brightly. "I woke up this morning a different person."

"A good night's sleep will do wonders for almost anybody," James commented.

Amy coughed delicately and let that pass.

James unfolded the evening paper and scanned the front page, looking up at Amy seconds later. He had a strange expression on his face.

"Please don't read the paper at the dinner table, dear," Beatrice said to him, unfolding her napkin.

Doreen Owens Malek

"What is it?" Amy asked James, ignoring her aunt.

He turned the paper so that Amy could see the headline.

MALIK BEY CAPTURED it read.

Chapter Eleven

Amy stared at the words, unable to respond, a falling sensation in the pit of her stomach.

"About time, too," Beatrice said huffily, snapping her napkin into her lap. "That man has been the scourge of the country long enough."

Amy opened her mouth, but nothing came out of it.

"I'm sure you're relieved to know that he's in custody, dear," Bea added to Amy.

James looked at his wife and then back at Amy.

"Amelia?" he said gently. "Are you all right?"

Amy swallowed, nodding.

"You've gone quite pale," Beatrice said to her. "I thought you said you were feeling better."

"I am," Amy replied, finally finding her voice.

"It's just a shock to know that he . . . has been arrested."

"He won't last long in the Sultan's bird cage," Bea said with satisfaction. "I predict that he'll be executed on the Feast of the Flowers."

"May I be excused?" Amy said suddenly, shoving back her chair and standing.

"But you haven't had a thing to eat!" Bea protested.

"I'll get something later," Amy said, turning and almost running from the room.

"That's peculiar," Bea said, shaking her head. "But who can predict the behavior of adolescent girls?"

James, who had a little more insight than his wife, and whose cousin Sarah had married her erstwhile captor, said nothing but followed Amy out of the room with his eyes.

Amy flew up the stairs, pausing on the landing to put her hand to her mouth and lean against the wall. She felt as if she were going to be ill, but managed to swallow her nausea and make it to her room. She sat on the edge of her bed and hugged herself, rocking, too stunned to cry.

It had finally happened. Malik had been caught, and it was all her fault. She didn't know the details yet, but for the news to make the evening paper, he must have been apprehended soon after he left her house that morning.

If he hadn't come into the city to see her, he

would still be a free man.

Amy wanted to do something, anything, but her mind refused to yield an idea. The Sultan was not going to release his most wanted criminal under any circumstances. Beatrice was right. He would hold Malik until the Feast of the Flowers and then execute him publicly on the national holiday. Hammid would delight in making an example of Malik, in showing his impressionable subjects what became of anyone who dared to oppose the Sultan's rule.

Amy got up suddenly and went to her writing desk, pulling out the sheets of British foolscap James had brought her from his office and uncapping her inkwell. She would write to Sarah. It was almost a month before the feast would be celebrated, and perhaps Kalid could get Amy in to see Malik before then. It would take a week for the letter to reach Bursa, but it was worth a try. Anything was worth a try, and at the moment she couldn't think of anything else.

Amy filled ten sheets of stationery with her fluid handwriting, pouring out her soul to Sarah, and when her fingers refused to function further, she folded the paper into an envelope and hid the letter in a book. When she looked up, she saw that it was eight o'clock; she had been writing for more than two hours.

She slipped into the hall and went downstairs, looking into the parlor. James and Bea were both reading by the fire. She walked down the hall to James's den, where the newspaper was lying discarded on his desk. She picked it up and took it into the foyer, reading the lead article by the light of the gas fixture overhead.

Malik had been seized at the home of Yuri's brother, who was described as a "known cohort of the rebel leader." Amy thought that someone must have seen him on his previous visit and decided to collect the reward. Or maybe Malik had been spotted elsewhere and then followed. It didn't matter now. He had been arrested because he had forsaken his safe haven in the hills in order to see her, and now she had to help him. Somehow.

The newspaper said that Malik had been taken to the imperial dungeon at Topkapi, there to await judgment.

Amy replaced the newspaper on James's desk and went back upstairs.

Everyone knew what that judgment would be.

Amy spent a sleepless night plotting and planning, to no avail; she was as powerless as the lowliest peasant in the Ottoman Empire. She appeared at breakfast, hollow-eyed but determined to carry on as if nothing had happened. She even forced down some food as Beatrice chattered on about the wonderful turnout for the Victoria Mission Ball and how the committee was going to use the proceeds. Amy was pushing a fragment of muffin around on her plate when she realized that James had spoken to her several times.

"Yes?" she said, looking up at him.

"You're in a fog this morning," he commented.

"I'm sorry. I didn't sleep very well."

"Is anything wrong, dear?" Bea asked.

Amy looked at her aunt—at her kind, well-meaning, freckled face—and thought about the yawning gulf between them.

What choice did Amy have but to lie?

"I'm fine. Just a little tired. Maybe the ball was more exhausting than I realized," Amy said.

"Speaking of the ball, I was about to tell you that Martin Fitzwater came to my office and asked for formal permission to call on you," James said.

Amy almost groaned aloud; it was all she could do to keep back the despairing sound.

"When?" she finally managed to say.

"Yesterday. I saw you dancing with him and expected his visit. I planned to tell you about it last night at dinner, but you may recall that you didn't stay."

Amy said nothing.

"Your reaction is less than enthusiastic," James observed.

"I'm just surprised."

"How could you possibly be surprised?" James asked archly. "The man was following you around the embassy ballroom like a spaniel puppy."

Beatrice giggled delightedly. Martin was her idea of a dream husband for Amy—wealthy, British, and well connected. The Woolcott stock would soar in the Western colony of Constantinople if Amy landed Martin Fitzwater.

"I thought he was dancing with other girls," Amy replied lamely.

"Only when he couldn't find you. Now what shall I tell him? I have no objection to his suit, but I don't want to encourage this young man if you aren't interested in him," James said.

"You could hardly do better than Martin, my dear," Bea added encouragingly. "He's a fine young officer with a splendid career ahead of him."

Amy sighed inwardly. What could she say? If she refused to see Martin, her relatives would certainly wonder why.

"Of course Martin may call on me," she said smoothly. "You can tell him he may send his card around during any of Aunt Bea's 'at home' afternoons. I'll be happy to visit with him."

Bea shot James a triumphant glance and then went back to her fruit compote. James watched Amy mutilating her muffin for a few seconds more and then said, "So what are your plans for the day, Amelia?"

"I have some letters to write this morning, and I thought this afternoon I might go to

Chumley's and see if any new books have arrived from the States."

"Ask if that suit pattern book I ordered from *The Delineator* has come in, would you?" Bea asked.

Amy nodded. She chewed diligently, tasting nothing, for a few minutes more and then said, "May I go up now? I really owe quite a few letters, I've been neglecting my correspondence lately."

"Go on, dear," Bea said.

After Amy had left, Bea confided to James, "I'm thrilled she's going to be seeing Martin Fitzwater, aren't you?"

"I don't think Amy is quite as thrilled as we are," James replied.

"What does that mean?" Bea demanded, annoyed at her husband's implied objection to her plans.

"Something is on Amy's mind. Any other young girl in her position would be delirious with joy at Martin's attentions, but I had the impression that Amy is going along with this scheme solely to please us."

"Don't be silly," Bea snapped. "She's just confused and lonely after the loss of her parents, not to mention the horrible experience she had when she first arrived in this country."

"I'm not sure that experience was so horrible," James muttered.

Beatrice stared at him, her fork suspended in

mid-air. "I beg your pardon?" she said stiffly.

"Did you see the expression on Amy's face last night when she heard that Bey had been captured? She wasn't overjoyed; she wasn't even gratified. She was upset. Very upset."

Beatrice was silent, thinking about it.

"And didn't you tell me that at your Mission tea she got into some tiff with Mrs. Ballinger? I believe you said that Amy was defending the rebels. Didn't that strike you as odd?"

"It did at the time," Bea said thoughtfully. "I guess I was so busy with the ball that I later dismissed it."

"Amy was gone for six weeks, Beatrice. She saw a lot of the rebel camp and the people there. And it was totally uncharacteristic of Bey to let her go, no matter what Kalid Shah said or did."

"What are you suggesting, James?" Bea asked, her eyes widening in horror. "That Amy had some sort of personal relationship with this man Bey?"

"Has," James said quietly. "Has."

"Oh, my God," Bea moaned, putting down her fork. "Do you mean she has a crush on him?"

James would have guessed from Amy's behavior that the affair had gone well beyond the crush stage, but there was a limit to how much Beatrice could take. "Yes," he said shortly.

"We have to put a stop to it immediately, James. What can we do?" Beatrice gasped. She began to tremble and half rose from her seat.

James held up his hand. "We don't have to do anything, Bea. The man is going to be dead within a month," he said firmly. "The Sultan's executioner will solve the problem for us."

Beatrice relaxed visibly, looking at her husband. James was right.

"I can't believe that she has deceived us this way, every day since she came to this house," Beatrice murmured, shaken by this new perspective on her niece.

"From Amy's point of view, she had no choice. It's not the sort of thing we could be expected to understand."

"Certainly not," Bea said indignantly.

"If my guess is correct, it would explain Amelia's lack of interest in your matchmaking schemes, as well as her other odd behavior," James said.

Bea nodded slowly.

"Now I don't want you to say a word about this to Amelia, Bea," James ordered his wife sternly. "No matter what you may feel personally about Amelia's behavior, chastising her about whatever relationship she may have with this outlaw is pointless at this juncture. There is no prospect of future difficulties. Bey will be out of the picture soon, and there's an end to it."

"And she'll get over him in time," Bea said, as much to herself as to James.

Doreen Owens Malek

"In time," James agreed.

Bea sighed heavily. "With myself as a notable exception, the women of our family certainly have a taste for these wild Turkish men," she said, sniffing.

"The women of our family have always done exactly as they pleased," James said in a tired voice, and poured himself another cup of coffee.

Amy's trip to the bookstore was an excuse to buy more newspapers, but after she had perused all of them, she knew no more than she had that morning. The only thing clear from the varying journalistic accounts was that Malik had been arrested and was now being held in the Sultan's dungeon. She discarded her purchases in a trash bin outside the store before climbing into the carriage to return to the house.

As the driver turned into the Woolcott drive, Amy saw that a coach was already there. She leaned forward to make out the insignia on the doors and her heart started beating faster.

It was the pasha of Bursa's coach.

Amy burst into the house and ran into the parlor, stopping short when she saw Sarah having tea with Beatrice.

"Oh, Sarah, I'm so glad to see you!" Amy cried, almost in tears of relief at seeing Kalid's wife.

"How about me?" Beatrice said crisply. "Aren't you glad to see me?"

Amy undid the bow on her cape, dropping the garment on a chair, then bent to kiss her aunt's cheek.

"Of course I am," she said, handing Bea the pattern book she had requested. "It's just that I wasn't expecting to see Sarah and it's such a lovely surprise."

"I had to come to Pera for some shopping and I thought I would drop in and see all of you," Sarah said smoothly, replacing her cup in its saucer. She was smiling as Amy kissed her, but when her eyes met the younger woman's, her gaze was serious.

"Listak, bring another cup for Miss Amelia," Beatrice said to the servant when she entered the room to clear the dishes.

"Oh, no, thank you," Amy said lightly. "I really don't want anything." The sooner the tea ceremony ended, the sooner she could get Sarah alone.

"Have my halberdiers been served in the kitchen?" Sarah asked Listak.

"Yes, miss," Listak replied, as she passed with a tray.

"Kalid insisted they come with me, but it's such a nuisance traveling everywhere with an armed guard."

"But necessary these days," Bea said pointedly.

The women chatted amiably, Beatrice still full of gossip about the ball, until Amy finally said, "Sarah, I wonder if you would like to take a walk around the garden? Aunt Bea has it looking so beautiful, and everything will be dying soon. It seems such a shame for you to miss it."

Sarah rose immediately, seizing her cue. "Oh, I would love to see it," she said warmly.

"Aunt Bea, would you like to come with us?" asked Amy, who knew Beatrice hated exercise of any kind.

"No, thank you. I'll just go back to the kitchen and see how dinner is coming along. Sarah will be dining with us and staying overnight."

"How nice," Amy said, edging toward the door. Sarah followed her, and once they were safely outside the house, Sarah took Amy's hands and said, "I came as soon as I heard."

"Is there any hope, Sarah? What does Kalid say?" Amy asked desperately.

Sarah shook her head and sighed. "Kalid has been involved in secret meetings for a week now, coming and going at all hours. He won't tell me what's happening, but I have reason to suspect it's something big."

"Is it something that could help Malik?"

"I just don't know."

"You don't sound optimistic."

Sarah shrugged. "Malik has been the most notorious criminal in the Empire for some time. Hammid will be anxious to make an example of him."

"So Malik will be condemned."

"I'm afraid so."

"And the dungeon at Topkapi is impenetrable?"

"If Malik is condemned, he'll be moved to the Pamukkale jail in the old city as soon as the execution is scheduled. It's tradition that state criminals be put to death there in full view of the people in the ancient square."

"Is it easier to escape from that jail?" Amy asked.

"Yes, I think so, but you can be certain that Malik will be heavily guarded all the time."

"But surely Anwar and his friends will try to free him," Amy said.

"They may try. I don't know if they can actually succeed."

Amy drew a deep breath. "Can I get in to see him?"

Sarah stared at her, speechless.

"Tell me. Is there any chance of it?" Amy demanded.

"Do you realize what you're asking?"

"If he's going to die, I want to see him one last time. Is it possible?"

"You would have to request the Sultan's permission, and why on earth would he grant it?"

"Maybe he would grant it to Kalid. And you," Amy said.

"Me?"

"I could go in disguised as you," Amy said.

Sarah closed her eyes.

"Think about it. If I were veiled and dressed in the Ottoman style, how would anyone at the jail know the difference? We're about the same size and our coloring is similar. If I showed up with Kalid, would anyone question that I was you?"

Sarah opened her eyes again. "Aren't you forgetting one thing? Kalid has not been on the best of terms with the Sultan—why would Hammid grant him this favor?"

"Isn't there a custom associated with the Feast of the Flowers called *feytva?* Each of the pashas asks the Sultan for one favor, and he cannot refuse."

"How do you know that?"

"Listak told me about it, and I read more about it later in the newspapers."

"I know what you are thinking, but Kalid can't ask the Sultan to release Malik. Pardoning capital criminals doesn't fall under the feytva. It dates back to the Byzantines, who incorporated the Roman tradition of granting favors on feast days—but *small* favors, like removing the ban on a forbidden marriage between two rival tribe members, or restoring a prepaid dowry to the bride's family when a betrothal is cancelled."

"But Kalid can ask to *visit* Malik just once,

and bring you with him. Except that I will be you."

"Kalid is not going to like it. He won't want to put you in danger."

"I'll take the chance."

"Hammid might not let me go in with Kalid," Sarah said.

"But Malik is Roxalena's brother-in-law."

"So?" Sarah said.

"Roxalena is your friend. She would want her friend to visit her husband's brother before he died, wouldn't she?"

Sarah sighed, shaking her head.

"You told me in the past that the Sultan was very indulgent toward his daughter, even honoring her whim to learn English. That's how you entered the harem and met Roxalena in the first place," Amy said.

"The Sultan was indulgent before Roxalena ran off with Osman Bey," Sarah replied dryly. "I doubt if he's much inclined to humor her wishes now."

"It's worth a try, isn't it?"

"Amy, you are talking about a man who killed the whole Bey family when he found out that Roxalena had married Osman. This plan is very doubtful."

"It's the only one I can come up with!" Amy said despairingly. "I wrote you a ten-page letter last night, trying to think of a way to help Malik, but I have no influence here. So if I can't save him, at least I can be with him for a short time before he dies. Kalid says the Sultan is very vain and likes to make grand gestures to show his district commissioners how benevolent he is. What better way to do that than to honor a pasha's request to visit a condemned criminal? What finer example of his indulgence and mercy?"

"And you want Kalid to say this to Abdul Hammid?"

"I'm sure Kalid will find his own way to say it, but please ask him to try."

Sarah was silent, thinking about it.

Amy bit her lip, trying not to cry. "I just can't let Malik go to his death with no word from me," she whispered.

Sarah put her arm around the younger woman and said, "I'll see what I can do."

"How will you let me know if permission is granted?" Amy asked.

"I'll send one of Kalid's fast riders with a message about the day and time. One of those horsemen can get from Bursa to your house in five hours."

"And what shall I tell Beatrice about where we are going?" Amy asked, wiping her eyes, which were tearing in spite of her best efforts to control herself.

"Tell her Kalid is taking us on a tour of the old city. Bea knows you haven't done much sightseeing. I'll bring the right clothes for you to change into during the carriage ride."

Amy nodded. Could her idea really work?

Sarah squeezed Amy's arm. "Don't count on this too much, Amelia. I can't mislead you—it's a long shot at best."

"I have to hope for something," Amy murmured.

"I know. I'll send word to you as soon as Kalid can see the Sultan. Now perk up and smile or Beatrice will be wondering what we've been doing out here."

The two women walked back to the house, arm in arm.

Malik stared up at the dripping ceiling of the dungeon, thinking about how many days he might have left to live. He was sprawled full-length on a dirt floor strewn with filthy straw, his feet manacled together and his hands tightly cuffed to an iron peg set in the stone wall.

He turned his head to look at the thin stream of lamplight filtering through a crack in the wall near the solid oak door. He had few regrets about his life; he had done what he wanted to do, and he knew that despite what Anwar had said the revolution would live on after he himself was dust. The people in his band had tasted freedom, and they would want more of it. Their victory in the Armenian mahalle had shown them that it was possible to dilute the Sultan's power; he was not an omnipotent being against whom they had no chance at all. They would grow in numbers and strength and eventually achieve their goal.

Malik was satisfied that his blood would be spilled in a just cause that would survive him.

His only concern was Amelia. He had made promises he couldn't keep, had led her to believe there was a future for them that now would never be. She was not the type to get over him easily; she might never get over him at all. He couldn't bear the thought that he had ruined her life, that she would grow old and embittered, grieving her lost love, denying herself the comfort of marriage and children because she had given her heart away in her youth. His final hope was that she could recover from her experience with him and go on with her life.

Malik closed his eyes, trying not to think about the implications of this wish. Another man would make love to her, hold her in his arms as they slept, father her children. Malik wasn't selfish enough to want Amelia to spend her life in mourning for him, but as long as he still breathed, the thought of someone else claiming her as he had curled his fingers into fists.

He shifted his mind from that subject; it produced an impotent fury that only drained his strength. He was not dead yet, so he directed his thoughts toward escape. He had been formally sentenced that morning, so his move to the jail near the docks was imminent. He knew he would be heavily guarded, but he was also more resourceful than any soldier the Sultan employed.

There was always a chance.

He remembered how he had been taken, surrounded by a force of ten armed men as he arrived at Yuri's house for his horse. He had yielded in order to live and possibly fight another day; to have resisted would have meant his death right there. He assumed he had finally been betrayed. Most of the Sultan's subjects were so poor that the only surprise lay in their ignoring the lure of the reward for so long. Malik knew poverty from personal experience; he knew what its rigors could force a person to do.

He understood only too well what had happened.

He shifted position in the straw, wondering how Amelia had learned of his arrest and what she was thinking now. He hoped that she wouldn't do anything foolish or dangerous, but he knew how impulsive she could be. Her courage was mostly a reckless determination that had to be channeled effectively, but in these circumstances she could easily go wild.

He heard the guard coming and quickly closed his eyes again, feigning sleep.

When he was alone again, he would make plans.

Amy heard the horse's hooves on the drive in

the late afternoon and came out of her room. She had been waiting for five days to hear from Sarah, five days of agony spent gleaning whatever information she could about Malik from newspapers and gossip. She stopped on the landing and watched Beatrice answer the door, then come back inside with a letter in her hand.

Amy walked down the stairs, restraining herself from running with an effort. She didn't want to look as if she were expecting to receive something.

Beatrice looked up and said, "This is for you, Amelia. It was just hand-delivered by a rider in Shah livery. It must be from Sarah." She gave Amy the envelope.

Amy folded it into the sleeve of her dress. She was dying to tear it open, but didn't want to read it in front of Bea and subject herself to questions.

"The Imperial postal service is no longer in operation?" Beatrice asked mildly, looking at James, who had just arrived home from his office and was hanging his hat on the rack in the hall.

"Sarah probably sent the rider on an errand to town and just asked him to drop this off," Amy said dismissively. She went into the library and got a book, pretending that was the reason for her sudden appearance, then went into the parlor.

Beatrice looked after her and murmured to James, "You don't think Sarah could be helping Amelia pursue . . ." She stopped short, amazed at what she was thinking.

"I'm sure Sarah is far too responsible for that," James said briskly, not sure at all. "Besides, Bey is incarcerated. His official condemnation was in the paper today. What can happen? Don't worry about it. Come up with me while I change for dinner. Are we having the mutton or the pork roast?"

Amy waited for Beatrice and her husband to go up the stairs, then ripped open the envelope.

"Permission has been granted," Sarah had written. "Kalid and I will be by for you at two on Friday the Fifteenth."

Amy refolded the letter and pressed it to her lips, closing her eyes. The Fifteenth was the next day.

Amy took the letter up to her room and destroyed it the same way she had destroyed the long letter she had written to Sarah. She tore it into small pieces and then charred each fragment with a candle flame until there was nothing left but a pile of ash, which she swept into the fireplace. Then she selected a dress which would be easy to change out of, draped it over a chair to air it for the next day, and went down to dinner.

It was a quiet meal, with all three participants absorbed in their own thoughts.

Doreen Owens Malek

"Sarah has offered to take me on a tour of the old city tomorrow afternoon," Amy finally announced as dessert was being served. "She's coming by for me around two."

James and Beatrice exchanged glances.

"That's nice, dear," Bea said, pouring caramel sauce over her slice of flan. "Is that why she wrote you?"

Amy nodded. "It was a last-minute decision for Sarah and Kalid to come to the city. Kalid has some business, and Sarah thought I might like to visit a few of the historical spots. I really haven't seen much beyond Pera since I've been here."

"Will you be back for dinner?" James asked.

"I'm sure I will be," Amy replied.

"Do you think Kalid and Sarah will want to stay here for the night?" Bea asked.

"They're staying at the American embassy," Amy lied hastily. "Kalid is meeting with Secretary Danforth."

Her relatives seemed to accept this, and Amy suppressed the familiar twinge of **guilt** she felt at lying to them.

Nothing was more important than getting in to see Malik.

Nothing.

Amy was waiting in the foyer when the Shah carriage pulled into the Woolcott drive the next afternoon. Kalid was mounted on his horse, rid-

322

ing behind the coach. He came to the door, observed the formalities with a characteristically reserved Beatrice, and handed Amy into the coach.

"I don't know how I let Sarah talk me into this," he muttered to Amy as she released his arm. "But then, she's been talking me into things for years."

"You won't be sorry," Amy said to him as she sat across from his wife.

"I'm already sorry," he said, looking meaningfully at Sarah. "If anything happens to either of you, I will hold myself responsible."

"If you were in Malik's shoes, wouldn't you want to see Sarah?" Amy demanded.

Kalid looked at her a long moment, then nodded.

"I suppose that's why I'm doing this," he said, and shut the carriage door.

"Is he angry?" Amy said to Sarah.

Sarah shook her head. "He's worried, and not just about this afternoon. He's involved in some plot against the Sultan. I'm not supposed to know about it, but of course I do. He thinks he's protecting me by not telling me about it, but I have my own sources." She picked up a bundle from the seat next to her and said, "Hurry and change. I have some things to tell you before we arrive."

Once Amy was attired in Sarah's Turkish ensemble and veiled to the eyes, Sarah said, "The guards at the jail will know Kalid by sight, of course, and they will assume that you are me, since they have been instructed to admit the pasha of Bursa and his wife. I will tell the driver to pull away so they don't see me sitting in the carriage, and then come back for you in ten minutes. Don't say anything, to Kalid or anyone else, until you are inside with Malik. The guards will undoubtedly remain with you during your visit, so make sure that you behave appropriately. You are supposed to be a friend of Malik's sister-in-law, not his lover, so bear that in mind."

Amy nodded.

"Do you have any questions?" Sarah asked.

"No." Amy folded her hands together in her lap; they were like ice.

"I am trusting you to be circumspect," Sarah added pointedly, looking at Amy.

"I promise I won't make a scene," Amy replied softly. "I can't thank you enough for your help in arranging this visit."

Sarah turned her head to look out the window. "While I was in the harem at Orchid Palace, Kalid was wounded in a bedouin raid, and for a while it looked as if he might die. I have always remembered how I felt then; it must approximate how you feel now. I want to help you, but I don't want you to do anything foolish. Be careful."

"I will."

The driver turned off the crowded main street and down a cobbled alley which ended at the water. Even from a distance, Amy could see the Sultan's halberdiers, outfitted more elaborately than Kalid's, standing at attention, two on either side of the main door. As they got closer to the low stone building, she could see the janissaries armed with pistols perched in lookouts stationed at regular intervals on the surrounding wall. It was a forbidding place, made all the more so by its lyrical name, *Pamukkale*, or "cloud castle," for the rock formations which formed a natural barrier between the prison and the bay.

The coach came to a stop before the prison and the halberdiers immediately presented their truncheons. Amy looked across at Sarah nervously.

"It's all right," Sarah said, moving back from the isinglas window. "That's just procedure. Kalid will tie up his horse; then he'll come to get you."

A short time later, Amy's door opened and Kalid said quietly, "Come with me. Don't say a word."

He looked quickly at Sarah, who whispered the words, "Good luck."

Amy descended from the carriage, and as soon as her feet touched the cobbled street, it pulled away, the horses' hooves clopping with a hollow sound on the paving stones. She looked after it, wondering if she and Kalid were both mad to have left its safety for the perilous encounter ahead.

Kalid took Amy's arm and steered her past the halberdiers, who stared straight ahead, and into the office of the jail, which was a bleak, windowless room containing a desk and a chair and a series of scarred wooden cabinets. A turbaned man in a gray uniform bowed to Kalid and said something in Turkish. Kalid replied curtly. The man bowed again, snapped his fingers, and two soldiers with rifles moved from the corners of the room to flank Kalid and Amy.

This, apparently, was their escort.

The turnkey removed an iron ring from the heavy belt at his waist and led the way down a dark hall where none of the outside sunlight penetrated; it was illuminated only by a flaring taper set into the flaking stone wall. The little group reached a massive oak door, double-barred and double-bolted, which the warden proceeded to unlock with a succession of keys. Finally he shifted the crossbars and the door swung open creakily, admitting them to a square, stone-paved room which contained four individual cells. Each cell featured a tiny, barred window near the ceiling and a narrow linen cot. Only one cell was occupied.

Amy sucked in her breath as she felt Kalid's steadying hand on her shoulder. Malik was lying face-down on his cot, his back to them, identifiable by his broad shoulders and thick black hair. The only other thing in his cell aside from the cot was a bucket on a wall peg.

"Has he been beaten?" Amy whispered, alarmed by Malik's slack posture.

"Not before a public execution," Kalid replied. "The Sultan would not want anyone to see the marks."

The warden rapped the bars on Malik's cell with his nightstick and said something in Turkish. Malik ignored him.

The warden spoke again, more sharply, and when Kalid saw that this would also be ineffective, he said in English, "It's Kalid Shah here, Malik."

Malik turned his head, and when he saw Kalid he sat up. Then his eyes moved to the woman standing next to Kalid.

Kalid said something in a soothing tone to the warden, and the turbaned man withdrew. He went through the door to his office, leaving the two guards and their rifles behind with the visitors.

Malik rose from the cot and came to stand facing Kalid, his hands gripping the bars. His cheeks were covered with beard stubble, his hair uncombed, his tunic ripped and stained.

"Amelia?" he said to Kalid. "How is she?"

Kalid looked at Amy, who lowered her veil just enough for Malik to see her face.

Malik's reaction was not what she had expected. He looked at her incredulously, then at Kalid.

"Why did you bring her?" he demanded of Kalid in English, his expression anguished. "I don't want her to see me like this!"

"Malik, I'm here!" Amy said, reaching her fingers through the bars. "You just asked for me, and I'm here!"

He turned away. "Go home, Amelia. This is no place for you."

Amy put her hand to her mouth, her eyes filling with tears. "Please, Malik—this is our only chance. Don't send me away."

One of the guards barked out an order behind them.

"He says we must speak in Turkish," Kalid translated.

Malik looked back at Amy, who put her hand over his on the bars and mouthed the English phrase, "I love you."

Malik closed his eyes.

Kalid said something to him in Turkish and Malik replied quietly. They exchanged a few phrases and then the guard who had spoken stepped forward and thrust the saber on his rifle in front of Kalid.

Kalid looked at Amy, who was staring at Malik, her fingers gripping the bars, tears streaming down her face. The guard jerked his head toward the door, indicating that their time was up.

Amy gestured to Malik, who wouldn't look at her. Then, just as she was turning away, despondent, he reached through the bars and seized her hand. He said something softly in Turkish, his eyes fixed on hers, then released her, stepping back.

The guard prodded Kalid toward the door with the tip of his saber.

Kalid lost patience and seized the saber, ripping the rifle from the guard's hand and smacking him in the head with its butt. The guard sprawled on the floor, unconscious, and as his companion turned to train his rifle on the visitors, Malik thrust his foot through the cell bars and tripped him.

When both men were prone, one insensible and the other distracted, Kalid faced Malik and whispered something quickly in a language Amy didn't understand. She saw Malik's face go blank with surprise, then change expression with lightning speed.

Before the second guard could rise, the warden burst through the door from his office at the commotion, pistol in hand. Kalid faced him down with the first guard's rifle, saying something surly in Turkish, kicking the guard's leg derisively with his boot.

The warden slowly lowered his pistol. Then he gestured for Kalid and Amy to walk past him, speaking sharply to the second guard, who put down his rifle and bent to lift his insensate companion.

Amy looked back at Malik, who was watching her. She put her closed fist to her chest, then opened her hand in a Yuruk gesture he had taught her which meant, "I give you my heart."

Malik pressed his lips together and looked down, struggling for control.

Kalid grabbed Amy bodily and shoved her through the door before the warden changed his mind. She lifted her veil to cover her face and stood quietly next to Kalid, trying to absorb all that had happened so quickly.

Kalid then entered into a fierce debate with the warden, complete with hand gestures and disgusted glances. Kalid simmered down only when the warden's tone turned conciliatory, then apologetic. The pasha finally ushered Amy out of the jail, propelling her down to the street before saying, "Are you all right, Amelia?"

Amy shook her head, unable to speak.

He put his arm around her and said, "I know that was very difficult for you. There was no way to make it easier."

"I'll never see Malik again," she murmured, her face ashen.

Kalid said nothing.

"I was so frightened when you got into that fight," she added, shivering.

"That arrogant bastard needed correcting," Kalid said tightly of the guard, as his coach came toward them down the street.

"Why didn't the second guard fire?" Amy asked.

"He was afraid to shoot the pasha of Bursa, as I thought he would be," Kalid replied.

"What did you whisper to Malik?" Amy asked. "What was that language?"

"The language was Arabic, and never mind what I said," Kalid replied shortly.

The shattering experience suddenly seemed to overwhelm Amy, and she began to shake harder, her knees sagging.

"Steady," Kalid said, his grip tightening. "Your ride is nearly here."

The coach glided to a stop, and Kalid lifted Amy almost bodily onto her seat.

Sarah took one look at the girl and said to her husband, "This was a mistake."

"She'll be all right," Kalid said. "She's tougher than you think."

"I can't send her back to Beatrice like this," Sarah said, glancing at her husband anxiously.

"I'll tell the driver to take you to the Trakya Hotel, and I'll follow you there," Kalid replied. "I'll book a suite and Amelia will have time to recover."

Kalid moved to withdraw from the coach, and Amy grabbed his hand.

"What did Malik say to me?" she inquired, finally asking the question she'd been avoiding. "When he spoke in Turkish before we left, what did he say?" She wasn't sure she wanted to know the answer.

Kalid glanced at Sarah, who nodded that he should reply.

"He said that he still meant everything he had ever told you, and that he would love you forever. If fate was not kind, you should go on with your life, but remember him as he would always remember you," Kalid said quietly.

Amy collapsed, sobbing, into Sarah's arms.

Chapter Twelve

The maid deposited a tea tray on a table in the parlor of the hotel suite, then turned to Sarah and curtsied.

"Will there be anything else, my lady?" she said in a cockney accent.

"That will be all, thank you," Sarah replied.

When the maid had left, Amy said to Sarah, sniffling, "My lady?"

"A British concession runs the hotel, and they frequently bring young girls over from England to serve on the domestic staff. The promise of adventure in an exotic foreign land, you know. The only problem is, the young ladies have a tendency to get confused about the local titles. Last year one of them called me 'your highness'."

Amy smiled wanly, then looked away.

"Feeling any better?" Sarah asked.

Amy bit her lip, tearing up again. "You know, I always had excellent self-control," she said, wiping her eyes with a corner of her lace handkerchief. "I didn't even cry at my parents' funeral. But ever since I met Malik, all I seem to do is cry. It's awful, whimpering constantly like a kicked puppy. I'm ashamed of myself, but I can't seem to stop."

"This has been a highly emotional time for you," Sarah said soothingly. "Don't be too hard on yourself."

"There's really no hope for him, is there?" Amy said despairingly. "What he said at the end of my visit sounded too much like good-bye."

"There's hope until he is dead," Sarah replied simply. "I wouldn't give up just yet. Malik is amazingly resourceful, and his men aren't just going to stand by and let him be executed without trying to stop it."

"But what can they do against the janissaries?" Amy cried. "There are too many of them, and they are too well armed."

"The rebels have been doing pretty well so far, and lately the janissaries have not been happy with the Sultan," Sarah answered. "Their wages have been cut, they are getting paid late or not at all, and their time off has been cut. The Sultan is putting his money into buying foreign property instead of maintaining them."

Sarah stopped, as if considering whether she should go on, then said, "There are rumblings of a palace revolt."

Amy stared at her. "I didn't know that."

Sarah nodded. "I think that's what Kalid's frequent disappearances are about; I suspect that's why he took off as soon as he deposited us here. He won't tell me anything, but I know he is trying to bring the rebels and the janissaries together in a common cause."

"How do you know?" Amy gasped.

"Kalid is not the only one who has spies," Sarah said dryly. "Most of the women who work at Orchid Palace have husbands who are involved with the rebels or the janissaries. The wives talk to me."

Amy clasped her hands together, hope brightening her features. "Oh, if only that were true! The Sultan would be nothing without the janissaries. His reign of terror would be over!"

Sarah held up her hand. "Now don't get too excited. What I'm telling you is mere conjecture on my part, a conclusion I reached from listening carefully and piecing things together. I just don't want you to give up when things might yet turn out well."

She stood and began to pace. "Kalid is betting that the Sultan will continue to be his own worst enemy. He's too stubborn to allow a parliament and too blind to realize that the janissaries might turn against him, even when they see him pouring a fortune into European markets while they put in overtime and wait weeks for their salaries. Kalid has been working for a long time for a bloodless solution to all of this, and I'm sure Malik's arrest has forced him to move up the timetable."

"To save Malik?" Amy whispered.

"Yes, and to prevent the degeneration into civil war that is sure to come unless somebody intervenes to stop it."

"How? How can it be stopped?"

"Kalid wants the Sultan to abdicate in favor of his younger brother. That would allow the title to remain within the same family and the figurehead to continue, but the brother is much more reasonable. To keep his head, he would make the concessions to democracy that Abdul Hammid is now refusing."

"Can Kalid convince them?"

Sarah shrugged doubtfully. "It would mean convincing two traditional enemies, the rebels and the janissaries, to work together. I don't know if even Kalid is that persuasive."

"And it has to happen fast, if Malik is to be saved," Amy murmured.

"My money is on Malik saving himself," Sarah said tartly. "His ability to escape from tight spots is legendary."

"You didn't see the inside of that jail," Amy replied. "It's like a strong box. There's no place to go. And he's guarded at all times by men with long-sight rifles, the new ones with barrel guides. I remember my father talking about them."

"Malik will find a way," Sarah said confidently.

Amy finally smiled. "You raise my spirits, Sarah. You have such a positive outlook."

"That's because I'm not in love with Malik and able to see the situation more clearly." She glanced at the table and said, "Our tea is probably cold. Shall I ring for another pot?"

"No, that's all right. I think I can go home now." Amy rose and picked up her cape. The Turkish gown and veil she had worn to the jail lay discarded on a chair.

"Are you sure you're composed enough to face Beatrice?" Sarah asked.

Amy nodded. "Thanks for giving me this time. Talking to you has really helped."

"Do you think I can send you back to the house alone in my carriage?" Sarah asked. "I don't want to go along because Beatrice is sure to ask me in and I want to be here when Kalid returns."

"That's fine."

"Kalid and I will be staying the night here if you need anything," Sarah said.

Amy nodded again. "Will you let me know if you learn more about Malik?" she asked. "Would Kalid let you send a rider from Bursa?"

Sarah patted her hand. "Don't worry about

that—you'll be the first to know. You'll just have to think of an explanation for Beatrice if a messenger arrives."

Amy sighed. "I have told Aunt Bea so many lies, I feel like Mephistopheles."

Sarah chuckled, and with a wry smile patted Amy's cheek. " 'Oh, that deceit should dwell in such a gorgeous palace,' " she said, obviously quoting someone.

"Is that Keats?" Amy asked.

"Shakespeare. He has a comment on almost every situation in life, and he's always right."

Amy smiled. "You'll forever be a teacher, Sarah."

"I'm afraid it's like the priesthood, a permanent condition," Sarah replied, rising and pulling the bell rope in a corner of the parlor. When the maid arrived, Sarah asked that her carriage be brought around to the front of the hotel.

"This will all be over soon," Sarah said, turning to face Amy. "The prospect of Malik's execution will force the rebels into action, so one way or another, we won't have much longer to wait."

Amy nodded, but did not say what she was thinking—that the amount of time didn't matter, because every second that Malik's fate hung in the balance was an eternity.

Kalid tied Khan's tether to a tree and looked around the clearing. He had arranged to meet

Anwar Talit here, in the hills beyond the city, but he wasn't confident that Malik Bey's lieutenant would show up at the appointed time. Talit had a reputation for being more impulsive and less reasonable than his friend, and he had to be pretty desperate to free Malik by now. Kalid didn't know Talit and felt that he was dealing with a volatile element in the mix; he had to reach Anwar and stop him from doing something that might damage his own plan with the janissaries.

If Kalid's strategy was to succeed, all three factions had to work together against the Sultan.

Kalid heard a rustling sound behind him and turned to face Talit, who was regarding him suspiciously, his eyes narrowed. He nodded once at Kalid's greeting, his expression glacial, and Kalid sighed inwardly.

He hoped he wouldn't have to waste too much time persuading Talit that they were now on the same side. Peasants like Bey's lieutenant grew up with the idea of the pasha of Bursa as the Sultan's man; unlike Malik, who had the foresight and the ability to compromise of a true leader, Talit might be unable to perceive that their relative positions had changed. If the Sultan was to be defeated, it was necessary for the rebels to work with aristocrats and janissaries alike toward the common goal.

"Your message said that you had a plan for

Malik's escape," Talit said shortly.

"You know I had promised to help Malik against the Sultan when the occasion arose," Kalid replied.

"He told me that," Talit said flatly, making it clear that he himself remained unconvinced.

Kalid waited a moment and then tried again. "I have been meeting with the captain of the Janissaries, Kemal Sorek, for the past two months," he said.

Talit spat on the ground.

"I know what you think of Hammid's private soldiers, but most of them want the Sultan deposed as badly as you do right now."

Talit was silent.

"It's the truth. They haven't been paid on time once during the past year and they are being worked to death. You haven't heard about this?"

Talit shrugged. "I've heard rumors," he said shortly. "In the Empire, there are always rumors."

"These have a sound foundation. Sorek is ready to turn."

Talit shook his head.

"You cannot get rid of Hammid alone, Talit," Kalid said impatiently. "You don't have enough men to do the job."

"We will."

"When? After Malik is dead?"

Talit eyed Kalid warily, then propped one booted foot up on a rock and leaned forward intently, his forearm across his knee. "What do you propose?"

"I propose that you don't try to break him out of Cloud Castle on your own. Wait until you can make a joint effort with me when the janissaries walk off the job."

Talit stared at him in amazement. "And when are they going to do that?"

"When they receive the word from me. They'll lay down their arms and get to safety before Sorek blows up the main arsenal at Topkapi."

Talit snorted. "You're dreaming."

Kalid cursed vehemently and threw up his hands. "Will you open your eyes and see that this is your chance?" he demanded. "Stop thinking of me as some overlord in a palace and the janissaries as the Sultan's secret police! Most of them have roots as poor as yours and are as disgusted with him as you are. In this instance we all want the same thing, and we can't get it unless we work together."

Talit didn't answer for a long moment. Then he said, "What is your plan regarding Malik?"

"We'll spring him when the Sultan is distracted by the revolt of his troops. I saw him in jail this afternoon and told him not to try to escape but to wait until we come for him."

Talit stared at him. "You take quite a bit on yourself, don't you?"

"I thought I could make you see reason."

"And reason is doing what you say?" Talit

countered challengingly.

"Reason is planning carefully and striking when the time is right, rather than staging a guerilla raid on a prison in the middle of a city where it has little chance of success."

Anwar examined Kalid measuringly. "What makes you think you can trust the janissaries? They don't have a reputation for keeping their word."

"They have a reputation for acting in their own best interest. Sorek assures me that his men are fed up and looking for a change. The Sultan's younger brother is not a megalomaniac like Abdul Hammid. The new Sultan would pay his soldiers on time and be grateful that they allowed him to keep his head."

"And convene a parliament?" Talit said.

Kalid nodded.

"And you think Sorek is telling you the truth?"

Kalid shrugged. "He's not Osman Bey, whose word I would take for anything, but Sorek is also not a fool. He sees the direction of the future."

Talit walked a short distance away, his head bent, his hands clasped behind him. Then he turned to face Kalid and asked, "How did you get in to see Malik?"

"Feytva. My position allowed me to ask for a favor. Amelia Ryder went with me disguised as my wife."

Anwar's expression softened a little. "How is she?"

"She was upset to see Malik in jail, but she'll be able to help us if we need her. She's a lot tougher than she looks."

"Yes, I know." Anwar looked down at his hands thoughtfully, then up at Kalid.

"What do you want me to do?" he said.

"I want you to go with me to see Sorek so we can get organized and act in concert. Several of the other pashas are with me in this. If Hammid sees that we and the rebels *and* his own army are all against him, he'll cave in and abdicate. He has no personal courage, but all his life he's had the backing of men stronger than himself. Without that, he's nothing. You'll achieve your goal and avoid the civil war we've all been dreading."

"You make it sound so simple."

"I didn't say it would be simple. Some of the janissaries will remain loyal to the Sultan even if Sorek goes against him, and you'll have to fight them."

"I've been fighting all my life, but if I commit my men to this plan, I have to know all the details before we see Sorek."

Kalid exhaled slowly. He hadn't allowed himself to consider what might happen if Talit wouldn't listen to him; now he was very relieved that he didn't have to face that challenge.

"All right," Kalid said. "This is what we're going to do."

Amy gazed into the pier glass in her room, adjusting the bodice of her shirtwaist and wondering how she was going to get through the long afternoon. She had not heard from Sarah during the past week, which meant there was nothing new on Malik's situation, and now Martin Fitzwater was coming for tea at Bea's suggestion. Amy felt as if she were participating in a charade, encouraging a suitor she had no intention of marrying, but she could only deal with one crisis at a time. If nibbling ginger snaps with Martin would keep everyone happy until Malik's fate was determined, she was prepared to go through with the performance.

Amy tucked up a stray strand of her hair and left her room, the ticking of the grandfather clock audible in the quiet foyer as she descended the stairs. The silver tray on the ormolu table was ready to receive Martin's card and the footman stood at attention just inside the door. Everything in sight was in a highly polished state of readiness, seemingly in wait for the visitor's arrival.

When Amy entered the parlor, she saw immediately that James was in his "man of the house" garb for the occasion, dressed in a frock coat accessorized with monocle and watch fob, smoking a cigar and reading the newspaper. Beatrice was bustling around the drop-leaf table arranging plates and cups; she looked up to smile widely at her niece.

"You look very nice, dear," she said.

"Thank you."

They both turned as the footman straightened, responding to the sound of a carriage on the drive.

Amy looked at the clock. As she might have expected, Martin was arriving exactly at three.

Beatrice moved to stand next to Amy in the hall as the footman opened the door.

Martin entered and bowed, first to Amy, then to Bea.

"Good afternoon, Mrs. Woolcott, Miss Ryder," he said. "Thank you for inviting me into your home."

Martin looked as if he were about to go on parade: his scarlet uniform was spotless, his black boots were polished to a high sheen, and the sword scabbard at his side glittered. He was carrying a sheaf of wildflowers wrapped in a regimental scarf.

"From Mrs. Ballinger's garden," he said, handing them to Amy. "It's the last of them, I'm afraid."

"How lovely. Thank you," Amy said.

"Let me take them," Bea said, "I'll add them to one of the vases inside."

They followed her into the parlor, where Martin made polite conversation with Beatrice until

Doreen Owens Malek

she vanished into the kitchen, then talked man to man with James about the state of Turkish politics while Amy poured tea. James finally took his leave and went into his study, leaving Amy and Martin alone.

"Your uncle is very interested in the local power plays," Martin said, selecting a tiny sandwich from the plate Amy offered him.

"They affect his business," Amy replied, raising her teacup and taking a sip.

"I imagine it must be difficult to run an enterprise like his in such volatile surroundings," Martin observed. "You never know who's going to be in charge from day to day."

"He manages to get along with everyone, but I think walking a tightrope all the time takes its toll on him." Amy replaced her cup in its saucer.

Martin nodded. "It isn't easy for any of us Westerners here. The differences between the cultures is so enormous." He stopped, then added, "But you must have discovered that for yourself."

"Yes."

"Have you recovered fully from the ordeal you experienced when you first arrived?" he asked delicately.

Amy didn't know what to say. Of course everyone in the Western enclave knew about her kidnapping, but she no longer thought of it as an 'ordeal', so she was at a loss for a response.

Martin mistook her hesitation and said

346

quickly, "Please forgive me. I didn't mean to introduce an unpleasant subject. Of course you don't want to discuss your abduction, and it was churlish of me to mention it."

"That's all right, Martin," Amy said quietly, relieved that he was too well mannered to pursue such a sensitive topic, even with a woman he regarded as a prospective wife.

"Have you been to any of the bazaars?" he asked brightly, obviously groping for an innocuous subject.

"Yes. I must say I found the experience rather overwhelming. There was too much to see on one trip."

"Then we must go back for a visit," Martin said lightly, holding her gaze and smiling.

Amy looked away from him, unwilling to agree yet loath to hurt his feelings. She wished she could explain why she was being so elusive, but knew she couldn't.

Beatrice appeared in the doorway with a tray of gooseberry tarts; Amy noticed that Listak had been banished and Bea was serving them herself.

Clearly her aunt wanted to keep track of the conversation.

"Please try one of these, Lieutenant. I made them myself," Bea said, placing the tray on the table in front of Martin. "My cook tends to have a heavy hand with pastry, and I didn't want to risk them."

Martin reached for one of the tarts and bit into it, nodding and smiling as he chewed. Amy looked away again, ashamed of herself. He was trying so hard, and she was such a lost cause; she felt sorry for him. The only thing that saved her from running from the room was the knowledge that if Martin ever learned the truth, he would not be sitting in her parlor, consuming her Aunt Bea's pastry.

Bea joined them and they all sipped tea for another twenty minutes, discussing mutual friends and local gossip. Then, after the proper interval had elapsed, Martin rose to take his leave.

"I would like your permission to return in two weeks' time," he said to Bea, "and enjoy your company once more."

James came in from the hall and Martin said to him, "Sir, I was just asking your wife if I might come back in a fortnight and visit with you again."

James looked at Amy.

"Of course," she said, thinking that in two weeks Malik might be dead, and in that event she wouldn't care what happened.

"Then we'll look forward to seeing you, Martin," James said, extending his hand.

Martin shook it, then bowed to the ladies.

Suddenly there was a loud commotion at the rear of the house. They all turned to look as Listak flew into the hall, her eyes huge and her hands clasped to her mouth. A tall figure came rushing after her, whirling to face the three in the parlor.

"Malik!" Amy gasped, too stunned at his sudden appearance to say anything more than his name.

He was filthy, his shirt ripped along the length of one sinewy arm, his forehead smeared with dirt, and his cheeks covered with black stubble.

"Amelia," he said, opening the half-exposed arm in an embracing gesture.

Amy, her whole body flooding with joy as she recovered from his dramatic appearance, ran to his side. His arm came around her tightly.

"How?" she said to him breathlessly. "How did you get here?"

"I'll tell you later. Go and get your bag," he said.

Amy ran for the stairs as James said to Malik, "You're not taking my niece anywhere."

Amy turned to see Malik hold up his hand in a conciliatory manner. "I don't want to hurt anyone here," he said, "but Amelia is coming with me. Now."

"The hell she is," Martin Fitzwater said grimly, reaching for his sword.

Malik drew a pistol from his waistband at the same instant and shot at Martin's feet. Martin jumped back as the report rang loudly, echoing in the confined space and kicking up a wood chip from the bare floor next to the carpet.

Beatrice shrieked and fell backward into a chair; Listak dove behind the stairwell, her apron flung over her head. James stood rooted to the rug in appalled silence.

Malik trained his weapon on all of them as Amy ran upstairs to her room, grabbed her canvas satchel, then flew back down to the hall to stand at Malik's side.

"Ready?" he said.

Amy nodded.

"Let's go." Malik grabbed Amy's hand and they turned toward the door in unison.

"Are you sure this is what you want, Amelia?" James called after them urgently.

Amy whirled to face him.

"Yes, it is," she said. She looked at Beatrice, who was sobbing now, unable to believe that all her careful plans had come to this awful end.

"Aunt Bea, please forgive me," Amy said. "Uncle James, try to understand. Martin, I know I misled you and I regret that, but I have to do this. I love Malik and I'm going with him."

"You love him?" Martin gasped. "This is your kidnapper!"

"And my lover. I don't expect you to understand, and I apologize to all three of you. I'm very sorry."

They stared back at her in silence; James looked merely sad, Bea was crying silently, and Martin was white with shock, his lips bloodless.

Malik tugged on Amy's hand.

"Please don't send anyone after us. Good-bye," Amy said to the trio in the parlor, then ran with Malik down the hall.

"Mehmet is tied up at the side of the house," Malik said as they burst out of the door and ran through the back garden.

"How did you get him here?" Amy asked breathlessly as he lifted her onto the horse and strapped her bag to the saddle.

"Anwar brought him to the jail," Malik replied. He settled behind her and kicked the horse's flanks, nudging Mehmet down the drive to the road.

"Where are we going?"

"Anwar has found us a safe house. It's about twenty miles from here. Just hang on to me and I'll explain what's happening when we get there."

The manicured streets of Pera were empty. Amy wondered what had happened to the ubiquitous janissaries; the patrols were gone, and an eerie silence had replaced the sound of clanging weapons and marching feet. Just as they left the Woolcotts' street, a tremendous explosion split the stillness and Mehmet reared, his forefeet flailing the air.

It took several seconds for Malik to control the horse, and in that time people began to pour out of their homes, babbling excitedly, running into the street, and pointing toward the water.

A number of smaller blasts followed in rapid succession as Amy turned to look past Malik's shoulder and saw a thick column of smoke rising toward the indigo sky.

"What was that?" she gasped.

"The gunpowder magazine at Topkapi," Malik replied grimly, still grappling with the restive horse. "The janissaries just blew it up."

Amy fell silent and grasped the pommel of the saddle more tightly, putting aside her questions for later as Mehmet settled down and they continued their ride. The startled population filling the streets paid them little attention; the residents gravitated in the opposite direction toward the park which offered an elevation and a better view of the harbor. Amy was glad they were so distracted that they didn't have the time to look closely at the two passing on horseback. She in her tea dress and Malik in his prison deshabille would have caused a commotion in themselves if the circumstances surrounding them at that moment had been less chaotic.

As they rode through the city, heading for the northern gate and the impenetrable hills which provided refuge for the rebels, Amy didn't see a single soldier. The janissaries had been a constant presence in Constantinople the whole time she had been there, and she found to her surprise that their sudden absence was unsettling. She had always resented them, since they made her feel as if she were living in a state of seige, but now she realized that there was no force in place to control the agitated population which swelled around them. Nobody knew what was happening, and the perpetually unhappy residents of the poorer sections gave every appearance of erupting into riots. She sighed with relief as Mehmet surged through the thinning suburbs and finally emerged onto the open plain with its scrub grass and thirsty trees. A silver moon rose while the sun set behind them, and the air grew chill.

Malik steered the horse upward into the foothills, where the track was almost lost in the undergrowth and only a native would know the way. Mehmet slowed, picking his way around boulders and leaping across crags, inching his way through the difficult terrain. Just when Amy was sure they would have to stop to rest the horse, she spotted the corner of a thatched roof through the trees. Malik turned Mehmet toward it, and as they came closer she saw that the hut was made of fieldstone with a door hewn from the local wood.

Malik reined Mehmet in and jumped to the ground, tying the horse to a tree and then lifting Amy down from the saddle. As she moved out of his arms, he pulled her back and said, "Stay here a moment. I thought I would never hold you again."

Amy put her head on his shoulder, clinging to him, finding the familiar spot under his breastbone where her nose usually rested. "You frightened me so much when I saw you at the jail," she whispered. "When you turned me away so harshly, I knew you believed you were going to die."

"Don't think about that now," he said, stroking her hair. "It's over and we're together."

"But for how long? You still haven't told me how you got out of jail, what happened to the janissaries—any of it."

"Let's go inside and I'll tell you everything."

The interior of the hut was stark, with just a table and two chairs, a bed, and a wooden storage chest on the dirt-packed floor. A fire was laid in the stone grate, and Malik knelt to light it as Amy closed the door behind them, leaving them in semi-darkness. He rose with a burning twig in his hand and lit the fat tallow candles standing in wooden cups on the table, glancing at Amy as she shivered.

"Are you cold?" he said, his hand automatically going to his shirtfront to remove what he was wearing and give it to her. Then he glanced down at his shirt, remembered that it was in rags, and grinned ruefully.

"I guess I'll have to keep you warm," he said, grabbing Amy and tumbling with her onto the bed. He pulled the faded, handstitched quilt over both of them and wrapped her in his arms. Gradually her shuddering ceased and she lay peacefully against him.

"Better?" he said, his lips touching her ear.

"Yes. I guess it was just a reaction to all of this—two hours ago I was having tea with Martin Fitzwater and now here I am with you."

"I should have shot that bastard when I had the chance," Malik said grimly.

"Oh, darling, don't be ridiculous," Amy murmured. "I was just going along with Aunt Bea's plans to buy some time."

"He's a lecher," Malik said darkly.

"And you're not?" Amy said smilingly, reaching up to touch his dirt-smeared, hair-covered cheek.

He turned his head to kiss her hand, his eyes looking very large and dark in the flickering candlelight. "Only for you."

"Are you going to tell me how you got out of jail?" Amy asked him.

"Anwar joined forces with Kalid Shah and they staged a raid on the jail at the same time the janissaries walked off the job," Malik replied.

Amy sat up and stared at him. "The janissaries walked off the job?" she repeated incredulously.

He nodded. "Most of them, anyway. The few that remained loyal to the Sultan gave us a bit of an argument, but there aren't enough of them to matter. As I said, the explosion you heard when we left Pera was Kemal Sorek torching the fuel dump at Topkapi."

Amy was stunned into silence. Finally she said, "Does this mean the Sultan has been deposed?"

Malik sighed. "It won't be that easy. He's still breathing, and he has a loyal group around him at the palace. We could have stormed it this afternoon, but Kalid wants to keep Hammid alive. He's afraid we'll be cut off by the West if we look like bloodthirsty assassins."

"That's reasonable, isn't it?"

Malik snorted. "Hammid has been murdering people for years, and it hasn't stopped the Western governments from sending ambassadors or doing business here." He paused. "If it had been up to me alone, I would have killed him."

"Even though it might have jeopardized the future of the new government you hope to form?" Amy asked.

Malik was silent. He was clearly torn between the two objectives—the old and deep-seated desire for personal revenge on the man who had killed his family, and the more recent goal of establishing a Turkish democracy, which could not long survive without foreign friends.

"So what is the plan?" Amy finally asked.

"As a first step, Kalid has sent word to the Sultan, offering to act as negotiator. He wants to get some concessions for us in return for restoring the janissaries."

"And you? What happens to you?" Amy said anxiously.

"I have to hide out for a few days until things cool down. Kalid said that my presence at the conference table would be too 'inflammatory'."

"Listen to him, Malik. He knows the Sultan and he knows what he's doing."

"I am listening to him," Malik said shortly. "That's why I'm here."

"But you'd rather be with Anwar?"

He pulled her back to him and kissed her. "I would always rather be with you," he said gently. "But after fighting for so long, it is hard to leave the end game to somebody else."

"In other words, you want to be there in person to shove your victory down Hammid's throat," Amy said dryly.

"It's not a victory yet," Malik replied.

"Why not? What can the Sultan do without his soldiers?"

"I don't know how long the janissaries will be with us. It's an uneasy alliance and could fall apart at any time."

Amy sighed, then hugged him tighter. "I know it's hard to wait and wonder," she said softly. "It's especially hard for someone like you."

He drew back and looked at her.

"You're not exactly the waiting type," Amy said, and he glanced away from her impatiently.

She tugged on his neck and pulled him back down to the bed. "I have an idea how to pass the time," she whispered, kissing the side of his throat.

"I'm filthy," he muttered, already unhooking her bodice.

"I don't care."

"Neither do I," he replied, and Amy could hear the smile in his voice.

Amy didn't mind the beard stubble, the jail smell, or the clothes that came off him in tattered layers. Underneath he was still Malik, and as the now blazing fire warmed the room, he made love to her hungrily, their time of separation making him ardent, demanding. As she lay in his arms afterward, gazing up at his carved profile, she almost had to pinch herself to make sure he was really there. She had gone from despair to joy in such a short time that she was still reeling from the quick change; it was like a miracle to feel his body next to hers. She snuggled closer to him and he stirred.

"Are you awake?" Amy asked.

"I'm asleep," he replied.

"You are not."

He opened one eye and looked at her. "Yes, I am."

"Malik, what will happen to you if the Sultan manages to regain his power?" she asked, ignoring him.

He sighed and rolled over on top of her, pinning her to the bed. "The revolt of his soldiers should have scared him enough to negotiate; I don't think he will ever again be what he was. But it's impossible to say what he'll do now. He's never been challenged before, and I don't know how he'll behave if he thinks he's cornered." He kissed her bare shoulder.

Amy said nothing. Malik might be out of jail, but she was still afraid for him. He had spearheaded the revolt, and if the Sultan retained any vestige of his former might he was not likely to forget that. Alarmed at her own thoughts, she realized that she would have preferred to hear that Hammid was dead.

"Don't look so worried," Malik said, reading her expression. "I'm in one piece, and we're a lot closer to getting rid of that monster than we were yesterday."

Amy held him against her and stroked his hair, hoping that he was right.

Malik suddenly raised his head and said, "Anwar told me he would leave some food here. I'm hungry."

"I thought you were asleep."

"Not any more." He got out of the bed, picked up his ragged pants from the floor, then dropped them again in disgust. He went to the wooden chest and began rummaging through it, tossing out several bundles, one containing soap and a hairbrush, another a couple of garments.

"Change of clothes," he said, donning the pants and tying the drawstring waist.

"That should come in handy."

"Ah-ha," Malik said, holding aloft a canvas bag. He untied the string at its mouth and produced two apples, a wheel of pita bread, and several hardening borek.

"Want one?" he said, displaying an apple.

Amy shook her head. "Aunt Beatrice had enough to feed an army when . . ." She stopped when she saw his expression change.

"When your suitor came to visit?" he said sourly, biting into the fruit.

"Don't start."

"He looks like a wax dummy in that uniform," Malik said.

"I thought you admired the British."

"Not when they're after my woman."

Amy slipped out of the bed, wrapping the quilt around her and kneeling next to him on the dirt floor. "Is that what I am?" she whispered, touching his cheek.

"That's what you are."

"Since I met you, I feel like a woman."

"You feel like a woman to me, too," he said teasingly, dropping the apple and wrestling her under him.

"Malik, I know you don't want me see how anxious you are," she said, looking up at him.

"I'm not anxious."

"Restless, then."

He bent his head and clenched his fists. "I want to know what's happening!" he blurted out, closing his eyes. "I've lived for this moment for years and I'm missing it!"

"Let Kalid do the talking. You know that's the right thing."

"Yes, but when I agreed to stay out of it, I didn't realize it would be this difficult."

"I know what you need," Amy said soothingly.

He smiled.

"I meant a nice, hot bath."

"Oh."

"I saw a rain barrel out back, and the fire is old enough now to heat the water."

He nodded and stood up, going outside for the water and then hanging the iron kettle on a peg over the roaring fire. Amy took out the soap and brush, picked up the clean shirt, and dusted it off ineffectually.

"I don't think that's going to help," Malik said ruefully, coming up behind her.

"You're lucky to have it at all, considering the condition of your own clothes."

"Someday soon all the people in this country will have enough of everything," he said softly, sitting on the edge of the bed.

"I know that's your dream," Amy responded, standing in front of him and putting her hands on his shoulders

He turned his head and kissed her fingers. "I hope it's coming true."

"It will. I can feel it. The Sultan's days are numbered."

He murmured something in Turkish, and Amy asked, "What was that?"

"How do you say it in English? It's the last word to all your prayers."

Amy smiled. "Amen."

He nodded. "Amen."

When the water was heated, Malik added some cold water from the barrel and soaped up, the firelight playing over his bare body as Amy watched. He had lost weight in jail, and the muscles were clearly defined under his skin, his ribcage visible. He was still beautiful, but if he dropped a few more pounds he would begin to look gaunt.

Amy resolved to fatten him up as quickly as possible.

Malik went back outside to rinse off on the grass, and Amy handed him the quilt. He bundled into it, rubbing briskly and glancing up at the emerging stars.

"It feels good to be clean," he admitted.

"Let me wash your hair now," Amy said.

He ran his hand through the ragged waves, his look rueful. "Pretty bad, eh?" he said.

"Pretty dusty. It looks gray."

"It probably *is* gray," he observed, following Amy back inside the hut and sitting on the edge of the bed.

She dipped into the kettle and wet down the dark mass of his hair, soaping it with the pine-smelling lump Anwar had supplied and massaging the thick tresses, digging her fingers into Malik's scalp.

"Feels good," he grunted. "See anything crawling out of there?"

Amy stepped back suddenly.

He laughed. "You can pick up a lot of miniature company in jail," he said.

"Let's not talk about it," Amy said, forcing his head forward and rinsing the back of his hair.

"Water's getting cold already," he said.

"Almost done." She rinsed again and ran her fingernail along a natural part in his hair.

"Looking for vermin?" he asked.

"Just making sure it's still black." She began to squeeze the moisture out of it with her fingers, since there was no towel and the quilt was already wet.

"I wish I had a razor," he said, rubbing his bearded jaw.

"I'll settle for just clean right now." Amy replied, admiring how his wet sable hair gleamed.

"I feel like a new man."

"I kind of liked the old one." She bent forward and wound her arms around his neck. "I missed you so much."

"I didn't miss you at all," he said teasingly, pulling her into his lap. "I liked the Sultan's jail. There were lots of like-minded people there for me to talk to—thieves, rapists, murderers . . ."

"You're none of those things," Amy murmured, resting her head on his shoulder.

"Hammid would disagree with you."

"His opinion no longer matters." She kissed him tenderly.

Malik rolled over onto the bed, pinning Amy under him. "I never would have predicted things would turn out this way," he said softly. "When I first met you, I saw you only as a means to an end. But you changed that very quickly."

"And when I first met you, my only goal in life was to get away from you," Amy countered.

"What's your goal now?" he asked, smiling, moving back onto his side

"Let me show you," Amy replied, reaching for the drawstring at his waist.

He closed his eyes as she loosened his pants and caressed him, then his breathing escalated as his skin flushed deeply. Finally he stayed her hand and said to her thickly, "You'll never touch another man this way."

"Never," she whispered.

He drew her to him fiercely, his lips against her hair. "I'll make sure you keep that promise," he said.

"I will. But it seems like we've been in love so long, Malik, and we've only been able to snatch little bits of time together," Amy said. "I want more. I want to be with you all the time, have a family, build a life together."

"We'll have everything we want, you'll see. Very soon," he said soothingly, and kissed her.

Amy responded avidly, and all conversation in the cottage stopped.

They spent the night in each other's arms, and just after dawn the next morning there was a knock at the cottage door.

Amy stirred in the semi-darkness, glancing at Malik, who sat up quickly, throwing off the sheet.

"Who is it?" Amy hissed in alarm.

"It's probably just Anwar. He's the only one who knows we're here."

We hope, Amy added silently, shivering and drawing the blanket over her shoulders. The fire was out, but her chill was not just a product of the temperature in the room. She watched Malik pull on his trousers and walk to the door; then she sighed with relief when she saw Anwar standing outside.

"What news?" Malik asked him.

Anwar glanced at Amy in the bed, then looked away quickly.

"I have a message from Kalid Shah," he said soberly. "He has received the Sultan's terms."

Malik waited.

"He will step down in favor of his brother, who will grant the formation of a parliament with elected representatives, if you will meet with Abdul Hammid at noon tomorrow."

Chapter Thirteen

"I can't believe you even listened to that nonsense!" Sarah said in an outraged tone to her husband.

"My role was to hear what the Sultan had to say," Kalid replied mildly. "I didn't indicate to him in any way that I agreed to accept his terms."

"You are not going to sacrifice that boy," Sarah declared in a strong voice. She had been reclining on a chaise in their bedroom and rose quickly, gathering her dressing gown about her.

"Of course not."

"The Sultan is ruthless. He knows that he is going to lose his throne, and he wants to take Malik with him. He'll be waiting for Osman's brother with a firing squad."

"Not if he wants to get out of this with his life. I think he's intelligent enough to imagine what will happen to him if he kills Malik Bey on the eve of this compromise."

"Then why make this demand?"

"Maybe he just wants to meet the man who has given him so much trouble."

"Is he that curious?" Sarah asked.

"Wouldn't you be? If you were one of the most powerful rulers in the world and you were about to be overthrown by an upstart peasant barely out of his teens?"

Sarah shook her head. She still didn't like it.

"I'll make it clear that if anything happens to Malik, the janissaries will not return and Hammid's imperial head will be back on the block again." Kalid sat on the edge of their bed and pulled on his boots.

"Maybe he doesn't care," Sarah said. "He's about to lose his position and his power. Maybe he doesn't want to live."

Kalid shook his head. "Hammid is a coward. Cowards always want to live. Anyway, I don't know if Malik will go."

"Malik will go."

Kalid looked at her.

"He's nothing if not courageous. Surely you have noticed that about him."

"You sound like you're the one in love with him instead of Amy," Kalid said tightly.

Sarah sat next to him on the bed and put her head on his shoulder.

"Are you jealous, you foolish man?" she said softly.

"I think I could be."

"Oh, Kalid, don't be ridiculous."

"Why ridiculous? You admit that you admire the kid's nerve, and it's been quite some time since I impressed you with my feats of derring-do."

"If you get us all through this to a democracy without a bloodbath, that will be quite enough derring-do for me."

He stared at the floor. "I'm tired, *kourista*," he said.

Sarah said nothing. He rarely commented on how he felt when in a crisis, but this time he really *looked* tired. He had been wearing himself out, occupying center stage in this clash of wills which could explode at any moment into real warfare, and the toll it had taken on him was visible.

A servant knocked and at Sarah's command entered the room. The girl was carrying a silver tray containing Kalid's Turkish coffee and a samovar for Sarah's tea.

"Set it on the table," Sarah said.

The girl put it on the serving stand and then vanished, closing the door quietly behind her.

"I won't let Malik go alone," Kalid said suddenly to Sarah. "Whatever happens."

Sarah kissed him. "Thank you."

He kissed her back, then pulled her down to the bed as their breakfast drinks cooled on the tray.

The Imperial Palace at Topkapi was almost deserted; the few janissaries who had remained loyal to the Sultan stood about, armed to the teeth, watching stolidly as Kalid and Malik walked through the vast hall leading to the Sultan's audience room.

In stark contrast to the soldiers who served the Sultan, they were unarmed.

At the end of a long, wide hall tiled with marble and hung with ornate tapestries stood a pair of doors, covered with gold leaf and overhung by a plaque which listed the Sultan's titles in enameled lapis script. As the vistors approached, the guards on either side presented arms. The doors swung open, revealing the Sultan seated on his throne at the far end of the reception hall. It seemed to Malik that it took a long time to cross the intricate bird-of-paradise carpet covering the mosaic floor and stand in front of the man who had been his enemy for so many years.

Abdul Hammid II, the Lion of the Desert, Defender of Allah and Master of the Two Continents, Ruler of Destinies and Sultan of the Sublime Porte, Shadow of God on Earth, looked back at him. Hammid, his graying black hair covered by a scarlet fez, dressed in his finest array, was alone in the room except for the two guards at the door. After studying Malik for some moments with obsidian eyes, he turned to Kalid and said, "Your presence was not requested for this audience, Kalid Shah."

"Nevertheless, I am here," Kalid said firmly.

"I wish to be alone with this brother of Osman Bey," the Sultan said.

Kalid opened his mouth to protest again, but Malik said to him quickly in English, "It's all right. You can wait for me outside in the hall."

Kalid looked at him, and Malik nodded. The Sultan waited until Kalid had left before saying to Malik, "You resemble your brother, but he is not so handsome. I assume you remember Osman, the thief who stole my daughter."

"He married her, for which you killed the rest of my family," Malik replied.

"He was not worthy!"

"That was for Roxalena to decide. Thinking like that has made you obsolete, *padishah,* and caused this revolution against you."

The Sultan sat back in his jewel-encrusted chair and fingered his moustache, still coal-black and thick. "So now you have won," he said flatly to Malik.

"The people have won," Malik replied.

Hammid smiled thinly. "You talk like a Westerner. Democracy is more difficult than the American newspapers make it sound. It is quarrelsome, inefficient, and very slow. After six months of it, you will be longing for the ordered and settled way of life of your ancestors which you discarded for rule by ignorant rabble."

"It will take time, but we will learn. And in future generations the rabble will be educated and capable of ruling themselves."

Hammid turned his head slowly, looking past him into the distance, and Malik suddenly saw the Sultan for what he really was: a weakling, a venal and overmatched man, thrust into his role by force of primogeniture, indulged and obeyed without question since childhood. Incapable of understanding change, he couldn't adjust to a world which had already left him behind. It must be almost impossible for him to accept that after ruling with a whim of iron for a generation, the most he could hope for in this situation was to escape it with his head.

"I have one further condition before I will abdicate in favor of my brother," the Sultan said, looking back at Malik. "I wanted to express it to you personally."

Malik waited.

"You will give me your word that you will have no public role in the formation of the new government. You will not run for office and will accept no official position offered by a plebiscite. That is my condition."

Malik was silent, rocked to his heels. It was a mean and petty request, typical of the Sultan's nature. Hammid was offering the one thing his opponent wanted, democracy for Turkey, if Malik would give up the only thing he now had: his leadership role in the revolution. Hammid would concede his defeat if doing so deprived Malik of the credit for the conquest.

Malik took a deep breath. "I agree," he said.

Hammid stared at him in surprise. He had misjudged his adversary. Again.

"Then it is done," Hammid said simply, after a long pause. "I will abdicate in favor of my brother, and your representatives will work with him in the formation of the congress."

"Kalid Shah will arrange the details." Malik turned and walked toward the doors.

"History will record my name in large letters, and your name will not appear at all," Hammid called after him.

Malik kept walking, then stopped before the closed doors.

Hammid gave the command, and they opened before him. Malik kept moving, but not until they closed behind him did he breathe a sigh of relief.

"What happened?" Kalid asked, rushing to his side.

Malik told him.

"That bastard," Kalid said heatedly. "He wants to deprive you of the glory of his removal and deprive the people of a figure to rally around, a central leader to unify them."

"It doesn't matter," Malik said. "Anwar and the others won't do anything without consulting me. Hammid knows he can't prevent me from working behind the scenes, but he thinks I'm as childish as he is and need the adulation of the masses."

"You deserve it," Kalid said quietly.

"I can live without it, as long as we get what we want." He smiled at Kalid for the first time that day.

Kalid smiled back, and the two men embraced.

"Now let's get to work," Kalid said.

The reception room at Orchid Palace was decorated for a wedding, but it was not to be a traditional Turkish one. The bride had insisted on a Western ceremony, with the rites conducted in English, and the groom had agreed. A minister from the British community in Constantinople had been brought to Bursa to perform the rites, and he waited anxiously before the banks of massed flowers. His prayerbook in hand, he glanced around anxiously at the opulent furnishings which until recently had belonged to the pasha, Kalid Shah, who now rented the palace and its contents from the newly established provisional government.

In an anteroom, Amy fiddled with her trailing veil of white net, staring into the cheval mirror as Sarah stood behind her, arranging the train on her pale peach silk dress. The gown's leg-of-mutton sleeves fit tightly from elbow to wrist and were complemented by a pointellated waistline and an illusion bodice of filmy chiffon. Amy had bought the ensemble in one of the exclusive shops in Pera, one of her last indulgences before assuming the role of pioneering legislator's wife.

Malik had kept his word to the Sultan, but he was the real force behind the new government and everybody knew it. He was happier than Amy had ever seen him, and she would be too, if only James and Beatrice had agreed to attend her wedding.

"There, it's perfect," Sarah said, stepping back to admire the modified bustle on the back of the gown.

Amy nodded.

Sarah put her hand on the younger woman's shoulder. "Don't fret about James and Bea," Sarah said, reading her mind. "They're conservative people, and it will take them a while to see Malik as anything other than a bandit who kidnapped one of their relatives. It took them a long time to accept Kalid too."

"I know, but this is not exactly what I pictured in my childhood daydreams. I thought I would be married at home, in a church, with all the family there and . . ." Her voice trailed off in disappointment.

"But then you wouldn't be marrying Malik,"

Sarah pointed out to her.

Amy brightened. "You're right. And there's no one on earth I would rather marry, so I guess that makes up for everything, doesn't it?"

"Of course." Sarah pulled on her white silk goves and picked up Amy's bouquet of creamy peonies, bound with trailing streamers of peach and ivory silk. Her own dress of celadon satin was bibbed and hemmed with three layers of *broderie anglaise*, and her daughter was similarly dressed, with white kid boots and lace bows in her hair. The two boys were attired as pages in black velvet suits, and had spent the last hour fingering their black silk ties importantly.

There was a tap on the dressing room door, and Sarah put down the bouquet to open it a crack. When she saw who it was she hissed, "Get out of here! You're not supposed to see the bride before the wedding."

"That's a Turkish tradition," Malik replied, trying to peer around Sarah to see his intended.

"It's a Western tradition too," Sarah replied crisply, blocking his path.

"Two minutes," he said.

"Sarah, who is it?" Amy called from her position before the mirror.

Sarah sighed and bowed to the inevitable, holding the door open and then calling over her shoulder, "I'll be back shortly."

Malik entered the room and then stopped at

the sight of Amy, who whirled to face him.

"You look gorgeous," he said softly.

"So do you," Amy whispered.

It was true. He was wearing a black tailcoat and trousers with a gray satin waistcoat, white shirt, and white satin bow tie.

"I look ridiculous," he said uncomfortably.

"You're very handsome," Amy said.

He ran his finger around his neck under his collar. "This thing is choking me."

"You look very healthy for someone who is suffocating," Amy replied, walking over to him and kissing his cheek.

"Can you believe this day has come?" he asked, holding her at arm's length and looking down into her face.

"There were times when I never thought it would," she admitted. "Now we will have everything."

"I already have everything. A free Turkey, and you for the rest of my life."

The door opened again and Sarah said, "James and Beatrice are here."

Amy glanced at her in amazement, and Sarah grinned.

"What happened?" Amy asked.

"James talked her into it," Sarah said impishly.

"Or dragged her out of the house and tied her to the seat of the carriage," Malik said dryly. He had not forgotten Bea's preference for Martin Fitzwater.

"Come on, you two lovebirds—everyone is out here waiting," Sarah said.

Malik lifted Sarah's hand to his lips and said, "Are you ready to become my wife?"

"If you're ready to become my husband."

Sarah stepped aside and the two young people walked past her to embrace their future.

Pure Temptation

Connie Mason

On Newsstands everywhere in July!

"Each new Connie Mason book is a prize!"
—Heather Graham

Chapter One

London 1795

Ghosts were so bloody unpredictable.

During his youthful years Jackson Graystoke had searched every nook and cranny of the crumbling stone mansion that he had inherited, looking for Lady Amelia's ghost, and he came up empty-handed. When he was a stripling he would have given his eyeteeth for a glimpse of the elusive lady who occasionally haunted the halls of Graystoke Manor. But certainly not now, not when he no longer believed that ghosts existed.

During the two-hundred-odd years following the death of Lady Amelia, who according to legend appeared only to those male Graystokes who walked the path to perdition, she had appeared infrequently, since few of her upstanding descendants throughout the years were debauched enough to need her help.

Until Black Jack Graystoke. The black sheep of the Graystoke family, he was a man dedicated to dissipation.

Rogue, bounder, rapscallion, rake, seducer of women. Men liked him, women loved him. And Lady Amelia, who hovered over his bed like an avenging angel, glared down upon him with obvious displeasure.

"Go away," Jack said irritably. He had just gotten to bed after a night at the gaming tables and had no time for an apparition who could or could not be a figment of his imagination. He knew he'd had too much to drink but didn't think he was *that* foxed.

Clothed in shimmering light and flowing garments, the ghost shook her head.

"What in the devil do you want?"

Lady Amelia merely stared at him through hollow eyes.

"Why now? Why have you chosen this time to appear when there was a day I would have welcomed a glimpse of you?" Jack was familiar with the legend of the family ghost, having heard it many, many times. "I'm too steeped in sin. Nothing you can do will save me from perdition."

Lady Amelia floated away toward the door.

Jack raised up on his elbow and saw that she was motioning to him. He groaned in dismay and fell back against the pillow, squeezing his eyes shut. When he opened them Lady Amelia was still there.

"Where am I to go? 'Tis raining out, for god's sake!" The windows rattled, confirming his words. Unfortunately, the rain had turned to pelting sleet, driven against the house by ice-laden wind. "Can't it wait till morning?"

Lady Amelia wrung her hands and appeared agitated. Obviously she wasn't going to go away. She shook her head and pointed toward the door again, even more determined that Jack should rouse himself and plunge into the blustery night.

"Bloody hell, is there no compromise?" Lady Amelia shook her head. "Very well, my lady, you win. Take me where you will; I can see there is no sleep for me this night."

The light surrounding Lady Amelia flickered as if in agreement. Then, before Jack's very eyes, the apparition evaporated through the closed door. Muttering an oath, Jack flung aside the covers and threw on his recently discarded clothes, taking particular care with his neck-cloth. He never appeared anywhere less than impeccably attired.

Still grumbling, Jack strode from the room, not surprised when he saw Lady Amelia waiting for him at the head of the stairs.

"Where in bloody hell am I supposed to go?" His handsome features, which women loved to distraction, bore a decidedly annoyed look.

Lady Amelia merely bowed her head and crooked her finger. He followed her floating figure down the stairs. She led him to the front door.

He hesitated at the door. "Do you realize what it's like out there? 'Tisn't fit for man or beast. Do you expect me to awaken my coachman on a night such as this?" Lady Amelia merely stared at him, as if to suggest he lacked a sense of adventure. Jack spit out an oath. "Oh, what the hell! I'll drive the carriage myself, if it will make you happy. All I ask is that you give me some idea where I am to go."

Lady Amelia seemed disinclined to offer further information as she backed away from the door. Her shimmering light dimmed, then went out.

"Wait! Don't go! You haven't told me . . ." It was too late. Lady Amelia had already disappeared in a wisp of smoke.

Thunderstruck, Jack stared at the empty space where Lady Amelia had stood just moments before. Had he imagined it all? Was Lady Amelia a figment of his rather fertile imagination? Perhaps, he thought ruefully, he was more foxed than he thought. He paused with his hand on the doorknob. What to do? If he was smart he'd go back to bed and treat this as a bad dream. Or he could accept the challenge and brave the inclement weather.

Black Jack Graystoke had yet to turn down a challenge. Ghost or dream, he was already awake and dressed. If nothing else he could go to White's Club and drink with his friends, some of whom would likely be out and about despite the weather. He wouldn't have returned home so early himself if he hadn't had the world's worst luck at cards tonight.

Needles of icy sleet blasted him as he opened the door and stepped outside. Bowing his head against the howling wind, Jack walked briskly to the carriage house and harnessed the handsome pair of grays he'd won in a card game to the shabby carriage, his only conveyance. Nearly everything Jack owned had been either won or lost at cards. His family, impoverished relatives of the young earl of Ailesbury on his mother's side, had left him nothing but an inherited baronetcy, a pile of debts and a crumbling mansion located in the heart of London's Hanover Square that had been in the family for over two hundred years. The mansion demanded so much of his resources that just the upkeep emptied his pockets.

Marriage to an heiress was Jack's only recourse and he was seriously thinking about ending his bachelorhood soon by marrying Lady Victoria Greene, a wealthy widow he'd been dallying with. A love match was out of the question. Everyone knew Black Jack Graystoke was too much of a rogue to offer undying love to any one lady.

Jack struck a light to the side lamps of the carriage, leaped up onto the box, took up the ribbons and guided the reluctant grays out of the gate. The sleet struck him forcefully and he buried his face in his collar, cursing Lady Amelia for his misery. He hadn't the foggiest idea why the ghost had sent him abroad on a night such as this and longed for a bracing brandy or something equally fortifying. Until he learned Lady Amelia's intention he might as well make the best of it. Jack drove through deserted windswept streets to White's Club and parked at the curb.

The warmth inside the club was inviting as Jack relinquished his cape to the doorman and strode into the brightly lit room. He was immediately greeted by his good friend, Lord Spencer Fenwick, heir to a dukedom.

"Jack, you old dog, I thought you'd gone home hours ago. What brings you out again in such foul weather? Do you anticipate a change of luck? Shall we find room at one of the gaming tables?"

"If my luck has changed, it's for the worse," Jack complained, thinking of Lady Amelia's unexpected haunting. "I'm in desperate need of a drink, Spence old chap," he said, placing an arm around his friend's padded shoulders.

On the way to the refreshment room, Jack found himself surrounded by simpering females, all eager for his attention. Tall, muscular and lithe as a stalking tiger, Black Jack was pure temptation to women of all ages. Wavy dark hair surrounding a bold masculine face and full tempting lips hinted at his sensual nature, but it was his wicked gray eyes that captured the ladies' fancy. Once Black Jack aimed his potent gaze at a woman, she was lost. The problem was that Jack saw no reason to focus those incredibly sexy eyes on any one woman.

"Drink up, Jack," Spence urged when they finally had drinks in hand. Jack needed no inducement to drown the memory of Lady Amelia in strong liquor. He must have been mad to have conjured up the family ghost he had all but forgotten years ago.

Hours later, both Spence and Jack were deep into their cups, nearly staggering, in fact. Spence had the rare good sense to suggest they call it a night and Jack agreed. Nothing good could come of this night, Jack decided, still annoyed at Lady Amelia for sending him out on such a raw night. Whatever did she have in mind for him? Probably mischief, he thought glumly, as if he needed any more mischief in his life. He was more than capable of dredging up enough of that commodity on his own.

"Wise of you to bring the carriage," Spence drawled as he reeled from the club on rubbery legs and spied Jack's team and carriage standing at the curb. "I walked, myself. How about a lift? Bloody raw night to be afoot."

None too steady himself, Jack wove an erratic path to the carriage. "Climb aboard, old chap, glad to give you a lift."

"Damned if I ain't tempted to walk," Spence grumbled when he noted Jack's unsteady gait.

"Drunk or sober, I can handle a carriage and team as well or better than any man alive," Jack boasted as he picked up the ribbons.

Spence had barely settled beside Jack when Jack slapped the reins against the horses' rumps and the carriage rattled off down the icy road with a jolt that shook Spence to the core.

"Bloody hell, Jack, are you trying to kill us?"

Jack laughed uproariously, until a barrage of icy pellets brought a measure of sobriety, making him realize that his recklessness could endanger not only himself but his good friend. He struggled to control the unruly grays now that they had their head and nearly succeeded when he felt a jolt.

"My God, what's that? Stop, Jack, we've hit something!" Hanging on for dear life, Spence peered over the side into the dark street while Jack fought the prancing grays. With great effort he brought the carriage to a screeching halt.

Jack's sodden brain had registered the small bump but had thought nothing of it until

Spence had cried out a warning. Had he hit something? Or someone? God forbid! Leaping down from the box, he felt sober as a judge as he frantically searched the rain-slicked street for . . . a body? He certainly hoped not.

The night was so dark and the carriage lamps so dim, Jack stumbled over the body before he saw it. "Bloody hell!"

"What is it?" Spence called from his perch on the box. "Did you find something?"

"Not something, someone," Jack said, dropping to his knees to examine the body. Searching frantically for injuries, his hands encountered two gently rounded mounds of woman's flesh. He inhaled sharply and removed his hands as if burned. "God's nightgown, a woman!"

Spence appeared at his elbow, staring in horror at the body lying in the gutter. "Is she dead?"

Jack's hands returned to the woman's chest. The faint but steady cadence of her heart told him she still lived. "She's alive, thank God."

"What do you suppose she's doing out on a night like this?" Spence wondered aloud.

"Plying her trade," Jack opined. "Only a whore would be out this late. What in the hell are we going to do with her?"

"We could leave her," Spence offered lamely.

"Not bloody likely," Jack responded, manfully accepting responsibility for the accident and any injuries the woman sustained.

"What do you suggest?"

"You could take her to Fenwick Hall, Spence, and see that her injuries are treated," Jack offered hopefully.

"Are you mad? My parents would skin me alive if I brought a whore into their home. I'm in line to inherit, for godsake!"

"Thank God I am no one of importance," Jack drawled with studied indifference.

Spence flushed, glad for the darkness that hid his stained cheeks. "I didn't mean that, old boy. But you aren't anyone's heir. You have no parents to tell you what to do. You don't give a fig about propriety. You're a free agent, Jack. You're the notorious Black Jack. Bringing a whore into your home would cause no raised eyebrows and only moderate scandal."

"Rightly so," Jack said with a hint of irritation. His reputation was already black—what was one more mark against him? "Damn you, Lady Amelia," he muttered beneath his breath. "If this is your idea of a joke, I don't appreciate your humor."

Spence looked at him curiously. "Who is Lady Amelia?"

"What? Oh, I didn't realize I spoke aloud. Lady Amelia is the family ghost. I think I've mentioned her on occasion."

"What has she to do with this?" Spence asked curiously.

Just then the woman groaned and began to

390

shiver uncontrollably, bringing the men's attention back to her. "We'd best get her off this icy street," Jack said, regaining his sense of chivalry. He'd never made a woman suffer in his life, no matter what her calling. "Help me lift her into the carriage. Careful," Jack chided when Spence staggered sideways. "Never mind, I'll do it myself." He pushed Spence aside and lifted the woman carefully, surprised that she weighed so little. In his arms, cradled against the broad expanse of his muscular chest, she seemed little more than a fragile child.

"Get inside," Jack ordered as he placed the injured woman in the carriage and stepped aside so Spence could enter. "Try to keep her comfortable until we reach Graystoke Manor."

Jack drove with more care than was his normal custom. His irresponsible behavior weighed heavily upon him. He'd often been criticized for his reckless ways, but somehow this incident emphasized his impulsive rush toward perdition. Not even Lady Amelia could save him from the course his life was taking.

The carriage entered the gates of Graystoke Manor just as a gray dawn lifted the night sky. The driving sleet had turned into gentle rain, and mauve streaks coloring the horizon gave hint of better weather in the coming days. The moment the carriage clattered to a halt, Jack leaped from the box and flung open the door.

"How is the woman?"

"Still unconscious."

"I'll carry her inside while you go for the doctor. I hope you have coin on you—I'm temporarily out of funds. If not, I'll figure out something. I don't care what it takes, just get the doctor here."

Jack took the woman into his arms and banged on the front door with his foot. In due time, a gaunt, sleepy-eyed servant wearing a hastily tied robe answered. He seemed not at all alarmed to see his employer returning home at dawn carrying an unconscious woman.

"Bring hot water and towels to my chamber, Pettibone," Jack ordered crisply. "There's been an unfortunate accident. Lord Fenwick has gone for the doctor."

"Right away, sir." Pettibone shuffled off, the hem of his robe trailing on the ground.

Once in his chamber, Jack carefully placed the woman in the center of his bed then stood back to take his first good look at her. He was more than a little disturbed to see that she was young and not the slattern he had expected. Her patrician features and dainty body belied her profession. Had she newly taken up whoring? he wondered, as his gaze roved over her petite form. Jack was no stranger to women of all kinds, and he thought he knew everything about them there was to know, but this woman—no, not woman, for she was no more than a girl—defied definition.

A mop of glorious dark red hair covered her shapely head and fell in a tangled mass about her narrow shoulders. Her features were finely wrought, and he was surprised to find himself contemplating the color of her eyes. Beneath her wet clothing, her body appeared slim and shapely. Though her face was bruised and swollen, which was his fault, he suspected, she was lovelier than he would have guessed at first glance.

"I suppose I'd best rid you of these soaking clothes," Jack said to no one in particular as he lifted the girl slightly and removed her wet cloak.

The dress beneath was no less dry and Jack was startled to see she was modestly robed in a demure woolen dress of inferior quality, sporting no ornament whatever. He'd never known a whore to dress in such drab clothing. One would expect to see women of her sort garbed in flaming scarlet with most of their bosoms exposed. Turning her slightly, he unfastened the row of buttons marching down her back and pulled the dress away from her body. The pervading dampness had rendered her chemise all but transparent, revealing lush breasts topped with ripe, cherry-red nipples. When he heard Pettibone open the bedroom door, he quickly slid back the quilt and pulled it over her.

"The water, sir," Pettibone said, presenting a steaming pitcher and stack of towels. "Will you be needing anything else, sir?"

"You're completely unflappable, aren't you, Pettibone?" Jack said with a hint of amusement. "I knew I acted wisely when I kept you on. Though I can little afford servants, I don't regret retaining your services."

Pettibone looked enormously pleased. "Living with you has taught me to expect anything, so nothing you do surprises me, sir. Will the lady be all right?"

"We won't know until the doctor examines her. Send him up the moment he arrives. Tell Fenwick to await me in the library. We would appreciate something to eat later."

Pettibone left the room and Jack turned back to the woman occupying his bed. She was shivering, and he placed another blanket over her, wondering how long she had been out in the brutal weather. Did she have no sense at all? Didn't she know she'd find little business on a night like this?

The disgruntled doctor, perturbed at being routed out of bed at such an ungodly hour, arrived a few moments later and shooed Jack out of the room. Jack left reluctantly, joining Spence in the library.

"Well, how is she?" Spence asked, smothering a yawn behind a lace-edged handkerchief.

"Still unconscious," Jack said, frowning. "I fear I may have done the woman irreparable harm. She's my responsibility now, though

Lord only knows what I'm going to do with the wench once she's recovered. It would be a travesty to send her back out in the streets. She's younger than we thought, Spence, and probably new at her trade. I may be a blackhearted rogue but I'm not a devil."

"Hire her on as a maid," Spence said, wagging his eyebrows suggestively. "Or keep her to warm your bed."

Jack sent him a black look. "As you well know, I can't afford a maid. As for warming my bed, I have no problems on that score. My tastes are rather discerning. I prefer women who don't ply their trade on the streets."

"Lord, Jack, I think you're stuck with the woman until she recuperates and you can send her on her way."

"The woman upstairs in that bed isn't going anywhere for a while, gentlemen." The doctor entered the library and plopped into an overstuffed chair that had seen better days.

"What's wrong with her, Doctor . . . I'm sorry, I didn't catch your name."

"Dudley. For starters, her left arm is broken. She has numerous bruises and most likely will develop pneumonia, which can be quite serious. Pretty little thing . . . Who is she and how did she get hurt?"

Jack hesitated, suddenly at a loss for words. For some obscure reason he didn't want to reveal the fact that the woman was quite likely a whore.

"She's a distant relative of Jack's, from the Irish side of the family. Her father is a baron. He sent his daughter to London to be introduced to society," Spence lied, warming to the subject. "She's Jack's ward. She was injured when her coach overturned on the outskirts of London. She had been lying out in the rain several hours before help arrived and she was brought here."

Jack groaned in dismay. Spence's fertile imagination would be the death of him one day.

Enormously pleased with his quick thinking, Spence sent Jack a smug grin. Jack's virulent scowl was anything but amused.

"That would explain the injuries," Doctor Dudley said. "I'll leave medicine and return tomorrow to put a cast on her arm. By then the swelling should have receded. She's likely to be in considerable pain, but laudanum should ease her. Barring unforeseen setbacks, Lady Moira should be right as rain in four to six weeks."

"You know her name?" Jack asked, sending Spence a fulminating look. "I don't recall mentioning it." He could cheerfully strangle his friend for getting him into this muddle. Relative, indeed.

"She awoke briefly while I was treating her. When I asked her name she told me it was Moira. Her Irish brogue is delightful. Since she is in no condition to answer questions, I decided to get them from you instead."

Spence had no idea Moira was really Irish when he wove his tale and was enormously pleased that his story held at least a thread of truth. On the other hand, Jack appeared ready to explode. Not only was Jack saddled with an injured whore, but he had claimed her as a relative, thanks to Spence Fenwick and his wicked sense of humor. Jack hoped Doctor Dudley would be discreet but feared the old man was inclined to gossip.

"Will you stay for breakfast, Doctor?" Jack invited courteously. He hoped the doctor would refuse, for he couldn't wait to get Spence alone and berate him soundly.

"No time," Dudley said, levering his bulk from the chair. "Office hours start early. I'll be back tomorrow evening to look in on the patient."

Pettibone appeared with a breakfast tray, which he set down on a table with a flourish. Sensing the doctor was ready to leave, he bowed and escorted him to the door, leaving Spence and Jack alone.

"You wretched oaf, you really threw the fat into the fire," Jack thundered. "Relative, indeed. Whatever possessed you to tell that old gossip that the whore upstairs is related to me?"

His mouth full of food, Spence grinned. " 'Tis a grand joke, eh, Jack? I outdid myself this time.

What a hoot. How many whores can you claim in your family?"

"None that I know of," Jack replied soberly. "And I'm not about to claim any now. Especially not for your amusement. One day your pranks are going to backfire."

Jack ate in silence. When he finished he threw his napkin down and rose abruptly.

"Where are you going?" Spence asked, setting down his fork.

"Upstairs to see the patient."

"Wait, I'm coming with you."

Moira was sleeping as innocently as a babe when the two men tiptoed into the bedchamber. But evidently she wasn't sleeping as soundly as they thought, for she opened her eyes and gazed up at them.

Rich, warm honey, Jack decided as he stared into her eyes. Not brown, not hazel, but pure amber with gold flecks.

"Who are you? What happened?" Her lilting voice was as enchanting as the doctor had indicated. "Where am I?"

Mesmerized, Jack had to clear his throat twice before he could answer. "You are in my home. Do you recall what happened, Moira?"

Moira's gaze turned inward, then grew murky. She recalled very well what had happened but it was nothing she wanted to tell these two strange men. "How do you know my name?" She tried to sit up, grasped her splinted arm and groaned. "Blessed Mother, I hurt."

"Don't move. Your arm is broken," Jack said. "Can you remember anything?" Moira shook her head. "My carriage ran you down last night. 'Twas a most unfortunate accident. I learned your name from Doctor Dudley. I'm Sir Jackson Graystoke and this is Lord Spencer Fenwick."

"Black Jack?" Moira asked, her eyes widening.

Jack's gray eyes sparkled with amusement. "I see you've heard of me."

Moira swallowed convulsively. "Aye. Though I believed none of the gossip, sir."

Jack tilted his head back and laughed. "You should have. You had no identification on you," he continued, "so I brought you to my home and summoned a doctor to treat your injuries. I'm sorry about the accident. If you have relatives in town I'll gladly contact them for you."

"There's no one in England. My brother and his family live in Ireland. He has three small children and a wife to support. I left home some weeks ago to find work in London and ease his burden."

"Is there anyone who should know about your accident?" Jack asked, skirting the issue of her obvious occupation. "An employer, perhaps?"

"I'm an unemployed domestic servant, sir," Moira replied.

"Unemployed?" Spence asked. "How have

you been supporting yourself?"

"Just recently unemployed," Moira amended. "I haven't had time yet to look for work. I have no money, sir, I fear I can't pay for the doctor."

For some reason her remark made Jack angry. "Have I asked you for money? Until you're well you're my responsibility." Deliberately he picked up a small bottle from the night table and poured a measure into a glass. "Doctor Dudley left laudanum for your pain. Drink," he ordered gruffly, holding the glass to her lips.

Moira sipped gingerly, made a face at the bitter taste and refused to take more. "Thank you, you're very kind."

"The soul of kindness is Black Jack," Spence said, smothering a laugh. "You're in good hands, my dear."

When Moira's lids dropped over her incredible amber eyes, Jack pushed Spence out the door and followed him into the hall, closing the door firmly behind them.

"Do you believe her?" Spence asked, openly skeptical. "What would a decent woman be doing out late at night? Why do you think her employer fired her? She'll be a proper beauty once all that swelling goes down. Do you suppose she was diddling the master or his sons?"

"I'm not about to speculate, Spence. What concerns me more is what I'm going to do with her once she recovers. Perhaps I should send her back to Ireland."

"Lord, she'd probably starve to death if conditions are as bad there as we've been led to believe. Famine, disease and crop failure have decimated the population."

"Confound it, Spence, must you be so damn practical? What do you suggest?"

A mischievous gleam came into Spence's blue eyes. He didn't envy his friend's predicament, but what a grand opportunity for a little devilment. Life had been bloody boring lately. Like most of his rich and idle friends Spence loved harmless mischief. That's why he and Black Jack were such fast friends. Both men possessed a perverse sense of humor.

"Very well, I do have an idea, though I guarantee you won't like it."

Jack's handsome features grew wary. "Spit it out, Spence."

"Little Moira may be a prostitute, but she isn't your ordinary one. She is daintily fashioned, well spoken and not in the least coarse. Her features, even swollen as they are, are refined and almost genteel. I've already planted the seed that she is a distant relative of yours." He paused for effect.

"Continue," Jack said, almost certain he wasn't going to like what Spence had to say.

"Why not pass Moira off as a lady?" Spence eagerly suggested. "Introduce her to society and find her a husband. What jolly good fun we'd have. You never did have any use for those macaroni dandies who mince about London wearing high heels and makeup. Why not introduce 'Lady' Moira to society and marry her off to one of those fancy puppies?"

At first Jack looked astounded. Then he began to laugh uproariously. "Your wicked sense of humor leaves me speechless, Spence. But your idea does have merit." He grew thoughtful, toying with the notion. "She will need substantial polishing."

"Remember, 'tis already established that she's a country girl. No one will expect her to be too accomplished."

"Granted she is surprisingly well spoken for a commoner, but making her into a lady will require time and energy. I'm not certain I wish to devote so much effort to the task."

Admittedly the notion of making a silk purse from a sow's ear piqued Black Jack's sense of the outrageous, and Spence knew it. Not only was Jack intrigued with the endless possibilities such a challenge presented, but the gambler in Jack saw a way to enrich his coffers.

"How about sweetening the stakes?" Jack proposed.

"I thought you'd come around," Spence chortled, slapping Jack's back jovially. "What an adventure, eh? One of us will be the richer for it; you'll get rid of the Irish baggage, and we'll both be able to sit back and spin tales about this for years to come. I'll put up two thousand pounds against your matched pair of grays that you can't pass the girl off as gentry and get her engaged within . . . oh . . . say three months."

"Three months," Jack repeated, rubbing his stubbly chin thoughtfully. Two thousand pounds was a lot of money. Then again, his grays were the only thing of value he possessed. "I don't know. It will be at least four weeks before she is capable of moving about in public."

"You can use the time to groom her," Spence suggested eagerly. "You're a sporting man, Jack, what do you say? Are you up to the challenge?"

Spence's good-natured goading made it impossible for Jack to refuse. "With one exception. The girl has to agree to our proposal. Otherwise the bet is off."

"Agreed," Spence said gleefully. "I have every confidence you can charm the girl into falling in with our harmless little charade. Returning to the streets cannot possibly compare to what can ultimately be hers if she marries well."

Chapter Two

Moira O'Toole did not drop off to sleep easily. She worried excessively about the kind of trouble she had gotten herself into. From the moment she had flung herself from Lord Roger Mayhew's moving coach and struck her head, she recalled nothing. From what she knew of men, which was blessed little, they were egotistical, lust-crazed wretches who demanded their way with helpess women. If they didn't get what they wanted, they found ways to make women suffer. Did Jackson Graystoke live up to his nickname? she wondered bleakly as she pictured the man whose bed she occupied. He pretended to be a gentleman but his intense gray eyes held the weariness of a man that had indulged freely and frequently in every vice known to man.

Was Black Jack—the very name made her shudder—a disciple of the infamous Hellfire Club like Lord Roger? She must be extremely careful, Moira told herself, or she'd find herself in another dangerous situation. Black Jack and his friend must never know her shameful secret. Moira had expected life in London to be difficult for a poor Irish immigrant but never did she expect to encounter such unmitigated evil.

Clutching the gold locket circling her neck on its delicate chain, Moira thought of her sainted mother and how she would have despaired to see her daughter in such desperate straights. The locket was a cherished heirloom, a legacy from Moira's grandmother, who had died giving birth to Mary, Moira's mother. Mary had always cherished the locket, for it bore the tiny faded likeness of a young man in uniform whom Mary had always assumed was her father, Moira's grandfather.

Haunted by her illegitimacy, Mary had given the locket to her daughter, Moira, explaining that it contained proof that she and her brother, Kevin, had noble blood flowing through their veins. Moira's mother had been told by the nuns who raised her that her father was an English nobleman who had deserted Mary's pregnant mother.

"Mother, what am I to do?" Moira asked despondently, expecting no answer and getting none. Her cheeks wet with tears, she closed her eyes and slipped effortlessly toward sleep. She did not see Lady Amelia's ghost hovering above the bed, but a tentative smile stretched Moira's lips as a comforting warmth engulfed her, wrapping her in protective arms.

Jack awoke long after the sun made a belated appearance in an overcast sky. He stretched and yawned, disoriented at finding himself lying in a guest bed. Total recall came instantly. At this very moment, his bed was occupied by a woman he had run down in his carriage. He groaned in dismay. He could hardly afford to support himself let alone assume responsibility for another human being. Yet what could he do? He had caused her injuries and and couldn't in all conscience throw her out on the street.

He rose quickly and rang for Pettibone. The servant, dressed somberly in unrelieved black, appeared almost immediately, bearing a tray containing a teapot and cup.

"Ah, Pettibone, you always seem to know just what I need. Though truth be told, a stiff brandy would serve me better. Something tells me I'm going to need fortifying today."

"Are you referring to the young woman, sir?"

"Then I wasn't dreaming." Jack sighed. "I was hoping . . . Never mind. Is the woman awake?"

"Aye, Miss Moira is indeed awake. I took her up a tray just moments ago. If I may be so bold, sir, you should engage a woman to see to her needs."

How in bloody hell am I supposed to pay for the services of a maid? Jack wanted to know.

Pettibone did not offer a solution to Jack's dilemma as he helped Jack dress and prepare for the day. By the time he finished eating his breakfast, he was ready to confront Moira about the idea he and Spence had hatched the day before. He knew it was a harebrained scheme, but the longer he thought about it the more the idea of passing off a woman of questionable virtue as a lady appealed to him. Making bloody fools of his peers filled him with wicked delight. And it did offer a solution to the perplexing problem concerning the future of the woman he had run down. The sooner he rid himself of the unwelcome burden the better.

Struggling from her bed, Moira used the chamber pot behind the screen and then returned to bed just moments before Jack rapped lightly on the door and barged into the chamber. He stood at the foot of the bed, legs spread wide, hands clasped behind his back, staring at her. Looking into his keenly intelligent gray eyes, Moira felt as if she had inadvertently dropped into the turbulent depths of a violent storm.

There was inherent strength in the bold lines of his face, she thought, as her gaze settled on his lips. They were firm and sensual, set above a square chin which suggested a stubborn nature. He was a compelling, self-confident presence, one Moira had learned to fear from her dealings with Lord Roger.

Jack unclasped his hands and stood with his arms akimbo, his lithe body so gracefully coordinated, Moira likened him to a stalking tiger.

"How are you feeling, Miss O'Toole?"

"Better, thank you. I'll be on my way in a day or two."

Jack's lips curled in amusement. "And just where do you think you're going?"

Moira's chin rose fractionally. "I won't impose on you any longer than necessary or accept charity. You've been very kind, but I must find work."

"With a broken arm? There is still the possibility of pneumonia. You don't even have a place to live, do you?"

Moira bit the soft underside of her lip. Everything Jack Graystoke said was true. Her life was in a shambles. Moreover, once she left the safety of Black Jack's house she'd likely find herself imprisoned in Newgate. But even that was preferable to being forced to participate in vile, heathenish rites.

Jack stared at Moira, enthralled by the silky-soft texture of her bright hair, so rich and heavy and lush it almost seemed alive. He couldn't recall ever seeing hair that exact shade of red before. Not exactly auburn, not really red, more like burnished copper. When she returned his gaze with mock bravado, her eyes reminded him of sweet, wild honey.

"Most domestics live in," she informed him. "I had no need for separate quarters."

Jack eyed her narrowly. "Except for a delightful lilt you speak flawless English. One could almost deduce that you have been educated beyond your station."

Moira hung on to her temper by a slim thread. She thought his lazy drawl sounded somewhat condescending. "My mother insisted that my brother and I be educated. She taught us at home, and when she and my father could afford it, they hired a tutor."

"I'm surprised they saw the need to educate you and your brother. It isn't as if you're gentry."

Refusing to be goaded, Moira's hand closed compulsively on her locket. She had only her mother's fanciful notion that she came from noble stock. "My family are poor dirt farmers. Kevin is trying to eke a living for his wife and children out of the drought-ravaged land left to him by our parents. Mama and Da died of typhus five years ago."

"Who was your last employer?" Jack inquired. "Why were you let go? What aren't you telling me? Perhaps I should speak with him . . ."

Moira blanched. "No! Don't bother, sir. I'll be gone soon."

Jack shifted uncomfortably. "You may have forgotten that it was my carriage that ran you down, but I haven't. I intend to take care of you until you're on your feet again."

Moira gulped nervously. "Take care of me?" She didn't even want to guess what he meant by that remark. "I can take care of myself." It was shameless of her to let him go on thinking he was responsible for her injuries, but she had no choice.

"That's all well and good, but I owe you my protection. If I hadn't been foxed and hellbent on driving at breakneck speed last night, I wouldn't have run you down. Do you have any plans for your future? A promise of employment, perhaps?"

Though his question was innocent enough, Moira suspected an ulterior motive. It was with good reason that this man was called Black Jack. "I left Ireland to find work and earn money to help out my brother. He's barely scraping by on the farm. My first employment didn't work out, but I'll find something soon."

What Moira didn't say was that it was unlikely she'd ever work as a servant again. Lord Roger had seen to that. Her only recourse was to return to Ireland and become another de-

411

pendent on her poor brother, not that Kevin would mind. He'd welcome her with open arms, and so would his wife, Katie.

"Your meager servant's pay isn't enough to help your brother substantially," Jack said, choosing his words carefully. Nor would a streetwalker's earnings, he thought but did not say. "Perhaps I can be of service."

Moira sent him a wary look. "How so, sir?" Her gaze lifted to the faded wallpaper, continuing on to the worn draperies and threadbare carpet. It appeared as if Jackson Graystoke wasn't well heeled enough to take care of his own affairs, let alone hers.

Noting the direction of her gaze, Jack shrugged philosophically. "I know what you're thinking, Miss O'Toole, and you're right. I'm nothing but an impoverished baronet who can't even see to the upkeep of his own home. My main source of income arrives via the gaming table and I must marry money soon or see my ancestral home fall down around my ears. But I'm not powerless to help you."

"Why do you care?"

"I have accepted responsibility for your injuries. What in God's name were you doing out so late on a raw night like last night?" He searched her face. "Were you meeting a lover?"

"What!" Her eyes blazed with outrage. "What makes you think that? I'm not like that. I thank you for your concern, but I'd rather not say."

Jack mulled over her words, deciding there was more to Moira O'Toole than met the eye. She claimed to be from the serving class, but she neither talked nor acted like any servant he knew.

"Doctor Dudley said you'd be unable to use your arm for at least four weeks so you may as well content yourself to remain here until you're able to function on your own. Meanwhile, I'll hire a maid to see to your needs."

"There is no need. I'll . . ."

"It's all settled, Miss O'Toole."

Before Moira could offer further protest, the jangle of a bell coming from somewhere in the far reaches of the old house caught her attention. She looked askance at Jack.

"Someone is at the door," Jack said in response to her unasked question. "Pettibone will see to it. He's the jack of all trades around here. Couldn't exist without him. Now, where were we? Ah, yes, I was about to ask if you have any preferences as to a maid."

Moira was on the verge of denying her need for a maid when Lord Fenwick burst into the chamber unannounced. "Ah, I see our little patient is alert this morning. Have you told her yet, Jack?"

Spence looked like a cat who had just swallowed a canary.

"Tell me what?" Moira asked sharply. Just what did Black Jack and his friend have in mind for her? Judging from the guilty expression on Jack's face it had to be something devious.

Jack sent Spence a blistering look. "Bloody hell, Spence, do you always speak without thinking? I haven't said a word yet to Miss O'Toole, but I would have come around to it eventually."

Moira certainly didn't like the sound of *that*. "I don't believe I'll stay after all." Had she jumped from the frying pan into the fire? She started to climb out of bed and remembered she was wearing naught but a threadbare shift. It suddenly occurred to her that if Jack Graystoke had no maid then he must have undressed her himself. Her face flamed scarlet and she jerked the covers up to her neck.

"We mean you no harm, Miss O'Toole," Jack assured her, though he could see she wasn't convinced. "What my precipitous friend here wanted to know was did I mention to you a plan we had discussed concerning your future."

"Plan? Why should you care about my future? I'm not . . ." she gulped, unwilling to say the word aloud, "what you think." Moira could tell by the way Jack talked that he thought her a fallen woman.

"It matters not one whit what you are, Miss O'Toole. As for your future, I told you I have assumed full responsibility for your accident. I merely want to right a wrong. There is nothing evil in my intent, so don't reject something that

414

could benefit you greatly. Hear me out."

What choice did she have? Moira wondered. She was injured and helpless in a strange bed, in a strange house, wearing naught but her shift. She had no money, nowhere to live and no one to turn to for help. So far Sir Jack Graystoke had made no demands on her, had in fact accepted full responsibility for her "accident" and offered amends. The least she could do was listen with an open mind.

"Very well, Sir Graystoke, what is this plan you and Lord Fenwick have devised for me?"

"First let me explain. Spence is in line for a dukedom and will do nothing to damage his reputation. He's a marquess in his own right. Thank God I do not aspire to so noble a rank. My young cousin, Ailesbury, is welcome to the title."

"Get on with it, Jack," Spence nagged. I'm sure Miss O'Toole has no interest in my family tree or your lack of title."

"Sorry. I merely wanted to impress upon Miss O'Toole that we mean her no harm." He turned to Moira, impaling her with the gray intensity of his eyes. "Since you are temporarily unemployable, Miss O'Toole, with no prospects of future work, Spence and I have come up with a solution to your dilemma."

Moira's warm golden gaze settled disconcertingly on Jack, making him decidedly uncomfortable. "I refuse to be used for vile purposes.

Others have tried and failed."

Jack stared at her through narrowed lids. What in bloody hell did she mean by that remark? What vile purposes was she referring to? "My dear Miss O'Toole, Spence and I have no designs on your person. You are perfectly safe with us."

Moira looked skeptical but gave him the benefit of the doubt. "Go on, sir, I'm listening."

"If you agree to the little escapade Spence and I propose, I can promise you a grand adventure. Moreover, if it works out as we expect, you will never have to worry about money again. You'll be able to better your own lot and provide for your brother's family."

Moira's eyes widened in disbelief. "How do you propose to do that?"

Jack perched on the edge of the bed, his eyes crinkling with amusement. "Have you ever wondered what it would like to be a lady? To belong to the gentry?"

Moira stiffened indignantly, taking his words as an insult. "I *am* a lady! I may not be gentry but that doesn't make me any less a lady."

The corner of Jack's mouth quirked upward. He had her now. "Prove it. Let's see if you've got what it takes to be accepted by London society."

Forgetting that she was scantily clad in a threadbare shift, Moira jerked upright, wincing in pain when her injured arm protested the sudden jolt. "Are you daft, sir? 'Tis highly unlikely

I'll be accepted by society, let alone mistaken for gentry."

Jack gave her a lazy grin. "Spence and I intend to prove you wrong. You *will* be accepted, Miss O'Toole. We'll coach you in etiquette, and when the time is right, you'll be introduced as my ward, a distant relative from Ireland. We'll make your father a baron, which will make you a lady. Lady Moira. How does that sound?"

"Outrageous."

"Spence and I will do our level best to see you married to an upstanding member of London society. One wealthy enough to keep you in grand style and provide funds for your brother. If that isn't enough inducement, just consider the endless hours of entertainment Spence and I will derive from our little charade."

Moira's thoughts scattered. What Sir Graystoke suggested was ludicrous. No wonder he was called Black Jack. His warped sense of humor would get them all in trouble. Pass her off as a relative, indeed. How could anyone believe she was gentry? Her mother had told her many times that her grandfather was highborn but there was no proof to substantiate her claim. That kind of thinking was dangerous. But so were the alternatives, which were definitely unpalatable. Finding another job without references was next to impossible. She had no funds with which to purchase passage to Ireland, even if she didn't want to burden her poor brother with another mouth to feed.

Actually, after careful consideration, Moira thought the idea that the two gentlemen proposed had some merit. The idea of marrying money had much to commend it. One possible drawback was having to deal with Black Jack on a daily basis until she left. The man was too arrogant, too handsome and too damn male!

"Well, what do you think of the idea?" Spence asked excitedly. He was literally hopping from foot to foot, waiting for Moira's decision.

"Why would you go to the trouble? There is more to this than an escape from boredom. What do you have to gain by passing me off as a lady?"

"A pair of . . ."

"Nothing," Jack interjected, abruptly cutting off Spence's sentence. He thought it best not to mention the wager he and Spence had agreed upon: his pair of grays against two thousand pounds. "We have your best interests at heart. The diversion your entry into society will provide will give us endless hours of amusement."

Jack's eyes roved over the upper part of Moira's body, bared when the blanket dropped to her waist. Her breasts were round and full, though not particularly large; he could see the darker aureoles push impudently against the thin material of her shift. A jolt of blatant lust made him want to reach out and encircle the fleshy mounds with his large hands. His fingers

418

tingled, imagining the warmth of her flesh against his palm. He blinked and looked away, surprised at the direction of his thoughts. Moira recognized the look in his eyes and yanked the covers up to her chin with her uninjured arm. She neither needed nor wanted *that* kind of attention.

"Amusement," Moira said bitterly. "Do the gentry think of naught else?"

Spence grinned. "What else is there?"

"Come now, Miss O'Toole, what do you say?" Jack asked with gruff impatience. "You've nothing to lose and everything to gain."

What did she have to lose? Moira wondered. What if she chanced to meet her former employers while she was out and about in society? What if she met Lord Roger at some social function or other? Perhaps he wouldn't recognize her dressed as a lady, she reflected hopefully. Due to their age, the elderly Mayhews attended few social events and as for Roger, tame amusements did not interest him. But there was always a possibility of their paths crossing. She'd just have to cross that bridge when she came to it.

"Very well," Moira reluctantly agreed. "Your scheme has some merit. I will do it to prove to you that I *am* a lady, that I'm as good as any woman born to the gentry. And to help me brother. But mostly because I do not wish to remain a burden to you."

419

Jack sent her a dark look. "I must marry money myself if I am to survive, but I will fulfill my responsibility where you're concerned. If not for me you would be hale and hearty today instead of recovering from injuries."

"Good show, Miss O'Toole!" Spence enthused, sending Moira a pleased look. "When you're ready, Jack will introduce you as a distant relative and let nature take its course. You're a beauty, Miss O'Toole. There is nothing coarse or common about you. If Jack wins we'll be toasting your engagement inside three months. But if I'm victorious . . ."

"That's enough, Spence!" Jack warned. "We've tired Miss O'Toole. I suggest we repair to the study and let her rest. We've plans to make."

"Don't we though," Spence said as Jack hustled him out the door.

Moira cradled her injured arm and pondered Jack's outrageous plan. She'd been a fool to agree, but what choice did she have? Despite Jack's argument to the contrary, clearly he did not want the added responsibility she represented. He thought he had run her down with his carriage, but she knew for a fact he couldn't have hurt her much more than she'd already been hurt when she'd flung herself from Lord Roger's coach. She felt guilty about lying to Jack about his involvement in her "accident," but she feared that telling the truth presented a far greater risk.

Moira was in so deep, she saw no way to extricate herself gracefully from this muddle. She'd see this through and prove to Black Jack Graystoke that being a lady did not depend upon one's birth.

Moira's thoughts scattered when she heard a discreet knock on the door. Moments later Pettibone poked his head into the room.

"Come in, Mr. Pettibone."

He stepped inside. "Can I get you anything, miss?"

"No, thank you. You've been more than kind. Have you been with Sir Graystoke long?"

"Aye, miss, a very long time."

Moira bit her lip then blurted out, "Is he as black-hearted as his name implies?"

For a moment Pettibone looked rattled, then he quickly recovered his dignity. "Not at all, miss. You mustn't believe everything you hear. I'll admit he can be a bit of a rogue at times, but I've never known him to knowingly hurt anyone, particularly a woman."

"Does he truly earn his living at the gaming tables?"

"True enough, miss. His folks left him little beyond this haunted mansion. And as you can see it's in a pitiful state of disrepair."

Moira's eyes grew round. "Haunted?"

"Indeed, miss. 'Tis said Lady Amelia Graystoke wanders the halls at night, so don't be alarmed if you see or hear anything out of the ordinary."

"Have you ever seen her?"

" 'Tis said Lady Amelia appears only to family members in desperate need of her help. 'Tis rumored she has saved more than one rakehell of the family. In recent years she's had little reason to appear and no one to redeem, until Black Jack, that is. But alas," the old man sighed, "as far as I know Lady Amelia has yet to appear to her wayward great, great grandson."

"Why does Lady Amelia haunt the Graystokes?" Moira asked curiously. Being Irish, ghosts and such had always intrigued her.

" 'Tis a sad story, miss," Pettibone said, warming to the subject. He enjoyed nothing better than displaying his knowledge of Graystoke family lore. "Lady Amelia's only son was a wastrel of the worst sort. He spent his days drinking, gambling, duelling and . . . er . . . visiting ladies of ill repute. 'Twas he who lost the family fortune. Lady Amelia finally managed to get him married to a lovely girl, but it didn't change his dissolute ways. He was killed in a duel days before the Graystoke heir was born."

"How sad," Moira sighed.

"Upon her death some years after that of her son, Lady Amelia made a deathbed promise. She vowed that no Graystoke heir would walk the same path as her wastrel son, even if she

422

had to haunt future generations of Graystokes to accomplish it. And the story goes that she has kept her vow, appearing only to those male Graystoke heirs who led debauched lives and were well on the road to perdition."

"Do you believe that tale?" Moira asked, thoroughly intrigued by Lady Amelia and her pledge to the future generations of Graystokes.

Pettibone shrugged. "Aye. There have been no wastrel males in the Graystoke family for several generations. Like as not it could be the result of Lady Amelia's intervention."

What he left unsaid was that Black Jack Graystoke surely qualified for Lady Amelia's help, and if Lady Amelia didn't intervene soon it may be too late for his rakehell master.

"Thank you for telling me, Mr. Pettibone."

"If there is nothing you wish, miss, I'll continue with my chores."

"I was wondering what happened to my clothing. I don't see them anywhere."

"They are being cleaned and mended. They'll be returned when the doctor says it's all right for you to leave your bed. He'll be here later today to place a cast on your arm."

After Pettibone left, Moira had much to think about, not the least of which was her handsome benefactor. Just how well-meaning was Jack Graystoke? she wondered. She wasn't so naive as to think that men did good deeds without expecting some kind of reward. Jack didn't strike her as an altruistic man who placed the needs of others above his own. Pleasure-seeking, self-indulgent, arrogant came to mind. Was amusement his only reason for wanting to pass her off as a lady and find her a husband?

Sweet Blessed Mother! Moira found it impossible to think of anything but Black Jack's sensual gray eyes. Eyes that held a tempting touch of wildness, of vital energy almost mesmerizing in its intensity. She was grateful for the lesson Lord Roger had taught her. No man was worthy of trust. She would remember that lesson in her dealings with Black Jack Graystoke.

"Doreen Malek's storytelling gifts keep us deliciously entertained!" —*Romantic Times*

When an innocent excursion to Constantinople takes an unexpected twist, Sarah Woolcott finds herself a prisoner of young and virile Kalid Shah. Headstrong and courageous, Sarah is determined to resist the handsome foreigner whose arrogance outrages her—even as his tantalizing touch promises exotic nights of fiery sensuality.

Never has Kalid Shah encountered a woman who enflames his desire like the blonde Westerner with the independent spirit. Although she spurns his passionate overtures, Kalid vows to tempt her with his masterful skills until she becomes a willing companion on their journey of exquisite ecstasy.

_3569-3 $4.99 US/$5.99 CAN

Trial by Fire

DOREEN OWENS MALEK
WRITING AS FAYE MORGAN

Bestselling Author Of *The Panther And The Pearl*

"Ms. Malek's marvelous storytelling gifts
keep us deliciously entertained!"
—*Romantic Times*

Linda Redfield doesn't stand a chance against prosecutor Jefferson T. Langford. After all, she is just another public defender, a street-smart professional from the wrong side of the tracks who earned her law degree from hard work and determination—not family money or connections. Langford has it all—wealth, position, power—everything Linda rebels against.

But justice's scales tip, and Linda enters an uneasy alliance with her courtroom adversary—as a partner in his law firm. Building a defense against Langford's charm and sensual appeal proves to be her toughest case by far—especially since he seems to take such pleasure in overruling her objections…one by one.

___3717-3 $3.99 US/$4.99 CAN

"Catherine Lanigan is in a class by herself: unequaled and simply fabulous!"
                                              —*Affaire de Coeur*

Even amid the spectacle and splendor of the carnival in Venice, the masked rogue is brazen, reckless, and dangerously risqué. As he steals Valentine St. James away from the costume ball at which her betrothal to a complete stranger is to be announced, the exquisite beauty revels in the illicit thrill of his touch, the tender passion in his kiss. But Valentine learns that illusion rules the festival when, at the stroke of midnight, her mysterious suitor reveals he is Lord Hawkeston, the very man she is to wed. Convinced her intended is an unrepentant scoundrel, Valentine wants to deny her maddening attraction for him, only to keep finding herself in his heated embrace. Yet is she truly losing her heart to the dashing peer—or is she being ruthlessly seduced?

_3942-7 $5.50 US/$7.50 CAN

TIMESWEPT PASSION... TIMELESS LOVE

The Reluctant Viking

SANDRA HILL

"*Picture yourself floating out of your body—floating...floating...floating...*" The hypnotic voice on the self-motivation tape is supposed to help Ruby Jordan solve her problems, not create new ones. Instead, she is lulled from a life full of a demanding business, a neglected home, and a failing marriage—to an era of hard-bodied warriors and fair maidens, fierce fighting and fiercer wooing. But the world ten centuries in the past doesn't prove to be all mead and mirth. Even as Ruby tries to update medieval times, she has to deal with a Norseman whose view of women is stuck in the Dark Ages. And what is worse, brawny Thork has her husband's face, habits, and desire to avoid Ruby. Determined not to lose the same man twice, Ruby plans a bold seduction that will conquer the reluctant Viking—and make him an eager captive of her love.

_51983-6 $4.99 US/$5.99 CAN

THE TARNISHED LADY
SANDRA HILL

Sandra Hill's romances are "delicious, witty, and funny!"
—Romantic Times

Banished from polite society for bearing a child out of wedlock, Lady Eadyth of Hawks' Lair spends her days hidden under a voluminous veil, tending her bees. But when her son's detested father threatens to reveal the boy's true paternity and seize her beloved lands, Lady Eadyth seeks a husband who will claim the child as his own.

Notorious for loving—and leaving—the most beautiful damsels in the land, Eirik of Ravenshire is England's most virile bachelor. Yet when a mysterious beekeeper offers him a vow of chaste matrimony in exchange for revenge against his most hated enemy, Eirik can't refuse. But the lucky knight's plans go awry when he succumbs to the sweet sting of the tarnished lady's love.

_3834-X $5.50 US/$7.50 CAN

Scoundrel

Debra Dier

"A sparkling jewel in the romantic adventure world of books!" *—Affaire de Coeur*

Emily Maitland doesn't wish to rush into a match with one of the insipid fops she has met in London. But since her parents insist she choose a suitor immediately, she gives her hand to Major Sheridan Blake. The gallant officer is everything Emily desires in a man: He is charming, dashing—and completely imaginary. Happy to be married to a fictitious husband, Emily certainly never expects a counterfeit Major Blake to appear in the flesh and claim her as his bride. Determined to expose the handsome rogue without revealing her own masquerade, Emily doesn't count on being swept up in the most fascinating intrigue of all: passionate love.

_3894-3 $5.50 US/$7.50 CAN